SCUTARIUS

Quintus Roman Thrillers
Book Five

Neil Denby

SAPERE
BOOKS

SCUTARIUS

Published by Sapere Books.

24 Trafalgar Road, Ilkley, LS29 8HH

saperebooks.com

ISBN: 978-0-85495-672-2

To my ever supportive family, for continuing to put up with me.

I: NAVIS ACTUARIA

'You, centurion. Board your men.'

Centurion Julius Quintus Quirinius looked up as the man on the dappled grey pointed to the nearest of the transports. He wore a crested helm and a rich red cloak, and was already turning away, the two junior officers that accompanied him looking back with disdain. Their horses were better dressed than Quintus' men.

Quintus was about to question the man who had issued the order, but he was already gone. Clearly, he believed in the strength of his authority. The centurion sighed and spoke to his companion Crassus, nodding in the direction of the staff officer.

'Board them, optio. The man on the horse with the new paludamentum says so.'

'But we are no sailors, Quintus. You know that as well as I do.'

'Look, Crassus, it has no sails. So we will not be sailing. Anyway, this water is as smooth as polished marble. There is no comparison to the seas that we have crossed.'

'And yet…' said Sextus, ominously. The third member of the group turned his head towards the dark clouds that gathered above the mountains. Sextus had joined the legions at the same time as Quintus. Although now classed as a veteran, he looked far too young to be a seasoned soldier. His face was clean-shaven and boyish, whilst his lorica laminata — the plated armour now universally worn on the orders of Caesar Augustus — shone brightly. His baltea and cingulum, the military belt that housed his sharp-edged pugio and the leather straps that protected the tops of his legs, looked like they had been newly issued. He lifted his helmet to gently stroke his hair — apparently it was out of place — then gently settled the helm again. The chinstrap hung loose. He smiled and shrugged as he noticed Crassus watching him. Quintus noted that somehow even his hair was cut fashionably.

'Do up the helmet, Sextus, then intercede for us. You know the formulae.' Quintus spoke respectfully enough that none could accuse him of mocking the gods. Sextus nodded, tied the chinstrap, then pulled his cloak over his head to say a prayer to great Neptune. Although he had no formal training as a priest or augur, the men turned to him on account of his upbringing, fostered by the Vestals.

The men, hurried on by Crassus, marched over the narrow gangplank. They followed their standard, the *signum* of the cohort, with its image of a black cow pawing a faded yellow field. This was Juno's cow, which echoed the black bull standard of Legio Nine.

They found themselves on an already crowded deck, being shouted at by everyone. Behind them cavalry horses snorted and blew. More swearing filled the air as they were ordered forward to make room.

The transports were wide and stubby, almost barges rather than ships, the carpenters hardly bothering to shape a bow. They were designed to make a single journey and would be firewood thereafter. Still they boasted two rows of oars, the auxiliaries below already in place, the blades of the oars poised to dip into the water.

Beside their vessel, more ships, already loaded, were being hauled into position. The water between the hulls churned dangerously, white-capped and angry. The oars — accompanied by many oaths — were used to keep the hulls apart. Water slopped through the lower oar holes and splashed up onto the deck. Though sailors ran along the decks using long sticks to push vessels away, another ship veered into them from the side with a crash and Quintus almost lost his grip.

'By great Jupiter's golden beard!' He cursed as he almost lost his balance, saving himself by clutching at the wet timber of the rail. 'Get me on dry land.'

'It's Neptune's favour you need, not Jupiter's,' laughed Sextus, who stood to his left. His head was now uncovered and he was miraculously unsplashed. 'It is water, after all.'

'There will be a nymph or nereid of the lake in charge,' said Quintus. 'It is to her I should direct my prayers.'

'Not prayers, but charms,' Sextus replied, placing a kiss on his fingertips and miming casting it into the water. They both laughed, then instinctively looked around for Tullius. They expected the voice of the double-scarred veteran with the long face to immediately upbraid them for making light of the gods, and demand an apology or a sacrifice. At the very least he would scowl at them and make the sign of the cornua, the horns, to ward off bad luck.

With sadness they remembered that of course he was not there. He had left them for the sunnier shores of Elysium when their marching camp was attacked by a force of Germani tribesmen and Roman deserters. He had died in the service of his comrades. His ashes were scattered and blown on the wind.

The two men caught each other's eye briefly, then cast their gazes down in sorrow. Quintus shook his head and mumbled a prayer.

'I miss him, too,' said Sextus, quietly.

'Miss who?' Red-haired, red-bearded Rufus, with his Gaulish moustaches and wolfskin cloak, appeared at Quintus' left shoulder, having failed to follow the exchange.

Rufus was the signifer, in charge of the cohort standard. He had served enough time to have lost two previous partners, to have had to send home meagre possessions in the case of one, nothing in the case of the other. He had sent wax tablets with loyal thoughts, wills that passed on possessions that no longer existed, and messages saying how honourably each man had died, whether he had or no. All of it had been painfully scrawled in his own poor hand. He looked with affection at Sextus, his third primus amicus in as many years. At least he had survived.

'Tullius,' said Sextus, in answer to Rufus' question. 'Mal Fortuna. I still expect him to teach us respect for the gods.'

'I know that's what he called himself,' said Quintus. 'But the gods twice saved his eye — and Marcus has survived him — even though Marcus was the last to be chosen by him.'

'Charon has a berth for us all, Macilentus,' said Rufus. 'We will meet again in the Elysian Fields.'

'I do not doubt it,' said Quintus.

Quintus, legionary recruit to Legio Nine Hispania, was known by his friends as Macilentus, meaning 'lanky', due to his height. There were few, if any, as tall as him in the legions. He had risen through the ranks and was now First Spear Centurion, leading an unlikely and woefully understrength cohort.

These soldiers now rocked unsteadily on a *navis actuaria*, a multi-oared ship built solely for transport and surrounded by many others of the same type. That morning the men had thought themselves anchored to dry land, ready to march around the lakeshore. Quintus had assumed that only part of the vast army was to be transported by boat. He was wrong.

'Not there, sir,' the legionary sailor with the long pole said diffidently.

'Of course,' Quintus replied, realising that where he stood he was in the man's way. He moved, forced to step nearer to where he did not want to be — the front.

As his own vessel found its place amidst a cacophony of commands, scraping again along the hull of another before lurching free, he held on to the unseasoned timber tightly, his grip turning his knuckles white. Quintus had been to sea before, of course, and had hated it. He had been in storms, in shipwrecks. His body recalled the sensation and shivered. He loathed the uncertainty, but more than that he hated the bucking of the ship, the keen edge of the wind, the sharp sting of salt water.

There was none of that here. He had been swimming in these waters. They might be cold, but they were fresh. Today no wind stirred their surface. They reflected the deep blue of the sky, the shadows of the mountains and the distant storm clouds that Sextus prayed would stay away. The lake was vast enough to be considered a sea. The mountains were cloaked in deep green firs, with hoary heads and bald crowns like a group of ancient senators.

'What is that?' Quintus loosened his grip to shade his eyes with his hand. Being a head taller than most of the men, he could see further. Even so, Crassus was ahead of him.

'Ships,' said Crassus, in a tone of resignation. 'Our crossing will not be unopposed.'

The grey shapes on the horizon at first looked like nothing more than a low cloud, or perhaps a flock of seabirds. But as they came closer, masts and sails could be seen. Tall masts and square sails. Officers on the command ships were already sounding the alarm. The strident sounds of cornua and deep-voiced buccinae rang out across the lake. The soldiers saw a series of flourishes from the standards on the right wing, echoed further down the line.

'The admiral has spoken,' said Sextus, sarcasm in his voice.

'He is no admiral,' said Crassus quietly, 'and we all know it. Nevertheless, our life is in his hands.'

He liked voyaging even less than Quintus. He had hoped this passage would be quick and unopposed. It looked like they would have to fight.

The ships reacted to their orders at different speeds. The Romans were no sailors — and Crassus was right, the admiral was no admiral. But he was a senator.

The drumbeat began slowly at first, mixed with many shouted orders and calls from those acting as lookouts and mariners. The ships had to disentangle themselves from each other, to create sufficient distance for the oars to bite. No single cadence dominated, each ship following its own drummer, the water between the ships boiling. Depths were reported, as were distances between ships, headings and directions. Warnings and instructions were tossed from ship to ship. All of these exchanges were accompanied by jests and insults. Soldiers and part-time sailors ran messages from one side of each ship to the other. Prayers and imprecations were thrown into the air; curses rained on other vessels for being too close or too slow.

As the ships cleared the shore and jostled to find their positions, the rhythm quickened to almost a march beat, a one-two, then the slightest of pauses, and a one-two again. Drummers caught the beat of other drummers and gradually a single rhythm emerged. Every ship first had space, then, with much shouting and swearing, found its place in the formation. Oars lifted, dipped and bit in unison, carving into the water like the many claws of some mythical monster. Slowly, the ungainly vessels began to move with purpose.

The ships each carried a single mast, held in place by strong, taut lines, yet they hoisted no sail. What winds there were on these waters appeared to be fickle, swinging from one direction to the other, bouncing from the sides of the steep mountains that surrounded the lake when they blew at all. The Romans knew that they were no mariners and preferred to trust the oars rather than Aeolus' breath.

To the crows that flapped above, the ships looked like insects with multiple legs, crawling out across the glassy surface. The birds protested about being disturbed, complained about the empty forest where trees that used to be their homes had stood, and landed briefly on the tops of the masts before lifting off again.

'We could have marched,' said Sextus glumly. 'We have no need to even be on the water. They would not dare attack so many on land.'

Nobody disagreed with him.

The drumbeat on Quintus' transport had become faster, more urgent. Their boat was outpacing the others, enough so that it would be the first to engage, the first to feel the brunt of the tribesmen's wrath. It could only be on the orders of a senior officer.

'Again,' muttered Sextus. 'We are on the sacrificial block again.'

'We are disposable,' said Quintus wearily. 'With the Ninth not here, we are of no legion, responsible to none but the general himself. He can risk us if he wishes.'

'Clearly he wishes,' confirmed Crassus, grounding his shield more firmly, squaring his shoulders, and settling his helmet more firmly on his head. 'But I do not. We will show him. This day we shall not die.'

Quintus' ship now began to pull further ahead of the following pack. More orders, specific orders, had been given: risk the new men, not the general's favourite legions. Or the horses. Or the carts or tents or slaves. With luck, the elite legionaries would not even have to fight.

Whilst the admiral was on the right, the general himself was on the left wing, far enough forward to claim leadership, but far enough back to be protected by other transports. His praetorians, all Germani themselves, would die to keep him alive. To them he was a living god.

In between these two, the ships had formed into the shape of an arrowhead. One stood proud at the very tip. Quintus and his men lined up on its deck, facing the approaching enemy.

II: PRAECEPTUM

Roman commanders did not do things by half measures. Tiberius Claudius Nero, son of Caesar Augustus, son of a god, had found a body of water in the way of his progress. It was a lake so wide that the other shore could not be seen. It was smooth as mirrored brass, shadowed by peaks whose tops vanished into the clouds.

He could go around it or over it. Being Roman, he chose the latter, so needed a fleet of transports. A great swathe of forest had been cut down and now floated on the water. Tiberius needed to move ten thousand legionary soldiers, both infantry and cavalry. Ten thousand auxiliary horsemen, archers and support troops went with them. Not to mention five thousand slaves, plus a multitude of carts and tents, a mountain of stock and grain, and an armoury of weapons, equipment and siege engines. So he needed a lot of ships and, for the moment, an admiral.

A shrill blast sounded from this admiral's ship. It was blown by the cornicen attached to his service, the long curve of the instrument resting on his shoulder, nestled in his wolfskin cloak. As he took the mouthpiece of the brass horn from his lips, the signal was echoed from vessel to vessel, signiferi reinforcing it with the dip and sway of standards, centurions and optiones reinforcing it with shoves and shouts.

It was the command to make ready for combat. The soldiers knew what it meant and fixed their feet more firmly against the timber. They lined up on the *signum* held by Rufus, the tattered and faded symbol attesting to the actions it had seen. At the other end of the line, a legionary held up the *pilus et manus* standard, the spear and open hand dressed in tassels and ribbons. The man who carried it was tall and broad-chested yet pale enough to be a ghost. Deep lines of care were etched on his forehead. He wore no facial hair.

He was Aquila, the former proud bearer of the legionary Eagle of the Fifth, and he wore no animal skin. Once he had worn a perpetual flickering smile on his boyish face, a sign of satisfaction with his own good fortune. Now he was permanently downcast, an aquilifer without an eagle. Tiberius had taken the rescued standard back and with it the spirit and spark of its bearer. To the other side of Aquila stood his own primus amicus, the rake and scoundrel Vetruvius. He was a womaniser, a gambler and a chancer, but a good man to have at your side in a fight.

There was enough room for two units, each eight men wide and five deep, side by side. The men planted their feet, bent their knees, squared their shoulders and tightened their grip on their shields.

The curved cornu was raised again, a single blast. 'Shields.'

As swiftly as wind in the trees, a movement spread across the vessels and a thousand solid scuta — long rectangular shields two thirds the height of a man — thumped onto the decks, rank upon rank of legionaries making sure that they were braced against the enemy.

The action made the vessels shake as if the breath of some mighty god had blown across them, the noise ringing and reverberating from the tall mountains that cast shadows on the lake. Another blast, and the front ranks levelled the heavy pila, long wooden spears with solid metal points, a bristling forest, ready to stop any foe that dared to come close enough.

The ships that approached were no longer grey shapes in the distance. The shadows first resolved into silhouettes, then into individual vessels with details like painted prows and brightly coloured sails. Though the Romans could not yet see the Germani faces, they could see that each ship held perhaps fifty men, sitting on either side of the mast. They could see oars dipping into the water in unison, sails bellied with the wind and the flotilla fairly speeding towards them.

These ships were smaller than the Roman vessels, with just a single bank of oars and, from what the Romans could see, no decks except for a short section at the rear, no doubt used for the steering paddle and its operator. Their sails were unfurled and, in contrast to the lumbering Roman transports, they moved swiftly and confidently on the water.

As the two fleets closed the voices of the warriors on the Germani vessels could be heard, men on deck shouting and gesturing, issuing challenges, waving weapons. All of it was in a language the Romans did not understand.

'What do they say?' Quintus called. 'We need Caius — where is he?'

'Not on this vessel, Quintus,' Sextus told him as he pointed. 'Centurion Felix is on the ship to our left — there. Caius and Marcus are both with him.'

Legionary Caius Sergio Nerva, late of Legio Five Alaudae, the Larks, was a veteran of many years' standing. He had enjoyed victory but also suffered much tragedy and dishonour, experiences that made him unsociable, distrustful and taciturn. He struggled to see why barbarian tribes rejected the civilisation that Rome promised, and was one of the few who tried to learn the language of his enemies, to try to understand.

'Pity,' said Quintus. 'We should know what they say of us.'

'I can guess,' said Sextus, smiling. 'Amongst the screams and caterwauling, there will be curses, insults, and no doubt suggestions as to the size of their manhoods compared to ours.'

'I hear the names of Týr and Wotan, well known to us. I am sure there are other gods of which we are not aware,' said Crassus.

'They also call the names of Maelo and of Dagaz,' said Sextus.

'Both dead.' Quintus was dismissive, although he knew the names carried power. The name of Dagaz in particular still caused a shudder. He was no god — in fact he had died by a woman's hand, stabbed through the eye with her hairpin as he tried to ravish her. An ignoble end. Quintus knew this; he had found the intertwined bodies.

But his death was not sufficiently proven to the Germani, so the man had become a legend and hero amongst his people. His name had become more powerful in death than it had been in life.

'You should have taken his head,' said Rufus, matter-of-factly.

'I know it,' replied Quintus, still cursing his own stupidity. Of course he should have taken the head. The body had, on his orders, been stripped of anything of value and flung into the dark waters of the Rhenus. But without the head, there was no proof of death. Since then many versions of the renegade leader had already emerged from the swirling depths of the great river. Many men inflated their own worth by claiming his mantle. Quintus had not defeated an enemy, but created a myth.

'We'll just have to kill him again,' said Sextus, with a wry smile. 'As many times as he claims to live, we will put an end to him.'

Crassus was about to respond but there was no time. Germani javelins were being hurled towards the Romans and their ship was the obvious first target. Many of the weapons splashed into the water well short of the hull, their leaf-shaped iron tips sinking them beneath the surface before their long wakes subsided. Some carried further and bit into the soft timber. Built with a single purpose and a single journey in mind, the transport had no ram or beak and made for an easy target. It would never have survived a lively wave on the open sea.

Tiberius had not expected to be opposed, yet here they were, faced with a fleet of small ships casting spears and slinging stones. The slingshots propelled the ammunition further than the spears could reach and the stones and lead pellets peppered the wall of shields, like hailstones driven on a storm wind. There were yelps as some found flesh or ricocheted from helmets. Noises from behind the soldiers betrayed that animals had been hit and hurt.

'No axes?' Quintus asked sarcastically, as he lifted his shield to fend off a javelin. As centurion, he stood ahead of the lines, ready to shout orders.

'They will not throw them. They are too precious,' said Crassus, who as a blacksmith knew a lot about the forging of weapons. 'They would sink even faster, long before they reached us.'

'You will feel the bite of an axe soon enough,' Sextus said. 'These ships are too small to ram us. These men intend to fight us on our own decks.'

The enemy ships were nimble. They sailed in no sort of formation, but like racing chariots in the Circus Maximus, they darted into any gaps that were left, vying with each other to be the first to engage with the enemy. The Roman transports were difficult to manoeuvre and would take an age to turn. They had no other tactic but to plough into the opposition.

The legionaries watched the advance with jaws set. They could do nothing, would do nothing, without orders. They muttered prayers, grasped good luck charms, sweated or shivered, silently cursed or called on the gods to protect them — they all had different ways to prepare their bodies and minds to meet danger.

Another shrill blast carried a call to action, a demand to respond to this insolent attack. Only the lead ships were currently capable of obeying.

'Ready spears,' Quintus ordered, and the front ranks hefted their javelins to shoulder height, shifted their weight to the back foot, and targeted the enemy. These were not lightweight javelins, but the heavy spears that they practised throwing on the Campus Martius.

'Front rank, *iacite pila*,' Quintus commanded. 'Throw spears.' The legionaries pulled back their arms and let fly. Three or four of the enemy ships were easily within range and a hail of spears thudded into the hulls of the first line of attackers. Some points stuck in the round shields of the Germani, some in the decks. Some even rent sails. Some lucky casts pinned fighters to their own decks or sent them spinning into the water. Wherever they landed, the shafts bent and broke as they were designed to do, making a shield heavy and useless, or creating a hazard.

The enemy threw overboard what it could, including shields, then lined the rails and jeered, redoubling their taunts and challenges. The first and second rank of Romans had changed places smoothly and a further volley flew. It was joined by more spears from the two ships that flanked Quintus, as they lumbered into range. Although the Germani were forced to duck and defend, they were soon on their feet again, gesticulating and taunting.

'Look at them. There are too many for each to have an oar,' said Quintus. 'These ships carry fighting men, not just sailors.'

'As do we,' said Sextus, gesturing to the troops and animals lined up on the deck behind them, a forest of tall shafts marking the infantry. 'We carry an army. We have enough spears to kill them where they stand.'

'You are right,' Quintus agreed.

Just then, ranks parted and men moved aside to let a runner through — an auxiliary, probably Egyptian, a messenger. He was breathless, holding out a small roll of what looked like goatskin vellum, which Quintus knew to be ridiculously expensive.

'It is a message, sir. It was sent from ship to ship tied to a javelin. It is for you. It bears the seal of the general.'

Quintus took it from him and unfurled it.

'I can read it for you if you wish, sir. And write a reply.'

'I can read,' Quintus snapped at him. Quickly he scanned the writing, then lifted his head to look at the messenger. 'No reply. Except to let General Tiberius know that we have received his orders.'

The man bowed and ran back the way he had come, the ranks closing behind him.

Quintus turned to the men and raised his voice. 'We are not going to spear them. These enemy intend to fight us on our own decks. They will try to board us, and we must let them.'

Crassus was puzzled. 'We can stop them easily.'

'But we won't,' said Quintus, waving the unrolled praeceptum. 'I have orders here if we are engaged. We are to leave them enough room to board, then kill them. Our master does not want them turning away because they cannot fight. He wants them fought and defeated. He does not want to be looking over his shoulder for these men. He wants them gone.'

'So we let them board?' Rufus was incredulous.

'We let them board,' Quintus confirmed.

III: NOLI DARE MISERICORDIAM

The open stretch of water between the opposing ships rapidly narrowed and the Germani javelins and sling stones began to cause greater damage. Instead of splashing into the water the weapons now hit timbers and shields and stuck, quivering. They were much more lightweight than the pila, but still capable of inflicting damage. If they flew with fortune behind them, they could pierce armour, although they would never damage a Roman shield.

The sharp stones and lead pellets caused multiple wounds, some merely annoying, others more serious. The stones were not small, and hurled at speed they could gouge a hole in exposed flesh. The pellets were smaller, but flew further and faster. Both reached the front lines, mostly thudding into the solid wood and leather of the scuta or spinning from their metal bosses. But sometimes they found a vulnerability, a forearm or a neck, an eye even.

'Back,' Quintus ordered. 'Step back. Two paces. Go.'

The lines of legionaries all stepped backwards. Moving as one was a skill acquired on the Campus Martius, and honed in countless drills and practices. At the rear, the decurion of cavalry, not anticipating the move, complained as his horses and men were forced to shuffle back to make room. The legionaries resumed their original positions, the signiferi still marking the ends of the front rank.

This was no retreat; it was more of an invitation to come aboard. What Quintus wanted was a space, a fighting platform designed to tempt the enemy. What he had created was a killing zone the width of the ship and six feet deep.

The first of the tribesmen, screaming, leapt for the open deck provided by the centurion. He grabbed the rail and climbed over it, at first teetering on the edge then, to a cheer from his comrades, gaining his balance. He was one of the religious zealots that believed his gods protected him, one of those that sought death in order to pave his way to the afterlife. His upper body was bare, with just the leather straps of the baldrics that held his weapons crossed on his chest. His long fair hair escaped raggedly from his cap and his beard was tasselled and plaited, decorated with shining shards of silver and bronze. He wore patterned trews and no armour other than the round headpiece. His mouth was open in a defiant scream.

He took a single long stride and swung his two-headed axe, choosing the nearest Roman with a standard. Instead of felling the *signum*, the blow hit the signifer's shield. The man behind it, Rufus, at first staggered backwards then managed to regain his balance. His movement temporarily opened a small gap in the line, enough for Sextus to take a half step forward and smash the heavy boss of his own shield into the side of the Germani warrior's head. The man's forged iron cap had loose cheekpieces. One of these took the brunt of the blow, but it was not enough to save him.

His gods did not favour him, not this day. The force of the blow broke his jaw; the cheekpiece twisted and ripped his ear, blood spraying and half blinding him. His shield, though sturdy, was lifted high to provide the balance for him to swing the axe. This made it useless to him, however well made it was.

The flesh of his upper body was unprotected apart from the leather straps that held his weaponry. A Roman pugio, the long knife swiftly drawn by Sextus, was punched deep into his chest. The warrior let the axe fall as this second blow made him stumble. A hefty shove from the legionary's shield was enough to send him tumbling from the deck. Sextus sheathed the blade and used his boot to send the fallen weapon spinning after its master. He smiled grimly at Rufus as both stepped back and redressed the line.

More tribesmen were leaping across the churning water between their ships and the transport, clambering over the rail, bracing themselves on the deck. They pummelled the line of shields with heavy blades, trying to batter their way through. They were armed not just with swords, but with hand axes and short javelins, chipping chunks of timber from the shields, trying to pry them apart or stab between them. Many of them wore the sort of mail shirt that Roman veterans tended to prefer; others wore pieces of armour clearly taken from Roman dead.

Although Quintus had stepped back close to his companions, he still stood alone in front of the shield wall, in his place as *pilus prior*, first spear centurion. 'Hold,' he commanded through gritted teeth. 'Brace!' The strength of the line was in its discipline. The formation was stronger than any individual. It was discipline that made the men defend, although their sword hands itched to draw their blades. It was discipline that made them absorb the blows to their shields and helms, that made them support injured comrades so that no gaps should appear, or quickly close gaps if a comrade fell. Quintus waited until the killing ground he had created was crowded with the enemy. Only then did he give the command to draw swords.

'*Gladium stringe.*'

The order to unsheathe blades was like encouraging a dog to bare its teeth. It was what the men had been waiting for. As one, the sharp-edged gladii, the Spanish swords, were drawn.

All with the right hand, all from the right side, arcing upwards between the shields in deadly unison, a line of sharp metal teeth. Only the centurion drew across his body. It was his privilege to stand alone.

All along the line of men Germani now fell. Though some had mail, many of them were wearing little protection but their faith in their gods. Their arms and legs were bare, their necks exposed, their headgear offering a scant and unreliable safeguard. The Roman swords stabbed and slashed, the legionaries aiming for the soft flesh where it was exposed, lunging at areas unprotected by bone or leather or armour. The aim was not to kill, but to disable, to put men out of the fight.

But these men, even when grievously injured, did not give up. Instead they fought even more ferociously. If they died in battle, they would go to their own version of Elysium; they would sit with their gods and heroes and feast for ever. All they had to do was to die with a blade in their hand.

This made them harder to fight. They did not care if they were injured; they only cared for a good death, a fighting death.

Quintus held his position in the centre, his sword arm darting out from behind the shield, cutting and withdrawing. A black axe, made haft and head from a single piece of iron, embedded itself in his shield. Whilst the attacker struggled to free it, Quintus swung his gladius and took the man's arm off at the wrist. The scream that followed was as full of rage as pain. The man smashed the boss of his round shield forward, meeting only the implacable face of Quintus' scutum. As a consequence, he was turned sideways, allowing a legionary blade to cut clean across his hams. He crashed to the deck, mortally wounded. The axe stayed in Quintus' shield, as much of an impediment to the attackers as to him.

Some legionaries inevitably fell as the sheer force of the attack beat them back, turning shields, creating gaps through which axe and spear could thrust. But these men were trained, professional. On a command from Quintus, the front row turned their shields sideways and stepped back a pace, even as the second row stepped forward. Within moments the men were at the rear of the formation, dealing with their wounded, taking a breath. At once the Germani faced a full shield wall of fresh men, uninjured, full of energy. Quintus, Rufus and Aquila remained where they were, Quintus in the centre, Rufus and Aquila guarding the standards at either end of the line.

There was no true hand-to-hand fighting — not yet, anyway. The Germani attack was more like the surf crashing against a rock, beaten back in disarray. It was akin to storming the wall of a city, which stood firm against its attackers. The noise of their challenges was now mixed with the groans of the dying and the deck beneath their feet was treacherous with blood and gore. Still more warriors clambered aboard.

The sails on the attacking ships were dropped and grapples deployed. Hooks and ropes that held the vessels to each other were locked closely together. Only a small channel, the water seemingly boiling, remained. It was easy to jump and men kept piling onto the Roman vessel, even though there was less and less room for them on the blood-slicked deck. They struggled to find purchase, to find room to swing a weapon. They struggled to join the advance, grasping at comrades to try and stay aboard.

The press was as Quintus had planned. The tribesmen were pushed and crushed from behind by their own people whilst dead and injured bodies impeded their way ahead. The shield wall still held, implacable, barring their way. They could not keep coming; there was no room and some now failed to clear the gap, falling back onto their own deck or into the water.

This was more like a land action fought on an enclosed battlefield made of slippery timber planks than any sort of sea battle. The fighting ground was the wide wooden deck of the transport, stained and slimy with blood, blocked with bodies.

Quintus continued to defend himself with shield and sword, using the shield as a weapon as well as for protection. One blow with it dislodged the enemy axe, taking a great splinter of wood with it. He barely noticed. His helmet took many a strike, his shoulder armour too. His shield still protected the rest of him. Only his arms were vulnerable, and on his forearms he now wore the metal wrist guards that Sextus had taken from a dead man and given to him.

The legionary formation held, the rows changing places again and again, so that every few moments a rested legionary faced the enemy, whilst the pile of writhing, groaning Germani bodies grew. On Quintus' command the ranks of fighters rotated until familiar faces finally reached the front. Sextus was still smiling, seemingly untouched, Vetruvius looked to have taken an injury to his sword arm, and Crassus was as solid as ever.

Crassus was broad-shouldered and muscular, with a bull's neck and a wrestler's strength. His curly black hair and southern features placed his origins firmly to the far side of Mare Nostrum. He had been a blacksmith in a village near Rome, was still a blacksmith in the legion, and vowed to be a blacksmith again in his own forge. Just as soon as he received his full service pension and the land that went with it — every soldier's dream since Divus Julius had promised it to all.

Now he smiled as he fought, teeth white in his leathery face. He remained the stable rock on which Quintus relied, the tree trunk on which he leant when storm winds blew. They protected each other, even as they continued to hold the enemy back.

The noise made by the attackers had not lessened. Still they screamed and cursed, their voices now mixed with the sounds of the dying. The legionaries had stayed silent, apart from grunts of effort and reinforcing orders. There was heavy breathing and short shouts: 'Maecenas, move.' 'Casca, step back.' 'Pollio, brace.' There was no energy wasted on curses and insults that the enemy would not even comprehend.

Fights were now taking place on other vessels. Quintus' height allowed him to see that the ships to either side of his had also been boarded. But only his ship appeared to have attracted more than one enemy vessel. Two had chosen to grapple with this, the lead ship of the formation, thinking it significant. They did not know that, as far as the admiral and general were concerned, it was no more than bait. Quintus knew that that meant they faced more than a hundred attacking warriors, fifty to each ship, plus the rowers if they left their oars.

His orders were to kill them all, to let none escape. *Noli dare misericordiam*: give no mercy, no quarter — the equivalent of the 'mournful note' on land.

Kill everything.

IV: AQUILA

Quintus judged the moment when he thought there was no room for any more of the enemy to board, then shouted the order to his own cornicen, who raised his battered instrument and blew. The centurion repeated the order aloud, emphasising it with a sword raised high.

'Slow advance in formation.'

Rufus and Aquila held the standards high at either end of the front rank. It was on these that the men dressed the line. Quintus remained in the centre, but stepped back to become one with the line of legionaries rather than standing in front of it. His chipped shield joined the others.

'Step!' He shouted the command, and was pleased to hear it repeated loudly across the deck as the caligae of the front rank crashed to the deck.

'Step!' He called again, and the standards at either end, the spear and hand and Juno's cow, again pulled the shield wall one pace forward. The only sound was the heavy tread of many feet. The ranks moved almost as one man, their smooth progress only stopped by the bodies lying beneath the legionaries' feet. These were not allowed to be a hindrance. They were stepped on or over if dead, and killed if they moved or moaned.

'Step!' Quintus ordered. The tribesmen found themselves jammed against the rail or teetering on the edge of the transport. They were left with a choice. Either they retreated back into their own boats — a leap across to a deck crowded by their compatriots — or they fell into the narrow stretch of water between the vessels. Neither option was easy. The

Germani did not want to retreat, nor did they want to drown. They redoubled their efforts to stay on board, shoving and jostling their fellows in desperation, elbowing companions out of the way with swearing and maledictions.

The Roman advance continued inexorably, and with every step the Germani were pushed towards the water, crashing into each other, falling over the low rail, barely finding the room to lift a weapon. One of their number swung his axe, but not at the Romans. He used it to cut one of the hawsers that held the ships together, then turned and chopped through the other. If these warriors had ever thought of retreating to the safety of their own decks, it was not now possible.

'They have loosed the hooks!' Crassus shouted, as the two smaller ships disengaged and began to drift away.

'They intend to die!' Quintus called. 'Let us aid them in their quest, men. Once more. Step!'

The press of shields moved forward and splashes signalled Germani fighters falling into the water. Rather than swimming towards their own boats, they attempted to climb back aboard, determined to fight. They grabbed hold of the clothing of their companions, tugging at them, preventing them from fighting, desperate to be back on their feet. The men still on board roughly pushed them off. They even cut off the grasping fingers. They could not fight with a brother hanging from their trews, and it was their own passage to the afterlife that was most important.

Quintus once more called the order to step, to advance, and again the machine rolled forward, leaving less and less space in which the Germani were penned. Still they swung axe and sword, still they wielded shields, still they had breath for curses and calls on their gods, even as they scrabbled for footholds on the deck, slipping backwards in the spilled blood and finally tumbling into the water.

The men remaining on the enemy boats could be seen hurrying to hoist their sails and use their oars to open the gap, the blades frantically splashing in the water. They were leaving the fighting men behind.

'Slaves or prisoners at the oars,' spat Rufus, with disdain. 'Look, they are abandoning them.' He was right; the space between the boats had already grown too wide to jump.

'Keen to leave their masters,' Sextus added, as he pulled one of their own spears from a body and flung it after them. 'Be glad that only free men row Roman ships.'

The press became too much for many of the Germani warriors, and they pitched backwards into the lake, try as they might to keep their feet. Gaps opened up on the deck, the remaining Germani standing to fight in ones and twos. A legionary took a half step forward, reaching to stab at the defeated enemy that was just out of his reach.

'Stay in line!' Crassus ordered sharply, his sword arm swinging round and crashing into the man's chest. 'We survive by staying in line.'

The legionary knew this. His move to step from the safety of the shield wall was a stupid one. He shook his head, the moment of madness passed, and he stepped back quickly. He knew that if both he and his optio survived, and the officer remembered, he might yet be flogged.

Another man, seemingly with the same idea, stepped out of the ranks and moved ahead of the legionaries. He was a tall man, wearing a wolfskin cloak, the animal's head snarling above his helmet.

'Who is that signifer?' Crassus demanded, recognising the cloak. 'Why does he carry no banner or standard?'

The signifer let his shield fall with a clatter and pushed the wolf's head back. With one hand he undid his helmet and pulled it from his head, dropping it to the deck. His hair, long and pale, and his face, pale and clean-shaven, were familiar.

'Aquila!' Quintus shouted, recognising his comrade. 'Back in line!'

But the man ignored him. With gladius drawn and raised in one hand, and pugio gripped in the other, Aquila stepped towards the remaining enemy warriors. They were temporarily amazed, and briefly opened a passage for this otherworldly apparition. Aquila stepped into the space and continued across the deck. At the edge he silently stepped into the air as if it was solid. He seemed to manage a pace, as if the ether would indeed hold his weight; then he faltered and fell, splashing into the churning waters below, joining the many Germani desperately trying to stay afloat as clothing and armour and injury pulled them down. No javelin or axe found its mark. The aquilifer just walked into Neptune's kingdom as if he was marching in front of a legion.

'Aquila!' Quintus shouted again, in desperation. But the water had already closed over the head of the aquilifer. He made no attempt to swim.

Quintus was stunned by the incident, they all were, but there was no time to try and understand. The Germani recovered quickly, filled the gap and renewed what was left of their attack.

'The standard!' Quintus called.

'I have it,' responded Vetruvius. 'It is safe.'

'Enough of this,' Quintus said to himself, then he ordered the cornicen, 'Blow *contendite vestra sponte.*'

The stirring notes, two short, one long, repeated, brought a rousing cheer from the men. The order to choose an individual opponent to battle gave them the chance to fight man-to-man, maybe even to gain war trophies — helms or swords or jewellery. Unlike their enemy, the Romans were more interested in wealth than heads.

The shields finally separated as legionaries picked their opponents. They worked in pairs, one man and his *amicus*, methodically crippling the warriors that remained standing. Some died of their wounds, while others were disarmed or fell to the deck, still resisting.

'You will have to kill them,' Quintus said, with a tone of respect for the enemy. 'They will not flee.'

'Then they die.' Crassus shoulder-charged one of the standing Germani overboard as he spoke. Others were falling all around him. There was space to breathe now, and the men could see the other ships. More and more of the attacking vessels were retreating, breaking off engagements and attempting to flee to safety.

'Bring me fire,' Quintus commanded. 'Our orders are to let none escape. Crassus, see if we can set them alight.'

Burning torches were hurriedly run from the back of the transport and lit at a brazier that glowed near the helmsman. The men carrying them were intercepted by the burly optio.

'Here, light these.' He held forth two spears, points wrapped in cloth. Crassus knew how to tame fire. His blacksmith's arms were criss-crossed with tiny burns, his face scarred with what looked like white scratches where cinders and sparks had landed. The spears ignited and he handed them back to their legionary owners. 'Cast them well,' he said. The men stepped forward as far as they could, avoiding the bodies, some of which still moved. They drew back their arms and released the spears as if they were competing on the Campus Martius. One spear fell short, skewering a body in the water then hissing into

34

steamy nothingness. Another stuck fast in the stern of the nearer vessel, still burning.

Crassus beckoned to other soldiers. 'Bring me more. Is there a champion here?'

The men knew what he was asking and one stepped forward. 'I took the laurels, sir. But only once.'

'Earn them now.' Crassus handed him a fiery spear. The man stepped over the bodies, bent his legs and raised his left arm in the classic stance. He uncoiled like a spring and sent the spear whistling towards the enemy. The legionary had clearly earned his accolade that day; the spear flew high and far. It pinned a furled sail, which blossomed into flame, the fire running along the folds to set the rest of the ship alight. A second ship, too close, caught sparks, the fires helped by the capricious breeze. The men aboard were already abandoning the vessels, flinging themselves into the water.

'Again,' Crassus urged, passing another spear across. Once more the man launched the burning weapon at the retreating ships that had minutes ago been roped to them. It disappeared into the space where the rowers sat.

'Some will escape,' Quintus said with a shrug. He was next to Rufus and Sextus. 'Not our fault. If they had let us have our Anatolians…'

He let the thought die on the air. The Anatolian archers, who had been of such value to the cohort, were somewhere to the rear, aboard another transport, on the orders of some idiot at headquarters. They were unable to even take part in the action.

'They would have picked them off,' said Sextus, in agreement. Screams were heard from inside the ships; flames bloomed from where the last spear had vanished. 'Some will be chained to the oars,' he added with indifference.

Many enemy ships along the line of engagement were either fired or sinking. Some had managed to escape and were rowing away. Not all the warriors had fought; only a minority of the ships had been in battle on either side. The majority of the Roman vessels took no part in the engagement except as spectators. The hottest of the fighting had been on the lead Roman ship and the two that flanked it. They had been attacked by four enemy craft in total. The other enemy ships had turned away long before they had been brought to battle. Quintus wondered whether these other vessels even held fighters.

The rest of the enemy ships were soon out of range, even for a champion. Legionaries on Quintus' own decks were throwing javelins towards the bodies in the water, hoping to finish the slaughter. Quintus spoke to his optio. 'Crassus, tell them to cease. They are wasting weapons. Let the bastards burn or drown. However they wish to reach their noble ends.' He turned in time to see the last of the Germani on deck being killed.

'Tell the men to take whatever they want,' he ordered unemotionally. 'There will not be much.'

V: PALLIUM LUPUS

Crassus supervised the clearing of the remainder of the dead from the deck. They had been efficiently stripped of anything of value — metal that looked like silver or bronze, armlets, torcs and amulets. Few weapons were taken; most were considered of such poor quality they were tipped into the lake. Leather buckets were filled with water and the timbers swilled down. Injured legionaries were taken to the rear, where Alba examined and bandaged wounds. Quintus had managed to retain the services of the capsarius. There was no medicus ordinarius on this ship, so this was the best they could hope for.

Many enemy ships still burned on the water, sparks and cinders sizzling as the wind carried them away. The rest swiftly faded across the lake. The air smelt of smoke and charred flesh. The cries of the burnt and drowned gradually subsided, to be replaced by the incongruous calls of the lake-dwelling flocks of birds whose peace had been disturbed.

The drumbeat was once more ordered, and the oarsmen dipped and pulled, the blades pushing floating bodies aside. The transports, big and lumbering, rolled over any of the Germani corpses and smoking detritus that was in their way. Those desperate hands that still managed to scrabble at the timbers were ignored or swept aside callously with spear butts or caligae.

'I hope they found their way to their own Elysian Fields,' mused Sextus, watching from the prow. 'But I do not understand why they bothered. They were never going to defeat a force so much bigger than themselves.'

'Honour and bravery?' Rufus suggested, without conviction.

'Neither.' Quintus shook his head. 'I think that this tribe wanted the invaders — us — to know that they have not submitted to Rome, that they would never submit to Rome. I do not understand why they are so opposed to being civilised.' There was no irony in his voice. One of the few things that they all believed in implicitly — along with the gods and fortune — was the mission of Rome to civilise barbarians. Why would these peoples not want order and discipline, regular food, roads and canals?

'Their fleet of small ships was not enough,' Quintus concluded. 'It did not matter how brave or honourable were the men within. It was never any more than a gesture of defiance.'

Sextus dared to raise the subject that they were all avoiding. 'What about Aquila? What happened? Did they enchant him? Was he possessed by spirits?'

'Perhaps he was possessed,' said Rufus. 'He gave Vetruvius the standard, but he gave me his leather satchel to hold. I have only now looked inside it. It holds the wills of many men with which he was entrusted. When he gave it to me, he took my wolfskin cloak from my back. He said that he was borrowing it. Because it was him, I allowed it. I thought that he must have a reason. I was stupid,' he added with a shake of his head. 'I should have seen what he was planning.'

'How could you have known?' Sextus said consolingly. He knew that Rufus' intervention would not have prevented Aquila taking his own life at some other time.

Rufus was saddened by his own loss. 'My *pallium lupus*, my wolf's cloak, is gone. I do not know how I will account for it.'

'No,' said Quintus, pointing to where something black had snagged on the transport. 'Though Aquila sank, the cloak lies on the water. He has left it for you. There.'

Gratefully, Rufus went down on his knees. Leaning over the rail, he used a spear to hook the cloak and bring it back on board. It was in a sorry state.

'I am glad you have it back,' said Quintus. 'The loss would have caused you much trouble with the quaestor.' He held the cloak up and peered at it with a critical eye. 'A task for the slaves, my friend.'

'He was attacking,' replied Sextus, though without conviction. 'He was armed, heading for the enemy.'

'He was aquilifer no more,' said Quintus, shaking his head. 'Though he stole your cloak, Rufus, you have your standard still. You are signifer still. Aquila was better than that; he was aquilifer to the legion. To him it was as if the eagle had been gifted to him by the gods. He became his famous father, the man who inspired the armies of Divus Julius. Though never promoted to it, he *became* the Aquilifer of the Fifth. Once Tiberius took the eagle from him, it was as if the gods had abandoned him, as if all the life had drained from him.'

'We noticed,' said Rufus, as he shook the worst of the water from the sodden cloak. He held up the skin to the light. It was heavy and awkward. 'He laughed no more, not even a smile, and he cursed the gods rather than praising them. He sulked for days on end.'

Sextus nodded in agreement. 'He was insubordinate, too. Stubborn. Slow to obey orders.'

'His own wolfskin he had to give up,' said Rufus quietly. 'The very thing that set him apart, that made him of those chosen by the gods. He was not made signifer officially, nor issued with an animal skin to carry the *signum*. It might have kept him alive.'

'I doubt it,' said Vetruvius, returning from having his sword arm bound. He still held the standard. 'He was keen to be rid of this life. If not now, he would have found another way.'

'Would you have stopped him had you known what he intended, Quintus?' Sextus asked.

'Probably not,' Quintus replied with a sigh. 'I am not sure that even he knew what he intended. Perhaps Neptune was calling him home. His father defied the sea gods; perhaps this is just the circle closing. I hope they record his death with honour.'

'It depends on who witnessed it,' muttered Rufus, still trying to squeeze water from his heavy cloak. 'If it was just us, then maybe he will find Elysium. Will the Vestals pay for him, Sextus?'

'I think so,' said the seer. 'He has much to recommend him. He stopped a mutiny in Hispania, he was the spearpoint at the relief of the winter fort in Germania, and he helped take the oppidum that held our commander. He led the men on many occasions. Look at the wills entrusted to him. They respected his leadership.'

'Let us hope that Charon grants him passage,' said Vetruvius, grasping the rail as the drumbeat quickened once more and the transport lurched forward. He held out the standard. 'Sir, I do not want this. It is an honour too high for me, even though it took me to the front of the queue for the capsarius.'

'It is yours for now. Protect it,' said Quintus.

There had been some casualties and deaths amongst the legionaries, but not many of either. Most of the flotilla, including the better appointed ships of both the admiral and the general, had seen no fighting at all. Their complements had not even drawn weapons.

A number of the enemy ships had escaped. Quintus suspected mutinies aboard, or slave oarsmen, considering the determination of the other warriors to die on Roman swords.

To Tiberius Claudius Nero, General, Praetor, son of Caesar Augustus, the attack was an affront. It had been his idea to sail across the lake, vast as it was, rather than struggle around it. He should have been allowed to do so calmly, rather than being interrupted by a rabble of tiny boats. And that any had escaped to fight another day rankled painfully.

Though still a young man, Tiberius had a reputation as a strict disciplinarian. It was inevitable that he would punish those he thought were at fault. That included the advisers who failed to persuade him otherwise, the captains of the transports, the centurions on the ships, of course. Quintus felt that he would be singled out. The lead ship had taken casualties and failed to totally destroy the enemy. Of course he must be at fault.

The transports, now unopposed, took more than a day to take the four legions and their auxiliaries, baggage and slaves across the lake. The construction of the camp on the far bank was started by the first arrivals and carried out in near silence, apart from barked orders.

The formation had been changed from an arrow, where Quintus' ship was at the point, to a crescent, the two wings carrying the senior officers apparently keen to outpace him. This meant that they were amongst the last to land, the camp already well established.

Tiberius blamed his staff officers for the action. They in turn blamed their subordinates. The centurions carried this resentment to their men. Many vine staffs were wielded by disgruntled officers. Many legionaries were harshly punished or demoted that day, purely because of the mood of the general.

One centurion, speaking out of turn, stood for a day and a night outside the general's tent, shamed. He wore no belt, so that his tunic hung like a woman's dress. He held in front of him one of the turfs that would be cut to build a rampart, his arms burning with the weight, his face with the humiliation. But, jealous of his rank and station, he did not let it drop. Once returned to duty, his men felt the sting of his vine staff for the slightest infraction.

The three other centuries of the understrength cohort, posted to other ships, joined them. They had also seen action, Centurion Felix of Century Four and his optio Marcus vying with Sextus and Rufus in the tales they told. Centurion Furius Lentulus and Centurion Marius each brought in fewer than a full complement of men from their centuries. When they heard of Aquila's strange demise, they were, more than anything, puzzled.

Marcus remembered the loss of his own primus amicus. Tullius had lost two previous brothers and saddled himself with the nickname Mal Fortuna, the unlucky one. Yet Marcus had accepted him and the two had become fast friends. Tullius' previous amicus had been falsely accused of cowardice and flogged to death in the punishment of *verberatio*, used to make an example before the men.

Marcus' own legionary brother had also been executed, killed by his own men in another brutal punishment. 'The sentence of *decimatio* is a rare one — to die violently at your comrades' hands, along with one in ten others,' he said now. 'But Ursus fell victim to it. An attack gone wrong, an officer lacking experience, an enemy allowed to escape. Does this sound familiar?'

'In that the punishment falls on the innocent?' Felix nodded in confirmation.

Quintus still carried Ursus' will and last wishes. Divus Julius himself had rewarded Ursus with a copper band for bravery in the days when mere legionaries had been allowed such recognition. The will, faded now, was kept in an ingenious pouch sewn close to Quintus' skin. The copper armband was kept with it. He touched them now for luck. Ursus had charged Quintus with taking his will back to his wife and child in Rome, and with keeping the comrades safe. Every time Quintus thought of the vow, he was ashamed by how much he had failed in the second of these tasks. Few of the original companions remained. Aquila was just the latest comrade he had lost.

'Tullius at least avenged his own friend,' said Sextus who, until Tullius had died, had been the only other to know this. 'He killed the centurion responsible for the lie that saw him condemned.'

'Aquila could hardly kill Tiberius for taking back what was his,' Rufus huffed. 'We have all lost brothers before. *Sic vita*, such is life.'

'But Aquila had seemed indestructible. A symbol of permanence.' Vetruvius shook his head sadly and retreated into a dark corner. He did not wish to speak any more of it.

'He prays, I think,' said Rufus. 'He hopes to help his friend across the Styx.'

Sextus shook his head. 'It is the waters of the river Lethe that Aquila will need — the waters of forgetfulness.'

'What did he hope to gain?' Felix asked. 'The eagle might have come back to him if he had been patient.'

'Unlikely,' said Marcus. 'It was never his. General Tiberius will have forgotten about it already.'

'Noble Tiberius of Caesar's own household,' said Rufus, jealously, deliberately moving the discussion away from Aquila. He pointed to the general's pavilions. 'I imagine there is much to envy in there.'

'Wine, I should think,' said Sextus, 'and fresh meat, and probably women.'

'Women would be good,' Rufus said wistfully. He had left his own 'wife' behind in Hispania, a woman with whom he had once hoped to raise a family. He had been punished, demoted, for his 'marriage'. Infantry soldiers were not encouraged to wed natives.

'I have seen inside. It is not exactly Spartan,' Quintus admitted with a smile. 'I do not want to see inside again, Rufus. Last time Tiberius demoted Aquila. Next time it could be me.'

VI: LEX EXERCITUS

Quintus' woefully truncated cohort barely registered next to the camps of the full legions, each snug within its own long ditch and mound defence. The typical square, dissected by two main roads, repeated itself again and again, crawling from the lakeside up into the hills. The first arrivals had claimed the best sites, nearest to water and wood. Those who came last camped on rocky or uneven ground, or had to negotiate the bogs that their compatriots had avoided. Auxiliaries who tried to claim good ground were barged away like vagrants in the city. There were many fights, unnecessary injuries and even deaths, making the resentment deeper.

The gates all faced away from the water, each with its own set of legionaries on guard. Quintus could see tent lines all along the side of the lake, vanishing into the distance. Smoke rose from innumerable fires. The camp squares each carried a collection of larger tents at their centre — the stores and armouries and officers' quarters. The biggest of these, the most luxurious, was the command pavilion where General Tiberius consulted his officers.

Quintus gave clear commands to the other three centurions in the cohort, and they marched the men smartly to their own campground, as if they were some sort of victorious procession. Furius Lentulus was an imposing figure. He had a full head of black hair, worn long, and a neat black beard. His arms and legs were also covered in black hair, which had earned him the name 'little Caesar' — the 'hairy one.' Clearly this was no longer acceptable as a nickname, so he insisted on the use of both of his names. As the commander of Century Two his rank was Second Spear Centurion of the cohort.

The cohort had barely three hundred men, some horses, though no cavalry, and a few auxiliaries and slaves. At least it still had its own signifer, who carried the *signum* on which flew Juno's cow — even though Rufus' wolfskin cloak dripped water. When a senior centurion suggested that considering their reduced numbers they give this up, Quintus insisted it was issued to this cohort of the Ninth Hispania specifically and, as the Ninth was not here, he would defend it and their right to fly it. Quintus had listened to his former commander Titus Flavius and others, so he knew how to issue orders as if born to it. He was well versed in acting the part of a noble, of one with *auctoritas*, and had perfected the tone of voice and supercilious gaze of the entitled. The centurion backed down, and their little corner was now marked with vexilla and guarded by legionaries.

At first light, as soon as the noise of cornicenes blowing to announce daybreak ceased, a centurion arrived at their area, fresh-minted with a bright red cloak and polished, undamaged helm. He was escorted by a pair of legionaries, also shiny.

'Centurion Julius Quintus Quirinius of the Ninth Hispania? The general will speak with you,' the visitor said, tapping his vine cane rhythmically on his hand. He did not wait for an answer, but turned on his heel, shaking his head and muttering scornfully, 'Not even a proper cohort.' He threw a look of disdain at the tattered and faded standard with its black on red figure no longer distinct.

Although Quintus knew that he would be expected forthwith, he did not feel like dogging the footsteps of this bundle of insolence. He was irritated that his own guards had

46

allowed the centurion in. Of course they had no right to stop him, they were all one, but they should at least have tried.

'Fetch Jovan and Maxim,' Quintus commanded the legionary who had brought the visitors in. 'Then get back to your post. Try not to let anyone else in.'

The two slaves came at a rapid pace. They had been gained by Quintus' contubernium back in Hispania and had managed to stay with the group. They were Macedonian fighting men, but had other skills as well. Jovan, with thick black hair and an even thicker beard, was literate and numerate, having been a factor once. Maxim shared the set of nose and chin and colouring of his cousin, but kept his beard carefully trimmed. He had been a farmer and had an affinity with animals. He and the husbandman in Quintus would have been friends in another life. Maxim arrived first, wiping his hands on a cloth. He had been preparing food. Jovan was not far behind him.

'I need to look presentable,' Quintus told them.

'Jovan, a tunic,' Maxim said to his cousin, seeing the state of the one that Quintus wore.

Jovan turned on his heel. He soon came running back, a freshly washed tunic under his arm. 'Sextus found it, sir. It is unblemished.'

'Of course he did,' laughed Quintus, unbuckling his belt and handing it to the slave. He pulled his own blood-stained and dirty tunic over his head and took the replacement from Jovan. As he pulled on the fresh linen, he turned to his amicus. 'What did I do wrong, Crassus?'

'Nothing, as far as I can see.'

'But Tiberius might see further. Think.'

Crassus was helping to clean his weapons. This was, of course, the role that Tullius would have insisted on taking. He might even have lent Quintus his own weapons. He was in borrowed gear anyway.

Centurion Felix lent his cloak — in much better condition than the one Quintus had. Centurion Furius Lentulus offered his helmet, but it did not fit Quintus. He could have kept it beneath his arm, but he would have looked distinctly foolish if ordered to don it. He decided to keep his own. The uneven crest — the result of a Germanic blow — would serve as a mark of honour. Or so he hoped.

He fastened his baltea over the tunic. Crassus lifted up the lorica laminata — now as clean as he could manage — and placed it over Quintus' shoulders. Jovan ducked round to the back to begin tying it on.

'Gladius,' said Quintus, and took the offered sword from Crassus, hanging the baldric across his shoulder.

'You let some of the tribesmen escape,' said Crassus. 'Perhaps that is why Tiberius wants to see you.'

'I did not let them. They chose to flee,' Quintus replied, as he shrugged his shoulders to settle tunic and armour and weaponry. He saw Crassus was about to speak. 'I know, I will need a better excuse than that.'

'I don't think it is a crime, Quintus.' Crassus was looking his friend up and down, to see if there was anything that might be improved. Jovan finished tying the armour.

Quintus shook his head. 'I think anything can be a crime in the army. The *lex exercitus* can be rewritten by commanders as they please. Cloak, Jovan.' The slave held up the *sagum*, the red cloak of war. Quintus took it and fastened it at the shoulder with a simple pin. Gold or silver, or anything that looked like it, might upset the general. 'Anything else?'

'Just the escaped Germani and —' Crassus hesitated — 'of course, Aquila. Tiberius may have heard how he died.'

'Honourably,' Quintus said firmly, taking the battered but shiny helm with its uneven crest from Crassus. He squared his shoulders. Though he shook inwardly as he prepared to obey the summons to the general's tent, he put on a cheery grin. 'Wish me *bon Fortuna*, both of you. No time for a sacrifice, but prayers would be useful.'

'Of course,' said Jovan, bowing his head. Crassus saluted, fist to heart.

Quintus' steps towards the general's pavilion were heavy. He picked up his vine cane as he left, not expecting to return with it, or his crest for that matter. He assumed that he was at least to be demoted. He thought hard about what he may or may not have done to earn the wrath of Tiberius. He was certain that such a summons could not mean anything good.

VII: SCUTARIUS

The centurions in front of the headquarters relieved Quintus of his gladius and pugio. It would not do to go armed into the general's presence. After a brief conversation they, rather apologetically, also took his vine rod.

'Helmet off,' said one, as he lifted the flap to allow Quintus into the opulent space within. Inside was bright with torches, even though it was day. Since he had been here before, the seasons had turned. Outside it was cold. The side of the tent was no longer open as it had been on his previous visit. Instead braziers burned and smoke swirled heavily. Four silent guards stood at regular spaces around the room. These were not legionaries, Quintus noted. They were Germani, half dressed as natives, but wearing cloaks as a Roman soldier would. They were probably each as tall as him and were certainly broader-shouldered. For once he felt small.

The rushes at his feet were fresh, the tent walls richly patterned and the general's suit of armour dazzled on its wooden dummy. It was shiny and silver, the breastplate beaten out to make its wearer look like an Adonis or a Hercules. In this room of the tent there was no furniture but the braziers.

'Forward,' said one of the praetorians gruffly, gesturing with a spear. This time Tiberius was not going to come out to greet Quintus as he had done before, nor, he guessed, offer him wine from a silver jug. Quintus ducked under the flap to enter the next space. It was much smaller, dominated by a scowling man sitting behind a desk. There were no other seats.

Quintus recognised Tiberius. He was a young man, with short, dark, curly hair framing a round face that carried the gentle scars of a childhood disease. He was too young to hold any of the high offices of state, even the most junior of magistracies, yet he was already praetor, by the leave of Caesar Augustus, his adoptive father. In a year or two he would be consul.

He might be young, but Quintus knew that he was already accomplished, lauded and laurel-wreathed. Before he had even put on his manly gown he had ridden the trace-horse at Augustus' triple triumph over the god killers of Divus Julius, over Dalmatia and over Antonius and the Egyptian queen at Actium. He was not one to let anyone — friend or enemy — stand in his way.

This time, unlike when Quintus had been in this tent before, there was no clasping of the arm, no greeting of brother to brother. Tiberius was clothed in a simple tunic and sitting on a curule chair behind a dark wooden desk. A wolf's pelt covered the chair. The general's substantial gold ring caught Quintus' eye. It was carved with the *lituus* or divining staff of the college of augurs. The hand that wore it grasped the wolfskin. The skin made Quintus think of Rufus and Aquila; perhaps his friend had worn it once.

'I think you have been here before, centurion?' Tiberius said abruptly. There was no greeting, no preamble.

The general spoke with a city accent, smooth and cultured. Quintus thought he must sound clumsy by comparison. He swallowed, his mouth dry. 'I have, sir. I brought you the Eagle of the Fifth.'

Tiberius shook his head. 'Not you. That was another, an aquilifer. Except he wasn't, was he?'

'Sir?' Quintus was unsure of his response.

'He wasn't an aquilifer,' said Tiberius. 'He was a pretender. A masquerader. An actor.'

Tiberius had recently celebrated the Ludi Romani. There had been theatre performances, so the idea of acting was on his mind.

'He had no right to either the rank or the respect, did he? No right to the wolfskin cloak or the title or the pay. Am I not right?'

The thought crossed Quintus' mind to say that Aquila had never received the pay. None of them had. He quickly smothered it. 'It is true, sir. He aspired to the post rather than being promoted to it. Our own commander gave him the care of the eagle. He took the rank and title for himself. On account of his father.'

'His father?' Tiberius was at least curious.

'His father, sir, was aquilifer to Divus Julius. He was aquilifer to the Tenth Equestris when Oceanus was first crossed.' Then he went too far, veering away from mere description. 'He it was who inspired the men to leave their ships and set foot on Britannia. He it was who stepped into the water with the eagle of the Tenth, urging the men to follow.'

'And would my grandfather not have had a say in this?' Tiberius asked, with an edge to his voice. Of course, Quintus realised, this was, through the workings of endorsement and adoption, the legal grandson of Divus Julius. He would not accept any criticism of the god.

'Of course, sir,' Quintus replied quickly. 'It was Divus Julius they were following, not the aquilifer.' *Although*, he thought, *the story is well known and attested to by General Caesar himself.*

Tiberius leaned back again. The look on his face, a slight smile, told Quintus that he had decided not to be offended. The smile did not reach his eyes. It seemed that this was a test. Perhaps just a game. Rumour had it that Tiberius liked his games.

The smile vanished. 'So your false aquilifer stepped into the water like his father — only without an eagle?'

Quintus did not know how to respond. Clearly a report had reached the ears of the general. He did not know how, but continued to be amazed at the information that Tiberius appeared to have at his fingertips. He looked at the floor.

'Was he sending a message?'

'A message, sir?'

'That he had the right to be aquilifer and I did not have the right to deprive him of it?'

'I do not think so, sir,' Quintus stuttered, flustered at this line of questioning. 'I cannot know his mind.'

'You know I rode beside my father in his great triumph, and that for the final act he rode too — no chariot for him. He used the parade to send a message, riding ahead of the magistrates, not behind them.'

'I know, sir. A subtle message,' Quintus said quietly.

Tiberius laughed with genuine amusement. 'About as subtle as one of my praetorians with an axe head.' Quintus noticed that the men heard the noise and took a half step forward, hands on weapons. Tiberius sent them back with a nonchalant wave. 'He wanted the message to be obvious. Did your aquilifer want the same?'

Quintus was so lacking in confidence that he found himself whispering, 'I don't think so, sir. Few saw him.'

After a pause that seemed to stretch out for a lifetime, Tiberius asked softly, 'Was it a good death, centurion?'

Quintus squared his shoulders and looked directly at the general. 'He had a blade in each hand and the enemy in front of him. I believe it was a good death, sir. I hope he has found Elysium.'

'Did he have coin to pay Charon his passage?'

'That I do not know, sir. But I think his passage was paid.'

Tiberius was curious and gestured for him to continue.

'One of my men was brought up as a ward of the Vestals,' Quintus explained. 'He says that they have promised to pay the fare for any soldier who falls in battle. I hope Aquila had his fare.' Privately, he guessed that Aquila had intended to die and would have placed a coin beneath his tongue.

'Let us hope so. Let us let him rest in Neptune's bosom.'

Again, Quintus did not know how to respond, so he merely stared at the rushes on the floor of the tent.

'You brought me men, centurion.' Tiberius tipped his head backwards. 'Look me in the eye,' he said sternly.

Quintus, with reluctance, raised his head and matched the general's gaze.

Tiberius continued, 'I put them on the front line deliberately. Advice I took from one on my staff. They were cowards, I was told. They had been deserters. The cohort was punished. And then there is the eagle. The eagle that your aquilifer friend carried was captured by the Germani. You retrieved it, so well done to you. But the shame of losing it runs deep, when I went to such trouble to bring back the eagles from Parthia — the ones lost by Licinius Crassus.'

Quintus knew this. It was one of the many shining achievements of the young commander. He had led a commission to investigate slave-farms in Italia, to stop their owners from kidnapping travellers and harbouring men avoiding military service. He had put foreign princes on their thrones. He had secured grain to feed Rome. He had brought back the lost eagles.

'I was told that they broke faith with our allies amongst the Germani. That they could not be trusted.' Tiberius paused. 'Yet I am now told that they fought well. That on the whole they did not die. Is this true?'

Quintus knew they were put at risk; they had not known that they were meant to die. 'We lost a few men, sir, including the aquilifer.'

'The aquilifer-that-wasn't, soldier. Remember that.'

Quintus nodded. He did not dare to drop his eyes to the floor again, so he fixed his gaze on a spot by Tiberius' head. A painted canvas. A particularly well wrought depiction of a naked river nymph, part of a large river scene.

Tiberius leant forward. 'Centurion, this action should not have happened. In the records, it will be as if this action never happened. There will be no rewards, no bonus pay, no deaths recorded. We should not have been opposed. My intelligence was that we should have been able to float across this lake in peace.' He shook his head in disappointment.

'It was not true. There will be floggings for those Romans who brought us this information, crucifixions for those tribesmen who informed them. These tribes are supposed to be allies, not enemies.' He paused, took a breath, then spoke more gently.

'I have lost good men. Not many, granted, but good men nonetheless. Their families will know they died honourably in service, but not that they drowned. They should believe they are in Elysium.'

He narrowed his eyes and drew his lips into a stern line. 'Your aquilifer-that-wasn't will not be amongst them. As far as I am concerned, he did not exist.'

Quintus would have objected, but knew that his life depended on what he said and what Tiberius said in the next few moments. He did not dare speak, nor move his fixed gaze from the nymph.

Tiberius rose and stepped from behind the desk. He was not as tall as Quintus; few men were. But he was built like a soldier, straight-shouldered and well proportioned. He deliberately blocked Quintus' view of the painting. 'Me, centurion,' he said. 'Concentrate on me.'

Quintus managed to look at him as he carried on. He realised that, against all expectation, he was having his rank confirmed. Tiberius had called him centurion. Perhaps Tiberius thought that he was bestowing a great honour on him. Perhaps he thought it a joke. Quintus did not know.

'Centurion, we captured some of the tribe that attacked my transports; they are called the Vindelici. They are supposed to be defeated, supposed to be allies now. We have taken many of their men and sent them back to Rome to see if they can be trained as legionaries.' He allowed himself a small smile. 'We know they make poor slaves. If they can be trained, they will be useful auxiliaries. The rest should be tamed.' He lifted Quintus' chin with his hand, studied his face, then let go.

'You and your men are useful. Deniable. Disposable. In the records, you do not exist. You sank when you crossed from Hispania, or died when the Germani defeated you. Or when they killed your commander and his women, and your own First Spear centurion.'

Quintus could not stop his mouth falling open. He gaped at the intelligence held by Tiberius. He wanted to know how he had come by such detailed information but did not dare ask.

'Close your mouth. I have my sources,' Tiberius said with a trace of humour. 'You will be my irregulars, my *irregulares milites*. You will find this nest of vipers that dares attack me and remove it. Do you understand?'

'Sir,' said Quintus.

'You will be my optio — my chosen one.' Tiberius paused. 'No, not optio, for I am no mere centurion. I think you will be my scutarius, my shield-bearer. You will scout the ground before my legions. You will pick up any caltrops, fill in any trenches, knock down any fences.'

Quintus was still not sure if he kept his rank. But then Tiberius confirmed it.

'You will command, centurion, although you will not have a century to your name, nor a crested helm. You will take no standards, no vexilla, no cornicenes. You will take no auxiliaries. You will take your swords, of course, but only partial armour.'

It was then that Quintus realised that his avoidance of death for some unnamed crime had only postponed the event. He was to die as a spy.

'You will be posing as Germani — tribesmen who have stripped the Roman soldiers that they killed. Your dress will be native. Your horses will be native ponies. You will find these Vindelici that stood against me and destroy them, all of them. Do you understand?'

'Sir.'

Tiberius put his hand on Quintus' shoulder, the first gesture of amity between them at this meeting. Now he smiled. 'You may take what men you wish, as long as they agree to go with you. Any that do not will be absorbed into one of my legions — Rapax, I think.' He threw this name into the shadows.

Quintus had not noticed the scribe standing nearby, but now he heard the scratch of his stylus.

Tiberius turned back. 'Your officers I will give a choice. They can join your renegades and irregulars and opt for an early death or decide that proper discipline in a proper legion would be better for them. For what it is worth, they can keep their ranks and titles — although the signiferi will be empty-handed. Do you accept the commission?'

Quintus did not expect to be asked for his compliance. Surely this was an order? Nevertheless, he nodded and said, 'Of course, sir. It is an honour.'

'No, it isn't,' said Tiberius bluntly. 'But have it your own way. You will not be sent off to the sound of brass and harness jingling. You will vanish in the night and your little corner of my camp will vanish with you. Your standards will become our standards, your wolfskins our wolfskins, your slaves and auxiliaries ours also.' He lifted a hand, as if a thought had just struck him. 'I will honour the standard of your cohort. It has seen much travel, much service. It will be packed away safely and either returned to the Ninth, or end up dedicated to Jupiter Optimus Maximus on the Capitoline. You will send it to this man.' He called beyond Quintus, 'Atticus.'

One of the centurions who guarded the entrance was instantly inside the tent, ready to serve. He looked down a distinctive long nose. Quintus compared the shiny armour, sleek folded cloak and unscarred face with his own appearance.

'Atticus will give you your orders,' Tiberius said. 'You will send the standard back with him. Leave me.'

The order was absolute. The men both left the general's presence, Quintus more than glad to do so.

'That is the last time you will see the general,' said Atticus as they stopped outside the tent, far enough away that neither guard nor anyone within the tent could hear them. 'At least until the mission is complete, and that is likely to take years. Nor will you often see me, although I will receive reports of your whereabouts and actions and I will pass on any new orders. There will be other go-betweens. Officially, you will not exist.'

Quintus nodded. 'I understand.'

'Your first mission is to find this branch of the Vindelici and destroy it — also any other tribes you find skulking, pretending they have not been conquered. Further orders will follow.'

'The men?'

'The general suggested three tents, twenty-four men. Plus the officers. No auxiliaries, no slaves. Native ponies. Native dress. Go now and choose the men. Then vanish quietly from the camp. Leave the standard with the remainder of the cohort. I will collect it. Be gone by morning. Succeed and more missions will follow.'

Quintus collected his weapons from the soldier that held them, as well as his vine rod. He was genuinely surprised to find that he still had a right to it. He turned and began the long walk back to the cohort that would soon no longer exist.

VIII: LUSTRATIO

Crassus and Sextus were waiting for him outside their camp. They were sitting on an outcrop of rock and rose as he approached. The looks on their faces betrayed their surprise.

'You still have your helmet,' said Sextus.

'And your vine staff,' said Crassus. 'So you have kept your rank?'

'Yes, Crassus, I have kept my rank,' said Quintus. 'Although I think it is now meaningless.' He sat with them, shook his head and sighed deeply. 'General Tiberius seems to be aware of everything we have done, my friends. It would seem that he has spies amongst the beasts of the forest and the birds of the air. He not only knew everything that happened on the water, but also all the events leading up to it. He knew of the death of the commander, of his women, of Galba even. He almost accused us of bad faith with the Germani tribe that led us astray. He knew the manner of Aquila's death. How do you explain it, Sextus? Does he have a direct link to the gods?'

Sextus shrugged. 'They do claim descent from Venus, so maybe it comes with being part of great Caesar's family?'

'Or maybe there are just too many men with wagging tongues.' Crassus, as ever, was more pragmatic.

'Come,' Quintus said, rising to walk back to their companions.

'Wait. Not yet. Sit down,' said Crassus. Quintus sat back down on the rock beside his friends. 'Why is your rank meaningless, Quintus? What has happened?'

'We are given a great honour,' Quintus said, his voice full of sarcasm. 'We are to find the tribe of Germani that dared to attack the ships and defeat them. Then we are to find other enemies and defeat them also. We are to help clear the path for the armies of Rome. Tiberius called us his scutarius, his shield-bearer.'

'That doesn't sound too bad,' Sextus began uncertainly.

'Not the cohort,' Quintus said bitterly. 'Not even a half-century. Three contubernia only, he said. We are to be spies, really, with no armour and no supplies. Our standards must be left behind. And we'll have no auxiliaries, no cornicenes, no slaves even. Worst of all, no identity. We are to masquerade as natives. We will be spies dressed in trews and furs. And we leave tonight. Those not with me will be scattered amongst the legions stationed here.'

'Me? You mean us,' Crassus said.

'Us,' repeated Sextus.

'Of course. Us,' said Quintus, realising that these men would always stand by him. 'But who else?'

'Rufus and Marcus, of course. They would not allow themselves to be left behind — and Rufus already looks the part,' grinned Sextus, referring to the redhead's wild hair and Gaulish moustaches.

'Even though Rufus is signifer and Marcus optio?' Quintus asked. 'Rufus will lose his wolfskin cloak, Marcus his crested helm and hastile.'

'Rank — and the symbols of rank — will never outweigh loyalty, not with them,' Crassus said with certainty.

Sextus nodded in agreement. 'Rufus will not wish to let the standard go, but he will have no choice. You say it must be left behind.'

'Those are my orders,' said Quintus. 'He may wish to stay with it.'

'Never,' chorused the other two together, shaking their heads.

'Nor will Marcus be concerned for rank,' said Sextus, who had made it his life's work never to seek any sort of promotion or responsibility. 'He has been up and down in the ranks before. He has been not just optio but centurion before, as you well know. He will manage.'

Quintus remembered how Marcus had once been senior to him, and how both of them had lost rank and pay through a brawl in a bathhouse. They had laughed about it since. They would both have been flogged and never promoted again had it not been for the storm that had scattered the fleet and washed them to Britannia. 'Marcus would not be left behind,' he agreed.

'That completes the tally of our original contubernium,' said Sextus.

'They will still be given the choice,' Quintus said seriously. 'As will all the others we will have to ask.' He set his jaw. 'I am not ordering any to go that do not wish it.'

'Name them,' said Crassus. 'If they are of Century One, I will tell you if they will go.'

'None of our few cavalry may go,' said Quintus, with disappointment. 'I am told they are needed here.'

'There are hardly any of them anyway. They will not be missed,' said Crassus dismissively. 'Who else, Quintus?'

'I would like Agnus the scout and Alba the capsarius for their skills. I would like Caius for his knowledge of the Germani language.'

'Vetruvius for his ability to cheat at dice?' Sextus laughed. 'I am sure you will have no problem filling your quota. They will all happily march into the arms of Father Dis with you.'

'I hope so,' said Quintus. 'Come, let's go and find out. We don't have a lot of time.' They all rose to their feet.

'Tiberius says I must give all the officers a clear choice,' said Quintus. 'That includes Rufus, as signifer, and you too Crassus, as optio. It also includes Marcus and Caius, both optiones.'

'As I have said, they will come,' Sextus concluded, glancing at Crassus to see if he would gainsay him. Crassus gave a little shake of his head. Of course he would join them.

'That accounts for the optiones,' said Sextus. 'What about the centurions?'

'If they are to keep their rank, the centurions may decide to stay with the legions,' said Crassus. 'I think Furius Lentulus and Marius may decline. I think Felix perhaps will not.'

Felix was centurion of the Fourth, the newest recruits at first insultingly, now affectionately, known as the rabbits. They had appropriated the term for themselves and were proud of it, as well as being fiercely loyal to their commander. He, in turn, was bold and enthusiastic and would not turn down the chance of an adventure. An assembly was called, and the men apprised of the offer.

'All ranks are to be kept, in name anyway,' explained Quintus. 'But if you think you are never going to be part of a legion again...' He allowed his voice to trail off. His contubernales already stood beside him.

'This is what the general is offering, men. Not glory, not even renown or reward, but an unmarked death on the blade of a native axe in a foreign forest. There is no dishonour in refusing.'

To his surprise, even with this bleak description, there were many men who were keen to go. There were men of the Fifth Alaudae who had been rescued from the forest, still seeking to redeem the loss of their eagle. There were those who were thought lucky, or to be good leaders, and those like Alba the capsarius and Caius the translator who brought skills. There were men who sought risk and adventure. Vetruvius the gambler was one such, especially as he had lost his amicus. He calculated that there would be a better chance of plunder in a small group of irregulars than in the vast anonymity of a legion. Felix the centurion was, as Quintus had hoped, another. He was allowed to choose some of his own to accompany him. Furius Lentulus and Marius, as expected, declined, hoping to keep their careers on track in the armies of Tiberius.

Quintus did not quite manage to stick to the stipulations he was given; there were too many volunteers. Three tents would be twenty-four men, as he had been told, but without slaves, they could sleep thirty. The officers would bunk elsewhere, which also swelled the numbers. They were not to wear full armour, but they reasoned that the pretend tribesmen could have attacked and stripped a Roman column, so some protection could be worn.

A delivery of native trews, crumpled linen shirts, skins and rough cloaks was met with laughter. These looked like a cart full of laundry on its way down to the Tiber, or the rags that Quintus had seen burned after their annihilation of a Germani tribe similar to that they were portraying. For the most part, the clothes were clean — slaves must have been tasked with washing them — but the tears in them revealed that they had been taken from dead men.

There were round shields too, short spears, daggers and native axes. Quintus handled one of the axes with disdain. He did not like them as a weapon; they were ungainly and inaccurate.

With the clothes there were, at least, too many of everything, meaning that the men had a choice — and a chance of finding something that would fit. The trews, in particular, proved difficult. None of the legionaries had ever worn anything so bizarre, and there was much amusement as they tried them on, securing them at the waist with leather ties. One or two tried to complete the look by cross-gartering them with leather, but gave up amidst gales of laughter. Short shirts took the place of tunics, furs took the place of cloaks and bare heads replaced helmets. The men still wore baltea and cingulum hidden beneath the native cloth. The belt was necessary to carry weapons, the straps necessary to protect their bodies. They also slung baldrics over the tunics to carry gladii. Again, they reasoned that such weapons could have been stripped from an 'enemy'. They had no wish to be without them.

Late in the afternoon Centurion Atticus appeared, seemingly to check on progress.

'You must look like natives, not Romans,' he chided, criticising the use of the belts and the satchels the men wore.

'Where do we keep rations?' Crassus asked, tapping the pouch.

'And how else do we keep these trews on?' Sextus asked, allowing his to fall comically to his knees. There was general laughter.

Atticus changed tack, gently striking Crassus' shoulder with his vine staff. 'The *baltea militares* half hidden under native garb — what about them?'

'We took them from a Roman patrol, if anyone asks,' said Crassus. 'Along with their swords,' he added quickly as he saw the centurion's eye fall on the weapons.

Atticus nodded. He accepted this. He understood the need to keep the gladii. Marcus bemoaned the lack of mail shirts. He had always preferred these to the new lorica laminata, but few of them remained; they had been replaced on the orders of Caesar Augustus.

'We could wear them beneath these shirts,' he suggested.

'You would get very hot, very quickly,' laughed Felix. 'I think you would boil inside them.'

Atticus smiled to himself; this seemed like a good group of men. He signalled and a slave approached, leading a string of ponies. There was also a cart. 'The cart, centurion, is for what you are leaving behind. The army will find it useful. The general will not give you cavalry horses, but you may take as many native ponies as you wish. If this is not enough, the Cantabrians have spare mounts.'

The Cantabrian auxiliaries, Quintus knew, were currently under guard. They had expressed a wish to join the expedition, and word of this had escaped. Legionaries had therefore been sent to ensure they remained.

'Into the cart,' he ordered, without enthusiasm. 'Helmets, cloaks, armour — anything you are not wearing.' The cart quickly filled up. Reluctantly, Felix placed his crested helmet in it carefully. With a wry smile, Quintus followed with his own, with its battered surface and damaged crest. 'At least when we return, I will have a new one,' he said to Marcus as the optio placed his own helmet in the cart.

'What about spare horses?' said Marcus. 'Or mules. Something to carry supplies and extra weapons. Surely they cannot deny us this.'

'They can deny us nothing,' laughed Vetruvius, piling his own gear into the cart. 'We leave at night, invisibly, with whatever we can carry. Then we no longer exist.'

A sacrifice was made to two-headed Father Janus, the god of beginnings and endings. The presence of four whole legions, along with auxiliaries and slaves, meant that Sextus found it easy to procure not just a ram, but a black ram — albeit a small and young one.

'Strictly speaking, it was not theft,' he explained. 'All the animals belong to all the army, and we are a part of the army.'

The rite was carried out carefully, with blade and stone and fire used to make the animal *sacrum*, sacred to the gods. The *exta* were examined and proved to be perfect. Blood was poured and dedicated to the earth. The gods having taken their portion, the men enjoyed eating the rest. This was their version of the *lustratio*, the great sacrifice that Tiberius would have carried out in Lugdunum before his army departed. For that, to gain the blessing of the gods, there would have been not just a ram, but a bull and a boar, throats slit in the sacred ceremony of *suovetaurilia* — a ceremony as old as Rome itself.

Darkness seemed to come later in the high mountains so, though impatient to be away, the group had to wait. Eventually, the sky turned a deep enough blue that Quintus judged it black and they slipped out of the camp, past guards who had clearly been instructed to look the other way.

The waters of the river were low enough for them to ride the ponies through. This was no broad-hipped Rhenus; this was but a tributary or lesser daughter of the great river, finding its way out from a corner of the lake. The flow of this stream in early autumn was shallow and slow, so the crossing took only minutes. They were all across before the moon had lifted itself above the topmost leafy branches. The men walked the horses away through the trees, beginning the climb away from the river.

IX: ANATOLIA ET CANTABRIA

Quintus, Crassus and Sextus were the last to cross. They stood on the bank and looked back at the line upon line of lights that marked the place from which they had come. They could smell meat cooking. They could hear the murmur of conversation. They could see the twinkling fires. The campaign season was over for this year. The legions of Tiberius could look forward to warm fires in the winter camp, with no more fighting until spring.

It was cool but Quintus' fur-trimmed leather cloak was on a packhorse, along with many of the others. Without his full armour he felt naked, vulnerable.

'Remember when we shared a cloak on that cold ground?' Crassus asked.

'I do, friend. We have shared much since,' replied Quintus, putting an arm around the shoulder of his amicus. When the cohort was first punished, the survivors had been sent outside the legionary camp and settled in a muddy field. The two friends had wrapped themselves in a single cloak.

'That glimpse of home through a mountain pass — is that the last time we will ever see anything of Rome?' Sextus asked.

'I hope not. I have vows to fulfil,' answered Quintus, squeezing the concealed package lodged in the pouch in his undershorts. It had been sewn by one of the Macedonians who now, against orders, could be seen creeping across the river.

'Come here,' Quintus commanded them.

'Escaped slaves,' joked Crassus, as the two cousins waded towards the legionaries. 'Better sound the alarm. It is Spartacus come back to life.'

'Sir, you need us,' whispered Maxim. 'I to cook and look after the animals, Jovan to count and read when necessary.'

'I can read,' said Quintus.

'And I can cook,' said Crassus.

'But not as well as I,' said Maxim confidently.

'Go,' said Quintus, indicating the way with a jerk of his head. He spoke in a stern tone that convinced no-one. 'We have not seen you.'

He sighed as the two slaves stumbled past, following the tracks and lights of the men. The three then turned their backs on the tented city that looked and smelt and sounded so much like their memories of home.

'We will be back in Rome one day,' Quintus said formally. 'By Jupiter Optimus Maximus and Ceres my protector, I swear it.'

'And I by Mars and Vulcan, my patron,' swore the blacksmith.

'And I by Mercury, the god of thieves and trickery,' swore Sextus with a smile. 'My own inspiration and protector.'

As the moon rose high enough for its light to finally reflect from the river, they began the climb, seeking the tracks of the Vindelici, the tribe who had dared to give challenge to Tiberius before escaping from the action on the water.

A guard not turning a blind eye would have seen a line of men in native garb snaking away up the hillside. Some walked, some were leading horses, and some were mounted on ponies. They would have scratched their heads, noticing the short tunics and trews favoured by the natives, but also seeing the gladius and pugio carried by each man. More doubt might have set in had they noticed the military caligae on the natives' feet. Even more curious was the small group of archers, clearly of some foreign race, bringing up the rear. The guards may have looked and shaken their heads, but none reported what they had been ordered not to see.

The climb up the hill was exposed, so the group had to move fast if they were to be out of sight before daylight. As soon as they were away from the river, the ground began to rise beneath their feet. They rode now, and Quintus urged his mount to the front, where Marcus led. 'East,' he ordered. 'Follow the contour if we can. East will take us back to the lake, back to the point towards which the ships fled. We should pick up the trail from there.'

East was difficult. The track they started out on went north, snaking upwards, climbing through the gnarled roots of the mountain. It was rough and narrow, but obvious, easy to follow. To the east the trees still grew thickly, close together. Where a wind-blown tree had fallen, or there was stony ground, bramble and holly grew. There was no clear trail.

'East it is,' said Marcus, reluctantly leaving the track for the more difficult ground. He turned the head of his pony, putting the last deep reds of the setting sun behind them.

The movement of the men across the mountainside was dictated by the terrain. They became less and less like a Roman patrol, and more and more like a group of natives. There were rocky outcrops which they had to decide whether to go over or around. There were narrow ravines, ripe for ambush. They tried hard never to lose height, knowing they would need extra energy to regain it. They found that almost inevitably they continued to gradually climb. Agnus, the scout, tried to stay ahead of the group and guide them away from rockfalls and obstructions, holding a torch up high and calling 'go left', 'go around' or 'drop down' as necessary.

They navigated ridges and furrows, deceptively smooth rock and wet grass. They needed to judge whether to ride or to walk; the ponies were often more sure-footed than they were. Sometimes they had to dismount, then their caligae could be treacherous on certain surfaces. They were all decisions of the moment, made instinctively, the earth beneath their feet dictating the rhythm of their progress.

As the first glimmerings of the morning light appeared ahead of them, snuffing out the stars, Quintus ordered the torches extinguished. By dawn they were high enough for the trees to be thinning and he worried that, exposed on the mountainside, any lights would betray their position. Though he searched for it, leaning his long body from the horse's back in an attempt to see further, he could see no sign of the camp.

'We must have turned a corner,' he said to Marcus, a sweep of his arm encompassing the thickly gathered treetops that marched down the steep hillside. 'I can see no sign of our vast army. I cannot even see the river.'

'The sun rises there.' Marcus pointed ahead of them, where gold light spread beneath a line of thin cloud. 'So we proceed still eastward — and the river is there.' Way down to the right, a small sliver of brightness reflecting the water could still be seen.

'We must cross their trail soon,' Quintus said, although he began to doubt it. 'They must have passed this way.'

The area they were traversing had turned into loose gravel, small stones bouncing away from the hooves of the horses. An area of flat ground, partially covered with scrubby grass and shaded by a rogue stand of tall spruces, provided an opportunity to rest. There was also fresh water trickling from the snows melting far above.

'We should stop,' said Felix. He had been riding up and down the column, talking with the men and gauging their mood. 'We should eat.'

'I agree,' said Quintus. 'Call a halt. We have yet to see who is actually part of our company.' He smiled. 'I think we may have gained some extra men.'

He was right, of course. When they gathered beneath the great trunks of the fir trees, there were four Anatolian archers and two slaves who had not been part of the original group. He knew about the slaves, of course. The archers were a bonus. He recognised one of them as a man he had spoken with before. He had tried to draw this man's great bow — without success. His comrades had laughed — not unkindly — at his efforts.

'You are most welcome,' Quintus said. 'Though I doubt there will be plunder or reward.'

'There will be fighting,' said one of them, his Latin heavily accented. He showed the overdeveloped bicep of his bow arm and added, 'My arm needs exercise or it will wither.'

Sextus and Crassus joined them, Sextus gingerly feeling the hard knot of muscle in the arm presented to him. 'You are from the shores of Mare Nostrum,' he said. 'Do you not miss the sea?'

'We are all from where we would call Phrygia, what you Romans call Anatolia,' said the man. He studied the smooth face of the questioner and the burn scars on Crassus' arms. He cocked his head to one side and asked, with a twinkle in his eye, 'Do you not miss the barber? And do you not miss the forge?'

They all laughed. 'You have them exactly,' Quintus said with amusement. 'You — and your sharp sight — are welcome.'

'We are being followed,' one of them said, lowering his voice conspiratorially. 'Three or four men only, with horses. They have stopped a half stade behind. I could shoot them for you.'

'Rufus!' Quintus called to the man nearest the back. 'Take a couple of men and see who dogs our footsteps.'

Rufus singled out three of the men. 'Two that side, one with me,' he ordered. They drew their swords and each took a wide arc, planning to catch the pursuers in the rear. A few minutes passed, and a commotion was heard, including some shouting, the words indistinguishable. Then there was, to the surprise of the listeners, definite laughter. Shortly Rufus' shock of red hair could be seen approaching. He was leading a small pony, heavily laden and flanked by two small olive-skinned strangers, also leading horses. When the whole party emerged there were four extra men and four ponies. The men were Cantabrians, the cohort's own auxiliaries, recruited in the province of Hispania.

'Remember me, master?' the leading man asked, showing the gaps in his teeth. 'I told you once that my grandfather fought against Hannibal.'

'And I told you that my grandfather fought *for* the Carthaginians,' said the other with a grin.

'I remember,' said Quintus, smiling at the memory. 'You are welcome, as are your ponies.'

'I thought you were under guard,' Felix said. 'Forbidden to leave the camp. Especially forbidden to join us.'

'My friend and I disagreed,' said the first man, gentling the pony he led by stroking its nose. 'We are free agents, whatever your generals tell us. We escaped. We want to fight. Will you have us?'

'Gladly,' said Quintus. 'Though our mission is secret.'

'What do you carry?' Felix asked, gesturing to the packs fastened across two of the horses.

'Food,' said the first man. 'A little grain, a little oil, a little wine. We did not know how long we would be on the road.'

'Nor how long we must follow behind before we joined you,' said the other.

'Oil and wine? You are more than welcome,' said Sextus, taking one of the ponies by the bridle. 'Let me find you a place to rest.'

'Go with him,' agreed Quintus, adding in mock serious tones, 'but do not trust him.' He raised his voice for the rest of the men. 'We stop here,' he announced. 'But it is only a stop, not a camp. No fires. Rest the horses, drink, eat. Sleep if you must. But we continue before the sun reaches its zenith.'

'So soon, and no fires?' Sextus asked, looking covetously at the pack on the pony he led.

'You know as well as I that a camp the size of the one we left will seek food and fuel for many miles far and wide. I do not want to be discovered by a foraging party and attacked as hostiles. Nor do I want to advertise our position with smoke,' Quintus told him.

Sextus nodded his understanding. He would still seek to befriend the Cantabrians, using his easy manner to charm them into sharing the food and wine.

'Pickets,' Quintus ordered. 'In pairs, in front, behind, to the left and right.' He pointed to legionaries as he spoke and they scrambled away. 'You will be relieved after an hour.'

Caius also approached the Cantabrians, curious to see if their language had the same roots as that of the Germani that he had learned. In many ways Caius Sergio Nerva was the antithesis of Sextus. He was coarse and bearded, his cheeks rough from too much sun and wind. In his lifetime he had drunk too much wine and posca, and it showed. He made friends slowly, then kept them close for life.

Caius had served in the army long enough to have helped the Fifth win its elephant emblem at the battle of Thapsus. He had re-enlisted after his discharge following Actium, then found himself on the losing side at the Clades Lolliana, the disaster on the Rhenus when the Fifth, badly led by general Lollius, had lost its eagle.

Tragedy and dishonour had made him taciturn, distrustful and short-tempered. He compensated for these shortcomings by attempting to learn the language of his enemies. It was a useful skill, and the men's respect for him had grown. He and Sextus had become unlikely friends. Between them they began to gently interrogate the Cantabrians about their cargo.

'Three hours, no more,' Quintus said to Crassus as the two squatted down to eat biscuit and drink water. Around them the men were sitting or squatting in small friendship groups.

'In spite of their native disguise, I think I could name most of them,' said Quintus.

'They are a good bunch of men,' said Crassus. 'A very good bunch of men.'

'But I think nowhere near enough for the task we have been given.' Quintus shook his head. The shadow on the pointed rock he had chosen as his timepiece was already shortening. 'Look, the time passes quickly. They have not slept.'

'They will be ready to fight, my friend,' Crassus reassured him. 'When it comes to it, they will be ready.'

X: VINDELICI

The enlarged company set off again before they had time to properly rest, the men grumbling, but still in good humour. They were keenly aware of the need to put miles between themselves and the legions of Tiberius. Felix and Alba watched the rear, lest other unexpected recruits — or enemy — approached.

For two days Agnus and Marcus went ahead as scouts, finding the easiest routes. On the whole, they were managing to keep going east. The two waited now on the trail, halting the column where the way dropped sharply down. Jumbled rock and rough undergrowth — trees and thorny bushes — blocked the path ahead. Agnus pointed down the hillside.

'Our easiest way is down, sir.'

'But we will no longer be in control of our direction.' Marcus shook his head. 'I think we have to climb. There was a fork in the path fifty or so paces back. It was rocky, but better than this.'

The three of them looked wordlessly at the steep downward slope. It would be difficult to manage, but not impossible. If they chose it, they would be travelling blind, having no idea of what lay around any corner. It could be fatal.

'Too much of a risk,' said Quintus. 'Especially as we have no idea where it would take us. Turn the men around, Marcus.'

'Back to the fork,' Marcus ordered. 'Take the other way, uphill, but east. Agnus, go on ahead. Go and look further along the track. Go on foot, but carefully. See what lies beyond.'

Agnus passed the column of men and found the fork. He ran easily up the slope, negotiating the fallen rocks, hopping from one to the other with uncanny balance.

'I swear he has mountain goat in him,' said Crassus, who watched until the scout vanished from his sight.

By the time the column had returned to the fork and started to climb, Agnus was back again. He was excited. 'Ships, Quintus,' he reported. 'Far below is an arm of the lake and I can see ships on the water. The lake stretches away for a great distance. It could almost be a sea.'

'The Vindelici?' Quintus asked. 'Is it them? How many?'

'I can only see two ships, but there may be more. There is also smoke from fires. I could see but a few men, near to the ships. They are Germani without doubt. We may have found our enemy.'

'Is there a way down? What does it look like?' Marcus demanded.

'It is steep, but the ponies will manage it.' The scout turned to Quintus. 'Sir, there is no way we can take them by surprise. This path goes up to a ridge. Once we reach it, we will be visible on the hillside.'

'Show me,' said Quintus and followed where Agnus led, both of them crouched low as they reached the ridge. The tall man had to almost bend double to match his scout. They peered over the top and Quintus realised that Agnus was right. They would be seen. They edged back, returning to the others.

'It is as he says, steep, but manageable. Our only hope is speed,' Quintus told them, then turned to Crassus, still his optio. 'Tell the men to leave all but arms and shields here. Speed and strength, greater strength than them — that's what we must have. We must come down on them in numbers and at a gallop. Once the charge has started, we will not be able to halt.'

The Anatolians shook their heads at the command. They were not known for their horsemanship. 'If it is permitted, we will watch the baggage and the slaves,' said one.

Quintus agreed, then turned to the group of heavily armed horsemen, dressed in native clothes. 'We will not be able to stop. We will have to trust to the gods.' He turned the head of his horse and urged it upwards. The others followed.

Even as the first of the ponies crested the ridge, it was obvious that they had been spotted. The Germani camp on the beach below was suddenly active. It was as if a child had disturbed an ants' nest with a stick. Men who had been strolling now ran in different directions, fetching material from the two boats drawn up on the beach, and loading it onto horses held by others. They threw equipment down to others who stood in the shallows, then those on the boats followed them, splashing into the water. Shouts could be heard, but not the substance of what was said. Soon the men were riding away from the lake. White smoke rising and swirling from beneath the overhang betrayed fires.

'Go!' Quintus shouted. 'No time to waste. Do not stop. Forward!'

The horsemen charged, picking up speed as they barrelled down the scarp. The slope was steep and dusty, the hooves of the ponies kicking up a cloud.

They placed their lives in the hands of Mars, god of war, Neptune, master of horses, and of course Fortuna, mistress of luck.

Even at this breakneck pace it took a good ten minutes to reach the bottom, negotiating twists and turns in the trod, and outcrops of rock and stubby plant growth. The mounts were given their heads as much as the terrain made it possible. The most dangerous part was where the steep slope met the flat beach, where the rough hillside turned into soft sand. Here the ponies could have tumbled headlong and broken their legs, but they proved surefooted and continued on the flat. However, some of the riders did not keep their seats. Those who were not as skilful as the beasts ended up on their backs.

As rapid as they were, by the time they arrived on the strand, they were disappointed. The beach was empty. There was no sign of the Vindelici, had it even been them, but a clear trail showed which way the tribesmen had fled.

Quintus, amongst the leading horses, threw out a command. 'Felix, Marcus, take your men and secure the ships. You men, follow me.' They rode in the direction the Vindelici had gone, following the enemy's trail as it wound away from the beach, hoofprints clear in the sand. Quintus followed them for only a few minutes before shaking his head in disappointment as the trail vanished. The ground turned rocky and the hoofprints were no more. Although the Germani probably had only a twenty-minute head start, it would be pointless to try to catch them at speed. The terrain made it a job for a tracker.

'At least we have found them,' he said to Crassus, as the two drew level on the smooth grey rock, their horses both panting and blowing. Behind them, they still had sight of the beach, the lake and the boats. In front of them was both more of the grey rock and loose gravel. They could see several tracks winding along a narrow valley, then beginning to climb up through the roots of the mountain. There was no sign of horsemen on any of them; even the dust of their passing must have settled. Following them would not be easy.

'Your skills are what we need, Agnus.'

'Providing they are of the Vindelici,' said the scout. 'Providing they are the ones who dared to attack Tiberius.'

Quintus nodded in agreement, wetting his lips and spitting away the powdery dirt their gallop had thrown up. 'It is them. It must be.' But there was just a trace of doubt in his voice. 'No point chasing them now. They will be riding hard. We can follow when we are regrouped. Let's see what they have left us in the ships.'

He turned the head of his pony and Crassus and Agnus followed. They cantered back to the spot where the two ships were drawn up on the beach. Only the sterns of the craft had been left in the water. It did not look an easy task to board them, but some men had managed it, climbing in off the back of their mounts. Marcus and Sextus were already peering out from one of them; Felix and others had clambered onto the second.

'There is no steering oar, no mast and no sail. The boats are useless,' Marcus shouted down, frustration in his voice.

'There is not even any rope.' Sextus' head appeared over the narrow side. 'They have taken everything that might have been of use.'

Felix and the men on the other boat confirmed that it was the same on their craft.

'What they have not taken, they have broken. The ship will not even float,' said Felix. 'They have chopped a great hole in it below the waterline.'

'This one is whole,' called Marcus. 'They must not have had time.'

'There is plenty of timber. We could patch them…' began another hopefully.

'We don't need the ships,' said Quintus, cutting him off. 'And clearly, nor did they. If there were other craft, they have sunk them or hidden them. No matter — we never had any intention of sailing anywhere. Better that we burn them so that the enemy cannot use them either, holed or not. Come down and bring anything that may be of use.'

Rufus was busy brushing himself down. His hair and moustaches were an uncharacteristic grey, full of sand and grit, despite his attempts to shake it out. He was one of those who had been thrown at the foot of the hill. His horse had reared and he had crashed from its back, glad of the protection afforded by the trews. He still rubbed the unprotected places where he had bounced on the ground.

'Rufus, those fires over there are still smoking. Bring brands. We can at least stop any of the Vindelici from trying to flee across the lake.'

The whole troop was now at the boats, milling around on horseback, weapons drawn, disappointed at not catching their prey. The Cantabrians seemed particularly vexed at having no-one to fight and rode their horses pointlessly up and down the beach in frustration, casting their short spears and then riding to retrieve them in impressive displays of horsemanship.

'It could have been thieves, stripping the boats,' said Rufus morosely. He had collected and then blown life into the smouldering branches, others helping him.

'You are right to be cautious,' Quintus said. 'Though I think it unlikely. These boats are very like the ones we fought on the lake, and this could easily be an arm of the same water. We have no idea how big it is. Thieves could just as easily have sailed the boats away. They would not have stayed to camp. Nor do I think they would have chopped holes in what they were stealing.' He wagged an amused finger at the redhead's dusty visage. 'Is there not water enough to wash in, my friend?'

'Very funny,' said Rufus laconically. 'Here.' He passed the brand to a man still on horseback, who in turn passed it up to Sextus on the stern of the first boat. He ordered that rowing benches be piled together then set them alight, adding further torches as they were passed up. Finally, as smoke swirled, he jumped down. Felix did the same on his vessel before being the last to clamber down from it. 'Clear!' he called. 'I am the last.'

Crassus took another flaming brand from Rufus and flung it over the ship's side, adding a prayer to the god of the forge, his own patron Vulcan, to speed the flames. '*Laudo Vulcanem.*'

Others took brands and followed, flinging as many sticks of fire as they could into both ships. At first there was just smoke spiralling upwards, then the first of many flames could be seen licking the air as the dry timbers above the waterline caught. If the Vindelici had ever thought about returning to the ships, now they could not.

Quintus smiled at the Cantabrians, who were still riding up and down, taking out their frustrations on their spears. 'Rufus, send the Cantabrians to fetch the Anatolians and the rest of the gear. They are better horsemen than any of us, and they seem to have too much energy. While they do that, we will water our own mounts at the lake — and wash the dirt and dust from our skin.' He pointed at a patch of rich green that spread along the margins of the water, back from the beach. 'There is good grass here for the ponies. Make sure they are fed as well as watered.'

'It will take them a good while to climb the hill and descend again at a sensible speed,' said Rufus. 'Perhaps we could swim?'

'As long as there are guards posted,' agreed Quintus, as he dismounted. 'And as long as you can get out of those clothes — and back into them — on your own.'

'We can help each other,' Rufus responded as both men and horses walked towards the water, well away from the ships, which now blazed fiercely, sparks spinning on the fresh breeze.

XI: ACTIAN APOLLO

Quintus let his pony be taken by another and turned Crassus towards the campsite, a hand on his shoulder. 'Let's see what they have left behind. It may give us a clue as to who they were, how long they were here, and what they intended to do.' Marcus and Felix joined them.

There were the remnants of four roughly constructed shelters of branches and twigs, all made in the same fashion — a split or forked trunk fixed upright, a long branch wedged into the split, the small branches and leafy twigs leant against it. At this time of year it was barely sufficient. In the midst of winter, they would need to build something much sturdier. There were four firepits.

'So there were not many of them,' Crassus surmised, estimating five or six to a fire. 'Twenty or thereabouts.'

'Many more than that escaped the action,' said Marcus. 'It was whole ships and crews that retreated from the attack. Where are they? Where are the other ships?'

'The rest of the men must have gone ahead already,' Quintus said. 'The ships are either sunk or hidden somewhere. These men, I suppose, were meant to strip these remaining vessels before returning to their settlement.'

Marcus kicked at a piece of smouldering wood. 'They have left nothing here. Perhaps we're doing their job for them? Perhaps they were meant to fire the ships?'

'Perhaps. Either way, the ships are burned, so that is an end to it.' Quintus looked around at the firepits and empty ground. 'You are right, though. Nothing here.'

'Something, perhaps.' Crassus had found a canvas bag, partially concealed. He opened it and looked inside. 'It is fodder for their horses.'

'For our horses, now. We will add it to our supplies.'

The four of them made their way back to the others and smiled at what they saw. A few of the men had stripped off and were splashing each other in the shallows. Not far from them the ships were now well alight, crackling and steaming and fizzing as fire found water.

'The smoke will be seen from a long way away, perhaps even the camp,' said Felix. 'Will they not investigate? I would.'

Quintus shook his head. 'They have no reason to investigate. And even if they do, we will be gone.' He looked up — the Cantabrians were almost at the crest of the hill. 'We leave when they return,' he shouted to the men in the lake, 'whether you are dressed or not!' They signalled their understanding and shortly waded out, running and flapping their arms to dry themselves before they started to awkwardly pull on the native gear.

'The water is too cold to stay in for more than a minute or two,' complained Rufus. 'Just long enough to wash my head.' He shook the water from his dust-free beard like a dog.

The Cantabrians were out of sight only briefly; they then descended the hill quickly. Though the Romans were good horsemen, the Hispanic riders were better, steering the short string of ponies left and right across the hillside — a more controlled descent than the previous mad gallop. They kept the Anatolians and the slaves in the middle of the formation, the better to shepherd them.

Once they arrived it did not take long for the company to be ready to resume the pursuit. They rearranged the gear, then mounted. As they looked back, the ships had burned low to their keels and their charred timbers now smoked, steaming where the wood met the water at the stern. Satisfied, Quintus signalled the men to set off after their quarry.

They rode fast, but carefully, Agnus sent forward to track the path ahead. The fleeing Germani had made no effort to cover their tracks. Wherever the ground was soft, or trees and bushes bordered the narrow trod, there was evidence of their passage, marks on the ground or broken growth. Agnus confirmed Crassus' first estimate of numbers. They followed no more than twenty or so horses. This would not have been enough to man both ships, so the main party had to have left some time previously. Some hoofprints were deeper than others, so some were, Quintus supposed, double-mounted. Still, it was a force that his troop could easily defeat.

He gave instructions to Agnus. 'We do not want to catch them; we want to track them. If it looks like we are getting too close, we will slow down. This is not a whole tribe, or anywhere near. I am sure that they are heading for their town, their base. That is where we need to be.'

'What do you expect?' Sextus rode alongside him. 'A collection of huts or a fully manned oppidum?'

'Hard to know,' Quintus replied. 'A collection of huts, yes. And a fence or ditch or both. We are deep in their territory, I know, but they fight amongst each other so much I would be surprised if it was not well defended.'

'Against their own people?'

Quintus cracked a lopsided grin. 'Against other tribes. Some Germani tribes hunt, some farm, some raid and enslave other tribes. It all depends on which one this is.'

'Predator or prey?' Sextus mused.

'If predator, they will be warriors and defending against enemies.' Marcus had ridden up on the other side and heard what Sextus had said. 'If prey, they will be defending themselves from raiders. Not sure which I'd prefer.'

'Prey, I think,' said Sextus. 'Prey is less likely to fight back.'

'We have nowhere near enough men for a siege, and no ballistae nor other siege weapons,' Marcus pointed out.

'There is only one weapon that will work,' said Sextus. 'Surprise, for which we will need the favour of the gods.'

'Well, my friend, you are the master of sacrifices and auguries,' chuckled Quintus. 'I expect you to win us the favour that we need. The gods were with us last time.'

They had attacked an oppidum before, waiting whilst their own omens allowed them to. They had laid low its initial defences with the use of cavalry and archers, brought down its gates with a battering ram wrought by Crassus, and finally finished it off with fire and the cold anger of the mournful note. This was the order to sack and burn, the order for no mercy, trumpeted by a brass cornu. An order necessary due to the treachery of the tribesmen. The victory had a heavy price on it. They had lost their two most senior commanders, the prefect taken prisoner and ending his own life, the First Spear centurion betrayed then killed by a defeated Germani leader seeking glory and Valhalla.

Sextus recalled the action now. 'For that attack we had cavalry; we had catapults of a sort. We had more men, more auxiliaries, more archers, more soldiers. We knew the oppidum was not fully manned.' His voice was gradually rising, full of pride as he spoke. 'We had standards and uniforms and cornicenes telling the enemy that he faced the might of Rome. We had an eagle.'

'We have enough.' Quintus turned left and right, assessing the company he led. He knew the individual strengths of many of them, but they were no army. They looked like no more than a bunch of brigands. He turned back to Sextus, speaking quietly. 'They will do, my friend. These men and the will of the gods will do. Read the auguries, read the stars and the flights of birds. Find a sign of victory. We will prevail.'

As they tracked their prey ever higher, seemingly right up through the foundations of the mountains, the weather became more and more unsettled. Flurries of cold rain were close cousins to sleet, and cool mists rose up the sides of the valleys. The wind that blew them away was bitter. They felt that they had left the last vestiges of autumn deep in the valley bottom and were climbing into winter. The trees thinned, and the ones that remained looked gaunt and unwell. Small patches of grass grew sparsely in breaks in the rocky ground. There was not enough for the ponies, and the fodder found on the beach was needed.

Higher still, the trees became not just sparse, but stunted, providing no cover. The legionaries now looked down into the canopies of the great spruces that had earlier provided shelter. The sky, in the periods between the rain, was bright and an unfeasible blue, as if the rain had washed it clean. With no mist, the men could see for miles, even to the tall mountains on the skyline. Though they climbed, they appeared to be travelling parallel with them, rather than towards them.

They rode up first one valley, then another, tracking the tribesmen much further than they had expected. There was water for men and horses, small streams and rivulets and waterfalls, often spilling over the rocks and making them slippery.

'This chase is taking longer than we ever thought it would,' said Quintus, as they stopped to pitch yet another camp.

'The men are restless,' Felix informed him. 'They can see no end to it.'

'I know, my friend. We need to stay on top of discipline.'

Both centurions had recognised tensions in the men. Some had even led to disputes. Quintus introduced punishments. Not floggings, of course. There were too few in the party for formal retribution, but reprimands were issued, impositions such as extra or unpopular duties, although often these seemed to just exacerbate the surly attitudes.

'We have a smouldering dispute to settle,' Felix said as they struck camp that morning. 'Two men have refused to accept an order that required co-operation. They were once friends, and are still officially contubernales and amicus one to the other.'

'That bond may only be broken by officers or death,' Quintus said, shaking his head. 'Bring them here.'

They arrived, muttering and jostling each other. Quintus called them to attention then asked tersely, 'You were insubordinate?' Both men started talking at once, each blaming the other. Quintus cut them off. 'Yes or no?'

They hung their heads and mumbled.

'I take that as a yes,' Quintus said. 'Though I wager neither of you can truly remember what began the dispute.'

'Let them fight it out, Quintus,' Felix suggested.

'Death for refusing an order, or single combat. What would you have?'

There was not really a choice. 'The fight, sir.'

That night, once the camp was established, the contest began. Vetruvius offered odds for each fighter and gathered stakes — or at least the promise of stakes, few having anything with which to wager. On Quintus' command, all weapons were banned — not just bladed ones — along with strangling and wrestling holds, but both fists and feet and even teeth could be used. The fight stopped when one or both of the men could fight no more.

The 'punishment' worked. The fight provided entertainment and raised the spirits of the men. The two combatants ended up bloody and bruised but otherwise mostly undamaged, laughing and hugging each other amidst promises of eternal brotherhood.

'I dedicate my victory to Actian Apollo,' laughed the winner.

'Beware of hubris,' warned Sextus. 'You are choosing exalted company. Caesar Augustus built a temple on the Palatine to honour the god after his victory at Actium.'

Alba saw to their wounds, but their rekindled friendship dampened most of their hurts and they dismissed him quickly.

'Are they fit to fight?' Quintus asked.

'They would fight to the death for each other, now, Mac,' said Alba. 'Such is the caprice of the gods.'

Again and again Agnus returned with news that yet another valley needed traversing, or another hill climbing. Sometimes there was more than a day between his reports. He picked out the best routes, the least dangerous, and advised whether to proceed on foot or horseback.

A wide shoulder of rock protruded in front of them, its steep stope shining with water. They could not go across it; the horses would find it impossible, the men almost so. They could go above it, but this would turn them north. The scar of the trod — worn by animals who could find no other route — could be seen snaking up the slope.

'What do you think, Marcus? Up or down?' Quintus asked.

'I think we have no choice,' Marcus said. 'If we want to keep going east, we have to go under it.'

XII: SUEBI

They set off at an easy pace. It was the first time they had travelled downhill in a while, so they were glad of the relief. The rock above revealed itself to be as massive and long and rugged as Agnus had said. It dipped in and out of the hillside, broken with vertical cracks and fissures, rich in green vegetation and dripping with water. It loomed over them like some great structure built in ancient times, like the Aurelian wall that surrounded the seven hills of Rome itself.

It cast a deep and oppressive shadow. Once under it, it was cooler than it had been above, no sun ever reaching beneath. Unconsciously they crouched and made themselves smaller underneath the overhang. The track was damp and flat, easy going for the ponies, and to start with they made good speed. They trudged along its length, conversation muted. It was only just wide enough for two to ride abreast.

Abruptly the rock ended and a spill of shale and loose stone tumbled across their path. It was as if a section of wall had collapsed into the valley. Broken stone and gravel ran down the mountainside like a river, swirling around those trees that it had failed to fell. From where they were, from where the track came to an end, there was a gap of perhaps fifty paces before it could be seen to start again. A faint trail crossed the scree slope where animals had worn a path.

'We will have to walk,' said Agnus, with a shrug. 'The scree is slippery and uneven, but the path resumes beyond it — and it is easier going once this is traversed. I have been across it once and returned safely.'

'Maybe,' muttered Marcus. 'But you are known to have mountain goats amongst your ancestors.'

'Single file,' Quintus ordered. 'The ground will hold the horses, providing they do not panic. They must be gentled.'

Agnus dismounted and took the bridle of his horse. He began to gingerly cross the slippery mass of loose stones and gravel. At each step, caligae sank in and a handful of tiny pebbles scurried down the rock. After he had traversed ten paces, Quintus urged the next of the legionaries onward. The horses were skittish and needed to be encouraged, but they grew in confidence once they had no choice but to keep going forward. The scree held, and soon there was a line of legionaries strung out, leading ponies. Their own heads were close to those of the beasts, as they mouthed soothing words. It was with a shout of triumph that Agnus once more gained firm ground on the other side. 'It is not too long,' he called encouragingly as the second legionary, with a sigh of relief, gained the path.

Quintus stood at the start of the crossing, like a shepherd with his flock, encouraging the men one by one onto the scree. Some faltered as the gravel gave way, but although this created noise — small stones falling in cascades like mini-avalanches — their caligae only sank down a little.

'Take care. Slowly,' Quintus kept repeating.

The overhang made him uneasy. It provided a perfect spot for an ambush, for an attack from above. He had wanted to post legionaries above them, on the top of the rock, but it was not possible; it was too massive. A mountain lion would have found it a perfect perch.

As most of the troop was spread across the scree and a few gained the far side, he signalled the auxiliaries forward. He was pleased. The crossing had gone more smoothly than he thought it would.

Suddenly, a Cantabrian was thrown from his horse and sent tumbling down the hillside before any of the others could react, his assailant bound up with him. This was no mountain lion, but a man, armed and clothed in fur. The assault on his companion was not so well executed. The target somehow remained on horseback, grappling fiercely with the tribesman who had leapt on him. He wrestled with the Germani and shoved him to the ground, then slumped over the high cantle, blood spreading, a blade sticking out from his side. There was shouting of challenges and war cries now that surprise was no longer needed as a third Cantabrian was assaulted from above.

This attacker missed his intended victim completely and fell heavily to the ground, already dead, stopped by the Anatolian arrow piercing his neck. The archers would not normally travel with bows strung but this was enemy territory, and two of them always had an arrow nocked. More tribesmen leapt down from the rock, armed with spear and sword. There was no need for any command to be shouted; the Romans not yet on the scree turned and ran back to where the ambush was happening, weapons drawn, ready to engage.

The attackers flung spears at the men, one fixing itself in a legionary's leg, another skittering past harmlessly on the rock. The legionaries nearest to the Cantabrians included Quintus and Marcus, who intended to be the last to cross the scree. The tribesman Quintus faced wielded two blades and screamed defiance. Quintus parried one blade and knocked the other from the man's grasp. The man raised his arm to strike and Quintus sank his gladius into the soft flesh beneath his armpit. The man crumpled. Marcus wounded another. They turned swiftly, ready to fight the other attackers, but the enemy had gone.

These Germani had no intention of fighting. There were only seven or eight of them, and three were already dead. They would have all been killed had they stayed to give battle. Quintus looked up at the rock face in anticipation of further attacks, but no more were coming.

'Keep going,' he called to the line of men still on the scree slope and the legionaries who had turned to fight. 'You men, go. Crassus, hurry them across. Marcus and I will deal with this.' The blacksmith hesitated and looked to be about to turn back. 'Go!' Quintus shouted.

Quintus believed that defeating this column was never the goal of the tribesmen. It was doubtful that they even realised it was Romans that they were attacking. They were thieves who had achieved what they had set out to do. They had separated the packhorses from their escort and driven them down the hill, following them with whoops and shouts of triumph. The man who had knocked the rider from his horse was up and making his way after the others, supporting his companion who, though injured, limped alongside him.

The wounded man did not go far. He dropped to one knee, and Quintus saw an arrow jutting out from his side. His companion let go of him and took only a step or two more before he too stumbled, a black fletching protruding from his back. The other two Anatolians had strung their bows and now all four followed in the tracks of the ambushers, leaping down the hillside with no regard for their own safety. The remaining Cantabrian followed them, his sharp curved mákhaira raised and ready to kill.

'Come on, Marcus!' Quintus shouted.

He and Marcus set off, scrambling down the slope and bouncing from tree to tree down the scree. They had swords in one hand, but needed the other to support themselves on the sparse tree trunks. They did not need to go far before coming across another body, pierced with an arrow. As they passed it, two of the Anatolians appeared beneath them, helping each other as they struggled up the slope.

With them was the Cantabrian, his sword bloodied and his face split with a grin. He spoke with a thick accent. 'No more, all gone.'

One of the Anatolians had better Latin. 'None survived, commander. There were just eight of them. They were after the supplies.'

'The packhorses?' Quintus asked.

The Anatolian shook his head. 'Gone, sir. Continued down the slope at a gallop. I do not think we could ever get to them — and if we could, we would never persuade them back up that hill.' He looked down to where his two comrades could now also be seen pulling themselves uphill.

'We need those supplies,' said Marcus firmly.

'They are gone, Marcus. Far below in the valley. We cannot even see the beasts,' said Quintus.

'They should not be abandoned so easily.'

'It is not easy,' Quintus said, a trace of annoyance in his tone. 'But it is necessary.'

Marcus was defensive. 'I could go after them.'

'No,' Quintus said as he turned to climb back up the slope. 'It would be a fool's errand.'

Marcus shook his head. He did not agree but held his tongue.

They struggled to gain the track again, where the wounded lay, both Cantabrian and legionary. Two of the Cantabrians were stunned, while the third carried a knife wound. Although the wounded man lived still, his companions thought that it would not be for long. They propped him carefully against the rock and soon pronounced him dead.

One of the Anatolians turned over the dead attacker to retrieve his arrow. 'They are not our quarry,' he said, as he withdrew the shaft. 'This one is not of the Vindelici. He is of the Suebi. The knot he wears in his hair betrays his bloodline.'

'But they don't belong here.' Marcus narrowed his eyes, puzzled. 'Was it not the Suebi who attacked the centurions of the Fifth — and was that not a long way from here?'

Quintus had the answer. 'Maelo led many tribes in that action, a sort of confederation in which the Suebi were but a part — but yes, you are right, Marcus. They are far from their hunting grounds.' He sighed. 'Rome has stirred the pot. Not every village or town will have bent the knee, but there will be none unaffected. If they are pushed out of their traditional grounds by Rome — or by tribes resettled by Rome — they must of necessity hunt elsewhere. These are raiders. Look at this man. He is starving.'

They looked down to where the Anatolian had turned the body over with the toe of his boot. He was right. The man's face was gaunt; his arm, where it protruded from his sleeve, was thin, the veins raised. His clothes were ragged.

'So they are stealing to eat,' Marcus concluded, almost with acceptance.

Quintus looked at him disapprovingly but said nothing, instead turning to the legionary with the spear injury. The man had pulled the weapon out and bound the wound roughly. 'I can cross, sir,' he told Quintus. 'I can make it to the capsarius.'

'Good,' Quintus replied with a nod.

The Cantabrians again began the traverse of the scree, leading their ponies. The wounded legionary limped after them, supported on the shoulder of a comrade. The rest, including the Anatolians, followed.

The men were glad to see their fellows and eager to know what had happened, but saddened by the loss of both the auxiliary and their provisions. Alba began treating the injuries, able to concentrate on the legionary as the Cantabrians were happy to look after themselves. They also turned down Sextus' offer of a prayer for their lost comrade. They managed to convey that an intervention with Roman gods would not be appropriate; they would invoke their own deities.

Alba cleaned the legionary's leg wound and bound it properly. 'A flesh wound,' he said. 'It will heal.'

Agnus was keen to lift the mood again and offered to ride ahead.

'I will find us a good place to camp,' he told Quintus.

Quintus would not permit the scout to travel alone, so at least one legionary always accompanied him, sometimes two, sometimes an auxiliary horseman. One of the Cantabrians this time offered to ride with him. Quintus sent two legionaries in addition.

The group returned quickly. The path had ended no more than half an hour away, the mountainside giving way to a wide expanse of grassland. There was water nearby, and cover from a stand of tall spruce trees that formed the edge of a wider forest.

'It looks like an excellent place to camp,' Agnus reported. 'There may even be game in the forest.'

'Good,' said Felix. He was still acting as praefectus castrorum, so supplies were his responsibility. 'We have little food left after that raid. We either have to make do with the meagre offerings that remain or we must hunt for meat. I prefer the latter course.'

'So do we all. We may have to rely on the Anatolians.' Quintus was grateful for the archers — they were excellent at bringing down game.

They arrived at the site, where Quintus ordered them to set up a proper marching camp, taking much more care with it than they had the last few evenings. The marauders who had driven off their packhorses could easily be part of a larger group. The ditch was dug just a little more deeply, the rampart was piled up just a little higher, and the guards that were posted were just a little more alert.

If there were raiders in the area — especially desperate, starving ones — they needed to be careful.

XIII: FORS FORTUNA

Quintus and Crassus looked at the land in front of the camp. For once it was almost flat, a wide-open area with three sides that sloped into shallow valleys. Here the grass was long, waving gently in the breeze, punctuated with copses of hazel and holly. It was capable of hiding whole troops of men and entire tribes of natives.

'It is ripe for ambush or treachery,' Quintus said. 'We need to be even more careful than usual. There could be more of these bands of robbers around.'

Despite their preparations, an uneasy atmosphere was noticeable in the camp. The attack reminded the men that they were in hostile territory. There were scurrying sounds behind them in the forest and the howling of wolves not far away. Two of the Anatolians returned after dark and were challenged sharply, and at sword point, even though they were well known and returning with game brought down for the pot. Felix intervened, telling the men to curb their enthusiasm and let the hunters in.

The following morning they awoke to dense, dark clouds and cold rain. They struck camp and set off early. The men were morose and fractious, the miserable weather only adding to their mood. Agnus and his escort went ahead. He returned sooner than expected.

'You are alone…?' Quintus began, looking beyond the scout. 'Has something happened to the others?'

'They are keeping watch over our quarry,' he said excitedly. 'The Vindelici have finally halted. Last night they camped as usual. This morning they should have moved. They did not.

Their fires are still lit, their shelters are still up, and their mounts are turned out to graze. It seems that they are waiting for something — perhaps they plan to meet another tribe? I do not know. I have left Vetruvius and a Cantabrian to watch them.'

Quintus raised his hand to call a halt but did not signal a dismount. 'It is definitely the Vindelici? And they have definitely stopped?'

'I could not name them as Vindelici — I cannot truly tell one Germani tribe from another — but I am certain they are the group that fled from the beach. The same riders that we have tracked from the lake. Last night I crept close enough to listen to their conversation. I could not understand what they said, but their mood was clear from the way they spoke and laughed. They are relaxed.' He looked around. 'It is a pity that Caius was not with us. We would have benefitted from his skill with their language. Vetruvius tried, but he is no linguist.'

'This is the first time you have been close enough to hear them clearly?'

'It is. I worried that if we had them in sight and if we could see and hear them, then they could see and hear us, if only they knew where to look. So until last night, we kept a long way back.' He shook his head. 'But they are not looking. They have dropped their guard. I think they may be somewhere near home.'

'Thank the gods,' said Marcus, with feeling. He had ridden to the head of the column to hear the report. 'I am getting cramp from constant riding.' Marcus preferred to walk, but they were travelling at the speed dictated by their prey, and on rough terrain. 'I need something positive to tell the men,' he explained. 'It seems that this may be it.'

'We will camp as close as we dare to our prey,' said Quintus. 'Tell the men, Marcus. Tell them also that the end of our quest may be in sight.'

Marcus nodded as Quintus turned back to his scout. 'Eat and drink, Agnus. Take some rest. But I want you back in sight of them before the end of today. More importantly, you should be within earshot. Take Caius with you this time and get close enough to hear them.'

Agnus saluted and went back down the line to find Caius. The mood of the men was lifted by the news. They were sore from riding and the cold and damp ate into their bones.

When it was not raining, the air was clear and sharp at this height, but the ground seemed to embrace the cold. Many mornings it glittered white with frost before cloud rolled in and drizzle melted it away. The men reluctantly had to admit that the furs and trews kept them warmer than tunics might have done. Nevertheless, they all missed their cloaks, especially at night.

By noon — guessed at, as the sun had not been seen all day — the troop had set up another camp. This, they hoped, was their last stop before tackling the enemy they had followed so many miles into his own country.

Quintus went to find Caius. 'Caius, your skills will be needed by the scout,' he said.

'So he has told me,' said the veteran. 'Although I am no interpreter.'

Quintus patted the man on the shoulder, a commander's gesture. 'The gist of what they are saying, Caius, that is all. How far to their settlement, if nothing else.'

'We will find out what we can, sir.'

Agnus and Caius took off together. By morning they had not returned.

It was again dull, although at least it had stopped raining and no frost had formed. The men breakfasted on limited rations, for once at a leisurely pace, and the horses were checked over by Crassus and Maxim. Some hunted, the party accompanied by the Anatolians bringing down a boar, a tusker of sufficient years to make it slow.

The boar was injured, stunned, but not dead. The men brought it back to the camp and approached Sextus, asking him to make sure the gods were pleased with their catch. The country, the weather and the attack had conspired to make them even more superstitious than usual. Sextus agreed and, head covered as *flamen*, offered a prayer to the gods as Marcus prepared to slit the beast's throat. The blood was to be an offering to Diana the huntress, a libation.

As Marcus stood poised with the knife, the boar held between his legs, a shout went up from the pickets. Agnus and Caius were on their way back in. At the shout, Marcus stopped. 'Do we need to wait?'

If he did not cut the animal, it could be slung over a horse whole and butchered later. They would still be able to eat it. More importantly, the ceremonial would be acceptable. If he started now, he would have to finish killing it and gutting it. If the sacrifice was interrupted once started, it would bring ill luck.

'Do we move tonight?' Quintus asked Agnus urgently as the scout approached the fires.

Agnus shook his head and raised his voice so all could hear. 'No, sir. I do not think we move tonight. They are not moving. They seem settled.'

Quintus trusted the answer. 'Go ahead, Marcus. The boar will be eaten tonight after all.'

Marcus smiled broadly and, invoking Diana, drew his knife across the boar's throat. Then he made the second cut down its long back as the watching company quietly expressed their pleasure. The ritual echoed that of the harvest, though it lacked incense and wine, and there were no cakes for Janus. Still, the men thought it the best they could do. Marcus cut out the heart and liver, holding them up. They were flawless. Once the ceremonial part was over, Sextus uncovered his head and Marcus handed the boar's carcass to the slaves to butcher and cook.

Quintus signalled the scout to carry on. 'We were there at first light, but so were others, sir. We could hear them, so we crouched down out of sight. We were confused. Whoever approached, it did not sound like warriors.'

'Or even men, Quintus, because they were not,' said Caius. 'They were women and children, babes in arms, even. There was squalling and cackling and laughing in equal measure.'

'The women carried food, drink and firewood as well as babes,' Agnus continued. 'The children who could walk brought faggots according to their age and size. The smallest ones had seen perhaps four or five winters and brought small sticks in bundles. The oldest were almost warriors, but not yet ready to shave, long-limbed and awkward. They carried larger bundles, seemingly vying with each other as to who could bear the heaviest load. They all placed their fuel together, building a great fire. At last there were some men of great age, too, white-haired. They came slowly in a group at the rear. Even they carried bundles of wood.'

'Fighting men?' Marcus asked.

'None but those that we have tracked.'

Marcus shook his head in puzzlement. 'Where are the warriors?'

'Perhaps they will arrive with a sacrificial beast — like our boar,' said Sextus. 'It is some festival or other,' he added, with conviction. 'A fire or fertility festival, perhaps? One that invokes family from youngest to oldest? It could be like Fors Fortuna or the Vestalia.'

'Not Fors Fortuna!' Felix exclaimed with mock horror. 'The festival of the goddess of fortune can go on for days. Revellers only return from the downstream temples to the Forum Boarium when food and drink runs out, or there is a sign from the heavens. Let us pray that this festival is not as long.'

'Vestalia can also be endless.' Sextus was more than familiar with the Roman festival of the hearth. As a boy fostered by the Vestal Virgins he had been regularly turned out of the temple for rites and celebrations, including this most important one that cleaned the hearth and renewed the flame. 'It lasts over a week without interruptions. If anything has to be repeated, it can be even more.'

'When we left they were building one great fire,' said Caius. 'Each piece of wood was laid with incantations. There were many gods invoked. I heard Týr and Wotan, Brokk and Heimdall. There was another called Freya — a mother-goddess, from what I could glean. There was no talk of battle or war. I could not even detect any mention of the lost ships. I could see no sacrificial animals, nothing dressed or garlanded — but of course, it may be that the warriors have to bring down a prize.'

'Perhaps they intend human sacrifice. Perhaps a child,' Sextus said darkly. 'It has been known, and you say there were plenty of children.'

This thought quietened them all for a moment. Even Rome had ceased live sacrifices of humans, the last being the burial of enemy Gauls beneath the Forum Boarium less than a hundred years since. At least the action had been condemned by the senate amid promises that such sacrifices would never happen again.

'It is none of our business what they do with their own,' Caius said.

'Maybe not,' said Quintus. 'But if we could prevent it…'

There was a general murmur of agreement.

'We could attack them now,' suggested Marcus. 'Whilst they are distracted by their ceremonies.'

'Except that the warriors are not there,' said Agnus. 'Or at least, only a few of them are.'

'Our orders are to destroy this branch, those that opposed Tiberius. We cannot claim to have done that if the warriors are not here.' Quintus became thoughtful. 'If their women and children and the aged are here, perhaps they have not come far. Perhaps their settlement is nearby.'

'Once they are within their walls, there is nothing we can do, Quintus,' insisted Marcus. 'We need to overwhelm them now.'

'Not whilst we cannot account for their warriors.'

'So we do not move tonight,' Marcus said, with clear disappointment. He wondered who was with him, who with Quintus. 'We need a council of sorts. All the officers.'

XIV: OPPIDUM

The six officers sat down together to eat. The two centurions and three optiones were joined by the signifer, Rufus. Somehow unpromoted common soldier Sextus was also in attendance.

'You may need auguries,' he said blandly when Felix queried his presence.

Marcus shrugged. 'Let him stay and listen. It will do no harm.'

Quintus accepted Sextus' presence, telling him to listen only, then began. 'I do not know what they are up to,' he said, as he chewed on a leg bone. 'But they have two choices. They either go or stay. If they go, that is easy. We follow, find their base and take it. If they stay, we must attack them where they are, whilst they are occupied with whatever it is they are doing.'

'We should attack them before they reach their settlement,' Marcus proposed at once.

'If it is near, and it houses the fighting men, then they will come at us from the rear whilst we are busy killing their women and children.' Crassus sounded disgusted. 'I may be dressed like a barbarian, but I have not yet become one.'

'How many warriors are there, Agnus?' Quintus asked.

'Only a few. Probably just those we chased from the beach. With the number of women and children there, there should be more.'

'I say we go after them tomorrow.' Marcus was sure of himself. 'If they are still there when we arrive, we attack. Especially if they are still occupied with their ritual. At the very least this will leave fewer of them to defend their settlement.'

There was general agreement. The men were tired of the inaction.

'And if they are on the move?' Caius asked.

'Then we follow and destroy them in their home,' said Quintus. 'In either case, the decision rests on what we find. We ride at first light.'

He wiped his greasy fingers on a rag, which he then threw into the fire. With a loud crackle it burst into a bright blaze, enough to make the men shy away. They were briefly taken aback by the ferocity of the flame.

'I think that may have taken my eyebrows,' said Felix.

'And my moustaches,' said Rufus, feeling what the others called his barbarian facial decorations.

Sextus also felt his carefully coiffed hair. 'Me, too. I am sure I am burned,' he moaned.

The little group broke up — there was more meat to be eaten, and the men would sleep better on full stomachs, knowing that soon they were going into action.

Ever since they had burned the ships and been swimming in the pristine but freezing waters of the lake, the men had become gloomier about what seemed like an endless chase. They were moving further and further away from their own people, vanishing into the lands of their enemy.

But the next morning, they were alert and excited, at last hard on the trail of the Vindelici. Before dawn they were packed up and mounted. The fires were extinguished and what remained of the meat was packaged. The skin of the beast was rolled up also. It was no use until it was dried. They crossed the grassy plain and descended into a valley, then followed a lively stream towards its source and began once again to climb.

Beneath their feet they could see thick mist rolling up the sides of the valley. It seemed to dampen the sounds around them — there was no birdsong, no animal calls, just the sound of running water. An hour into the journey they were met by a man riding hard in the opposite direction. The Anatolians immediately nocked their arrows, but Quintus waved them to stand down. It was Vetruvius, returning from his watch.

'Quintus, they have gone,' he said hoarsely, keeping his voice down.

'Speak up,' said Quintus. 'Let us all hear.'

Vetruvius understood. He raised his voice and his chin. 'Yesterday eve they lit a great bonfire. There was a lot of eating and drinking. There was singing and much dancing around the fire. They were celebrating something, but I could not tell you what. Early this morning, with the fire still smouldering and the sun yet to rise, they all left. At first I thought it was just a few, so I waited. But then I realised it was everyone. Women, children, animals — they all traipsed off.'

'Did their warriors come?'

'No, the company stayed as it was when the women and children arrived. There was no sign of any more fighting men.'

'Where were they going?'

'I know which direction they went in; they are following a shallow valley, the same stream that runs here. The Cantabrian has stayed with them, tracking them. But little skill is needed for this. They are moving slowly and noisily, clearly fearing no enemy. I think we will not lose them. I think they are near home.'

'Did you see them sacrifice?' Quintus asked.

'I saw nothing sacrificed but the timber in the fire. No bird or beast. They just built the bonfire, lit it and danced round it, chanting and singing.'

'Your thoughts, Sextus?'

Sextus understood what Quintus was asking him. He shook his head. 'I cannot divine the reason. It was neither a full moon nor a new moon, neither equinox nor solstice. I am puzzled. There were no new stars that I could see. There was no hairy star like the one that announced the death of Divine Julius. It was too cloudy for shooting stars last night. If there were sacrifices or any religious practices, it sounds like they were carried out secretly.'

Vetruvius agreed. 'This is possible — sometimes rites are not for everyone.'

Quintus nodded. 'There are the strange ceremonies attached to the Good Goddess, the mysteries kept from men — there could well be sacrifices.'

'Or it could be something only they know, only they can see,' said Sextus. 'It could be as simple as a safe homecoming, as complex as a dynastic wedding.'

'Whatever it was, it is over. Lead on,' Quintus commanded Vetruvius. 'We will follow slowly and carefully at a distance. I do not want to spook them. I do want to know where their warriors are before we attack.'

Agnus and a Cantabrian provided a bridge between pursuer and pursued, reporting on progress. For two more days and nights, the Vindelici remained the pursued, though they did not know it. There was still no sign of any more fighting men than those few who had fled from the boats.

The tribe moved unhurriedly, confident in their own country, setting up sprawling camps with many fires at night. 'They are not totally careless,' Agnus pointed out. 'There are guards, some of them mere youths. Look.' He indicated where his sharp eyes had picked out armed men on horseback at regular intervals. They rode to either side of the group and on the far bank of the river. He was right; some appeared to be very young. 'They also take up position at night. But still all seem to be relaxed and unhurried.'

Quintus and Crassus rode side by side at the front of the column. They had climbed out of the valley along an animal trod that took them onto a sharp ridge from which they could see their prey. Far below, in the crook of a wide valley, many families moved in a leisurely fashion. They could hear singing. From time to time, haunting tunes rose up the valley sides.

'What do they sing, Agnus?' asked Crassus.

'We do not know,' said the scout. 'The words, the few that we can make out, have defeated Caius' simple knowledge of their tongue.'

'They clearly feel safe,' Quintus said. 'To them the tribesmen that galloped down the hill towards their lakeside camp must be, as far as they could determine, Germani warriors — raiders, probably ship stealers. That such marauding bands are present is evidenced by the group that attacked our auxiliaries and drove off our packhorses and supplies. The Vindelici must know that such men will not follow into someone else's home territory. I think that they are home, Crassus, and happy to be here — hence the songs.'

'So the tribe considers itself safe and travels at a pedestrian pace. For the most part, people walk their ponies — the families travel on foot — and they have children, babies even, also the old. This will slow them even more.'

'We have missed our chance,' Marcus grumbled. 'We should have fallen on them before there were such numbers.'

The group eventually turned to follow another valley, this one even narrower and home to a white-water stream that ran noisily over stones. The change of direction meant that the legionaries could no longer watch from the safety of height. They had to descend back into the valley. This time, there was no trod. Instead, it was a difficult traverse of rugged ground down which they had to walk the horses. Then they turned to follow in the enemy's footsteps. The ground was rough and climbed steeply, the trail crossing and recrossing the stream. The pace of the Vindelici diminished further and Agnus was forced to counsel caution, lest they close too fast. A short time later, he returned and urged a halt.

'I can see where they are headed, their village, or town,' he reported. 'It is set in a bend of the river and, like all their towns, it is raised above the surrounding land. There is no attempt to hide it. Approach any further now and we will be seen. There is no cover in front of it, no rocks or walls. Trees either never grew here or have been felled.'

'We camp back there,' Quintus told Crassus, indicating a short way back along the trail. Here they had passed through a wider part of the valley, with an area of flat floor. A few stunted trees — bushes really — would provide scant fuel.

'No fires yet, not until we are sure the smoke will not give away our position. Felix and I will go with Agnus to see what lies ahead. Caius, you too are with us.'

As Crassus turned the column, the two centurions and Caius joined Agnus and the Cantabrian, making their careful way on foot to the last spot with cover before the settlement. Darkness was beginning to close in as they arrived, and a thick evening mist had risen, though it stayed not far above ankle height. This caused them to doubt their footing and slow their pace.

The oppidum, for that was what it surely was, sat on a rise in the ground. From where they stood they could not gauge its size. It was squat and black, backlit against the pale sky and the setting sun. There were no true hills here, but the valley floor sloped upwards and then flattened out again, a plateau ideal for defence. 'That hill might even be manmade,' said Quintus. 'It does not look natural.'

Felix nodded agreement. 'It does not. But that does not make it any less effective.'

The oppidum sat in a great curve of the river, so that attack would be difficult on the three sides protected by water. The fourth, the side they faced, had cleared bare ground before it. A well-worn track led towards the opening through which the people of the Vindelici entered. The gateway formed a rectangle of pale light in the dark facade, extinguished as the gates were pulled closed behind the last of the travelling party. The sun sank below the horizon at the same moment, making the legionaries shiver as darkness fell.

Torches marked the corners of the palisade, with others flickering above the tall towers that carried the gates. These pinpoints served to delineate the shape, a dark grey silhouette on a blue-black field, seeming to float in the mist that gathered around its base. As yet, there was no moon, and only a few stray stars winked to life above their heads.

'There is not even enough cover for a rabbit,' said Felix. Quintus was about to question him when he clarified, 'No, I mean an actual rabbit, not one of my men.' The others chuckled softly, remembering the nickname that Felix' century claimed.

'We need to get closer,' said Quintus. 'Somehow we need a better look at it. It does not seem as fearsome as any oppidum we have seen before. Sextus is not here — do any of you know when the moon will rise?'

Felix and Agnus did not. Nor did Caius. He had to translate for the Cantabrian, who did not have enough Latin to understand the question. The man held up two fingers in response.

'In two hours or at the second hour, sir,' said Caius, shaking his head. 'I do not know which.'

'Probably two hours. Give him our thanks anyway,' said Quintus. The Cantabrian understood and made a salute to confirm it.

'Whichever it is, it is not yet. That means we can take our chance to get a closer look in the dark.'

XV: FOSSA

'The tribesmen have only just arrived,' Felix said. 'This is the time when they will be least on their guard. They will be looking to unpack, to find their own hearths, to eat and rest.'

Quintus knew what Felix was suggesting. He also knew that if he put this to the other officers, they would also be keen to attack; they would remind him of the mission given to them by Tiberius. But it was this mission that had prevented him from attacking thus far. He needed this tribe in one place, in order to destroy them. If they were allowed to scatter, the mission would have failed.

Quintus looked at the oppidum. *Not yet*, he thought. He had learned caution from Centurion Galba, his former commander and First Spear.

'We need greater knowledge,' he said to the other men. 'In the time we have before the moon rises, we need to know if this oppidum is assailable. Agnus, you come with me; we can move like shadows in the night. Felix, Caius, you are hardly insubstantial — go back to the men and ready them. If we are not back when the moon rises, lead them into the attack. Take the Cantabrian with you.'

Felix and Caius saluted and quickly vanished into the darkness, taking the auxiliary with them. Quintus looked upwards at the dark sky with its few pinpoints of light. 'We can risk an hour at most, Agnus. You are the scout — what do you suggest?'

'We must become beasts. We must be like scavengers or hunters of the night. We must look like them, move like them.'

114

Quintus heard the grin in the man's voice. 'We must hope that they do not decide to hunt us like them.'

'Agreed,' said Quintus drily.

'First,' said Agnus, 'we must check for anything that might reflect the light, even starlight — and that includes skin. We must put it off if it is clothing or weapons; we must use dirt to blacken it otherwise.'

They first darkened their faces and arms, then inspected each other for anything else that might reveal them to the enemy. For once they were glad to be wearing trews, rather than being bare-legged.

'Anything that might make a noise, including weapons, should also be put off,' Agnus added.

'I will keep my blades,' said Quintus. 'I would rather take my chances wearing them than leave them behind.'

'We just need to make sure that no metal touches metal,' said Agnus. 'Then, we proceed on all fours, our furs on our backs and over our heads. And we do not move in a straight line. We move erratically and stop to graze, or to react to danger.' He looked at the oppidum. 'With your permission, I will take this side. I think the climb the other side will be easier.'

Quintus smiled briefly to himself but took no offence, though he thought he could have managed either. In the dark two strange shapes set off across the open ground.

Of course, with their noses to the ground, the legionaries discovered that the area was not as totally lacking in cover as it had seemed. There were small rises, furrows where perhaps a field had been worked, shallow streams, and gaunt shrubs. They darted from one skeletal bush to another, to a tiny rise or depression, stopping to take stock as any prey animal would.

Once he reached the base of the hill on which the oppidum was raised, Quintus realised that it was not a difficult climb. He was also less exposed than on the approach; he would not be visible unless someone looked straight down at him. He hoped that the eyes of any guards would be on the approaches. He had looked for guards, had tried to spot movement on his way across, but had seen none. The torches on the palisade had not moved. Perhaps the inhabitants, deep in their own country, felt safe enough to post no watch.

His progress was stopped abruptly by a deep ditch, a fossa, which seemed to run all the way around the oppidum, beneath its perimeter. The oppidum itself was marked not by a wall, but by a wooden fence, the inhabitants no doubt thinking that, with the ditch, a wall was unnecessary. He slithered forward on his belly to look over the side.

It was deep, the height of a tall man and twice as wide. He could not quite see what was in the bottom, but knew that the rain that had been falling constantly over the past few days would have left puddles. Perhaps it was filled with water anyway, as part of the defence. He took a pebble and dared to cast it into the ditch. It splashed.

How had the Vindelici crossed the ditch? He had seen them enter the oppidum, so there had to be a way. He crept to within sight of the gates and was pleased by what he could see. There was no bridge or temporary crossing that could be removed. Instead, the ditch was filled in where the trail crossed it. At least here was a point of entry, although this of course would be guarded.

It was too dark to accurately assess the state of the wooden fence, but from one point he could see the flicker of fires from within. So the fence was not as solid as it looked from a distance. Further round, a bigger gap allowed him to see inside. There were some thatched huts and a larger central fire. He hesitated to call it a town; it was not big enough.

He returned in the same manner as he had arrived, on all fours, zigzagging from side to side, until, with a sigh of relief, he was once more at the place from which they had set out. They had not been long; the stars had barely moved, and the moon was still not risen. The scout was already at the rendezvous.

'What do you think, Agnus?'

'It is not as well built or as well kept as the oppidum we destroyed when our commander fell. Nor is it as big. I could see gaps at the bottom of the fence big enough for small animals like deer and foxes to enter, but they would have to cross the ditch first. The ditch is a better defence than anything we have encountered before. Did it continue on your side?'

'It did, but only after the gate. Where the gate is, the ditch is filled in. That is its weakest point.'

Quickly they loped back to where the rest of the troop waited. Some of the men were clearly disappointed to see the two scouts, preferring a battle to the siege they now expected. A siege would demand a lot of men and time; they did not have men to spare and winter was fast approaching. They would be unlikely to succeed.

Quintus again called a council of his officers.

'Divine Julius would of course fill the trench in,' Marcus began.

'Not only that — I am sure that he would dig another trench, even deeper, all the way round, so as to stop anyone from escaping,' laughed Sextus. 'He had both trench and walls at Alesia.'

'He did,' Quintus agreed. 'He also had legions. Legions with siege engines, ballistae and onagers — and engineers to operate them. We have none of those. We cannot take it by siege; we have neither the men nor the machinery.' Crassus was about to object, but Quintus held a hand up to stop him. 'I know you would try, my friend, but we do not have the time to build engines, even if we had carpenters and engineers. Our only chance is to somehow persuade them to open the gates.'

Felix nodded. 'I agree. We do not have the strength to force an entry.'

'We could have destroyed them whilst they were on the move,' Marcus said sourly.

'And leave them behind us? To harry Tiberius further?' Felix countered. 'Our mission is to destroy them — and that means in their base. We had to wait until they were back in the nest.'

Quintus was glad of the intervention.

The men within earshot nodded, including a reluctant Marcus. No-one wanted to be responsible for discord. A silence fell as they chewed on pork bones and stared at the crackling flames of the campfire.

'We could set fire to it,' said Crassus quietly.

'We could,' agreed Quintus. 'If we can set fire to the buildings, it will force them to leave. The palisade will burn, and the huts are wooden, thatched with straw. The fence looked to be in poor repair — at the bottom there are gaps where it has rotted. It will have suffered from the predations of beetle and worm. I am sure that it will burn.'

'We can use the pork fat,' said Rufus, his hand going to where his moustaches had been singed earlier. 'The pork fat burns like a funeral pyre — and it spreads if you try to douse it with water. We can use fat-soaked rags.'

'Excellent,' said Quintus, delighted. He called to the slaves. 'Maxim, get as much of the pork fat as you can from what is left of the meat, and soak linen in it. The Cantabrian who was killed has no need of his horse blanket or spare linen anymore. Beg it from his comrades.'

Maxim saluted his understanding and called to his cousin. The Cantabrians gave up what was spare and together they began to tear and soak.

'All we need is a way to deliver the fire.' Felix was thoughtful. 'You have been up to the palisade, Quintus. Could you cross the ditch? Could you reach the wall to set fires? It would be risky.'

'With men who are lithe enough to move softly and silently, who are capable of crossing the ditch and climbing out, yes.' He knew the type of man he meant. Not Felix and Marcus, who were sitting across from him. Marcus had the broad chest of a wrestler. As for Felix, it was said that no oxen were needed on the farm belonging to his father, as Felix could pull the plough himself.

It was he who spoke next. 'We have auxiliaries. There is no need for such risk if the archers can make the range. Do you think they can?'

'With fire arrows, I don't know.' Quintus called the auxiliaries across.

The leader of the Anatolian archers joined the council diffidently. Though no commoner in his own land and captain of many in the army, he was not used to being consulted by his Roman masters. He took pride in the ability of his archers. He listened, then weighed the soaked rag in his hand and spoke carefully.

'I know the range. I am confident that we can make it if we are able to creep close enough.'

'How close?' Quintus asked. He did not wish to lose men by taking unnecessary risks, even auxiliaries. These men could be the key to his taking of the oppidum.

'It is about half our normal range.' The Anatolian looked upwards. 'We need to be in position before the moon rises.'

Quintus stood and looked at the sky. He tugged his tunic straight. 'Maxim, Jovan, hurry. The archers need your rags.'

The Anatolian stood. 'Do not worry,' he said in a heavy accent. 'We will not fail.'

Suddenly, with the decision made, there was a flurry of activity. The slaves soaked the rest of the rags and stuffed them into leather bags for each archer. The leader of the archers went to brief his companions. Marcus sought out tinder and flint. The others looked nervously at the sky, praying that the moon would wait.

After a brief discussion with Agnus, Quintus determined that the western palisade was weakest. That would also give the legionaries the advantage of having the rising sun at their backs when they played their part.

Equipped, the archers set off at a jog. They wore linen shirts beneath a belted tunic and their own baggy leggings, tucked into tall hide boots. All were in sombre colours, deep blues and blacks, and their faces were darkened. They skirted around the edge of the forest and only crossed open ground when they had almost reached the river. They kept low until the leader threw up a hand to halt them. Each took the bundle he was carrying, along with flint and tinder, and settled down to await the dawn, motionless shadows in the landscape.

Not long afterwards, clouds bubbled up as the moon rose.

'Two hours,' said Caius, as he watched the half-moon scud in and out of the cloud. 'The Cantabrian was right.'

Back in the camp, Quintus ordered the lighting of many fires in front of the trees where they were camped. The intention was for it to look like a great troop of enemy was established here, and to draw eyes away from the archers. He wanted the Vindelici on guard, alert to danger, but looking where he wanted them to look. It was part of the strategy. It was important that they saw where the danger was coming from, the fires set to the southwest of the oppidum, across the open plain.

Quintus knew that he did not have the numbers for a direct assault. He did not even have the numbers to be able to rely on surprise. This oppidum had to be taken by subterfuge, by careful planning and a dose of luck. They all prayed to Jupiter Optimus Maximus, to Mars, and individually to their own guardian deities.

Then they waited and watched for daylight in the east.

XVI: CARNIFEX

The torchlights on the palisade were still flickering as the first pale light of dawn broke, outlining the oppidum like a dark and jagged tooth on the horizon, a tooth floating in a milky mist.

Out of the haze came what looked like a flurry of small shooting stars, arcing across from the west, each pinpoint flying brightly through the air. Another group followed it from nearby, and then another.

Each Anatolian arrow with its fiery cargo thudded into the base of the fence. Where it hit there was smouldering at first, then an eruption of yellow flame. Several fires were already starting to grow and spread. To begin with, there was no reaction from inside the oppidum.

'It has not worked. It has not burned through to the inside,' Felix hissed to Quintus as they watched. They were each squatting at the head of a column of men, also crouched.

'Vulcan would not let us down,' said Crassus, defending his patron.

'Patience,' Quintus counselled. 'It is the first and most crucial part of the plan, it must work. Listen.'

Though they could not see anything, they began to hear what was happening inside. Cries and panicked animal noises told them that the inhabitants were alerted to the fires. The bleating of sheep, the squealing of swine and the honking of geese rose above the human shouts.

These noises were joined by the crackling of flames. Smoke billowed up above the western rampart and, as the sun cleared the horizon, a cold wind from the north began to shred the mist and fan the fires.

The legionaries could hear hissing as water was thrown on the fires, then voices calling out in alarm. Instead of quenching them, the water seemed to enrage the flames.

Rufus was about to comment but Quintus put a finger to his lips. 'It is your addition — the pig fat,' he said quietly. 'It is making the flames flash and flare.'

Not only did the pig fat burn well but it had an aversion to water, and reacted angrily to it. When doused the rags erupted, burning with a fierce flame, crackling, spitting and sputtering.

At two of the places where fires had caught, the flames had already climbed towards the top of the palisade, following edges of dry timber. Smoke rose from inside also.

'The fire has spread to the huts,' said Quintus.

'It sounds as if it has scared the livestock,' said Felix. 'I think they are running amok.'

'Now,' Quintus commanded on seeing the flames leap even higher and hearing the cacophony coming from inside. 'Attack.'

The waiting troops set off at a run due east, until they were alongside the river. They then turned north, so that the attack approached from the eastern flank of the oppidum, the opposite side from where the arrows had flown.

Their numbers were small. There was less than half a century in total, certainly not enough to storm such a fortress, yet they ran across the open ground and up the hill as if they meant to batter down the gates. Behind them the fires continued to burn in the woodland, as if there was a great horde waiting to follow this puny raid.

The men were in a rough column of two, limiting their vulnerability by presenting as little of their bodies as possible to the enemy. Felix led one column, Quintus the other. Felix had twenty men, including the legionary with the spear wound to his leg, who insisted on joining the attack, and the three Cantabrian auxiliaries. Quintus had a smaller troop, just sixteen men including himself. His wing included Crassus, Sextus and Rufus along with the veterans Marcus and Caius. Felix had many men of Century Four — his own rabbits loyal to him — and some of those who had been serving with the Fifth Alaudae when it was defeated. They were still keen to redeem their honour.

The men were ordered not to attack like Romans, so there was no sense of order, no formation of shields and spears. They were also encouraged to make as much noise as possible. They charged as Germani would charge, in a group, shouting the names of the gods that they had learned — Týr and Wotan and Heimdall — waving blades and shields in the air, and running as fast as they could towards the palisade and the gates. The only difference was a subtle one; the advance was to two distinct points, one nearer to the gate than the other.

Missiles were thrown from the gate towers, stones ricocheted off shields and the hard ground, and javelins were skilfully turned aside, plunging into the earth. To Quintus' relief, the Germani did not seem to have any archers. Inevitably, some of the troop were hit and fell, but most gained the square of land that crossed the ditch and began to beat on the gates. Quintus and his column battered the eastern leaf, Felix the other. They wielded native weapons, mostly short spears and axes forged in one piece. They protected themselves as best they could with round, leather-covered shields.

'How long?' Felix shouted.

'Not yet,' came the reply. 'Let the fires take hold.'

Their attack had hardly been opposed — clearly the fire had taken the attention of the inhabitants. The two groups of attackers now crouched as close to the gates as they could, whilst stones and other debris were thrown from above. They held their shields above their heads as missiles landed on them. They beat hard on the gates and shouted curses and the names of Germani gods even louder. They waved spears and thudded axes into the timbers.

Judging the moment Quintus shouted, 'Now, Felix!'

As one, Felix and his men left off their battering and turned to run back the way they had come. They held their shields behind them for protection, over their shoulders. This was hardly necessary as the defenders, shocked by the sudden capitulation, merely cheered and waved their arms in the air. Felix and the men scattered, running down the track away from the gates, shouting and gesticulating. They ran for the cover of the oak grove and vanished into it whilst those on the palisade shouted defiance and victory.

They had not escaped without losses; three bodies lay unmoving. One of the Cantabrians had fallen to an enemy spear and lay pinned to the earth, clearly dead. Two legionaries also failed to rise.

As soon as the retreat into the trees was complete, the fires there began to go out in great clouds of black smoke. Clearly the invading army, defeated, was leaving. The smoke thinned and was blown away on the breeze. There was sizzling and crackling as the fires dimmed and died, then silence.

Although no sound came from the grove, a great tumult of bleating and honking and human voices came from the oppidum. The fire there had not diminished.

One of the gates swung open, the left one, so the legionaries knew that the bar had been lifted. The gap was instantly filled with smoke and the sounds became louder. A few faces peered out, to make sure it was now safe and, after a cursory inspection of the erstwhile battlefield, they could be seen standing back and beckoning to those inside, offering them a means of escape.

First to come through the open gate were swine, sheep and geese, the pigs running towards the river, the sheep milling about in a tight group. The geese beat their wings and loudly called their indignation at being turned out of doors. Women and children followed, some youngsters with sticks to drive the beasts, some mothers carrying young ones at their bosom. Some older children shepherded younger ones. Behind them the fires continued to smoke and roar.

Quintus waited until the animals and these people had passed and then shouted the order. He and his men had concealed themselves to either side of the gate, using the corner formed where the gate tower met the palisade as a hiding place. Now they discarded the native axes and instead drew their own blades. For hand-to-hand fighting, they wanted to feel the weight of a gladius in hand.

'To me!' Quintus shouted. He and his men had only one task — to keep the gate from closing until Felix returned. If the gate was open, then they would have a chance to take the oppidum. On Quintus' signal, they pushed the gate wide and stood with their backs firmly to it, using the round shields to protect themselves.

The first tribesmen to try and dislodge them were careless, thinking that these invaders were no more than renegade tribesmen. They did not give them sufficient respect and died for it. The next wave approached more warily.

'They are boys,' Quintus exclaimed, shocked.

'Boys and old men,' Crassus added, as he cut one of them down.

Felix waited for the gate to open and, as soon as he saw it, charged up the slope, this time emerging from the grove on horseback, at the head of a group of mounted men. Up the track, through the animals, birds and refugees, they galloped. These men too had discarded native weapons, preferring their own swords to Germani axes.

Felix did not have enough men for a proper attack. This was going to be *contendite vestra sponte* from the start, the command for each man to choose his opponent and fight one-on-one, or nearly so. He had the momentum of his charge. He had the element of surprise. He had the support of the Anatolians, who moved round from the west and now shot arrow after arrow into the defenders.

The young men and their grandfathers defending the oppidum now shouted in fury, wielding long swords and their own short axes. But they were torn between repelling the attack and dousing the flames. Many abandoned their attempts to quench the fire which roared behind them, the smoke growing ever thicker. Others stayed, throwing pail after pail of water and earth at the flames.

The other gate, the one furthest from the fire, was pushed open and a group of ponies galloped out. The horses were ridden by young men, boys barely of fighting age, incensed at this assault. Youths ran with short spears alongside them, shouting with rage. Some of their voices were piping still. They charged down the track, screaming defiance, but found no-one at the bottom of the hill to fight. The enemy were already at the gates, which were breached and lying open.

After these riders more women and children emerged to run down the hill. There were more animals, too. It looked like the inhabitants were abandoning the stronghold. The Romans merely had to keep up the pretence that they were an invading army. If the Germani realised that they fought only a few handfuls of fighters, then their confidence would soon return.

The centurions were still wondering where the tribe's warriors were.

One of the boy riders halted at the foot of the hill, shouting. He pulled up his pony and turned back towards the gate. He galloped forward and, lifting his spear, looked directly at Quintus' position. But the spear never flew, and the boy's eyes darkened as an arrow jutted out of his chest. Another, a runner with a javelin, stopped as if he had run into a wall, a black-fletched barb wheeling him backwards. Another of the ponies turned sharply, the horse rearing onto its hind legs then galloping back towards the gate whilst its rider screamed challenges. An arrow found the poor beast's neck and the horse fell, crushing its rider beneath it, blocking the gate.

Amongst the youths some women came out to fight too, wielding sword and spear alongside their sons. They were not as strong, perhaps, but nimbler, able to dart under a defence and then out again, stinging as they went. They had to be treated the same way — as warriors.

Quintus hated the slaughter. These were not warriors.

Pompeius Magnus had in his youth been called the *carnifex adulescentulus*, the juvenile butcher. Quintus felt like the butcher of adolescents and innocents.

XVII: MARS

This was not how the legionaries preferred to fight. They preferred order and discipline behind a solid wall of scuta. They preferred cavalry to guard their wings. They preferred auxiliaries who could take the brunt of the attack. They preferred an enemy that they could battle with honour. Not women. Not children.

They would expect to fight in the reek of the hot sweat from their comrades around them. They demanded enemies that came at them with ferocity and fury. They needed signals and discipline from officers and strategists. Thinking was not a skill that came naturally to the legionary — he was not paid to make decisions.

They wanted orders relayed by cornicenes and signiferi, by brass and banner. They wanted the manoeuvres practised in the Campus Martius. They wanted a flank protected by a comrade dedicated to the survival of both of them.

The men fought in pairs, back-to-back, each soldier protecting his comrade's flank. They also had the invaluable support of the bowmen. The Anatolian archers came up the hill and sheltered behind the bodies of fallen horses as they shot death into the tribesmen. They were near enough to be able to pick a target, and few arrows went to waste.

Neither side had much armour, though some stolen pieces were worn — some of the enemy even had shirts of ring mail. For many of the Germani, the display of bare flesh was meant as a sign of courage, a lack of fear in the face of death. The young men emulated their fathers in this, baring their hairless chests.

These youths had the bravery and foolhardiness of the young. Few of them yet sported a beard, yet they were willing to sacrifice themselves for glory. There were old men fighting, too. They were brave but slow; fewer strikes were needed to fell them. Yet, blade in hand, they died with smiles on their lips, joining the great feast of heroes at last.

There was little science to this sort of combat. The surgeons of Divus Julius had marked the soft spots of men, but it did not take surgeons to know what was vulnerable.

Thus, in the cold air, as a chilly rain was blown on the stiff breeze, flesh was sliced, blood spurted and sprayed and eyesight was blurred not just by rain, but by the sweat that flew from every man's brow.

Quintus was back-to-back with Sextus rather than his own amicus, Crassus. To his right Marcus and Caius fought, while Rufus was paired with the blacksmith. Though his height would have given him a view of the battlefield, the film of rain would not permit Quintus to see further than the length of his arm. His world was bounded by blood and death.

He stabbed and cut with his gladius, happy to have not abandoned the sword in their quest for authenticity. In his other hand he held a Germani round shield, hardly big enough to cover his heart, yet with an iron edge that was a weapon in itself. He fought now at close quarters, smelling the odour of the men he felled, and feeling the heat of their breath on his cheek as he cut and parried.

'Sextus,' he gasped, as the legionary appeared to go down under a rain of blows from his pigtailed opponent. The young man had swung a cavalry sword, but Sextus had seen it coming, deflected it, then stabbed the man hard through his belly button.

'Still here,' he wheezed as he rose. The Germani fighter dropped to his knees, clutching his guts.

Quintus finished the job with a slice across the man's throat, then parried a blow from his own attacker. The force from the two-handed sword, a long, straight double-edged blade, pushed him backwards, but the weight of the sword meant the fighter needed two hands to wield it, so carried no shield. The size of the sword meant that it took time to lift it again — time that the warrior did not have. Quintus stepped in under the weapon, inside the defence. His gladius cut deep into the attacker's sword arm, only halted by bone, then slashed a dark rent across the youth's exposed middle.

The enemy did not die at once, but his sword was no longer a threat. Desperate to keep hold of it, he snatched at it with his other hand as it fell, grabbed it by the blade, not seeming to feel pain as it cut into the flesh of his palm. He died on his knees, sword gripped firmly.

There was a lull in the fighting. For now, no more enemies came, although the sounds of combat had not moved far away.

They were positioned with their backs to the open gate, a quick glance telling Quintus that his men still stood. The Germani had backed off, tried to regroup, but in so doing had exposed themselves to the deadly arrows. Many lay dead before the gates, with black fletchings protruding from their bodies.

'What was the boy doing?' Quintus asked.

'Without his sword, he wanders forever as a shade,' said Sextus. 'With it he joins his own gods and heroes at the feast that will only end with Ragnarok.'

'Ragnarok?'

'The ending of the world, of all worlds.'

Quintus caught the youth in the jaw with his shield. He fell forward, but did not loosen the grip on the weapon. 'He is dead. See, he smiles, he must be at the feast.'

Sextus nodded and grunted, turned to see who was next. Another tribesman, trailing blood and fury, threw himself at the little group of legionaries, sword raised, hoping to take some of this strange foe with him to Valhalla. He gasped as an arrow hit him before his steps brought him close enough to threaten. The curse the man uttered died on his lips as breath and life departed. He fell heavily onto the corpse of his pigtailed comrade.

For now, at least, he was the last. Quintus raised his head and lowered his weapons. He looked around to see dead and dying on the ground. There were still some of the tribesmen on their feet, wielding weapons, but there were two or three Romans to each. Any threat would be quickly extinguished.

'We must have taken prisoners,' Sextus said. 'Some of the women and younger children at least.'

'I think not,' said Felix, who arrived at the gates still mounted. He pointed down the hill. 'I have been to the hillside with riders. There were boats in the river. The women and younger children have mostly vanished. Many old men took their own lives. They have abandoned the animals.'

'The fighting men?'

'Not here. There were nowhere near as many as we thought. There seemed to be groups of old men and groups of young ones — few in between. Few of the sort that we would fear. Our losses are not great. Theirs are catastrophic.'

'We can take no prisoners, Felix,' said Quintus darkly. 'We cannot guard them or feed them. They cannot live.'

'I have not stopped them from escaping,' said Felix. 'Not the ones who ran. I do not think that any will surrender.' He shrugged. '*Sic vita.*'

Quintus nodded his understanding. They were meant to destroy this particular nest of hornets so that noble Tiberius would not be troubled by them again. In this at least they had succeeded. The enemy no longer fought; many of them had fled. The fire still burned brightly in the oppidum.

'Gather the men, Felix. Call them from wherever they are and bring them to muster here, at the gate. Let the women and children run, if they will. They will not trouble us or General Tiberius.'

'Shall I set men to douse the fires?'

'I think not. The place will be no use to us. After tonight, we return to the legions. But you should set men to catch some of the livestock. It will be a useful addition to our food — especially since the raid on our supplies.'

On the western side of the circle of the palisade, the flames had petered out due to lack of fuel. A great black gap was burned in the fence, as if a fell beast had taken a bite out of it. At either end Quintus could see two tall columns of smoke, merging above into a single eddying cloud. At the base of the bite was a ramshackle collection of glowing charcoal sticks that would once have been the animal pens.

Stores and winter fodder had also fuelled the flames. The remnants of storehouses and barrels mingled with rags of sacking floating on the breeze and chunks of burning thatch. From time to time there was a crash as a building collapsed in a spray of sparks and cinders.

As far as Quintus could see, there was no further fighting taking place, but many of the enemy fallen were not dead. He could still hear groans and the names of gods being called upon.

At Felix's command the men were gathering on the hill beneath the gateway, some on foot, some on horseback. The Anatolians came, their bows still primed. The Cantabrians mourned another fallen comrade. As each small group arrived, Quintus sent them to carry out specific tasks, such as seeing to the injured and capturing as much of the livestock as they could.

One job he assigned to many of the men was less than pleasant, but it had to be done.

'Kill any that survive,' he ordered. 'They belong to blood-red Mars. You are welcome to any wealth that you find, but I do not think there will be much. We can take no prisoners.'

XVIII: RES EXERCITUS

There were, inevitably, some injuries to Quintus' own men. Those hurt were helped by comrades where necessary. Some failed to move.

'Find me the capsarius,' Quintus ordered.

Alba came running. He was with Agnus, the scout, and now joined his commander to survey the carnage. They were themselves bruised and bloodied. Alba looked to have taken a serious wound to his face. Blood stained his neck, spreading to his shoulders and back.

'Alba. You are injured,' Quintus observed with concern.

'It is nothing,' said the capsarius. He touched the side of his head. 'A flesh wound. The ear is such a little thing, but it bleeds profusely. It will stop.'

'You are sure?'

Alba nodded, using the centurion's nickname for reassurance. 'Trust me, Mac.'

'The fire took hold impressively.' Agnus gestured at the still burning oppidum.

'Not all our doing,' said Quintus. 'There was something piled against the fence — hay or grain — something that sparked. There were stores there. Look, some still burn. And the pig fat helped.' He turned back to the capsarius. 'Alba, if you are sure that you will mend, go and tend to our wounded. Agnus, find the Macedonians. Tell Jovan to make a tally of the men we have lost and to bring it to me.'

Both men saluted and left. Quintus watched the others. Crassus, Rufus, Vetruvius and Caius moved swiftly from body to body, performing the duties of mercy and lifting anything that shone brightly from the victims.

'Take care it is only the enemy,' admonished Quintus, raising his voice. Both sides in the conflict were dressed in a similar fashion.

'Caligae and gladius for ours,' Vetruvius called back. 'And I know their faces.' Then he grinned as he held up a silver torc.

'He will share it,' insisted Rufus in a low growl as he and Crassus joined the group.

'He will,' said Crassus, his voice muffled. He spat a wad of blood onto the ground. 'Nothing to worry about,' he said to Quintus, seeing the look of concern on his friend's face.

Quintus left the men to their tasks and, with Felix, walked down towards the river. The shapes of the two centurions were distinctive, instantly recognisable. Quintus was very tall, making him look thin, though he was not, earning him his nickname of Macilentus. Felix was also tall, but not as tall as his fellow officer, and more heavily built.

They had arrived at their commands by different routes. Quintus had worked his way up to centurion mostly through the deaths in battle of those above him. Felix was the type of soldier that the army recruited to aspire to the rank, a solid man, steady of thought and action, commanding respect. He was a city man, born within the Servian walls. His father had served in the army for over twenty years. Discharged when Caesar Augustus rationalised the legions, he had been rewarded with farmland in Campania.

On his father's death, Felix inherited the farm. He hated farming, hated the uncertainty of wind and weather, the caprices of both gods and grain markets. He was forced to take on both the land and his father's obligations in the local community. He did not want either and so joined the legions as soon as he could, leaving the management to a freedman.

Both men needed to wash away the taste and smell of the battle. They squatted by the water, well away from where the bodies were being tipped in. As they splashed their necks and faces, Quintus picked up a strange tongue.

'What is that? I do not recognise it.'

'It does not sound Germanic,' Felix replied, but drew his sword anyway as they moved to investigate. Pushing aside long river grasses, they came across two men sitting and laughing together on a tiny beach hollowed out of the bank. They could only see their backs — they were not washing, but sharing a waterskin. Quintus did not recognise them as legionaries. He caught the cadence and emotion of the language, but could not understand the words. Felix was right; it was not Germanic.

Finally, Quintus grasped it — it was a form of Greek, and these men, he was shocked to admit, were Maxim and Jovan. The Macedonian slaves had, with the addition of Germani clothes and Roman blades, turned smoothly into the Macedonian warriors that the farmer and the factor had once been.

'Valé friends.' Quintus and Felix approached the men, who looked at them with apprehension.

'You have tasks for us, masters?' The two men dropped to one knee, an automatic gesture of submission. They had been caught acting as free men.

'I sent for you. I need a list of the dead and injured,' said Quintus sternly.

'I will deliver it at once,' said Jovan, his eyes still fixed on the ground.

'And I, dominus?'

'You have a blade, Maxim. Your cousin too.'

'Taken from the field, dominus. We mean nothing by it.' Their anxiety was apparent, because they knew that there were many who would not condone the arming of slaves. Long-faced Tullius, now dead, was one such. Veteran and optio Marcus another. Centurion Felix, who looked at them now down his long nose, was probably a third. But they also hoped and dreamed that Quintus might recognise their service and free them.

'We joined the battle, master. At its end. We could not just stand by. We killed some of the enemy. We feel like men again.' Looking up, Maxim saw the look on his master's face, a mixture of surprise and, to his amazement, perhaps approval. He nudged his cousin and quickly they offered up their swords to the officers, hilts first. They were not Roman, but shorter Germani blades.

After a long pause, Quintus spoke. 'Keep your weapons. I do not object.' He looked at Felix. 'I will make sure that no others object either.'

Felix shrugged. Though he did not approve, he would not oppose Quintus.

'I thank you for your service,' Quintus continued. 'But know that I cannot free you. You are not mine to liberate. You are *res exercitus*, the property of the army. I cannot erase the mark you wear beneath that headband.' He touched the scrap of cloth that Jovan used to hide the slave mark etched on his forehead. 'Only Augustus Caesar can free you, or perhaps one of his sons. General Tiberius is nearer than Rome, which is where great Caesar will be. I can report your actions, make recommendations, but that is all.' Quintus opened his arms and turned his palms upwards in a gesture of futility.

The Macedonians nodded sad acknowledgement.

'Finish your wash, and your tales,' he said. 'Then resume your work. We all have duties. I will inform the men of the matter of your arms.'

As they walked away, Quintus braced himself for criticism from Felix. Felix sensed it and spoke before his comrade did. 'I will not gainsay it, friend. But it is both your decision and your responsibility.'

'I know it.' Quintus lowered his voice to a whisper. 'I hope I am right.'

'Centurion!'

The two men stood quickly, spinning round to see from where the shout had come. Felix turned towards the gates. 'We are not finished, Quintus,' he called, pointing up the hill. 'Look.'

The left-hand gate of the oppidum, the one not blocked by a dead horse and rider, was being slowly pushed closed from within. Several men, the distinctive figure of Marcus at their head, were already jogging up the hill towards the movement.

'Who are they?' Quintus shouted. 'Boys? Women?'

'We'll find out soon enough,' Felix replied. 'They will never close the other gate.'

'Come,' Quintus commanded, using his sword to sweep a broad gesture towards the opening. Those within sight responded, and a few minutes later, a troop of ten or more men, plus the Anatolian archers, joined Marcus and approached the gate at a run. They pushed it open with little resistance, those enemy attempting to close it seemingly giving up the effort. Cautiously, they advanced inside to see youths running and hiding.

'Leave them,' Quintus ordered. 'I have no idea what they were attempting.'

Not all agreed with such an order, some men shaking their heads, the Anatolians particularly perplexed at being told not to shoot them. Fugitives carried information and could bring reinforcements. Still, none questioned the command.

Marcus had run on ahead. 'Here!' he shouted. 'Enemy.'

But what he found was no threat. A number of old men and women had decided against flight. Instead they sat motionless in the doorways of their huts, swords in hand.

'They are as brave as the conscript fathers ever were,' said Quintus with a half-smile, remembering the courage of the Roman patricians in the face of the Gauls. 'Do not stroke their beards — instead send them on to Valhalla.'

Crassus reported from the other side. 'There are young men also. Some of the proud youths have stabbed each other, embracing in a mutual death pact.'

'Honour, or shame, or both?' Rufus asked.

'To prevent enslavement, I assume,' said Quintus. 'After all, we are just another tribe to them.'

'And to enter the halls of their heroes,' said Crassus. 'Valhalla holds a great attraction for these people. It is all the things that Elysium is to us, but with no ferryman to charge for passage, or Cerberus to bar the way. We should leave them where they fell. I think we have no more use for this place; it is full of evil spirits. We should let it burn.' The smoke was beginning to clear, blown away on the breeze.

The floating ash was rapidly being replaced by soft snow, huge flakes gently spiralling to the ground. Apart from the now subdued sounds of fire, reminiscent of a hearth at home, it was eerily quiet, the snow muffling all natural sounds. Quintus repeated his orders. 'Make your list, Jovan, then you and Maxim can help the capsarius.'

As the slaves left, Quintus' eyes were drawn to a quick movement. From the direction of the burnt palisade a lithe figure ran low and stealthily, holding a burning brand in each hand. He ran away from the gates, turning down what Quintus took to be the main street.

'Movement, there!' Quintus called, pointing, and an Anatolian arrow was immediately ready.

'Bring him down! He carries fire!' Quintus shouted to the nearest archer. The man did not hesitate but immediately shot the runner. The man fell, the two burning torches sputtering on the ground. Another Germani runner appeared from the shadows and bent to pick one of them up.

'Him, too.'

The Anatolian shot and the man fell.

'Come on. Let's see what they were doing.' Quintus beckoned the men to follow and ran to where the brands were now smoking, and the men who had been carrying them lay still.

XIX: PRAETORIANS

From where the bodies lay the Romans could see into the centre of the oppidum. There stood a longhouse, sturdily built under a thatched roof. The fire had not reached it. To their amazement and consternation, in front of its firmly closed door and around its perimeter, stood a group of fully armed Vindelici.

These were not youths or boys; these were men. Here were at least some of the missing warriors. They stood firmly shoulder to shoulder, round shields held in a line. Though they must have seen their foes, they made no attempt to engage them, no attempt to move. A glance told Quintus that this must be their version of the praetorians — their best men. They were big, muscular, well-armed and looked grim and determined. These were the men that they should have been facing at the gates. Clearly they were under some dreadful compulsion to stay where they were.

'What are they doing, Quintus?' Marcus stood with his sword unsheathed, breathing hard. He was clearly amazed.

'Defending the building, I think. Obviously refusing us entry to this place was more important to them than resisting us at the gates.'

'Is this where they were bringing the torches?' Felix looked at the two sprawled bodies.

'It looks like it. They seek to destroy whatever is inside the building.'

Scorch marks on the base of the building showed that they had tried to fire it but it had failed to ignite. It looked better made than the palisade, with no gaps where the fire could take hold. Its thatched roof was white now, topped with a thin covering of snow.

The men guarding the closed door shouted challenges and curses at this enemy that had come from nowhere. They waved both weapons and fists, but they did not advance. It seemed that they hoped to frighten the enemy away. The curses might have had an effect on a genuine Germani tribe. A brother tribe would no doubt have understood the warnings and the dire consequences threatened. This tribe of invaders seemed impervious to them.

'What are they guarding so ferociously?' Quintus asked as the men made no attempt to approach. His own men stood ready, swords drawn.

'It must be a temple or shrine of some sort,' said Felix. 'I hear the names of many of their gods.'

'We have seen the like before,' said Rufus, remembering a temple in a forest where severed human heads were left as offerings. 'Dedicated to Wotan or Týr, it is from one of these that we rescued the Eagle of the Fifth.'

'Then there will be wealth within,' Felix said. 'It seems we must cut them down.' He raised his gladius and settled his shield on his arm — a stance of challenge shadowed by the men. Still no enemy moved.

'Stand back, Felix,' said Quintus. 'No point taking the risk. Archers.'

The Anatolians nocked and shot arrows into the men directly in front of the doors. The men fell, their weapons rolling uselessly on the floor. The other guards still did not try to attack; instead they closed the gaps, stepping over their comrades, still calling curses down on the heads of these people. As yet more legionaries arrived, the Romans formed a horseshoe shape, encircling the front of the building, facing the enemy. Still the warriors made no move to fight, though they shouted more maledictions and insults.

'This is unheard-of discipline for barbarians,' Quintus said. 'They wait for our attack.'

'It looks like we could just let the auxiliaries shoot them,' Marcus said.

'Not with honour,' said Felix, stepping forward and making a sword thrust in an attempt to induce a response. The Germani chosen was not much smaller than the centurion, but he moved with speed and agility. He parried the blow with nonchalance, then instinctively lifted his own blade to respond. In lifting his arm, he exposed bare flesh, into which Felix thrust his gladius. He moved as if to resist, then stopped himself and stood back, stoic. He fell, blood bubbling from his punctured lung.

Still the others did not attack, but cursed and closed the gaps instead, a human shield before the door. 'At least he made to fight,' said Felix as he stood back.

Marcus also challenged an opponent. He drew his blade and approached the man nearest to him, goading him to fight. When the man moved, Marcus struck, a swift, straight thrust under the shield, drawing a bloom of bright red. The enemy took the blow, raised his shield and sword and took a half-step towards Marcus. His companion grabbed his arm, muttered something unintelligible, and pulled him back. Though the tribesman bled profusely, he remained standing.

'Felix, Marcus, we do not need to take the risk,' said Quintus. 'It seems they will not move to attack or even to defend themselves. Honour or not, the auxiliaries can take care of them.'

'Very well, commander. Auxiliaries and spears,' growled Felix, then raised his voice. 'Cut them down.'

A volley of javelins and arrows felled a number of the tribesmen, although deft use of shields saved some. They were caught in a second volley. Eerily, many did not even cry out. They held each other up where they could, pulled each other back into the line, making sure the doors were always guarded.

At last there was but one uninjured. His shield had stopped many arrows, but javelins had missed him and he remained standing directly in front of the opening. He was a giant — fair-headed and blond-bearded, his bare chest carrying many scars. His feet were planted wide apart. He grasped a short sword in one hand — something that looked like a gladius — and a round shield in the other, the broken shafts of arrows sticking out from it. He bellowed curses and shook his weapons, but remained firmly in front of the door, unwilling to take the fight to his enemy.

Finally he fell to two more arrows, shot into him from close range, and to legionary swords that stabbed into soft flesh at thigh and stomach and sent him to his knees. At the last, he leant on his shield as it bit into the ground and dropped his weapon. This seemed to give him new life, as he grabbed for it desperately. Finally, now on just one knee, he managed to seize the blade. He held it to himself as if cradling a child, the hilt grasped in two hands, the blade turned to the floor.

'It is his key to Valhalla,' said Sextus. 'Let him leave.'

Marcus pushed at the shield with the point of his sword and the man keeled over. The silence was eerie, made deeper by the increasing amounts of snow.

Felix was reluctant to sheathe his sword. There could be more men inside — but the door had to be opened. He looked at the fallen warriors with sadness. 'They are gone. Let's see what silver and gold they were protecting.'

He pushed the last of the warriors out of the way. Others pulled the dead from in front of the doors. Rufus stamped out the torches that still smouldered. Felix pushed the double doors open and men crowded to see inside.

'Stand back,' Quintus ordered. 'Step away, you are blocking the light.'

As the doorway was cleared, the red light of the dying day fell into the windowless interior. It barely lit the centre of the hut, leaving the sides and far end in dark shadow, but it was enough. Finally, as their eyes adjusted, Quintus and Felix could see the treasures within the hut. They were both amazed and disappointed.

'I expected a pile of silver cups and trinkets,' said Felix.

'Or a shrine with offerings,' said Quintus.

'I feared it would be another pile of heads,' Crassus said.

'Heads?' Felix was curious.

'That's what we found the last time we entered one of these temples. Severed heads. They offered the heads of their enemies to their god and displayed them in a cave.'

Felix shook his own head, baffled by such practices.

'Is she alive, do you think?' Quintus asked.

The object of the centurion's question was a woman, sitting stock-still in front of them. She was in a chair raised up on a dais, itself within a great pile of logs and branches. She was clad in layers of fur and leather, closely wrapped around her body. More furs were tightly cross-gartered with leather thongs on her legs. Her height could not be gauged and her face was devoid of any emotion. It was framed by a wealth of pale hair that hung long and unbound down her back. Her head bore a thin circlet of white metal, probably silver. Her eyes were closed and she was not breathing. Her brow was smooth; she was not old, but not young either.

She was surrounded by faggots and fuel, not exactly in the bonfire, but on it. She was clearly prepared to burn. By an irony that could only be by the design of the gods — hers or theirs — the fire had failed to flourish. It had scorched the edges of the pile, leaving brown and black marks, but it had not taken hold, though wisps of smoke rose still. Clearly it was to here that the runners had been delivering the burning torches.

Through the open doorway behind the men the sun dipped low. It painted the sky a deep, dull red, seen through the filter of the fast-falling snow. All other colour was bled from the land but for this eerie tone, as if Mars and Father Dis had agreed to banish all other shades from the world.

The woman held a great sword in her hand. It was almost a cavalry sword, except it had no curve. It was long, straight and double-edged, with a jewel set as a pommel into the top of the hilt. It glinted, reflecting the blood-red light. Her hands were placed on either side of the sword's hilt guard, its blade tip resting on the fuel meant to end her.

Felix made to approach the woman, but Quintus raised an arm. 'Wait,' he said. 'There is sorcery here. I have seen the powers of the druids of Britannia, my friend. She may yet be dangerous.'

'She may also be dead,' scoffed Felix, although he went no further. 'They may have killed her. Certainly she intended to burn, and they to burn her.'

'Disarm her!' Sextus shouted over Quintus' shoulder. He was a shadow in the doorway, barely able to see the woman, but unwilling to come closer. 'Do no harm to her. She may be just a sacrificial victim, but it looks like she was something more, something special. She could be a priestess or seer, or a witch perhaps, so be careful. Remember, without the sword she cannot enter Valhalla, so take it from her.'

'She may have already left,' said Quintus, attempting almost nonchalantly to bat the sword away with his own. The clang as the blades clashed was louder than anything they had expected, loud enough to make them alert and on guard. The great sword shuddered but otherwise did not move. Quintus had thought that the force of his stroke would make the woman drop the blade, but her grip was vice-like and the great sword remained, effortlessly blocking his blow. Her eyes opened.

'There is magic here,' said Sextus, stepping back. 'I sense it.'

XX: CORNUA

The woman lifted her head. She was alive. She blinked and her eyes focused. She looked at her assailants and immediately began a long and ululating wail, high enough that dogs pricked their ears and men covered theirs.

'What is it?' Crassus shouted.

'Nothing,' Quintus replied over the racket. 'She lives, that is all.' He stepped closer and with a struggle wrested the sword out of the woman's hands. She resisted but did not rise. He prised her fingers from the hilt as she spat and cursed and continued the piercing wail. The keening grew louder and began to contain words, including the names of gods he recognised.

'Search her for other weapons, Crassus. You and Sextus bind her. Marcus, get rid of this.'

Marcus took the sword gingerly, as if it might burn him, and left the building.

The men lifted her from the chair and a rough but thorough search ensued. 'Only this,' Crassus reported, holding up a long dagger that the woman had worn on her belt. She was now lying on her front on the ground, the wailing muffled. 'She is otherwise unarmed. The only metal on her is the circlet she wears on her head and the hammer that hangs at her neck.'

'The headband you can have. Leave the hammer,' insisted Sextus. He knew the significance of the symbol. 'It is a religious thing. It will not harm us, but she will believe it protects her. Superstition really.'

Sextus' hand went to the amulet he wore at his throat. His childhood bulla, which he still carried for good fortune. None had ever sponsored him for a manly gown so he kept it still, at least partly in the forlorn hope that it might one day lead him back to his real parents. 'If you take it, she will feel abandoned by her gods, and therefore be more likely to be violent and dangerous.'

The woman struggled as Crassus took the circlet and then bound her hands and feet tightly. He sat her up and the volume increased. 'Should I gag her?'

'I think she would bite a chunk from your neck before you could, Crassus. Let her wail. She seems to be coming out of some sort of trance. She was surprised by our presence; I think she was surprised not to be in Valhalla. Leave her where she is and shut the door on her. She is unarmed and going nowhere, and we need to dampen the noise.'

Felix and Crassus pulled the doors closed. The sound, though much reduced, was still audible; it still carried far enough down the hill to scare birds and beasts in the forest.

'We should silence her!' Sextus shouted over the din.

'We should understand her,' said Quintus. 'She may be the reason why we took this oppidum with such ease. The men protected her rather than the settlement, rather than their own families. I think there are still at least some men missing. She must be important. Find me Caius — we might at least find out what she is saying. Crassus, take the rest of the men and search this place.'

'This?' Crassus asked, the glint of silver in his hand.

'Keep it safe,' said Quintus. 'Although it is poor reward.' He swept his arm to encompass both sides of the burnt oppidum. 'Kill any that remain in hiding. You know that we can take no prisoners.' He beckoned his amicus to him and spoke quietly. 'If there are boys still, let them flee if you can. The tale of Germani tribe versus Germani tribe should be told. But there should not be too many — and no warriors, should you find any more.'

Crassus nodded. He understood that this was a mercy, that children were to be allowed to live providing they ran. Not all commanders would agree with him, Quintus knew that. His own mentor, Galba, would have killed everyone in the town, regardless of age or sex. He would have argued that unprotected children would die in the forests anyway. Quintus preferred to let the gods make those decisions. Crassus would help them.

'What you said, Quintus — Germani versus Germani,' said Felix. 'Witnesses must not be aware that we are not of the tribes. They must think us to be Germani. We must convince them of it.'

'I know,' Quintus said quietly. 'I know what you are saying. We must take heads. Both for the sake of any witnesses that flee, and for any others that come across this oppidum. There could be parties out hunting or making mischief. Tribesmen could return here. Somewhere there are more warriors.'

'The Cantabrians and Anatolians are ahead of you,' said Sextus, pointing down the slope to where shadows moved in the deep red gloom. 'The auxiliaries are already removing heads.'

'They do not ride with the trophies, do they?' Felix asked.

'The Germani tend to sling the heads over their horse's necks, or even place them as door guards,' said Sextus. 'No worse than Rome. Except we display them in the Forum.'

Quintus knew this to be the case. 'I saw the heads in various states of decomposition on the Rostra on my infrequent visits to Rome as a boy. I have never understood why they were always politicians and "state enemies", never criminals.' He pointed to the hillside. 'At least they don't ride with them.

Look, they fling them into the river. I am not sure what sort of rite it is they are conducting, but it has the same effect. The headless corpses we leave on the field. The heads can feed the fish.'

The keening sound continued to rise and fall behind them. It was enough to prevent the men from thinking clearly.

'Sextus, I have changed my mind,' Quintus said. 'Though she may bite and spit, gag her. Take men with you. Then bring her to the camp. Felix and I will be there to take reports and a tally of the dead and injured. Then we decide our next move. If we find out who she is, she may play a part in that decision.'

Mounts were brought by Vetruvius for the centurions and the captive. The woman they slung across the horse, her moans now muffled. They left the gates behind and set off down the hill, passing torches and moving from place to place as men checked on the bodies.

Some of the enemy bodies they passed were already without their heads. It did not bother them — this was how it must be. A sound alerted them to the capsarius, who was waving from the far side of the field as two men lifted a third — injured — onto a horse's back. Quintus acknowledged him.

'Is it bad, Alba?'

'Not bad, centurion. Some losses, some injuries. Some will die; some will mend. *Sic vita.*' He shrugged.

'That one?' Quintus nodded towards the man slumped across the horse.

The capsarius smiled. 'He will mend, but he will walk with a limp.'

Once the mountain tops lost their golden light, the darkness that night was absolute, the snow thick. The men had to move but a step or two away from the fires for the flames to appear as if they were in the distance, islands of light cloaked in a sea of black.

The men hastened to finish. None were keen to stay near the field of battle, even less to be within the confines of the settlement. It stood empty, as far as they could tell — apart from the shades of the dead.

'We cannot stay here,' Sextus said. 'The lemurés, the vengeful ghosts of the dead, will be roaming tonight. The men know this.'

From the camp in the woods they could see both the outline of the oppidum and the last light of the day still shining on the mountains. In this place dark came to the valleys long before the peaks, and the orange tint of the sun could still be seen highlighting the distant tops.

Jovan brought Quintus the tally. Three dead, three injured sufficiently that they were likely to die, the rest with cuts and bruises that would mend.

There was no official assembly, no cornicen to call it, but they all drifted together at the same time out of deeply ingrained habit. Sextus sacrificed in thanks for victory.

Quintus addressed them with words of congratulation and praise. He told them that they had taken a prisoner, a priestess of the Vindelici, and that she might be of use. He promised that the deaths would be properly noted by the state, that their comrades would share a funeral, if their contubernales agreed.

Quintus sighed as he said this. They could not afford to lose men — and he was quietly informed by the optiones that some of those hurt had been careless and had taken unnecessary risks. The men were losing their edge. He needed to speak to Marcus about extra drills. He was grateful for the auxiliaries, and even grateful that the slaves bore arms.

For their own dead, though they were few, the Romans built a pyre. The men said a prayer, lit the kindling, and watched it burn. They felt little. Sextus acted as *flamen*, and now had oil on his hands and ash in his hair. The ritual of death was carried out too often to have great significance for any but the dead's closest companions. It was a thing that had to be done if their comrades were to reach the Elysian Fields. Each of the dead carried an obol for Charon the ferryman beneath his tongue. Each had left a will of some sort with his amicus or commander.

It was a thing not done well, nor done badly. It was just done. Only one of the dead was recognised by Quintus: Cotta, lately of the Fifth Alaudae, bearer of the noble name of the Cornelii. Cotta's grandfather had been surnamed Cornelius by Sulla Felix when he brought ten thousand slaves and freedmen into his family. Quintus remembered the story. Perhaps the man had a son — that much he did not know. Perhaps his line was extinct. Unlike the great families, the lesser tended not to adopt the sons of other houses. As the flames curled and danced upwards, Quintus hoped that Cotta Cornelius had a son to carry on the name. After the funerals Quintus promised the men that in the morning they could return to the legions.

'It was too easy.' Later the centurion addressed the small group that sat with him. 'There were nowhere near enough people here to represent a tribe. It is not a tenth of what I would expect, even for an oppidum this size. There were barely enough to crew the ships we burned.'

'But we have punished those who dared defy Tiberius on the water,' said Felix. 'And that was our aim.'

'Those few, yes,' Quintus agreed. 'But they have friends and relatives, sons and uncles. There must be more. We are not safe here — there is the rest of this population to come home, and the rest of the Vindelici to follow and avenge them.'

'Surely they will avenge their compatriots on other Germani,' Marcus said, the sweep of his arm encompassing them all. 'Look at us. We are a tribe of their cousins attacking a poorly defended outpost. The young ones you let go will carry the message. Their attackers were not Roman, as far as they know. For that reason alone, we are safe.'

'Except we still look like their enemy,' said Vetruvius, patting his furs and trews.

'And we have their princess, or priestess, or sorceress captive,' said Sextus. 'She must be a powerful figure for them to guard her so fiercely. She is a queen or chieftain of some sort — I am sure of it.'

'She could just be an offering,' said Marcus. 'Trussed up like any other sacrificial victim.'

'I don't think so. She has an arrogance, a haughtiness — at least she does when she is not keening and railing against her captivity,' Caius added. 'Yet they would have burned her without our intervention.'

'She could still be a sacrifice,' Marcus countered.

'Her people sacrificed themselves for her — the warriors guarding her pyre, the old people in the doorways, the young killing each other,' Caius said. 'Their deaths were dedicated to her. Perhaps she is no sacrifice, but to them a goddess. We should be careful.'

Under the trees the men huddled close to the flames. Though they banked them up, the fires seemed reluctant to part with their heat. Many made the warding sign against bad luck, the *cornua*. They would be glad to leave this place.

XXI: EFWICH

The captive, still struggling, was brought to the camp and left trussed and gagged on the ground, there being nowhere to confine her. Even through the gag, she tried to wail.

Quintus needed to find out who she was and why they were so keen to burn her — and she so eager to burn. He walked across, telling Caius to give her water. Caius removed the gag in order to make her drink, but she began the cry again. Men looked at him with disapproval and, with a sigh of resignation, he replaced the gag.

'Who is she? What is she? And why is she so special that they would defend her so?' Quintus demanded. 'Do we kill her or keep her?'

'I think I know her name,' said Caius. 'There is a noise which when howled we take to be her name or station. She repeats it often and says *I am* before it, as if we should know who she is and respect her for it. The Germani are named as daughter- or son-of-their-father. She is, we think, Efwich Sigurdsdottir — Efwich, daughter of Sigurd.' He shrugged. 'Sadly, knowing her father's name does not help us to know her.'

'Is she not a sorceress or witch?' Sextus asked. 'That sword, and those noises — is it not magic?'

Quintus was not uneducated. He had been taught his letters by his father at the same time as he had learned his numbers, the latter essential for trading on market days. He knew of the stories of Circe and her powers, of Erichtho, who had brought doom to a son of Pompeius Magnus. He shivered involuntarily. He had no counter to witchcraft.

'She makes no such claim,' said Caius. 'Apart from her name, she has told us little. Hardly anything she says is understandable. She spits and curses, bites and struggles with her bonds. She tries desperately to reach a blade, any blade. She will end her own life with an eating knife if she has half a chance. We can make out the names of the gods of Germania that we know, Wotan and Týr, Heimdall and Thor and Freya. Other sounds might be other gods she entreats. But she is no witch. She threatens us with her menfolk, not magic. She says her husband and sons will avenge her. But she does not name them. Of course, if she is a chieftain of sorts, they may also be chiefs and warriors.'

'We will find out tomorrow,' said Quintus. 'We leave early and she comes with us. Our mission is fulfilled. We will go and find General Tiberius and the legions. For now, Caius, see if we can at least stop her from ending her own life.'

Quintus remained on edge, aware of the restless spirits that roamed not far away, aware that the men shared his misgivings. As all tried to sleep, they could not avoid the work of the day. The wind blew from the north, not strong but cold and laden with snow. It brought with it not just the raw edge of the high mountains but the smell of the burnt oppidum. The sounds of crows and magpies fighting over morsels filled his ears.

By morning the snow had ceased. The odd blade of grass poked through the trampled path from grove to gate. The wind dropped and the sky turned a sickly dull yellow colour. Felix stayed to oversee the striking of the camp. Quintus took Crassus and a group of legionaries for a final check of the oppidum. There could be food still, and there were definitely horses. Crassus would be able to advise whether or not the rest would burn.

They found no silver and it appeared that the flaming arrows had set fire to the winter store of grain by the palisade. There were several barrels of a bitter drink that made the Romans grimace when they tried it. There was also a small amount of food for both the men and the horses. They gained a few ponies, small beasts but tough.

Some of the livestock released was also rounded up. The men would eat well for a good while. That night they would be feasting on pork and lamb, much of it prepared by a disappointed Maxim and Jovan. The Macedonians were back cooking and cleaning, with sad looks on their faces, but with swords at their sides. At least Quintus had given the word. They were permitted.

Quintus and the troop investigated the longhouse but found nothing of interest. Outside he felt a fresh snowfall, cold and wet against his skin. At first, there were just a few — one or two — seemingly stray flakes that brushed his cheek but when he turned towards the gate he was taken aback by its appearance. The yellow sky had turned grey, draining colour from everything. The atmosphere around him was a kind of liquid fog, dense and impenetrable. Quintus would have recognised it as a blizzard had there been a gale to drive it. As it was, no wind blew, and it was as if a heavy blanket had been thrown over, blotting out all sight and sound.

Though Quintus and Crassus stood shoulder to shoulder, they could only vaguely see and hear each other through the murk. The snowfall muffled everything under its thickening shroud of white.

They rushed towards the gates. The horses and the men appeared as spectres, their outlines blurred. At the gateway they could barely see beyond the oppidum. There was no sign of the forest or stream. No hillside, no enemy dead. It was not even possible to make out the ditch.

'We must take cover.' Quintus' voice was muffled by the snow, but the men saw his frantic gestures through the haze and pulled the beasts to follow. They made it to the door of the longhouse, which stood open, already half blocked by snow. They tumbled over the threshold, the ponies slipping and sliding but finally inside. There was no way that they would ever be able to close the door.

'We wait it out,' said Quintus. 'There is nothing else we can do.'

They watched as the blizzard filled the doorway. Although they knew it to be before noon, it was dark. Some of the men used the fuel of the pyre to make a fire, one of them carrying flint and tinder, but the smoke from it at once became a nuisance, making them cough and choke. Quintus ordered it extinguished. Anyway, it was not particularly cold. The snow seemed to insulate the building.

The legionaries talked quietly amongst themselves. Vetruvius found something that could be used as knucklebones and began a game of chance. Quintus and Crassus held a stilted conversation — there was nothing to talk about — before Crassus moved away to gentle the horses. Gradually the darkness of the snow gave way to the true dark of the coming night.

'We may have to spend the night here,' said Quintus. 'So we may yet need the fire, for light if nothing else.'

Vetruvius, having fleeced the men of many hours of duty — there being nothing else to wager — looked out of the gap. 'There are lights, sir. There are lights moving outside.' He began to clear away some of the snow piled up in the doorway.

'It could be the Germani come back for us.' One of the men tugged at his arm to stop him.

'It could be the lemurés of the defeated,' said another.

'You think that spectres would come bearing flaming torches?' Crassus said sharply. 'The Germani, maybe. Vetruvius, take care.'

Vetruvius went back to removing snow. 'They are calling. Sir, it is in Latin. They are not Germani. They are our comrades.'

'Quintus!' Crassus called his amicus across. 'What do you think?'

The lights bobbed in the yard outside, even through the still falling snow.

'It is our comrades. Vetruvius, shout to them. Come on, men. Dig. Dig your way through this doorway.'

Their calls were heard by the men in the yard, Felix and Marcus at their head. At once the men seized their trenching tools, digging a way through the drifts.

'Quintus?' Felix's face appeared in the gap above the snow.

'Felix, it is good to see you.'

'We thought the blizzard might have taken you. Come quickly — we have made a path, but it will not last long.'

'The camp?'

'Still stands. The snow came before we had struck the tents. The fires are lit, Quintus.'

As soon as the entrance was cleared Quintus and his companions came out. The horses were reluctant, but Crassus found cloth to bind their eyes and persuaded them on. Felix was right; the way that they had made was rapidly vanishing.

The troop struggled down the hill. Back in the camp the Macedonians were keeping one large blaze tended, but elsewhere the snow continued to accumulate, blurring all edges.

'As soon as it started, I realised we would not move tonight,' said Felix as the two centurions thawed out by the fire. 'Nor tomorrow, I think.'

'It will be better further down in the valleys,' said Quintus hopefully. 'We move at first light — or as soon as this blizzard ceases.' He looked around. 'I hope we have pickets posted.'

'We have,' Felix confirmed.

Quintus patted Felix's shoulder. 'I knew the camp would be in good hands. I am going to eat, then sleep.'

But Quintus could not sleep. He tossed restlessly in the tent before, with a groan of frustration, he rose and went outside. His thoughts were murky and his head hurt. He felt like he carried a great weight on his head, like Atlas with the world on his shoulders. The air was thick, oppressive, hard to breathe yet bitterly cold.

Snow fell on snow on snow. Quintus held his hands out in front of him, letting the great flakes gently land on his fingers. They were big enough not to melt at once. He was convinced that if he held his palms out long enough, the snow would defeat his body heat and settle.

He looked around for a place where he might sit, but all he could see was unrelenting whites and greys. The fire no longer burned bright, but glowed and hissed gently.

Crassus had seen Quintus leave the tent, thinking he was off to relieve himself. When he did not return, he rose and joined the centurion outside, though he had to feel his way through the darkness. He touched his friend firmly on the arm to announce his presence.

'Come,' said Crassus, and held open the flap of the tent. 'There is room in the doorway.'

Quintus was annoyed. 'Someone should be tending that,' he said.

'I will find someone,' said Crassus.

When he returned, Quintus looked at him quizzically. 'There was someone, Quintus. He had gone to relieve himself. He was away for hardly any time at all. He is there now.'

Quintus harrumphed.

They squatted together. Behind them was the noise and heat of the sleeping men; before them was the silence and cold of the snow. Theirs was one of two tents now over-occupied thanks to the injured, who shared the third canvas with Alba and Rufus as his assistant. Should they need ministering to in the night, the capsarius could do so without disturbing the others.

Somewhere close by the woman moaned. She was not welcome in any of the tents, so the slaves had rigged up a temporary shelter for her, and her alone. It kept the snow off her; she was still tied and might be cold, but she would not die of it. Crassus was more concerned for the horses. They should each have a blanket, the shelter of trees, a nosebag of hay.

Quintus heard her moan. 'I need to know her part in this,' he said suddenly.

'She did not cause the snowfall,' said Crassus, in amazement. 'You cannot believe that.'

'I do not know what I believe, but I need to know who she is.' He was terse. 'I have a feeling that she brings ill fortune.' He was restless still, and once more rose to his feet. 'Come, Crassus, old friend, find me Caius. Wake him — and her. It must be morning.'

XXII: ERSTER SCHNEE

Crassus sighed. He did not believe that it was anywhere near morning. The heavily falling snow made the veil between day and night uncertain. Nevertheless, he reluctantly complied, fetching Caius first from one of the other tents, then making him help drag the woman to the fireside. She opened her mouth, seemingly about to resume her wailing, but Caius made a quick chopping motion with his hand and spoke swiftly and sharply to her. She seemed to hesitate, then desisted.

Crassus sent the man tending the fire away and used his blacksmith's skills to bring it to life. Before long it was blazing, an oasis of light and heat as the snow continued to tumble down. The three Romans pulled their furs over their heads, and Crassus found a spare blanket for the woman. She looked at him with disdain.

'Find out who she is,' ordered Quintus.

'I am Efwich Sigurdsdottir,' she said clearly. 'I understand some of your tongue. Your man understands some of mine.' Through Caius she asked her own question. 'Who are you?'

'Tell her she does not need to know,' said Quintus firmly.

She ignored him and spoke in a mixture of poor Latin and her own language.

'She says that we speak Latin and wear the boots of the legionaries,' Caius translated. 'It is always the boots that give the Romans away. She says we are not of the Germani. She thought us perhaps to be Raeti or Helvetii come down from the high mountains to raid. Then she knew we could be neither.'

'How?' Crassus asked.

'Because we allowed some of the boys to live, even to escape. She says the Raeti kill all the males in the tribes they raid. I am not sure I have this right, sir, but it seems to me that she says they use magic, some form of divination, to determine whether pregnant women are carrying males, and kill these in the womb.'

'The Helvetii the same?'

The woman grinned through even white teeth. 'She says you have too little mountain craft to be from the Alpen lands. She says you have been caught by first snow, and have burnt the only shelter available to you.' He paused and checked again what she had said. 'She says you will surely die.'

'We will all surely die one day,' said Quintus, in exasperation. 'But I do not intend to do it here. What does she mean by "first snow"?'

Caius and the woman exchanged words and phrases. Frustrated, she burst out to Quintus, 'Erster Schnee — how can you not know what it means? The gods send it to cleanse the land. All war stops. All trade. All marriages. Everything. Until the green comes again. It is the harbinger of winter. And it can be measured in feet rather than thumbs.'

Caius continued with growing confidence. 'I have it, sir. The festival of fire they celebrated on the road. This is the last rite before First Snow. Then they batten down for winter.' He gestured upward. 'This is First Snow. This is the time to bring in the animals, pile up the fodder, close the gates.' He paused, not wanting to pass on what else he had learned. Quintus waved him to go on. 'She says had we been truly of the Germanic race, we would know. First Snow blocks the passes and prevents all travel. Now we are trapped here until the spring melt.'

The woman watched the exchange between the two Romans and chuckled, gurgling something guttural amid the laughter.

'Well?' Quintus demanded.

'She says only a fool would be caught by it,' said Caius quietly.

This just made Quintus angry. 'Only a fool would die by their own hand,' he spat at her. 'Only a fool would let their warriors die for them.' He turned to Caius. 'What was she doing? Why was she set to burn?'

She smiled again. With the efforts of Caius and her ragged Latin, what she said was unwoven. 'My death would save my people. Save the Vindelici. My sacrifice would bring the gods to our aid. Better, it would ignite a blood feud. When our warriors returned, they would be honour-bound to destroy the invader utterly. Whatever tribe was attacking us, they would be blood enemies for three generations, even to the son of my son's son. There would be vengeance.'

'Then without your sacrifice, there is no revenge. There is peace.'

'Not with honour there is not. My son will avenge me. My son is a famous warrior. He is away fighting, but he will be back.' She looked into the flames with longing. 'It is a pity the fire was not set.' She leant dangerously close to it.

'But you have recognised us as Roman,' said Quintus. 'You could not hope to take vengeance on Rome.'

She laughed. 'You Romans are so arrogant. Of course we could avenge ourselves. We are no tiny tribe, but a great nation. We have taken your eagles before.'

This stung because it was true. Quintus knew it to be true.

'She wants to know if we are deserters,' Caius said. 'We march with no eagles and no uniforms. Apparently her husband is a great leader who has taken deserters into his ranks before. She says he could do so again.'

'Who is her husband?' Quintus demanded.

A long exchange took place between Caius and Efwich. Seemingly Caius doubted what she said and demanded she explain it in a different way. Eventually, though he shook his head in disbelief, he turned to Quintus.

'I think her husband is Maelo, and her son is Dagaz,' he said quietly. 'I have checked and she insists. If we are deserters, she offers to recommend us to Maelo's forces.'

'Maelo,' said Quintus quietly. 'The chieftain of all tribes and none, who demanded the loyalty of many renegade Germani. Maelo, who crossed the Rhenus and caused havoc. Maelo, who destroyed the centurions and officers of the Fifth, crucified them, took their heads and sent their commander fleeing. Maelo, who destroyed a legion and captured the Eagle of the Fifth.' He shook his head. 'It is a name I thought I would never hear again, the name of a dead man. Clearly, he is not.'

He paused. 'Dagaz, her so-called son, is another matter. I saw his body. Stupidly, I did not take the head to display on a spear or pole, to prove the man's death. Thus a legend has grown that he still lives, and many claiming to be Dagaz prowl the right bank of the great river. He is a legend. It is difficult to destroy a legend. So you are wife to a traitor and mother to a dead man?' Quintus asked the woman.

She whispered something to Caius, punctuated with a little laugh and a gesture in the direction of the heavens.

'What does she want?' Quintus snapped.

'She asks that we release her hands so that she can warm them at the fire. She says there is nowhere for her to go, nowhere for any of us to go. Not after the first snow. She says we should have known, should have fled the valley when we could. She also says her husband will be back as soon as it thaws.'

'Keep her bound. Keep her from the fire. She is likely to throw herself in it.'

There was a long pause, a deep silence, broken at last by Crassus. 'So perhaps we must winter here. Perhaps it is the will of the gods that we did not complete the burning of the oppidum.'

'Was it also their will that we should let the stock animals free, destroy the winter grain store and burn down the very walls that we might seek to use for protection?' Quintus was not bitter but spoke honestly.

'Then there is a challenge,' Crassus countered. 'We have overcome challenges before. We will see our path more clearly in the morning light.'

The woman spoke with Caius again, this time with more urgency. 'She says to kill her, that she does not wish to suffer another winter. Especially not with her home burned. She was prepared to go to Valhalla before the snowfall; she is even more ready now. She just wishes to be gone from this life.'

'And with her death to cause a never-ending war of vengeance between her people and Rome. I think not. Anyway, it is not her choice,' said Quintus flatly. 'I have a better use for her. If it turns out that she is Maelo's woman and Dagaz's mother, she will make a great prize for a Triumph. Maybe prize enough for General Tiberius to give us our uniforms back, to put us under the colours once more. She is worth more to us alive than dead.' He looked sideways at her. Her wrists were still bound, but her hands stretched out towards the fire.

'She is worth more to Tiberius than her weight in gold,' Quintus went on. 'There has been no such hostage since Divus

Julius had Vercingetorix in chains and strangled before the Curia. She will buy our return.'

'Women and Triumphs have not fared well,' said Crassus, half to himself. 'The sister of the Egyptian queen was applauded by the crowd when she marched before General Caesar.'

'This is not Arsinoë,' said Quintus abruptly. 'This is the mother and husband of rebels, no queen of the Ptolemies.' He turned to Caius. 'Tell her that she will not die, not yet anyway. But that when she does, it will be a great and honourable death.'

She muttered something urgent-sounding and Caius repeated the question.

'Yes, I will make certain that she has a blade in her hand. She can join her ancestors — and her son — in Valhalla.'

The silence between them was only punctuated by the hissing of the fire. Quintus looked at the sky hopefully, but there was no sign of light. 'It is early still. We have what we needed; we know she is valuable, Caius. Lodge her in one of the tents until morning finally comes. We will see to her accommodations in daylight. There will be room with the capsarius and the injured.' Though the makeshift shelter kept out the worst of the weather and she was wrapped in leather and furs, she would be safer in a tent.

'I will stay close to her,' said Caius. He half pushed, half walked the woman into the tent and made her lie down inside it. There was plenty of space between her and the men. Alba was awake and about to question the intrusion when Caius put a finger to his lips and whispered, 'By the commander's order.'

Rufus, there as assistant to Alba, spoke anyway — quietly and forcefully. 'If she starts that wailing amongst injured men, I will personally throttle her.'

Caius made a salute and bowed his head. 'Tiberius Junii of the tribe of Collina, I hear and obey. I will tell her.' Rufus was not used to being addressed by his proper name, and it surprised him into silence. He turned his back on Caius and the prisoner.

Crassus went in search of more firewood. Quintus stared into the flames, praying for the real end of the interminable night.

XXIII: DIES FEBRUATUS

Quintus could not rest. He was too awake, too alert to go back to sleep.

Instead he sat close to the revived fire and covered his head against the continuing snowfall. Remarkably, it was no longer cold, the snow seeming to act as a blanket and the wind being non-existent. He felt sleepy. He let his eyes close and dreamed of his future. He knew now who the woman was, and her worth to him. He must keep her safe. He imagined himself if not in the Triumph, then at least in an honoured place amongst the crowds watching as Tiberius rode along the Via Sacra, dressed as Jupiter Optimus Maximus, face reddened to more closely resemble the god. And in his train, amongst gold, silver, slaves, exotic animals and representations of victory, there rode a captive woman, chained. He imagined himself proudly holding the chain.

At the climax of the Triumph, as the crowd cheered Tiberius and his men again acclaimed him imperator, her chariot drew to a halt next to the Carcer. Here the triumphator ordered her strangled — the only stipulation that she be allowed to hold a blade of some sort as she died, a promise made on a legionary's honour, so sacred.

Quintus would receive a great reward, gold or silver, perhaps the very sword she held as she died, and maybe even a tribunate, a proper command. He would go on to become a great hero, a leader of men. His conscience, however, was insistent, whispering, *What about Ursus? What about his son? What about your vow?*

Ursus will be remembered and honoured, his will taken to his wife and child, their ownership of his farm confirmed, he told himself. *The rest of the men I will safely lead back to barracks in Rome. They will be in the Triumph also. Even the dead will be remembered, Nox and Lux and Tullius.* He felt for the hard metal of the armlet, the award that carried his vow.

'Quintus,' Crassus said, a little too loudly. He was piling more fuel onto the fire. 'Are you awake? Why do you speak of Nox and Lux? Sleep in this cold and you could die.'

Quintus opened his eyes to the spectral scene before him. The fire, which he had thought aflame with welcome warmth, was little more than a fading glow, holding no heat.

'A dream, Crassus. A vision, perhaps. I suddenly felt warm and weary.'

'That is how you die in the cold,' said Crassus tersely. 'Even I am struggling to keep this fire alive.'

Quintus made a sound of agreement, near enough to apology to mollify his friend. Allowing himself to fall into reverie, he had almost fallen asleep. He realised that this would be a painless but certain death in this weather. A stupid, careless death.

He shook his head to clear it and opened his eyes wide. The sky was still dark. A ghostly white shroud lay across all, a mantle that continued to grow thicker. He stood up and brushed snow from his furs. 'Is it morning, Crassus? I cannot tell.'

'Nor I,' Crassus admitted. He stood up and pointed eastward. 'The sky seems a little lighter over there.'

One by one the other men rose out of habit, first amongst them Felix and Marcus. Caius had failed to find sleep, instead watching over the prisoner, who seemed determined to stay awake.

The men emerged from the tents, made darker within by the thick snow that had to be shaken from them.

Quintus spoke loudly enough for all to hear. 'We have established that the prisoner is a chieftain of some sort, which makes her valuable to General Tiberius. She is to be kept alive and guarded.' He turned to Caius, who sat in the entrance to Alba's tent. 'You and another must watch her every hour of the day and night. Take it in turns to sleep. If we can take her down the mountain, back to the legions, she could adorn Tiberius' Triumph when he returns to Rome.'

He shared the rest of the information with the other centurion. 'Felix, she is mother to Dagaz and wife to Maelo. She could be our ticket to redemption and restoration.'

'You are right,' said Felix. 'If we can keep her alive and caged.'

Caius nodded. 'I understand what she is worth, sir. Vetruvius will help me.'

Sextus was another who had risen. He overheard part of the conversation and marvelled at the woman's worth.

Quintus did not rely on Sextus' abilities, but he did make use of them sometimes. 'How did you not see how important she is?' he demanded, lifting his eyes to the sky. 'How did you not see this coming?'

Sextus smiled from deep within his furs. 'I do not forecast the weather, Quintus.'

'But the fire festival? The coming of winter? Did you not see its significance?'

'None of us did.' Sextus shook his head and trudged away along the path trodden flat by others.

The camp itself was busy. Men encouraged the fires back to life and built them high. They provided oases of heat and light, spitting and hissing gently as they defeated the snow. Meat was cooking on them and the Macedonians had a pot of grain porridge brewing. Alba emerged with the good news that none of the injured were worse, and at least one was much improved. Rufus reported that the woman seemed to have finally fallen asleep.

'We will have to winter here,' Quintus said with despondency. 'Not here, but in the oppidum. There is shelter there still. We did not burn the longhouse.'

'And we do not need the palisade — except perhaps for wild animals,' Crassus said. 'No enemy will come at us whilst this snow lies.'

'And as soon as it is gone, so are we.'

Sextus, on his return, was horrified. 'We cannot stay there. It is haunted — worse than that, cursed. The shades of the dead walk there. It is a place of nightmares.'

Quintus drew him to one side and spoke quietly. 'You will have to purify it, my friend. You know the rites of Lupercalia; you must banish all evil spirits, all malignancy. Can you do it?'

Sextus was indignant. '*Dies Februatus* is for purifying the City of Rome, not some barbarian village.'

'If we are to survive this winter, it is our only shelter,' Quintus snapped. 'The woman says this is just "first snow"; there will be more to come. Can you do it?'

Sextus took the centurion by the shoulders and put his face close. Quintus could feel the warmth of his breath, the wet of his spittle. 'With a priesthood and a he-goat and a couple of Vestal Virgins, of course I can,' he hissed. 'Do we have such things?' He would have stomped off in a sulk, but there was nowhere for him to go.

Quintus bit back his anger. He spoke slowly, deliberately. 'You know we don't, Sextus. You will just have to make do. It must be done, or we will all die here.'

'Die where?' Marcus had been almost within earshot and had heard a part of the altercation.

'We die here, of cold, if Sextus cannot purify the oppidum.'

'We need no Germani building, Quintus. There is nothing wrong with a good, sturdy army tent. We have survived winters before.'

'I can do it,' Sextus said. 'I will do it as soon as this snow stops.' He smiled at Marcus. 'You can pitch your tent outside the walls if you wish.'

Marcus made a grumpy noise and moved away. 'Nothing wrong with canvas,' he muttered.

'What do you need?' Quintus asked.

'Water and fire and blood — all possible. Myrtle, unlikely. And for this snow to cease.'

They both looked upwards. The sky was still grey with the huge flakes. For now, their world was bounded by the edges of the campsite. There was a rough track leading to a pit dug for bodily wastes, and the bright oases that were the fires. All the rest was white.

They needed to fetch timber to feed the fires and meat and grain to feed themselves. They needed to ensure the horses were safe and well. Otherwise, their only other concern was to try and remain warm and dry. They would not be entering the oppidum on this day.

The little light that marked the day soon faded. Men were set to watch the fires, to keep feeding them. They slept in shifts and waited.

It was three days before the stars finally shone. The sky, black as obsidian, was smooth and cloudless. Quintus gazed in wonder at the white pinpoints above reflected in the landscape below. The world was grown tranquil and muted. There was no noise of wind or weather, nor of brook or beck. There was no song of bird or cry of animal. Distant whumps punctuated the silence as branches dropped their load of snow or broke under its weight.

The campsite was tamped down by many feet, with the busiest routes wider and flatter than others. All around its edges was a wall of snow, banked up high.

'It has stopped,' Quintus said with relief.

Agnus, standing close by, agreed. 'I think you are right. We can finally move.'

'We cannot,' Quintus said. 'But in the morning, if it is still clear, Sextus can.'

The morning broke with a clear sky and achingly bright sun. Quintus and Sextus climbed to the top of the wall of snow and looked out. To the west, a thin grey line of mist separated the softened contours of the land from the empty expanse of the sky. To the north, the outline of the oppidum could be seen stark against the pale blue of the heavens.

Once more Quintus asked, 'What do you need?'

'A way up there; a he-goat — failing that, a ram; two men, preferably a Fabian and a Julian or a Quinctilian.'

'You know there are none such here.'

'Rufus is of the Junii — that is close enough. Vetruvius is of the Cornelii. Both noble houses. You and I are not noble enough, Quintus.' Sextus smiled. 'But as commander, you should be there.' He paused. 'What about the sacrifice? Do you think any of the animals survived?'

'Some were still inside the walls. They could have huddled together; there was some fodder, and they will have licked the snow for water. Maybe. Had we known how the snow would fall, we could have brought them down here.'

'Except here we have no food for them,' said Sextus flatly. 'Without a live animal, all our efforts are pointless. The men will be Luperci; they will need to be bloodied.'

'There were geese,' Quintus said desperately. 'And if all else fails, there are ponies.'

'The gods will provide,' said Sextus. Quintus could not tell whether he was being serious.

He called Rufus and Vetruvius to him and told them that they had a role to play in the purification. To them he added four of the brawniest men and told them to bring trenching tools.

Their job was to carve a way through the snow to the oppidum. They worked up a great sweat, digging out a trench whose walls came up to their shoulders. The snow they dug needed to be disposed of, and the only place for it was to either side of the trench, making the walls even taller.

As they made headway up the hill, now and again they came across humps in the ground. These were not tree trunks but bodies, frozen in place. Where they could, they went around them.

'They can stay where they are,' said Quintus. 'They will not trouble us, and animals will not trouble them until the thaw.' Others, which could not be avoided, needed to be dug out and moved, flung out of the trench that they blocked.

The trench wound its way uphill until it reached the still open entrance of the oppidum. The mound that marked the horse and rider was still blocking one of the gates.

'That will have to be moved,' said Sextus. 'It is too close.'

The corpses of both man and animal had been attacked by beasts before the snow had covered them. Moving them was a messy and time-consuming business. In the meantime, Sextus set up his altar and lit a fire beneath it, taking dry kindling from within one of the huts.

Rufus had found some of the animals inside — in a sorry state, but alive, huddled out of habit where they would have been penned. He brought Sextus a bedraggled sheep.

'Neither goat nor ram, Sextus. There are none such. Surely Juno will understand?'

'We shall see,' said Sextus, taking the animal from him.

XXIV: CASTRA INIMICA

The ceremony — days long and full of joy on the Palatine — was over swiftly. The animal was despatched, its blood smeared on the foreheads of the two men. The exta were burned and the gateway of the oppidum sprinkled with blood and water.

'You should run round the walls beating yourselves with the flayed skin,' Sextus informed them. 'Just run inside, shout and flap your arms.'

The men looked at him as if he had lost his wits, but he insisted. 'Watch,' he told Quintus as Rufus and Vetruvius each set off in a different direction, waving their arms and shouting as they stumbled through the snow.

The effect was what Sextus had hoped for. The noise and movement was enough to disturb a great host of crows and magpies that had taken to the oppidum to scavenge and roost. Their flight, noisily vacating the buildings, was enough to convince the men that here were the spirits of the dead, leaving the oppidum, that here was the proof that the purification had succeeded. Sextus smiled to himself. He was confident that they would carry the word back to the others.

Rufus and Vetruvius returned to the gate laughing and giddy. They had fallen over in the snow several times, but they had seen the great flock of birds lift, had seen the lemurés fly away. Quintus sent them to fetch the others, reminding Vetruvius of his responsibilities in guarding the woman.

Led by Felix, the remainder of the men arrived to take stock of their winter home. Within there were animals to rescue and feed, and more bodies. Those found within the oppidum needed to be removed. Some of these were stiff, lying where they had fallen in buildings. Some lay in the open, blanketed in white. Some had been attacked by birds or beasts before the snow shrouded them. A few of the dead tribesmen before the gates were headless, a precaution now no longer necessary to maintain the subterfuge that these Romans were Germani. No-one was likely to come across them until the spring thaw. Still, they needed to be cleared from in front of the oppidum and from within the walls.

'Carve a way to the river,' Felix ordered. 'We may need it for freshwater, so dump them downstream. Let the current take them.'

The river, though sluggish and narrowed by the banks of snow to either side, flowed still. It received the bodies with hardly a splash. They cleared a space in front of the longhouse then managed to pull open its doors. Inside was the great pile of wood that had been used to make the woman's erstwhile pyre. Felix carried out further investigations around the oppidum then sent Agnus to report back to Quintus.

'The longhouse is habitable, sir,' said the scout. 'The roof and walls have stayed intact. There is timber for fires; there are also sacks of grain untouched by the fire. Centurion Felix thinks some of the stock animals may recover, those that found shelter. He thinks we should bring them inside. There is fresh water in the river, and also an unlimited supply of melted snow.'

'Alba, Rufus,' Quintus called. 'Use whatever men you need and take the injured up to the longhouse in the oppidum. Crassus, Sextus, see to the horses. Take the auxiliaries with you. Maxim, Jovan, take the cooking gear and any food, and go with Crassus. See what you can do with the animals that have survived. You may cook those that will not.'

The oppidum was far too big for the meagre numbers that had trudged up the hill, even with horses and auxiliaries. Quintus decided they would all sleep in the longhouse; its roof had held and its walls were sturdy. It was also big enough to bring in the animals and the horses. They could pen and stable them at the back.

'They will have to be managed and exercised,' Quintus warned the Cantabrians, making sure that Crassus also heard. 'And mucked out,' he added for the benefit of the Macedonians. They nodded acknowledgement.

He posted guards at the gates and towers of what was left of the palisade and also at the doors of the longhouse — but he did not expect any enemy action. The only tribesmen anywhere near were the few boys who had run away throwing stones and insults. If they had been caught in the snow, they would surely have died. Otherwise they would be far away.

Finally, the only people left to move were the woman and her guards. 'Caius, Vetruvius, take her. Make certain that she is securely tied. I want to make sure that there is somewhere to put her where she will not be tempted to escape.'

The two men complied. The woman's hands were tightly bound, but her feet they left untied, so that she might walk. They noted that she was better protected than most of them, with her thick woollen trews and a tunic that seemed to be made of a single hide, all cross-gartered, belted and fur-trimmed.

Quintus called an assembly of all the men and addressed them from a raised area created with a mound of packed snow. They stood inside the longhouse whilst he stood just outside the doorway.

'Discipline is necessary for us to endure,' he said. 'Your tents have come up the hill with you. Pitch them if you wish.' He gestured at the buildings. 'This will be our home for the winter. We have a place to sleep, here, in this longhouse. We do not yet have a place to exercise or to sacrifice. We do not even have a place for a latrine. All these things are necessary. It was also necessary that the place was purified, cleared of any malignant spirits and bearers of ill luck. Legionary Pupillus Sextilius of the Esquilina has carried out the necessary sacrifices and lustrations.'

He was going to point out that the lemurés had been seen leaving in the form of the crows, but decided to let the men make that connection for themselves. That way, it was more powerful. 'I have chosen Sextus as your augur and interpreter of signs. He is not of the college of augurs, nor a *flamen*, but he was raised by the Vestals and knows the formulae for many rituals, great and small. Before we even begin our tasks today, he will lead a sacrifice to Janus. After all, this is a new beginning.'

He turned to Sextus. 'We have no dates, figs or honey to offer. Can you once more find something appropriate?'

Sextus saluted. He would have to be inventive.

Quintus indicated the two men standing to either side of the woman, who still managed to look proud. 'This woman, this one captive is precious to us. She is of great value to General Tiberius. We need to guard her and keep her safe.' He laughed. 'If nothing else, she is the only way in which you and your pay will be united.'

The men laughed with him, then looked at the woman and shrugged. It should not be too difficult to keep her from harm, providing she did not try to harm herself.

'There is one rule with her that must not be broken. She must never be allowed a blade of any sort. She will not try to take her own life unless it is with a blade. So be wary anywhere near her, keep close watch on gladius and pugio. She will eat with her fingers or a spoon, and all sharp objects are to be moved far from her reach.' He smiled patronisingly at the prisoner. 'I will keep you safe from yourself, Efwich Sigurdsdottir.'

She reacted to her name with a raised eyebrow and a lift of her chin.

Quintus put a hand on the shoulder of his fellow centurion. 'Centurion Felix will still be our praefectus castrorum. He is in charge of all things to do with the fortress and its preservation. Food, fodder, timber and maintenance, guard duties.' He cracked a wry smile. 'Even latrine duties.' The men laughed in response.

'We need to keep wild animals and all illnesses at bay. The space in front of the longhouse will be kept swept for exercises and assemblies. The gates will be cleared of snow and anything else that blocks them. We need to be able to close them. The gaps where fire took hold of the palisade will be sealed against roaming beasts and foul weather. No more than that, Felix.' He spoke directly to his fellow centurion. 'I do not expect us to have to defend this place, but it would be good if the wolves could not enter. Make use of the auxiliaries if you wish; bowmen guarding the approaches would be good, and the Cantabrians will need a space to exercise their mounts. Ours, too, Crassus?'

'Ours, too,' Crassus confirmed. He and Felix both saluted and Quintus turned his attention to Marcus.

'Optio Marcus here will lead in all things to do with discipline. He is in charge of training and exercise and —' he looked at Marcus quizzically — 'perhaps some sport? Wrestling or boxing or feats of strength?'

Marcus nodded enthusiastically, recalling with a mime the rope-pulling game that they had played with the Britons.

'It is he who will inspect your kit. Not just the rags of fur and leather you wear,' Quintus added quickly as the men grumbled. 'But your gladius and pugio, what spears and shields you still possess, and yourselves. Your blades will be sharp, your furs and linen will be clean, your leather polished and supple. Though we are in a barbarian fortress, we do not have to live like them.'

He gestured at Maxim and Jovan. 'The slaves will help. They may be armed, and by my authority remain so, but they are still slaves.' The Macedonians bowed their heads from the neck.

'Alba remains our capsarius. Go to him with hurts or illness.' His voice took on a tone of admonishment. 'But only major ones. Do not trouble him with minor aches or injuries. Those you can endure. Rufus assists him. I hope the injured men will soon be back amongst us. Alba?'

'They make progress, sir,' Alba said.

'No more will die?'

'I think not, but it is in the hands of the gods.'

Quintus nodded. 'We will remember our gods and festivals as best we can.' He brought another man forward. 'Agnus, you remain our chief scout. As soon as you can, you will ride out with comrades to see how far the snow extends and to make sure that no enemy approaches.'

Agnus acknowledged the charge with a nod.

'Caius and Vetruvius, guard our prize.' Quintus spoke directly to them. 'She is valuable and dangerous, so you have no other duties. If you need others to help you, ask.'

Quintus knew that there was precedent for what he did next — consulting the men. Divus Julius had done it, Pompeius Magnus had done it; Marcus Antonius and Sulla Felix had done it. He asked, 'Men, are there any questions or concerns, any suggestions as to how we can improve our situation?'

The men were about to spend winter in an enemy fortress, surrounded by snow. Rome, General Tiberius and his legions, would probably decide they were lost when they did not return. It did not matter: they were dispensable. But the men could be allowed a voice. They needed to be a family, even more close-knit than a legion. Quintus braced himself for criticisms of his actions, his command.

None came. With relief, he realised that while they were not about to acclaim him imperator, they were not going to undermine him. He dismissed the assembly.

XXV: SOL INVICTUS

Felix began by directing the men in the primary tasks that needed to be carried out. The oppidum was searched thoroughly, first for any remaining occupants, of which there were none. Next, they sought out any foodstuffs, fodder and other material, like timber and straw, that could be used for survival. The men found some open stores of grain and animal feed and brought them into the longhouse. They also found a barrel of apples, along with a few sacks of other fruit. In one hut they found more apples and, to their delight, a sow and her young responsible for scattering them. These, too, were moved.

The longhouse had a firepit at its centre, with the smoke expected to find its way along the rafters to a hole set in the apex of the wall. The rafters were soot-blackened and there were no windows, but the arrangement meant that once the slaves had the fire burning, the building became warm. The fire also gave light; otherwise the only light came from propping the doors open. A couple of the smaller huts were checked for soundness and brought into use for the livestock.

In one of the huts Sextus found what he at first took to be a pile of rags in a basket; then he realised that curled within was a brindled dog. He reached down for it, expecting it to either be dead or, if alive, to bite. But it lived, and its limpid grey eyes looked up at him with despair and no sign of violence. A movement beneath it revealed it to be a bitch, somehow still suckling a single pup. When Quintus lifted the dog, it felt limp and light as a leaf in a stream. Beneath it lay three more pups, dead. Pink and shrivelled, they had not managed to survive.

'Here,' Sextus said to the nearest soldier. 'Take these to the capsarius. Their survival may be a lucky omen.'

That evening, Sextus honoured Janus by pouring a libation of the bitter drink that the Germani made. He covered his head and they burned coals in a makeshift censer. All was carried out solemnly enough for both gods and men.

Overnight the snow threatened to return, the stars extinguished by cloud and a few large flakes drifting down. Those inside the longhouse, with its fire burning merrily, thanked the gods that they were not on guard duty. Those outside, keeping watch at the gates and towers of the palisade, wished they were inside. Those guarding the doors, propped half open, were close enough to see the fire, but too far away to feel it. Quintus was proud that they kept their discipline and their gaze outward.

The half-moon rising low and late showed the cloud scurrying away and the air clear and frosty. By morning it seemed that, for now at least, the snow would not begin again.

Some wildlife returned. Wolves were heard calling to each other across the white wastelands of the valleys. Small birds fluttered in, sparrow and wren, robin and blackbird. They saw the smoke emerging from the longhouse and sensed the return of men. They came seeking sustenance: crumb or wheatear or discarded food. Finches gathered on the roof and pecked at the straw.

'There must be food there, seeds and insects that we cannot see,' Sextus observed, as he and Rufus returned from washing in the river. 'Finches are precious to Mercury. They bring good fortune.'

'They sense food and warmth,' Rufus responded. 'Who can blame them?'

So, as the days grew shorter and the nights darker, the routine of the camp was established. It snowed intermittently, but nothing like as great an amount as in that first snow that almost buried them. Guards were changed, latrines filled in and fresh ones dug. Streets and exercise spaces in the oppidum were cleared of snow and kept swept. A long ride was kept for the horses.

Marcus arranged bouts of swordsmanship, wrestling and boxing along with javelin-throwing contests and foot races. Sadly, there was no rope strong enough for the pulling contest. In between, the soldiers rehearsed the moves learned on the Campus Martius. The injured men recovered slowly. The animals, dogs included, thrived, the puppy growing thick, white fur. The pigs were fed with leavings, the soldiers keen to eat them, but even keener to fatten them first. They looked forward to a midwinter feast.

Alba had no interest in the hound and its pup, so they attached themselves to Rufus. He pretended harshness with them but was discovered feeding them titbits and talking to them.

'Your shell has softened,' said Alba.

'How could it not? Look at them,' said Rufus. The mother had a long nose and liquid brown eyes. She fixed him with a loyal gaze, whilst her pup rolled onto its back, expecting a tummy tickle. The mother was not a large dog, more of a ratter than a hunter, and of no discernible breed. The father must have been big and pale, for it looked like that was what the pup would become.

The weapons of the previous dwellers were collected and stacked in another hut. Quintus took the blacksmith there with him to make use of his expertise. Crassus picked up the blades one by one, discarding them with disdain.

'Poor quality. Badly made. Weak metal. This one is even rusted.' Then, with a cry of astonishment, he pulled out a long straight sword. It was the great sword that Efwich had been about to take to Valhalla. Crassus was surprised at its quality.

'This is Norican iron,' he exclaimed. 'Look at the blade — turned and hammered and tempered again and again. This is an expensive blade from a master smith. And set in the hilt is a stone of some kind.' He wiped the dirt from the hilt with his hand and the stone caught the light. It was blue and green, reflecting the colours of earth and sky. He shook his head. 'Sadly, it is not a jewel, my friend, merely a piece of polished stone.'

Quintus smiled. 'It belonged to a chieftain. Do you want it?'

'No,' snorted Crassus, 'I do not think it will be a lucky blade. I merely admired its craftsmanship. Anyway, what would I do with a cavalry blade?' He looked from the sword in his hands to Quintus. 'Pity to waste it, though. Perhaps the Cantabrians?'

'You can bring them here when we have finished — there may be other things they could use.'

'There are axes here,' said Crassus. 'They will come in useful for cutting firewood.'

'Before long we may have to venture down the mountain for timber,' said Quintus. 'There is little that grows at this height. In the meantime, we burn whatever we find within the palisade, though not the palisade itself. There are wolves out there. The axes will be useful for demolishing huts and byres.'

Sextus appeared at the entrance to the hut and helped them stack the blades they had chosen. 'I will bring the Cantabrians here,' he said, weighing one of the axes in his hand. 'Do you really think we will run out of firewood?'

'I think we may,' said Quintus. 'It is going to be a long winter.'

Sextus made a crude calendar with a sharp stick and an area of carefully smoothed snow. He drew a circle around the stick, defining this boundary with smaller sticks set at regular intervals. He commanded that none venture inside on pain of death. When the sun set on the night of their first day, he took a black stone and marked on his circle the position of the shadow it cast. On the second night he did the same. In this way he plotted the march of the sun across the heavens.

'What does it do?' Quintus asked as he stared at it with curiosity. Crassus was with him and also eyed it suspiciously, expecting some sorcery or trickery — especially as Sextus was involved.

'It doesn't *do* anything,' laughed Sextus. 'It is just an indicator. Where the shadow falls at sunset shows the position of the sun in the sky.' He gestured theatrically. 'At midwinter it will cease to move that way and begin to return. Then we will know that winter is half over. I especially want to see when the sun stands still — Sol Invictus, the day that marks midwinter, when the sun pauses in its movement across the sky and is then reborn. The following day it begins its return journey. Then we know that we are heading once more for spring, for light and warmth.' He shook his head and looked out at the snow. 'Although this land seems to have little of the latter.'

'We can celebrate the festival of Sol Invictus, the midwinter festival,' said Crassus, adding hopefully, 'Perhaps we might even eat some of the stock.'

Caius and Vetruvius kept watch over Efwich, taking it in turns to sleep. For much of the time her wrists and ankles were bound. It was not long before both were convinced that she would not try to escape.

The prisoner was kept separate from the longhouse, in a hut of her own, even though this meant that a second fire had to be lit. She was not just a prisoner, of course, but also the only woman for a hundred square miles. And there were many men here. Quintus tried to talk to her using a combination of her poor Latin and Caius' limited knowledge of the Germani language. It seemed that they had the same conversation every time, until the presence of Caius was no longer needed.

She was permanently angry with him. 'Why do you keep me captive? Why do you not let me join my warriors at the feast? They have all passed into the hall of heroes, yet I am here trussed. Why?' she demanded.

'Because you will be a great ornament to our general,' Quintus explained. 'Tiberius is son to Caesar Augustus, who is the son of a god.'

'Men and gods seldom mix their seed,' she interrupted, scoffing. 'Even in our pantheon. Are you sure?'

'Of course I am sure,' Quintus insisted, though in his heart he was doubtful. 'Many portents were seen, not least an eagle ascending to heaven from his pyre and a bright star appearing in the sky to show that he had ascended.'

She was dismissive. 'I have heard of this god Julius. He was but a man. My son would defeat him if he lived.'

'Your son, if Dagaz was your son, is dead. I saw him with my own eyes. He was killed by a woman he was attempting to ravish. I am only sorry that I did not take his head — in your fashion — and carry it with me to prove his death.'

'I do not believe your story. That was not my son — he would not threaten a mere woman.' She shook her head. 'He is a man of honour, like his father.'

'His father?' Quintus laughed. 'His father is a man of treachery. He attacked his ally with no warning.'

'His ally was in the process of betraying him.'

And so the conversation would go on, she declaring that both her son and her husband were honourable and alive, he insisting that they were treacherous, and that at least one of them was dead.

Their arguments became almost friendly. Her hut was warm, and Quintus sometimes shared food with her. She tried to get him to like the bitter drink, but he could not, saying that it tasted like sour wine. He sat close to her, and she did not object. One soft evening, when night sat on the cusp of darkness, he put a hand on her thigh and she smiled. He almost dropped his guard and she almost took his pugio from him. He recoiled in shock as she bared her teeth. How stupid of him.

'Almost,' she hissed angrily. 'I am not for you, Roman. But your dagger could have been for me.'

'Caius, Vetruvius, see to her,' Quintus snapped.

Suddenly the hut was no longer somewhere he wanted to be. He walked down to the river to splash cold water on his foolish head.

He visited her no more as the days, shorter and shorter, passed slowly. When it snowed, which it did often, Felix had a roster of legionaries clear the public areas, especially the exercitus, the space in front of the gates and the tract where the horses were run. The route to the clearing in which they had camped was also kept open. Moving the snowfall before it froze was a priority, otherwise many areas became too slippery for the hobnailed caligae. Neither the drills held for the men nor the exercise needed for the horses were possible if ice formed which, overnight, it sometimes did.

Sextus tracked the shadow of his stick across the smoothed ground. It moved and moved and then, one day, it stopped, one flat black stone placed on top of another. Then it began its trip back in the opposite direction.

Hogs were slaughtered, fires built up and a great feast eaten to celebrate the victory of the undying sun, Sol Invictus. A great fire blazed to announce that here, in this oppidum of the enemy high in the foothills, a spark of Rome was surviving.

After the feasting, the mood of the men at first lifted. Then, as the days did not seem to grow any longer and the cold became even more intense, they descended into bouts of chafing and ill temper.

Agnus and his comrades were sent out every few days to look for signs of a thaw. They rode down the high-sided corridor that led to their original campsite, returning each day with news that the snow still held fast.

XXVI: SALIX

'This day is particularly miserable,' Quintus complained one morning, when between the thick cloud, the light snow and the usual morning mist, the light of day barely broke.

Crassus agreed. 'It is indeed grey, my friend. Perhaps a day to remain by the fireside?'

But it was on this day, gloomy as it was, that Agnus galloped through the opened gates and up to Quintus with unfeigned joy and excitement. Even before dismounting, he blurted out, 'Sir, the clearing where we camped is almost bare ground. There is slush instead of frozen earth. We could hear snow crashing from tree branches in the valley. Winter is ending. Spring is coming.'

Men heard what he said and stopped what they were doing. Soon a group had gathered just behind Quintus. Agnus continued excitedly, 'It is as if the mountain is pulling up its skirts. Here at this level the snow is still thick and slow to thaw. Not much further down, the water is already running free and the land is once more turning green. Our pathway has high sides up by the oppidum; it is still a tunnel, almost. Half a mile further down it is clear.'

'Hear that, Salix?' Rufus said happily to the puppy in his arms. He had named it after the woven willow basket in which it had been found. 'Quintus, does it mean we can escape?'

'Maybe the sun *is* climbing noticeably higher,' Felix added. 'It's just that with this cloud we cannot see it.'

Sextus had placed no stone on his calendar for four days as no sunset shadow had been cast.

Many other voices joined in with the questions. Quintus raised his hand and spoke clearly. 'An assembly tonight, men. To hear the news officially. This that you hear is but rumour; the man has yet to report officially to his commander.' He threw a stern glance at Agnus. 'Dismount, scout. Follow me.' Few but Crassus saw the wink that accompanied the order.

Agnus slid off the horse, one of his companions taking its reins. He realised he was being chastised. 'Apologies, sir. I should have reported to you privately first.'

Quintus waved a hand in dismissal. He could barely rein in his delight. They entered the longhouse. Quintus had established himself a sort of command post in a corner. There were stools here, and they sat. Felix joined them.

'How clear is it, Agnus?' Quintus asked. 'If we can move into it and down the slopes, then surely the enemy can move up it. It may not be long before the occupants come here to see what happened to their comrades over the winter.'

'Some of the boys we let free may have found their fathers,' said Felix. 'Their families will surely seek us. If we can move, we need to do it soon.'

'We can leave.' Agnus spoke with certainty. 'I think the thaw will reach the gates within a week.'

'Then we march at last,' said Quintus. 'Felix, I will tell the men tonight, but you can start making arrangements. Pass the word to Marcus also.'

Felix left and within an hour a new atmosphere of purpose could be felt in the camp.

As the grey afternoon light began to fade to black, legionaries put their shoulders to the great gates of the oppidum. This might be the last time they shut them. The oppidum had been hard and unwelcoming. Though the Romans had some meat and grain, they felt trapped.

Sextus and Crassus watched the gates swinging closed. 'It is one thing to be in a place, to remain in that place of your own free will,' Sextus said. 'It is another to be forbidden to leave, or unable to leave. When I was permitted to go from the Temple of Vesta as a boy, I felt free. I knew I was not a prisoner. Here, I have been confined, and such confinement is hard to bear.'

Crassus agreed. 'I was never allowed to leave the forge as a boy, not on my own. All my waking hours were spent working. It has felt much the same here.'

At the start of the winter there had been hunting parties, but it was difficult to make any progress through the packed snow, and the game was not worth the effort. The Anatolians and their deadly arrows had more success than any. The brindled bitch had run with the hunters a few times, but then, during one chase, she had failed to return. The Anatolians had searched, but she was nowhere to be found.

After this, Rufus attempted to train the puppy, which suddenly had long legs and an even longer stride, loping beside its master. He failed, but the beast brought joy to the men, with its inquisitive nature and innocence.

When the men tried fishing where the river ran narrow between the banks of snow, the fish were elusive, staying deep whilst Salix sniffed at the snow at the edges of the water. She jumped away and barked whenever the surface broke.

The gates had long since been cleared of blockages but still failed to swing smoothly, even though their hinges were greased with pig fat. They had been too badly damaged. Once they were shut, and the next roster of guards posted, the assembly would be called. The men were excited. They anticipated an order to move, to vacate this place at last. Their calls to each other were jocular as they struggled to shut the gates.

Suddenly the tone changed. Crassus and Sextus turned at the sound of other raised voices, calls of alarm rather than merriment, then a scream and the sound of something crashing to the ground. They drew their swords swiftly and turned to face the noise, which came from inside the oppidum. They barely registered that what furiously raced towards them was a horse, before it brushed them aside, its flanks sending Sextus reeling. On its back were two figures. One held a long sword in her hand, which Crassus recognised at once. The one who wielded it was instantly recognisable from the fair hair flying around her head. The other, mounted behind her, appeared to be a tribesman, dressed in furs. The gates were still open just wide enough to let the horse through and, within seconds, it was gone.

Men cursing and waving swords surrounded Crassus as he helped Sextus to his feet.

'Horses!' Quintus was there now and barked the order. 'Open the gates. Bring her back.'

'The other?' Crassus asked. 'Who is he? How did a tribesman enter?'

'It is no tribesman,' exclaimed Caius, running behind the others, his face and ear bloodied. 'It is Vetruvius. He has betrayed us and taken the woman.'

The few horses that they had were not kept ready to ride, apart from the one Agnus habitually used. He and Crassus rushed to saddle the rest. The Cantabrians had no need of such accoutrements and were already at the gate.

'Go. Follow,' Quintus ordered. 'We will be behind you. Agnus, you go too.'

Agnus saluted and pulled himself up onto his horse, turning its head for the gates. He was first through, with the Cantabrians galloping out in his wake. Men on foot went running behind them. Soon the bigger cavalry horses followed, Quintus riding one of them. But the already poor light was fading, and the shadows were growing dark and deep.

They did not need light to travel along the path that they had first cut to the oppidum. This had been kept clear by shifting snow whenever it fell and flinging it onto the banks. When the men reached the clearing in which they had first camped, Quintus could see that Agnus was right. The snow had all but gone, replaced by mud.

Here the hunt changed into a tracking exercise. The pursuers slowed; they had not paused to collect torches, so the men were forced to tread carefully. Darkness was soon complete, and many unseen dangers lurked amongst the deeply shadowed drifts and the meltwater flowing between them. There could be rocks, drops, streams and all manner of hazards. They needed light to pick up the tracks.

Quintus commanded two of the Cantabrians, 'Go back and fetch torches. Tell centurion Felix to secure the fortress — on my command.' The horsemen turned and vanished into the night.

'By the time they arrive, the fugitives will have made good their escape,' Crassus said.

'She chose her time well,' said Quintus. 'She must have been prepared.'

'And armed,' said Crassus. 'With the blade that I gave to the Cantabrians. How did she manage to steal it?'

Quintus shook his head. 'We may never know, although I will beat it out of Vetruvius if we catch him.'

'We should keep going on foot, but carefully.'

Quintus signalled agreement. 'Dismount,' he ordered the riders. 'Agnus, come to the front. Track them.'

The going was slow without torches, and they had not gone far before the horsemen returned from the oppidum, pinpricks of light along the path marking their progress.

'Wait for them,' Quintus ordered. 'We will do better — and proceed faster — following the tracks with the aid of light.'

The auxiliaries had brought many unlit torches which were quickly aflame so that a line of lights was soon snaking down the mountain. With them was Rufus, with Salix straining on a long leash. 'Perhaps she can track,' the redhead said. 'I offered her a piece of Vetruvius' clothing. She seems keen to follow its scent.'

In places the ground was steep; the fugitives must have relied on the sure-footedness of their horse in the dark. In other places, their tracks were lost on smooth rock and the pursuers had to search a wide arc to find where they had gone.

The hunters proceeded on foot, walking the horses. They needed to be able to see the signs on the ground, rather than following at speed. Salix, moving like a pale ghost in the dark, often found the trail first. Sometimes they were forced to climb over and around obstacles, but more often they descended, the sound of the river clear and constant but far below them.

Agnus had been right; after only a little while, the snow was all but gone. Beneath the straggly trees that they passed, the ground was bare. A sickle moon rose, but provided little help, its light filtered by the trees and hidden by the clouds that still scudded across the sky. It was no hunter's moon, no helper sent by Diana.

They crossed rock and rough ground, new grass and mud, small streams and gullies bringing snow melt down the mountain. In places the path was so narrow the hunters were strung out behind, Rufus and the dog always at the front.

With a raised hand, Quintus called a halt. 'We do not need all of us. Go back,' he commanded all but a few legionaries and most of the Cantabrians. 'Rufus, stay.'

His optio was the one he chose to lead the others back. 'Return to the fortress, Crassus. Tell Felix to prepare the men for departure. Tell him to pack up the camp. As soon as I return, we will leave. This is no chase that will end in a fight; it is a hunt. The prey may turn on us, but it does not have such claws that we need so many hunters.'

'I will stay if you will allow it,' pleaded Caius. 'I was her guard.'

'You failed in your duty.' Quintus spoke harshly, without sympathy. 'You will go back to the oppidum and await your punishment.' He spat out the last order venomously. 'Do not dare to desert.'

Caius knew that it would be useless arguing and, shoulders slumped, he turned back and joined Crassus.

As the waning moon dipped, Quintus, Agnus, Rufus and Salix continued hour after hour through the black night. Sextus was on foot behind them with two Cantabrians, mákhairai drawn. They all walked their horses. The rest had long gone. Entering a rocky clearing, they paused on the hard ground and swept the torches around its perimeter. The spot seemed to be surrounded by stunted trees. The dog strained towards a spot beneath the tightly packed trunks. Agnus bent close to the earth, torch in hand.

'They must have passed here,' said Quintus, in frustration. 'There is nowhere else for them to have gone. There must be a gap in the trees.'

'Here,' said Agnus at last, bending back a wiry shrub. 'Salix has found it. This is no tree; it is but a bush.'

'Does their trail lie beyond it?' Quintus asked.

'It does, sir. The path is clear. The ground begins to rise again. They must have slowed down.'

'I hope so,' said Quintus, jaw set. 'I will not go back without her.'

He followed Agnus, brushing past the shrub to see a narrow, wet track winding steeply upwards. There were hoofprints to see, but no footprints.

'Are they still riding?' Quintus asked incredulously, looking at the tracks.

'It would seem so. She must be a better horsewoman than we knew,' said Agnus. 'Look, they are no longer galloping, but they are still mounted. From the depth of these tracks, I would say two of them still.'

'Follow,' ordered Quintus, his mouth set in a stern line. 'I will have her back. And I will kill him.'

XXVII: MALEDICITE IOVI OMNIBUS DIISQUE

As they climbed, night began to give way to day. The sky grew lighter and the stars disappeared, but Quintus' rage only grew darker.

Though hungry, wet and tired, the men forged on. The slope that they climbed was steep and long, the path running straight through lines of tall trees. At last they could see the crest of the track and the sky beyond, framed by dark trunks. Near the top Agnus paused. Rufus watched the dog sniff in circles on the ground.

'They stopped here and dismounted,' he said. 'Look, there are footprints alongside the hoofprints. It looks like they rested.'

Agnus pointed ahead to what looked like the end of the climb. 'The horse is tired; it is carrying two of them. We should see them from the brow of the hill.'

'Sir,' said one of the Cantabrians, approaching Quintus, 'we can ride on this ground; our ponies are sure-footed.'

'We can, too,' said Sextus. 'It is only grass.'

'Then mount,' said Quintus. 'If they can ride, so can we.' He shook his head in frustration. 'They cannot be far.'

They began at a trot, then a canter, urging the horses to gather speed as Salix, a spectral flash of golden fur, outpaced them. At the top, the slope finally flattened out to a broad stretch of spring grass, wet from the morning's dew in the shadow of the trees. It led gradually downwards. They shaded their eyes and peered as far as they could, but there was no sign of their quarry.

'We must be closing in on them,' Quintus said. 'We must catch sight of them soon. Unless they have turned off this track. Agnus?'

Agnus studied the land. 'It does not seem possible, sir. There is hardly room for a man between these trees, let alone a horse.' He dismounted. 'Their tracks are still here.'

He walked along the track a little further then raised a hand. 'Here,' he said. 'They walked but a little way, then they mounted. They are on horseback again.'

The little troop once more set out, the canter turning into a steady gallop. The grass, wet and slippery, would be an enemy to caligae, but the horses easily coped with it. They covered the ground quickly, but still there was no sign of their prey. They had no need of their tracking skills anymore; the path formed a broad avenue, flattening out across boggy ground where the horse's hoofprints were clear. Salix still led, running on ahead and then back to them, tireless.

They splashed through the bog and then the way sloped slightly upwards. It narrowed as the trees crowded ever more tightly to either side of it. There was only one way the fugitives could have gone. On Quintus' urging, the men began to go even faster.

Suddenly, shouts and commands in different languages rang out as the men struggled to bring the horses to a halt. The beasts reared and pawed the air with their front hooves. Clods of earth were kicked up. Salix stopped dead and barked at the empty air. Curses sounded loudly and echoed from the trees. The horses were stopped, blowing and snorting, the riders gentling them.

The land had suddenly and unexpectedly slipped away, creating a sheer drop beyond a jagged edge of rock and earth. Divots and small stones kicked up by the horses' hooves went bouncing over the cliff edge, vanishing into the depths. The dog lay on its front, legs splayed, nose pointing forward. The path itself appeared to lead straight over the precipice.

The men dismounted quickly, Quintus handing his reins to Rufus. Carefully he moved towards the cliff edge and peered over. There were wiry shrubs and small trees growing out of the cliff face, sufficient to block his view. Far below he could hear the sound of rushing water. He lay flat on his belly and edged his way out until he could see. Deep in the ravine the river ran white, gushing out from the forest's edge and tumbling down between black rocks. Great trees had been brought down the mountain by it and were jammed and jumbled where it turned and narrowed, struggling to bubble past them. The blood of Quintus' anger suffused his cheeks as he saw what else swirled in the water.

Efwich, Vetruvius and their horse all lay smashed and broken amidst branch and bough. Vetruvius was stretched on a rock and twitching still, his face turned to the heavens. Beside him glinted the silver headband. His mouth was opening and closing soundlessly. Either he was not quite dead, or the rushing waters were playing tricks. The horse was certainly dead, half of its body in the swirling river, the rest stretched across a fallen tree, its neck twisted at a bizarre angle.

Efwich, too, was dead, lying in an impossible position, face down, arms and legs arranged oddly, her head in the water, her unbound hair streaming in its flow. Her left arm lay across a rock, the hand empty. Her right arm stretched out in front of her. In her fist she grasped the unsheathed sword of the oppidum, the cavalry blade with its blue-green hilt decoration.

With this, Quintus knew, her entry into the feasting halls of Valhalla was guaranteed. She had sacrificed herself. She had called down vengeance on Rome for at least three generations. The shining stone winked up at him insolently.

Quintus stood up, shaking with rage. He railed at the gods. *'Maledicite Iovi omnibus diisque!'* he shouted. 'Curse Jupiter and all the gods.' His anger exploded. He swore loudly, spitting and waving his fists. He cursed Vetruvius and Efwich, cursed all the men of the Fifth, the whole country of the Germani and their sky-spawned gods. He cursed the sun and the moon, the mountains and the plains, the river and the sky, the grass and the trees. He cursed his birth, his station and his luck. He cursed Mercury, the trickster god, enough to make Sextus flinch and Salix seek sanctuary with her master.

'Quintus, stop,' Sextus said urgently. 'The gods will hear.'

'I want them to damn well hear!' Quintus shouted. 'This was our way back; this was our redemption. This would have won us the favour of Tiberius. Instead, I am betrayed by one of our own. One that I trusted to keep her safe.' His fists opened and closed. He was struggling to stay coherent through his fury. 'They are down there, Sextus. Both of them. A good cavalry horse destroyed, a traitorous legionary and a princess of the Germani dead. A hostage that would have graced the triumphal procession of noble Tiberius. She even has a blade — the sword we found her with originally. She was our way back. Now we have nothing. Why should I not call the wrath of the gods down on us?'

Sextus took a step back. He had never witnessed such a fit of temper in his friend. He did not know how to respond.

He did not need to. Quintus had run out of curses. Instead, tears welling, he turned to look hopelessly at the place where his quarry had galloped over the edge. He roared, raising his fists to the empty sky. Sextus moved towards Agnus and Rufus, placing a hand on each man's shoulder and steering them away from him, whilst the Cantabrians, fearing the madness of the centurion, stood back.

'Our chase is over,' Sextus told his comrades. 'Our quarry lies at the foot of this cliff, horse and riders both. Quintus is too full of rage to approach yet. Let him cool down. He is taking the mighty gods to task.' He made the sign of the horns. 'I would not wish to be Caius when the centurion catches up with him.'

'They rode over the edge?' Rufus asked, dumbfounded. 'Deliberately?' He had picked up the dog, which now licked his face enthusiastically, unaware of the fate of its quarry.

'Almost certainly,' said Sextus. 'The end of this track is obvious; it does not look like an accident. We were only at risk because we galloped.'

'Perhaps it is what she planned all along,' Agnus said in a whisper. 'A noble death at her own hands, rather than capture.'

Sextus shook his head. 'I do not know their beliefs, but a headlong plunge from a cliff into a rocky chasm does not seem especially noble to me. She had a blade, though. Perhaps for her that was enough.'

They waited a good while until Quintus finally collected himself.

'There is nothing to be done,' the centurion said at last through gritted teeth. 'Even the sword she carried stays out of our reach. The gods of this river can have it.' He took a deep breath and drew himself up to his full height. His face and neck were no longer red. 'I did not mean to frighten you.' He patted Salix's head and spoke gently to the hound by way of apology. Then he looked at the men. 'Mount up,' he commanded. 'We return to the oppidum. I will find out from

Caius what spells she cast. I will know what it was that turned the gods against us.'

'It is Týr and Wotan who oppose us in this land. It is they you should curse, not our gods, not even Mercury,' said Sextus softly.

Quintus bridled at the rebuke, mild as it was, then took another deep breath. 'I am sorry,' he declaimed, arms open, face turned to the heavens. 'If I have offended, I apologise.' He paused and looked at his friend. 'I will offer Mercury a black cockerel when we are back in Rome, Sextus. Is that enough?'

Sextus guessed that no answer was required, so he nodded but kept his peace. He would make sure a sacrifice was made long before they were back in front of Mercury's temple in the Circus Maximus.

Their journey back was made in almost total silence. Once Agnus managed to convey to the Cantabrians what had happened to their prey, there was no need for further conversation. The sky was once more clouded, matching their mood. Quintus rode at the front, setting a punishing pace. He was keen to begin his interrogation of Caius.

It was a faster journey, with no halts for tracking or to choose between paths. The dog still ran ahead, seemingly impossible to tire. Towards the end, though they climbed, the small fir trees had already shaken off the snow and the ground was only patched with areas of white. Tracks that had seemed treacherous in the dark were now easily traversed at a canter.

The final few miles uphill had to be taken at a walk. Quintus was forced to slow down, recognising that his horse was as tired and hungry as the men and could not be pushed to go faster. Even the dog walked. Once they came to the campsite and the clear path up to the oppidum, he ordered the men to dismount.

By the time they reached the closed gates, darkness was beginning to fall. There were guards with torches on the parapet, and one of the gates was swung open once their challenge was answered. Quintus dismissed the party and the Cantabrians took charge of all the horses, leading them away to be fed and rested.

Felix was waiting to greet the men and realised at once that they brought back no captives. 'Where are they, Quintus?' he asked. 'Where are our fugitives?' He did not dare ask if they had escaped.

'Dead,' said Quintus flatly. 'And not by our hand, but their own. Either by accident or design, they galloped off the edge of a cliff and lie now in a deep chasm, washed by the waters of the river.' Felix shook his head in disbelief. Quintus continued, 'The woman Efwich had a tribesman's sword in her hand, one that had been stored here in the oppidum. It was meant to be given to the Cantabrians.'

He paused, then issued orders. 'Felix, I want to know how this weapon walked from the auxiliaries to the woman. Find out. And bring the veteran Caius to me. He failed in his duty. I will find out how and why.'

XXVIII: CAIUS SERGIO NERVA

Caius was expecting to be summoned as soon as Quintus returned. He had not been held in any sort of confinement — there was no place to confine a man in the oppidum. Instead he was left free of duties, cold-shouldered by men who knew of his failure.

Alba cleaned the injuries to his face and head — they were not serious, but now the veteran's craggy face, usually florid, was pale with anticipation as he was brought to the centurion for interrogation. Quintus sat face to face with him, not in the torchlit corner of the longhouse, but in the hut that had held the weapons. He saw that Caius perspired and bade him sit easy. He used a kindly tone, but Caius knew that within his centurion, iron justice waited for him. He was offered no food or drink, not even water. He knew that he babbled but could not help himself.

'She never made any move to run away, none that I knew of, anyway,' said the veteran. 'There was no thought of her escaping. Even when she went to the latrines, she was escorted and on a leash. The rest of the time she was kept bound as you ordered.'

'You took it in turns to watch her?'

'At night, yes. But during the day, we both sat with her. We talked, but that was all. She never tried to persuade us to release her, never even asked for freedom.' He shook his head in bafflement. 'I do not understand what happened to Vetruvius.'

'I do. I, too, sat with her. She made me comfortable, made me drop my guard, tried to steal my pugio. She only ever thought of escape.'

Caius was shocked at the admission. 'We just talked,' he said. 'She never tried anything with me.'

'No. She had her victim pegged. Clearly she saw Vetruvius as her way out. What did you talk about?'

'Many things,' said Caius. 'She told us the reason behind the noise she made, the wail of anguish when she was captured. It was, she said, a warning to the gods in Valhalla that a great warrior was about to arrive. She must have thought of herself as such a warrior. She told us of the great hall of the heroes in Valhalla, of how the honourably fallen warriors feasted there until the world's end. Of how those who did not fall in battle were banished to suffer in another realm, a land of ice, fog and darkness. In turn we told her of Elysium and the Isles of the Blessed; of Charon's boat and the payment required; of Mercury's guiding hand; of the ghosts that wandered in agony on the nearer shore.' He shook his head. 'Our lands of the dead did not seem so different to hers.'

'This sounds harmless enough,' said Quintus. 'What else?'

'What else?' Caius repeated, as if finding it difficult to recall. 'We tried to learn more of each other's languages. I taught her the names of household things — chair and stool, couch and table. She taught me their names for weapons — spear and sword and shield. We both, Vetruvius and I, taught her games of chance. We taught her to gamble at knucklebones, though she had nothing with which to place a wager.' Once more he shook his head.

'So you played games with her. You made a friend of her.' Quintus' voice now carried menace.

'No, sir, not friends. Just passing the time. We tried to find out more about their customs, their numbers, their cities. Information to help us, to help Rome. It was a sort of soft interrogation.'

Quintus was sceptical that anything useful would have come of such a conversation. 'And you discovered…?'

'That they are an ancient people and, if what she said was true, widespread and vast in number. She told stories of lands where her cousins ruled, lands beyond the shores of Oceanus.' This time the head shake was vigorous. 'Neither of us believed her, but Vetruvius tried to match her fables with stories of our own. Of Romulus and Remus and the foundation of Rome and of the hut that miraculously still stands near the forum. Of the fall of Tarquinius Superbus, the last king.'

The words tripped over each other as Caius sought to defend himself. 'We told her of the Senate, at which she cackled. One strong voice is the only way to govern, she said, not many voices each seeking mastery. One voice and strength. She would not believe him when he described the size of the city and its sites — the great theatre of Pompey, the Mausoleum on the Campus Martius that contains nothing but Marcellus; the Curia, the Rostra, the temple of Great Jupiter.'

'Stop!' Quintus snapped suddenly. 'I have heard enough of your games. You were supposed to be guarding her, not entertaining her. My patience is at an end. Tell me truthfully: how did she turn Vetruvius? How did she come by the sword? How did she escape?'

'I don't know how she turned him, sir. But it was he who betrayed us, not me.' Caius dropped to his knees before his commander, stretching his neck forward. 'Nevertheless, I have failed you, sir. I have failed all of us. I should die.'

Felix had entered quietly. 'He is right,' he said. 'The Cantabrian captain tells me that he claimed the sword for himself. A gift from you, as he understood it, the Romans having no use for it. Then a man came, one who said he was an officer. He said that the commander had asked for the sword, that it should never have been taken. Reluctantly, the Cantabrian handed it back.' Felix looked at Caius, kneeling with his head bent. 'This man was betrayed. The Cantabrian described the man who came to him — without doubt it was Vetruvius. I imagine he obtained the horse in the same way. He was capable of deception, that much we all know from gambling with him.'

'He struck me from behind,' said Caius, his voice muffled. 'He called her his darling as he urged her to mount. She used witchcraft on him, I am sure. I think perhaps they had become lovers. Or planned to.'

'Under your gaze?' Quintus was scathing. 'This could happen on your watch?'

Caius remained silent.

'He is guilty,' Quintus said.

'Agreed,' said Felix. 'But of what? Perhaps of nothing more than trusting a friend.'

Quintus, eyes hard, faced his fellow centurion. 'Take him, Felix. Keep him confined. I will deal with him later. There will be an assembly at first light, and a punishment detail. Afterwards we will leave this place.'

That night Quintus found himself once more sleepless, wandering the bounds of the oppidum throughout the hours of darkness. The place was not quiet. Men moved around with purpose, collecting materials and foodstuffs. Horses were being moved and their saddlebags packed. There were several fires. Quintus looked to the heavens for guidance, but found none there, the stars hidden behind a veil of thick cloud.

Dawn came slowly. It was not so much first light as a patch of darkness in the east becoming less dense. During the night the spring thaw had crept much closer to the oppidum. The ridges and furrows on the corridor of snow that led to the campsite were smooth and glistened in the light. Down the track itself, already wider, water ran. It would not be long before the snow had vanished completely.

Quintus felt hungry and was drawn to the smells of cooking emanating from the various fires. He took meat from one group, speaking softly to the men. In the longhouse, Crassus and Felix joined him. The three of them sat by the remnants of the fire, where the slaves were cooking long strips of meat wound around green sticks. The legionaries had eaten many of these, but some remained in the embers. Quintus and his companions were happy to chew on them. This morning the fire would at last be allowed to die completely.

The doors were propped wide to allow the morning light to enter and shadows of men and horses could be seen moving outside. There was mist, of course, but it did not rise above the knees of the men. Quintus and Felix were in discussion.

'We have no means to mete out any punishment but extra duties or death,' Felix was saying. 'Extra duties are hardly possible if we are leaving. Death is too great a price to pay for what Caius did.'

'To start with, I will take away his rank and seniority,' Quintus said.

'You could even dock his pay,' suggested Felix with a smile. They had not been paid in months.

'It is not enough,' said Quintus, ignoring the lighter tone attempted by his comrade. 'He was naive. His guard was undermined when he was drawn into games and conversations. But he was also duped — by both Vetruvius and the woman. Dereliction of duty is death, as surely as falling asleep on guard.'

A silence grew between them. Eventually, Felix broke it. 'Naivety is hardly a reason to pronounce death. Many of us as young soldiers would have been executed if it was.'

'He is no young soldier, Felix. He is called again to the colours — a veteran, one of the evocati.'

'Still, death is too harsh a penalty for Caius' offence,' Felix insisted. 'And you know it would demoralise the men.'

'Twenty lashes,' Quintus said, as if offering the opening bid in a haggle.

'Perhaps ten,' said Felix softly, putting a hand on Quintus' shoulder. 'Twenty could kill him. We said we do not want him dead.'

'Ten then, for failing his comrades. I will do it myself,' insisted Quintus stubbornly. 'Caius is an optio; he cannot whip himself.'

'He was,' Felix pointed out. 'You will have deprived him of all rank and station. He will be just a common soldier. As your optio, let Crassus do it.'

'Am I to be opposed at every turn?' Quintus complained. He squared his shoulders. The negotiation was at an end. 'Very well,' he agreed reluctantly and called his amicus over.

'As optio, it will fall to you to flog Caius,' he told him. 'Ten lashes, Felix and I agreed, for failing in his duty. But it must be real, Crassus. You must make sure you do not hold back. The punishment is deserved.'

'I know my duty, commander,' said the blacksmith.

'Commander indeed,' scoffed Quintus, as Crassus saluted him. 'I remember the tent of General Tiberius — its size, its hangings, its floor coverings, its guards. That is a commander.' He spoke sadly, looking at the floor, all the anger drained from him. 'I command nothing but a bunch of renegades dressed as barbarians — and now I must punish one of them. I will at least call the assembly myself.' He rose and made for the door.

'We do not even have a whip,' Crassus said quietly to Felix. 'We have punished none this winter, except lightly with switches and canes.'

'The reins of a horse will have to serve. Make something,' said Felix, rising to leave.

XXIX: JANUS PRIMUS VESTA EXTREMISQUE

The assembly gathered outside the front doors of the longhouse. Horses and men were loaded with packs. A cold wind blowing from the east made them eager to move. They stood impatiently as Quintus spoke.

'We have had few assemblies. There has been no need,' he said. 'But this morning there is need. We must sacrifice to Father Janus and take the haruspices before we set out. If the gods want us to stay, they will tell us.' The men mumbled assent at this. It was normal and necessary.

'There is also a punishment to carry out.' He gestured and two men, the punishment detail, brought Caius forward. He did not resist. Quintus pointed.

'This man allowed his friend to deceive him. This friend, Lucius Cornelius Vetruvius of Tarentum, is dead, killed by the chieftain we held for general Tiberius. The captive who we could have used to buy our way back into favour. She was the only bargaining counter we had in seeking the favour of Caesar Augustus' son.' He paused to let the facts sink in, although every man was aware of what had happened.

'Now she is gone. She rode the horse that she stole over a cliff. Along with the legionary she deceived, she died. Even the beast died. Whether this plunge was by accident or design, we will never know.'

He turned his gaze on Caius. 'Caius Sergio Nerva, evocatus and optio of the Third, you are hereby stripped of all rank, station and seniority. Your pay for the winter months is forfeit.

You will be flogged, ten lashes for your failure to carry out your duties.'

Caius merely bowed his head in submission. There was no yoke for him, not even a whipping post. Instead he knelt on the ground, his back bent, his hands clasped together in front of him. He was clothed in just Germani trews; his long shirt had been removed, exposing his back. Baltea and cingulum had been set aside. Crassus was also stripped to the waist. He judged that the tunic and furs of the Germani would hamper him. He still wore his baltea and cingulum, but his chest was bare, showing the scars of the forge where he had worked as a boy, the inevitable burns and brands. There were also scars of battle, healed strikes on his arms and legs and bull-like neck, plus the two deep scars at the base of his spine, sustained in Hispania when he had been attacked from behind. Unconsciously, he pulled up the waistband of his undershorts to hide these.

Deep within his mind lay other scars — scars from the violent years he had shared with his father, once he had returned from the legions. Scars from the disappearance of his brother in the cesspits of the city, and the hurt and anguish of his mother. He did not like to inflict pain and avoided being the one to mete out punishment if he could. But he was an optio and this was his duty. It was a duty to Quintus also — one of the few who knew the blacksmith's past.

He held the simple whip in his hand. It had three tongues made up of reins and no handle; instead it was wrapped around Crassus' fist. He had tied knots at the end of each tongue to help it travel and to reflect the usual configuration of the short-handled scourge. It was no flagrum; it had no sharp metal attached. This was not intended to take the skin from Caius' back.

Crassus was efficient, counting the blows aloud. The first raised a welt on Caius' broad back; the second crossed it and blood glistened. The third raised another welt further down. A cruel man would make sure the stripes crossed often. Crassus did not try, but nor did he hold back.

Caius did not cry out.

Ten lashes for dereliction of duty was a light sentence, but the officers had decided that they had no wish to kill the man. They needed him to be able to march. Crassus called 'ten' as the final blow cracked. He stood back, unwrapping the thongs from his hand, ready to return the reins to their owners.

Alba stood nearby with a pail of water, icy from the river. He splashed it on the ex-optio's back. Caius now groaned — he had managed to remain conscious. His comrades grasped his arms to help him up, but he batted them away. He was determined to rise to his feet himself. He struggled and staggered as he pulled himself upright, turned to Quintus and, fist to heart, saluted. Only when Quintus had returned the salute and turned away did he allow his comrades to help. They escorted him away.

'It was not his fault,' Quintus said quietly.

'But he had to be punished,' said Felix. Crassus merely grunted acquiescence as he pulled his tunic back on.

Sextus stood waiting to one side, head covered, with a sacrificial stone, a sharp knife and yet another wood pigeon. 'A ram for Janus would be better,' he said. 'But this is an ending too, so Vesta will share. *Janus primus Vesta extremisque.* The gods will understand.'

The sacrifice was quickly done and the bird opened. Sextus hardly looked before exclaiming that the exta were perfect, the haruspices good. The remains of the bird were carefully placed on the dying embers of the longhouse fire: food for the gods.

Quintus mounted up and led the troop back down the track. They were neither entirely cavalry nor entirely infantry, but they were still a formidable force, with the legionaries to the fore, ahead of the great bows of the Anatolians and the sharp mákhairai of the Cantabrians.

Alba had lost two patients during the winter, both badly injured at the storming of the oppidum. Other injuries had healed. Quintus was confident that there were no groups of tribesmen near that could stand against them. He was not confident that this would be the case for long.

The thaw continued apace and now some of the bodies of the tribesmen, frozen for a season, were starting to emerge from the snow. This was an unwelcome reminder of the previous action, and many of the men made the warding sign of the cornua as they passed. Sextus clutched the unbroken bulla at his neck, Quintus the precious armband of Ursus. They left the fortress behind quickly, some riding, some marching.

As they made their way down the hill to their initial campsite, Quintus looked back at their winter home. Already it was vanishing, draped in the swirling fog that haunted every riverbank in Germania. He could see the shadow of the oppidum, a grey and forbidding mass slipping silently into the mist. He shuddered. He was glad to be away from it. Below lay forest and stream, green fields and spring. They might not make it back to Rome this season, but they would be able to report to General Tiberius that the tribesmen who had dared to attack him on the water had been dealt with. They had fulfilled their mission.

There was no need to tell him that the woman they had lost was the mother of one renegade and wife of another, that she was to be a gift to him. There was no need to mention her at all. He would have the word passed.

'Double time,' he commanded, and the group, still clothed as tribesmen, swiftly left the hill behind.

From their original camp above the treeline, there seemed to be a single obvious path, one already beaten down by feet and hooves. But Quintus knew from the pursuit that these were his tracks, and that this led only to a cliff edge.

'This starts well enough,' he said. 'But we must find another path before it reaches the cliff. At the foot of the cliff is a river which, though swollen with snow melt, I do not think is the mighty Rhenus. For one thing, it is too near.' He was talking to Crassus, who rode alongside him. 'For another, it is too narrow.'

'The waterfalls near Tiberius' camp were wide,' said Crassus, as they passed out of the flat area that had been the site of their camp. 'They were also fast and fierce. We could hear them from a great distance.'

'The river into which Efwich plunged was also fast flowing. But it was narrow, tumbling over rocks, bouncing off the walls of the deep gorge that confined it. It was a young and merry river, not slow and stately one. And I do not think it flows in the right direction. The other is of no use to us?'

By this he meant the river that flowed past to the west, the one which held the oppidum in one of its curves as if in the crook of an elbow.

'It is not. It soon disappears, slipping like a serpent into the forest, trees growing down to the water's edge. We would be hard put to follow it on foot. It would be impossible for the horses. If we had boats, we might make some headway down it. It is where the fugitives from the oppidum went.'

'We could build barges, I suppose — but I would be fearful of rounding a bend and vanishing over a waterfall.'

'The twists and turns of these rivers have long since defeated my sense of direction,' smiled the blacksmith. 'We should follow the sun and the stars. They at least are constant.'

'True. But when we follow them they take us in a straight line, whereas the gods of this country conspire to strew valleys and hills and rivers in our path, so we are forever knocked off course.' Even as Quintus said this, they had to take a detour around a fallen tree, its roots dripping with the soft mud from which it had been recently pulled. 'Even things like this push us off course.'

'If we can find a river we can follow,' said Crassus, as they resumed the track beyond the fallen tree, 'its course downhill must take it to a bigger river, and then a bigger one again. The last of these must surely be the largest, the Rhenus. And with that river we must find Tiberius and the army.'

They did not find it easy. With difficulty they negotiated the first few miles of the track until they reached the clearing, where Agnus had struggled to find the fugitives' trail. Quintus called a halt, pointing beyond the brush.

'That way lies a broad track, Crassus, but one that plunges over a cliff edge. That is where the renegade woman and her traitorous helper plunged to their deaths.' He would not afford either the respect of using their name. 'We must take this track.' He pointed to an almost invisible trod winding into the forest. 'And we must go with care. We walk the horses.' He dismounted and led the way.

As they gradually lost height, the trees grew more thickly, trunks sometimes almost touching each other. Many branches had been brought down by the weight of the winter's snow, and sometimes whole trees had crashed to the ground, blocking their way. Above them was a canopy formed of the branches of great conifers, which had lost little of their green over the winter. Where these were prevalent, they blotted out the sky, especially at night, so that neither stars nor moon could be seen. Sometimes the men came across groves of other trees, oak and ash, birch and beech, and these at least still let light through their bright spring growth.

Snow and slush had destroyed paths, in places turning them into quagmires. Though it was Quintus' instinct to continue in as straight a line as possible, hacking through obstructions or squelching through mud to maintain direction, sometimes the fallen trees were too big, the roots too tangled; sometimes the ground was so wet that it was impassable. Then, with mattock and axe, they had to fight a way through or around.

Where they had hoped to find familiar ground — the valleys and hills that they had traversed in their pursuit of the Vindelici, and eventually the lake where they had burned the ships — nothing looked as it had when they had passed before. The winter weather had changed contours, established rivers where there had been dry valleys, and caused landslides and mudslides. Now, new green growth had changed the face of the country.

They were undoubtedly lost.

XXX: LEMURÉS

At least they ate extremely well. There was an abundance of fish in the rivers. Game was so plentiful that they left the least favoured cuts of the animals they shared or shot. This caused problems, wolves and other creatures being drawn to the leavings, and so Felix, still erstwhile praefectus castrorum, had to order such leftovers to be buried.

The reason for the verdant growth was clear — it rained incessantly. Whilst high above the canopy there might be sunlight, it seldom filtered down through the leaves and branches. Paths turned to water, clearings to quagmires. Several times they reached a flooded river they could not ford, or a ravine too deep to cross. They were forced to work their way upstream to try and find a place where the waters did not run so wide or so fierce, or where the ravine narrowed. Inevitably, they veered far from their original course and lost their way.

Shortly after the latest of these crossings, which had sapped the energy of all the men, one of Felix's rabbits — young, fit and strong — first paled and then struggled with his breath. Inexplicably to the capsarius, he then died. He blamed the lemurés of the men whose bodies they had left unburied at the oppidum.

The men were struggling even with campfires so, instead of a pyre, they dug at the earth and laid him in a shallow grave. The rain and apparent lack of progress towards Tiberius had already dampened the men's spirits. This death and funeral made them even more depressed, bad-tempered with each other and the animals. Even the dog, normally joyful, now moped around with her tail between her legs. It seemed that the ghosts of the dead had found them and now tormented them.

Comrades became short with each other, snapping nastily. There were fights, but they were small affairs. The men knew that anything serious could explode into mutiny. Quintus witnessed one of these and shook his head. He had no idea what it was about; he just saw two legionaries nose to nose, almost hissing at each other. One had clearly had enough and turned on his heel. The other threw some parting shot at his retreating back and, turning, saw Quintus watching.

'Sir…' he began.

'I don't want to know,' said Quintus tersely. 'Just make sure he makes it safely back to camp.'

The man saluted, although he was clearly disappointed that he had not been able to make his case.

In the early morning Quintus remembered the man's deeply tanned face, his sparse dark beard, the scar above his eye. He remembered the look of righteous anger twisting the man's mouth downwards — the mouth that now spoke to him as the morning light crept into the clearing.

'Sir, he did not return. I looked for him, sir.' He twisted his focale between his hands as though wringing it out. 'I thought he was still angry and had decided to stay away to try me. When he did not return this morning, I went to look. I found him then — what was left of him.'

Quintus looked down at the body laid out before him. It was headless and almost naked, stripped of anything useful. The capsarius was leaning over it, working a leaf-shaped iron blade out of its chest.

'Caught in the ribs, sir. His assailant broke off the shaft trying to remove it.'

'A Germani weapon?'

'Without doubt, sir.'

'It was not my fault, sir. He decided to be on his own. I am not to blame.' The man pleaded as much with his own conscience as with his centurion.

Quintus silenced him with a gesture. 'Take him. Wrap him and bury him with honour, as an amicus should.'

The legionary, clearly both bereft and full of guilt, lifted the body tenderly and withdrew.

'Centurion Quintus?' The man who had been in the shadows approached meekly. It was one of the Cantabrians, whether he whose father had fought for Hannibal or he whose father had fought against the Carthaginian general, Quintus could not tell.

'What is it?'

'Two of our horses, precious to us, are missing. Taken in the night.' He held up a hand. 'We do not seek replacements. We just thought you should know.'

'Thank you,' Quintus replied before another demanded his attention. This time it was Rufus.

'Salix has found another man, Quintus. Wounded, not dead.' He looked at Alba. 'He needs help — and I will need help to bring him here.'

'Capsarius, go,' Quintus commanded, then turned to the Cantabrian. 'We have been too careless, my friend. These are enemy lands. My fault. It is time we were more cautious.'

Felix, standing nearby, grunted approval. 'I will see to it.'

Marcus, at his shoulder, glared at Quintus.

'What is it?' Quintus asked abruptly.

Marcus had not planned to speak. He knew his words would be accusatory. Still he blurted it out. 'It must be those boys you let go so easily. I warned you they would be back to haunt us.'

'It does not have to be them,' Quintus argued. 'It could be other Germani, other tribesmen.'

'Perhaps it is just evil spirits? Lemurés?' Marcus was caustic. 'What do you think? Lurking in ones and twos? Stealing horses? Killing and injuring individual legionaries? I think this is no tribe.'

'I suppose you would have liked me to slaughter them,' Quintus spat back. 'I am no Divus Julius or Sulla Felix.'

'No. You are not.' Marcus spoke with contempt.

Quintus grabbed him by the shoulder and spun him around, fire in his eyes.

'Not here.'

A stern voice cut through the anger that gripped both of the men. Sextus had witnessed such a meeting of tempers before on their way to Britannia. It had cost both Marcus and Quintus their rank, pay and position. Here it would cost them discipline, and the respect of their men.

'Save it until later, and do it in private, if you must,' Sextus added in low tones. 'Although I would hope that it is not necessary.'

The two men looked at each other for a long time, then Quintus said quietly, 'I could not have killed them in cold blood, Marcus. In battle or in flight is different.'

'Such decisions are part of the burden of command,' Marcus replied flatly.

The danger had passed. Like two circling wolves, they backed away from each other.

Rufus and Alba returned, holding another injured legionary, his leg cut badly, his sword in his hand, bloodied.

'He was attacked whilst he squatted,' Alba reported. 'It was sheer luck that he had drawn his sword.'

'Not luck,' Marcus grunted. 'Training. Preparation. Discipline.'

'Bind the wound,' Quintus commanded. 'How bad is it, Alba?'

'It is deep,' the capsarius replied. 'It is also full of mud and debris. I will have to clean it.' He looked at the patient. 'It will be painful.'

'Call an assembly, Optio Marcus,' Quintus said coldly. 'I will speak with the men whilst this injury is dressed.'

The assembly was nowhere near as disciplined as it should have been. The men had clearly lost their sense of comradeship, their shared direction. They even began to grumble at the indignity of being called together before finishing their breakfast — forgetting that legionary assemblies were often held before fires were lit. Quintus climbed up onto a rock, Felix standing beside him.

'Silence,' he ordered sternly, then waited until it was totally quiet. 'You are legionaries. Whatever rags you wear, you are soldiers of Rome. Straighten your lines, straighten your backs, and take some pride in who you are.'

He paused again, whilst the men shuffled into better order. As optiones, Marcus and Crassus chivvied the men, but only gently. They feared that if they pushed too hard, there might be a reaction, even a mutiny. Tempers were running hot.

'We have become slack, lacking in discipline and basic sense. You have left your *disciplina militaris* by the wayside,' Quintus continued. He looked directly at the man who had discovered the headless body. The man looked away. 'As a result, there is one man dead and one injured, and some of our auxiliaries' horses have been stolen. I do not know who it is. It is not the lemurés of the Germani dead. It could be the boys from the oppidum that we let go — that *I* let go. It could be —' and here he looked hard at Marcus, daring him to contradict him — 'a small group of tribesmen. Foragers or hunters, perhaps — we have seen bears and heard wolves. Whoever it is, it is our fault that they have been able to strike. We have been acting like children instead of soldiers. If we act like children, we will die.' He changed his tone to one of hope rather than reprimand. 'Men, we will find the legions. We will find General Tiberius, never doubt it. But only if we keep our discipline.'

He paused and looked around, hoping to catch expressions of pride, of comradeship. Some looked at the ground in shame; some looked at him with defiance. It did not matter. They would conform or die; they just had to realise that.

'Centurion Felix,' Quintus invited.

Felix spoke no less forcibly. 'Remember the basic rules of enemy territory. Always armed, blade drawn when away from the camp. Never alone — even to the latrines.' He looked towards the injured man. 'Especially to the latrines. We go in pairs and watch over each other. When we move, we set pickets at the front and rear. We leave nothing regarding safety to chance. At night we dig ditches and post guards. We have become slack. Remember, however we may look, we are Roman soldiers still.'

The men were not, as they had expected to be, dismissed. Instead, Crassus and Marcus gave each group a task before letting them fall out: ditches and defences, guard duty, forward scouting parties, rear pickets and defenders. There were a few moans, but not many. Marcus knew from experience that what the men needed was order. Work gave them order.

'This man will need a litter,' Alba informed Marcus. 'He cannot march; he cannot sit a horse.' A simple stretcher was made and the men took turns to carry it.

'I don't know what we will do with him if we have to cross another river,' the capsarius said. 'For he certainly cannot swim.'

That night, the rain finally stopped and the skies cleared. There was a better feel to the camp that they set up. Trenching tools were used to dig ditches, stakes were sharpened and put in the ground, points upwards, to snare the unwary. Men moved in pairs in whatever task they undertook. Guards were set and all camped close together, auxiliaries included.

Quintus called Sextus across to look at the stars, to see if there were any clues as to which way they should be heading. But the constellations defeated the seer. There were patchy clouds that obscured parts of the sky, but he had hoped to be able to find the Great Bear, or Draco, or the Hunter. But none of these were clear, or were not where they should be in relation to other stars. As the moon, waxing, rose, its light dimmed what stars could be seen and he gave up.

'I cannot tell how far we have travelled,' he said, 'so I cannot say how far we have to go. We rode a long way to the lake shore, and a long way from the lake to the oppidum. For all I know, we have passed the lake on our return journey.' In despair he added, 'Quintus, to be honest, for all I know, we have crossed the Rhenus and are on the other side of it.'

'Not possible.' Quintus shook his head. 'Not possible.' But he knew that Sextus might well speak true. They had been forced to climb hills when they really wanted to descend, to go around mountains when they wanted to go over. They had crossed many rivers and streams, including those they had been forced to swim.

The Rhenus could easily have been one of them, narrowed through rocky terrain, or made shallow and fordable.

'Which way?' Quintus asked.

'South,' said Sextus. 'We can do no better than to go south. Wherever we are in this gods-forsaken land, if we go south we must meet Mare Nostrum. Once we reach the sea, we can find our way home.'

In their hearts both knew that this was a wish unlikely to be fulfilled in the near future. Whilst the coast might be a mere fifty miles away, it could just as easily be five hundred. They had seen no sign of gulls and had caught no smell of the salt sea. They had seen no flat horizon, even from the highest hills that the lookouts had climbed.

XXXI: COLLEGIUM AUGURIUM

There were, for the next few days at least, no further incidents and no further losses. The Cantabrians managed without the two horses. The Anatolians, bows unstrung and strings stowed to protect them from the wet, stayed close to them. The injured man struggled uncomfortably on his stretcher. He did not complain but seemed to be covered in a sheen of cold sweat. The man whose amicus had been killed marched with eyes downcast. He would remain guilty until he could find a time and place to make a sacrifice, both to his dead brother's shade and to Clementia for forgiveness.

Marcus and Crassus maintained strict discipline and the mood of the men changed. Subtly, their irritation with each other turned into a quiet resentment of authority. This, Marcus avowed, was as it should be. The mood swung from possible insurrection to no more than disgruntlement directed at the officers. Marcus grunted approval. He still only spoke to Quintus with great and enforced formality, his ire at their argument still hot. Quintus responded in kind, speaking loftily to his friend as if he were an unwanted newcomer to the company. Their contubernales merely sighed, hoping for a thaw before they had to face anything serious.

The man on the stretcher became full of fear when, beneath its bandages, the wound began to smell. Removing the cloth, Alba found it putrefying, giving off a stink like rotten eggs that turned his stomach. He worked throughout the night, cutting away the dead and dying flesh whilst the man was held down. He bit on a piece of wood to stifle any groans from the pain.

Alba cut right back to pink skin and fresh blood, salved the wound and bandaged it anew.

On the following night, when they stopped, Alba shook his head. His efforts had been to no avail. Even with the bandages in place, he could smell the stench of rotting flesh.

'If he is to survive, he needs to have his leg removed below the knee,' he told Quintus. 'I have no saws, so I could not cut the bone. I could separate the flesh behind the knee with a sharp blade — I would have to use a pugio to do it.'

'Shame we no longer have Tullius in our ranks,' Quintus said with regret. 'His was always the sharpest and cleanest dagger. Shall I tell him, Alba?'

Alba nodded. 'You are his commander, sir.'

Quintus approached the man, who tried to sit up and salute. 'Stay down, friend.' He paused, then plunged on. 'You know what I am going to tell you, even though the capsarius has done his best. If you are going to survive, you need to lose the leg.' He jerked his head towards Alba. 'He can do it, legionary. I have seen him do it before on the battlefield.'

'And did his patients survive?' The legionary's attempt at humour was a brave one.

'Some.' Quintus was blunt but truthful. He knew that in the terrain they were in and the way they were operating, an amputation would be a death sentence. The man knew it too.

'I do not have a will, sir,' he said quietly. 'I would like my people to have what little is coming to me.'

'Jovan!' Quintus called the Macedonian across, then turned back to the legionary. 'This man was a factor in a former life. He will take your words and write them down. I will hold them for you.'

'I thank you, sir,' the man said with great sincerity, 'but if you don't mind, there being no aquilifer, I would like the signifer to hold them. I have made a friend of him over the past few days.'

Rufus was called over. He and Jovan sat down by the light of the fire with the man and took down his words. There was, to their surprise, land — a farm that had been gifted to his father, also a soldier, on his retirement, one of the many benefices of Divus Julius. This land was managed on his behalf by a freedman and a couple of household slaves. There were also offerings to be made in the City to Mars, to Ceres for good harvests and to his household spirits.

'Rufus, as signifer, would you keep this and take it to my family in Brundisium?' he asked.

'I will,' Rufus agreed. 'But it is not necessary. You will be able to take it yourself.'

The man shook his head.

Sextus and Rufus sat with him as night fell, Sextus babbling on about where he had ended up living in Rome.

'At one time I lived on the fifth floor of an apartment block,' he said, describing one of the tenements that Quintus knew had sprung up in the shadow of the Esquiline hill. 'Five dwellings, one on top of the other.'

'Not possible,' said the patient. He had spent little time in Rome and had never seen a proper second storey, let alone several.

'Twice,' Sextus insisted, which the patient immediately misunderstood.

'Ten levels!' the man exclaimed. 'Now I know that you are making it up. Not even the gods have ten levels.'

'No,' Sextus laughed, 'not ten levels, but twice I lived on the fifth level. The first time the entire block collapsed — luckily whilst I was not there, although I lost the few possessions that I had left behind. Nothing of real value — like most, I carried everything I believed to be worth anything with me, on my person.'

Rufus brought water to the man's lips. He was sitting awkwardly, his leg straight out in front of him, but he appeared to feel little pain. 'So the whole thing fell down?' he asked.

'Yes. They often did, or burned. There were even those teetering above me, though I do not think there were more than six levels anywhere.'

'Six!' The man spluttered, astonished.

Jovan, who had remained with them, shook his head. He did not believe it. 'An exaggeration, master, surely,' he whispered to Rufus.

'Perhaps, perhaps not,' Rufus said. 'I have heard of such things falling down, but never of anyone living in them.'

'Indeed. Six,' Sextus confirmed. 'There is not enough land for all those that want it. Although on the other side of the valley, the ancient families have gardens, grounds, pools, fountains, olive groves and more room than they can use. And the not so ancient new money — rich families, traders and successful crooks.'

'How did you cope, living piled on top of each other whilst the rich and powerful looked down their noses at you?' Rufus asked.

'I stayed clean,' Sextus said simply, 'and I tried to make sure I always had a slave in attendance, even if he was a borrowed man. It was an effort, but I had people who owed me favours. It meant that when I walked in the shadow of the Esquiline, the cut-throats and vagabonds knew that I had a sword at my back, that I had friends. They left me alone.' His eyes glazed over as he remembered the worse times and mumbled, 'For the most part.'

A quiet grew between them. The injured man had taken water but refused food, and he eventually waved his companions away, claiming the need for sleep. They left him, Rufus tucking the will away safely.

In the morning the man was gone. He had his own gladius and pugio. Sextus owned up to having given him a coin.

'Rufus, have Jovan add to the will that he died in service,' Quintus instructed the signifer.

Quintus and Felix rode side by side, the men strung out behind them in a column of two, the auxiliaries and slaves bringing up the rear. Their progress was slow. They trudged in grey weather, through wet undergrowth and mud. There were sudden dips and deep holes in the earth — badgers or foxes, perhaps. There were roots and brambles that crossed and twisted and made it dangerous to ride.

They reached the banks of a great slow-moving river, its surface unruffled by anything but the soft pockmarking of the rain.

Quintus raised his hand, calling a halt. 'There is not enough light left today,' he said to Felix. 'Tomorrow we must try to cross.' They were on a sandy bank where for once the trees did not grow all the way to the waterline.

'The wet ground will not make it easy, but we can camp here,' said Felix, signalling to the men to dismount.

Quintus called the scout. 'Agnus, take another with you and go and see what lies along this river. See if there is anywhere where it is easier to cross.'

Agnus saluted and gestured to Alba, and the pair rode off upstream, passing the two men who were wearily marking out the bounds of the castra. The optiones made the legionaries dig a trench and build a proper marching camp, however temporary their stay was going to be. As they finished marking out, the rain miraculously stopped and the sky cleared.

Behind them, the sun was low, dipping towards the treetops. For a moment the men's attention was taken by a murmuration of starlings that rose into the pale sky, sweeping into intricate shapes. The mass of birds swept back and forth like so many legionary banners blown by Aeolus' breath, twisting and writhing in patterns that darkened and lightened as skeins danced across each other.

Hundreds, perhaps thousands, of the little birds formed waves and spirals, curves and ripples, looping and swirling around each other, the noise of their chattering rising and falling as they flew. The men watched the display in fascinated silence, their comments reduced to whispers.

'Does it mean anything?' Rufus asked Sextus anxiously.

'It means that they are seeking a place to roost before dark, nothing more,' Sextus replied with a touch of frustration in his voice. 'Not everything has to have a meaning, my friend. Not all birds need to be subject to augury. It is the fault of the priesthood, of course, and the Collegium Augurium. You know that nothing can begin or end without a sacrifice and an interpretation, without the positive or negative auspices seen in the flights of birds. Every time they give a reading, of course, there is payment.' He smiled at his friend. 'Do you think there is a connection?'

Rufus was stubborn. 'There are many things that need interpretation. Owls flying in daylight, sacred geese honking, birds flying in patterns, stars falling from the sky.' He waved an arm upwards.

Sextus shook his head. 'They are not all honest. The augurs spend their lives deciding whether this or that day is auspicious for public business. Look at how Antonius behaved, closing down the Senate whenever he felt like it.'

Crassus was even more acerbic. 'Caesar's Master of Horse was famous for many things, not least his tendency to abuse his membership of the College of Augurs — to pull his toga over his head and declare the omens were bad whenever a decision seemed to be going against him.'

'And yet he had the right…' Rufus' response was that of the majority of Roman soldiers, who knew that to offend the gods would at least bring ill fortune, or at worst, death.

Crassus remained practical. He was dismissive of omens not directly sanctioned by the state. Sextus was equally sanguine.

'You can see whatever you wish in the flights of birds — the augurs certainly do. But these birds will be here, with this same performance every night, and the fate of the world will not alter.'

XXXII: BARCAE

Alba reappeared with Agnus, trotting along the riverbank on the black colt that he had gained from its previous owner, a Germani chieftain. The scout was excited.

'Sir, there is a group of tribesmen further down the bank, perhaps a mile away. They seem to be guarding *barcae*, rafts or barges.'

Quintus sighed. This would probably mean that they could not camp here, and the work done so far was wasted. He waved a hand at the men to stop digging. 'How many?'

'I could count no more than ten. We could easily overcome them,' said Alba. 'They are not alert, sir. They talk loudly and have a huge fire, and there are no pickets posted. Clearly they feel themselves safe.' He looked across to where the men had stopped working. 'I can see no problem with us camping here, providing we post pickets. There are not enough of them to pose a threat.'

'Guarding rafts?' Quintus mused. 'I wonder, is it some sort of trading post? Show me.'

He rode with the scout and the capsarius to a high point, where they tied the horses. Carefully, they crept forward to see what was happening on the bank. The group of Germani was impossible to miss, and making no attempt to hide their presence. A large and sprawling fire burned near the water's edge, crackling noisily, tongues of flame licking upwards. There were perhaps ten men visible. Four sat at their own — much smaller — cooking fire, while others wandered in and out of the trees. Their barges sat on the water, big enough to transport Quintus' troop. There were shadows of men moving near them.

'Why so large?' Quintus asked, indicating the bonfire. 'It is not necessary for warmth, and they do not appear to be cooking on it.'

'It is too hot a fire for cooking,' Agnus said with a smile. 'I think it must be a signal fire. I can only think that it sends a message to the opposite bank of the river: *we are here; we are safe.* I can see no other function for it.'

Alba looked out over the water. 'It looks deep and still. There might be islands, but I see nothing on them.' It was hard to tell. The light of the fire reflected off the water's surface, merging with the last rays of the setting sun.

With sunset, the starlings finished their performance and took to perching noisily in the trees.

'Listen,' said Agnus. 'Not to the birds. There's something else, Quintus.'

It was a sound that Quintus had not noticed before, which now became obvious. It was a discordant chorus, the harsh croak of bullfrogs calling to each other across the water.

'Frogs,' he said. 'I hear them. Is that what you mean?'

'It is. Frogs do not like rivers. They do not like moving water. I think that this is no river, Quintus. I think perhaps we have found ourselves a lake. Perhaps marshland, but it has grown in size. Look down at where the trail leads into the water. This lake spends much of its life smaller than it is now.'

Quintus nodded in agreement. The track led straight into the water. Storms and torrents of rain did not just happen at sea. There had been heavy rainfall here, and the water lapped up the line of the path. Perhaps by late summer it would be dry. 'It is not our lake, though. I wish it was,' he said. 'It is much further from the tall mountains and much more encroached on by trees. But it is obvious that the water is not flowing.'

He was right. There was no sign of a current, just gentle ripples on the surface. In the foreground, short reeds broke its surface; behind them stands of tall bullrushes rose, their heads nodding brown, crowded at their base with lush grasses clumped and twisted together. There was a large island of rushes in the centre, with two smaller clumps to either side. Quintus looked down at the place where the barges were drawn up.

'A long-term crossing, I think, fixed. Is there a rope?' Quintus asked. If a raft crossing was permanent, it was often marked with a rope, tautened across the water and used by the boatman to pull the barge or raft across. It was easier than using just a pole, and it meant that navigation — even in fog and mist — was not necessary.

'I see no rope,' said Agnus. 'I think they will pole across.'

'Who is the signal fire for?'

'The rest of their number must be on the far side of the lake,' Alba said. 'But I can see no trace of them. I can see no lights, no fires.'

'No ships,' said Quintus quietly. 'No sudden rescue. Agnus, those rafts are ours. We will use them to cross this lake. Stay here, both of you. Watch what they do; watch the far bank. As soon as it is full dark, one of you come back to the camp and report what you see.'

Quintus hurried back to their camp and confirmed the halt to its construction. 'We may yet be camping on the other side tonight, Felix. But they are not to drop their guard.'

Only a little later Alba returned to the castra and, thanks to the new atmosphere of discipline, he was challenged. He passed inside and found Quintus.

'Agnus has remained, sir, but it is full dark and the moon has not yet risen, so we can barely see our hands before our faces. There is an answering bonfire on the far bank. It shows only as a pinprick of light, it is that far away, but it is there. The tribesmen on this bank would be able to see it. We can assume that the tribesmen on the far back can see this one.'

Quintus gathered his chosen troop to him. Crassus, of course, as well as Sextus, Rufus, Marcus and Alba, plus four others. Felix led the rest of the men, including the still-shamed Caius, to where the barges lay at anchor further along the bank. Quintus also had the services of the auxiliaries; the Cantabrians were masters of close combat, and the Anatolian archers were able to provide cover. The Macedonians were tasked with looking after the horses.

The dark beneath the trees was absolute, with the bonfire providing a beacon for them to follow. Its bright flames could be seen through the trees, as well as the shadows of the men feeding it.

They all crept as close as they dared to the enemy. Quintus silently pointed out an individual target for each of the legionaries then, in a signal they all knew — his arm first raised straight then dropped — they acted in concert, each rushing to snuff out his chosen target. The aim was to kill each tribesman swiftly and efficiently, not allowing them time to react.

Whether it was the sharp iron of a gladius thrust through the back and into the heart, whilst the left hand stifled sound, or a blade drawn swiftly across the throat, each ensured a quick and silent death. The idea was that they would avoid a fight. Mostly this was achieved, but not in all cases.

Five of the legionaries found their marks and killed silently and efficiently. Elsewhere there were brief struggles. Sextus' victim was slightly further away and had half-turned before the legionary reached him. The blade found the soft flesh of the man's belly, but Sextus could not prevent him from crying out, or from trying to draw his weapon. Crassus, spinning around from the man he had killed with his pugio, took the tribesman by the hair and drew the bloodied blade across his throat.

There was another man not counted in the original number, who appeared out of the darkness carrying fuel to feed the fire. One of the Anatolians, not having time to nock, ran shouting at him, his short blade raised. Quintus did not know if the victim knew what was happening or merely reacted through instinct. He dropped the timber he was carrying, drew his blade and stabbed. The Anatolian died but, before he hit the ground, two arrows thwacked into his assailant's chest.

Silently and slowly, the man keeled over into the fire, the loose edges of his clothing already smoking as he fell.

The shouts alerted the other Germani and, down by the barges, the attack did not go as smoothly. A quick glance at the scene by the bonfire reassured Quintus that no more adversaries remained, and he called the men to support Felix. There were sounds of splashing and shouting coming from the mooring place. Two tribesmen were caught as they ran back to the fire for help, running straight into Crassus and Sextus.

At the bank, the mooring ropes of one barge had been severed and tribesmen were attempting to push it out into the water. Again an arrow felled one of them.

'Hold!' Quintus ordered. 'Do not shoot. He is one of ours.'

He had spotted that the other head in the water was that of Marcus. It was too dark to make out hair or features, but Quintus knew the way the man moved, the shape of him. He had served with the optio for long enough to recognise him even in this light. Marcus was trying to stop the barge from drifting away in the breeze.

'Help him,' Quintus ordered and, at once, legionaries splashed into the water to make sure the vessel was not lost.

By the other barge, the fight continued in the darkness; it was impossible to tell who was battling who. There were shouts in Latin and Germani along with many groans and splashes.

'Stand back until we can recognise our own,' Quintus commanded. His few men stood off in a semi-circle, cutting down tribesmen who attempted to escape. The sound of fighting lessened and, finally, ceased.

To Quintus' relief, the broad figure of Felix and the lithe shape of Agnus emerged from the gloom, each leading legionaries. They were bloodied but, they assured the centurion, unhurt.

'You men, bring light,' Quintus ordered two of the legionaries, who trotted back to the fire to make torches. 'You two, fetch the Macedonians and the horses,' he ordered two more. 'Felix, let's count our losses and see what we have gained.'

Jovan and Maxim appeared, leading the few horses and the Cantabrian ponies that were left. The dead Anatolian's fellows were already seeing to his funeral rites. For once the auxiliaries had a choice — they could commit his body to earth, water or fire. They chose fire. They wrapped the body so that its face was covered, placed it on a makeshift stretcher of timber and lowered it into the flames. Then they fed the fire until it blazed high into the night.

'Jovan, Maxim, tie the horses, then make sure that the fire remains ablaze. Their compatriots on the other bank must not suspect anything is amiss.' Quintus turned to the capsarius. 'Alba, how many have we lost?'

'Just two are dead, sir.' He nodded in the direction of the bonfire. 'Plus the archer. Two others are badly enough injured to be unable to fight — for now. Their survival is in the hands of the gods.'

'Make sure that Jovan keeps a record of their names. They died honourably in action. Now let's see what it was for. What have we gained?'

The men carried torches, which Quintus and Crassus took down to the waterside. There were two vessels, big and flat — almost big enough to take all of them and their animals.

'Is there enough space for the horses?' Quintus asked Crassus.

'Yes. And the dog,' said the blacksmith. 'Perhaps not all the men.'

Quintus shrugged. 'If they cannot accommodate us all, some of the men will have to swim. They can hold onto the side.' He looked across the lake. 'It is not so far.'

XXXIII: THEATRUM POMPEII

Quintus knew that all the legionaries could swim, whether they liked to or not, for it was a part of their training. They could swim through rivers, or they could build bridges. Water, their generals had decreed long ago, should not halt the passage of arms. By the gods, Divus Julius had even built a bridge over the great river Rhenus so that his cavalry could cross and punish the Germani. He then demolished it, to show how easy it was. Quintus did not wish to start bridge-building, the *barcae* would have to do.

There were no ropes slung across the lake — perhaps it was too far — but there were long poles laid on the bank. They would have to pole the rafts across. Marcus was busy tying up the craft that had been freed by its owner, making sure it was secure. Quintus looked across towards the opposite bank to a pinprick of light where the other half of this operation had their homes. He called a council of his officers.

'If we go tonight — now — we can steer by that fire,' Felix suggested, pointing to the faint glow on the far bank. 'We can steer away from it, so that we do not meet the brothers of these Germani. I do not think that we will be able to see it in the morning, so we might unwittingly land in the midst of them.'

'But if we go now, this fire will die,' Marcus said. 'However much we bank it up, it will signal to them that their men are not feeding it. They will be prepared for us. Unless we leave someone behind.' His eyes strayed to the wounded men.

Crassus saw which way his eyes had wandered. 'These wounded men need treating,' he said, indicating the men that

Alba was inspecting. 'And the Anatolians are still conducting funeral rites. We should wait until morning, all of us. We can note where that fire is and steer clear of it.'

'If we stay, we can use their camp,' said Sextus. 'But we will need to clear the dead away. I do not want any more ghosts and demons dogging our footsteps.'

Quintus opened his mouth to speak when a huge splash and the sound of reeds being flattened and broken came from the water. The legionaries, expecting a Germani attack, were instantly disciplined and ready. There was no time for any sort of deployment or tactics, but four swords were already drawn when an immense bird, a heron or stork, half walked and half flew across the water towards them, its huge flapping wings and high-pitched cry filling the air. It finally managed to lift itself just before it ran into them. It tumbled noisily over their heads, dripping water.

The soldiers found themselves looking foolish, blades drawn against an unarmed avian foe that had disappeared, a bird that they had not even managed to down for the pot. They stood for a few moments, waiting for the inevitable attack from the tribesmen, but it did not come. It was no enemy advance that had disturbed the bird; instead behind it came a dark and wet figure, but one that bore a wagging tail rather than a sharp sword.

'Salix!' Crassus was first to recognise the beast. First one, then the others broke into laughter. Salix ran to Rufus and shook her fur, wetting him.

'At least we showed discipline,' said Marcus, smiling grimly. 'We must be doing something right.'

'It must be considered an omen,' said Crassus as the dog ran up to him, shaking the water from its fur. 'But what in Hades does it mean, Sextus?'

The seer had no chance to respond, as Quintus spoke first. He was no member of the College of Augurs, but he knew how augury worked. If he gave his interpretation first, that was what would be accepted. 'It means that we stay. We do not move tonight.'

The disturbance passed; the night was once more silent over the water. Quintus straightened an imaginary tunic beneath his ragged disguise, tugged down on a non-existent breastplate and tightened his belt — all unnecessary, but all physical signs of a decision made.

'We stay here, we keep this fire lit, and we leave as soon as there is enough light for us to navigate away from the camp on the other bank. We will set pickets, but we will dig no trenches, build no ramparts. We stay close to each other at all times. No-one walks alone, not even briefly. If it is a trading post, there could be traders arriving at first light. We must watch the track keenly. We will load the barges before sunup, ready to go when we can still see the fire on the far shore, and set a course to land beyond it. There will not be much sleep tonight.'

They slept roughly, cloaks wound around them, no camp or attempt at defences made — a grave omission, Quintus knew, but they needed a quick start even before the morning's first light.

There was Germani food and drink — although it was the bitter drink that the tribesmen favoured and which was little to the Roman's liking. There was also, beneath a shelter, a small store of fodder, although the camp did not seem to have any horses. 'It could be for horses that arrive from the other side,' said Crassus. 'Or even for the mounts of those that come to trade. It is ours now. I will load it onto the barges and have the horses ready to board. They will be more willing to go if there is food.'

The night was brief, and Quintus' prediction accurate — there was little rest to be had. Felix made the watches short so that all would serve, whilst others helped the slaves with the fire. Alba stayed awake tending to the two badly injured men until Marcus relieved him.

'I will watch them for a while. You try to rest, capsarius.'

'Thank you, Marcus. I would normally expect Rufus to relieve me. He has taken on the role of medic's assistant.'

'He has other duties. I think he is assistant to the hound.' Marcus pointed to where Rufus was combing twigs out of the dog's fur.

Alba smiled and rolled himself up in his cloak where he could feel the fire.

Crassus loaded the fodder and then, using handfuls of hay, coaxed the horses onto the barges.

'I would rather they had nosebags,' he told Quintus, but there were none here and no time to fashion any. The animals stood towards the centre of each raft, heads down and calm. It was dark still, the moon failing to penetrate the cloud and the light of the fire blotting out any stars there might have been. A soft mist began to lift from the water, almost as if a fire had been lit beneath it.

'This will help,' Quintus said.

When there was light enough to see by, though the sun had yet to rise, Quintus ordered the camp abandoned. Most of the men boarded the two vessels with many prayers and invocations. The barges seemed to float on clouds rather than water and this, along with the unfamiliar early morning sounds of the lakeshore, made the men shiver. They were not afraid but believed that the favour of the gods would always keep them safe and should always be requested. Four of the men, drawn by lot, stripped off their furs and slipped into the water.

They would swim to either side of each barge, holding onto it and helping to steer it. They included Rufus and Caius.

Quintus and Crassus were last to board. Quintus looked at the two loaded barges and asked his friend, 'What have we become? An act in the Theatrum Pompeii? We are now fewer than a third of a century, yet we have auxiliaries — two separate sets of auxiliaries — as well as two centurions, two optiones and a signifer without a banner to his name. We have our own capsarius. We even have slaves and a canine mascot.' He smiled at the sight of Salix, who sat upright at the front of the lead vessel, looking as if she was steering the barge. He turned back to the blacksmith. 'It is no wonder that we struggle to keep discipline in what few ranks we have. There will be more officers than men if we carry on as we are.'

They shoved off, using the long poles to push the barges away from the shore. The horses whinnied but were calmed — by Crassus on one barge and Agnus, with the help of Maxim, on the other. Sextus first drew back in alarm, then sighed to himself as the still figure of a heron appeared out of the mist, its beady eye fixed on the water.

Behind them the fire flared fiercely, but it would not do so for long, even though they had put everything of the camp that could be burned onto it. Quintus was surprised it was still blazing so brightly. For now the tribesmen on the far bank would not know that anything was amiss.

'Did you record the names of the dead?' Quintus asked Jovan.

'I did,' replied the Macedonian.

'What of the injured, Alba? Will they survive?'

It was not the capsarius who answered.

'They elected to stay, centurion. To feed the fire. Their wills are, I believe, with the signifer. They did not want to slow us down. Sir.' Marcus was deliberately over-polite; the pause between the end of his statement and the 'sir' that followed it was full of meaning. Quintus knew that he was being insubordinate; he guessed that the men left behind had been given little or no choice. He also recognised that this should have been his decision, but that he had failed to make it. Effectively, Marcus was pointing out his shortcomings as a commander.

They spent the day on the water, hemmed in by the thick white mist that sat on the lake. The tallest of them — which of course included Quintus — could see above it, could even feel the warmth of the sun. But being able to see did not help. There was nothing to see but a blanket of white, endlessly stretching before them. There was no sign of a tree or bank by which they could steer.

The signal fire and camp rapidly vanished; no other could be seen. By peering above the mist, Quintus could call directions based solely on the position of the sun. He on one barge, Felix on the other, tried to keep the barges moving in the same direction, ever south. The men took turns to use the heavy poles and worried at times when they could no longer feel the bed of the lake, although some said that was a good sign, as they must be near the middle of it. When that happened, the men in the water propelled the barges by swimming.

Towards the middle of the afternoon the sun finally began to burn off the stubborn mist, and the far bank loomed starkly before them, still a long way distant. They had no idea where they were in relation to the enemy camp and had no sight of either of the signal fires.

'Head for the shore,' Quintus ordered, no longer the only pair of eyes that could see the bank. 'We need to be on land before this day is out.'

XXXIV: RHENUS?

The first that they knew of the presence of the enemy was a spear splashing into the water just ahead of the leading barge, another just behind it. A third spear swiftly followed these two, this one burying its head in the timbers of the second barge, making the horses skitter and shy. Then they heard the sounds of men's voices raised in anger.

Their pursuers were flitting in and out of the trees on the shore. Stones splashed into the water to either side of the barges, threatening to take out an eye.

'Shields!' Felix shouted. His barge was nearer to the shore, and so more vulnerable.

Quintus repeated the order for his own vessel. 'Defend yourselves; these are not mere pebbles they are slinging at us.' One skittered across the deck in front of him, a lead pellet, cleverly designed to travel further and faster than mere stones.

He looked, and there seemed to be many tribesmen, certainly more than Quintus and his weary and depleted troop might resist if they faced them on foot. They would just have to escape their wrath by staying on the water.

'We cannot land!' he shouted to the other barge. 'Follow the shore. There must be a place where they cannot pursue.'

'The opposite bank had stretches where the trees came right down to the water, or where soft ground meant that marsh and reed had spread,' said Crassus. 'It was in one of these that the heron had its nest. There must be others.' Another volley of spears reminded them that the enemy was close.

'Let's hope that they do not have boats of their own, Crassus. Anything with oars or sails would be more manoeuvrable and catch us easily.'

'It would also be smaller, Quintus. We could defeat them one by one. If they had warships they would be alongside by now.'

Before them a spit of land jutted out into the lake, a barrier that would block their progress if they could not sail around it, and that would bring the angry tribesmen nearer.

'Past that headland,' Quintus ordered. He pointed to two legionaries. 'You and you — in the water.'

Rufus and Caius were already swimming to either side, pushing the barge away from the spit of land. The two men detailed by the centurion dropped into the water to help. Felix saw what was happening and repeated the action on his own vessel. Gradually the two barges turned. Just when it looked as if they would come up hard against the spit, Crassus shouted, 'Pole, quickly! I have found the bottom.' The other men with poles thrust them deep.

'Shove!' Marcus shouted, as he put his weight against his own pole. The barge moved and the pole was almost left behind, but the ungainly vessel finally cleared the spit. Quintus sighed with relief as he saw the reeds pass by. They had been close to running aground.

To the other side, a great featureless expanse of water stretched out in front of them, hardly a ripple disturbing its surface. The land beside and behind them receded as the poles bit deep into the lakebed, but no other bank or trees could be seen ahead. Although their pursuers could follow them onto the spit, they could not shadow them any further without doing so on the water.

Quintus looked at Sextus questioningly. Sextus understood. He stretched over the side, cupping the water in his hand and tasting it. 'Fresh, still, Quintus. It is not seawater.' Quintus sighed with relief.

Half an hour out from the spit, Marcus called, 'We have lost the bottom, Quintus. We cannot pole any more for now.' He lifted the pole from the water and rested it on the stern of the barge.

The spit of land and the trees behind it gradually fell away as the swimmers slowly moved the barges. The sun sank out of sight where their enemies had been, lighting up the cloud-riven sky.

Quintus ordered the men out of the water, so they could dry in the warmth of the evening. They needed fires for hot food, but did not dare light them, for fear of setting the craft alight. Boats designed to spend the night on the water had raised areas and iron grates to contain fires. This had nothing of the sort. It was an uncomfortable night under the star-strewn sky.

The rising sun revealed them to be still marooned, floating in a wide stretch of water. Marcus tasted it and reported it as still fresh. The barges were being tugged south, gently but insistently. The breeze that came out of the north also pushed them inexorably in the same direction. In the night Quintus had let them drift; now he once more sent men into the water.

'We are making good speed,' said Sextus as he joined Quintus at the bows, bringing the centurion one of the twice-baked biscuits that were currently the main ration for the men. 'There is even a bow wave of sorts.' They both looked at the tiny white disturbance in the water.

A few twigs and branches floated past, which could have been moved by the wind. Then a log, too big for the breath of this wind, first caught up with them, then spiralled past. Quintus watched as it overtook them and continued on southward.

'That is more of a tree than a mere branch,' he said. 'There is a current pulling it.'

'It is a river,' Sextus said. 'I am sure of it. Flowing out of the lake. It may even be the source of the river we seek.'

'The Rhenus,' Quintus said. 'General Tiberius. Have the gods really smiled on us for once?' The craft was gathering speed, the swimmers holding on rather than pushing. 'Try the poles,' he ordered. 'If they bite, fetch the men out of the water. We do not want to be carried away on this current. There could be rocks and rapids; there could even be waterfalls. We have seen the like before. The current is going south; we need to pole across it, west, until we find the far bank.'

On his barge Felix and Marcus grabbed a pole each, and they thrust them deep into the water. 'Nothing!' Marcus shouted.

Crassus and Rufus were doing the same on their barge. 'A bite,' called Crassus. 'I touched the bottom.'

They all tried again. 'Me, too,' called Felix, then, 'Out, out, you men. Get yourselves on board.'

'Look!' cried Quintus. 'Trees, a riverbank.'

Across from the barges a line of grey could be seen on the water, at first looking like no more than cloud. Then an uneven line of more solid shapes appeared, which turned out to be the tops of a forest. Finally, individual trees emerged, and the bank beneath them eroded with bush and shrub. They poled desperately, turning the flat bow of the vessels towards the greenery even as the speed at which they were drawn south increased.

'There!' Quintus pointed ahead. 'Make for that spot.'

It was a spit of land like the one they had passed the day before, but this one stuck out into the river from the western bank. It was the shape of an elbow, like the bar across a harbour mouth. If they could steer the barge within its ambit, it would enfold them and bring them to a stop in calm water.

The barges were difficult to steer, especially with the current pulling so hard at them.

'We are not going to make it,' said Caius, standing at the front of the barge.

'We are,' said Quintus, standing next to him and willing the vessels into the makeshift harbour.

'The gods are with us,' Sextus reassured him.

Marcus heard. The craft were dangerously close together and he cursed, shoving his pole deep into the riverbed and heaving. He could have shoved the other barge away, saved his own vessel and let Quintus take his chances, but he refrained, managing to move his craft out of the way without touching the other. 'Strong men are what we need, Sextus, and luck. Pray that training is stronger than this current, if you think that will help.'

The barge bumped against the peninsula and turned dangerously to continue its journey down the river. The shove that Marcus gave to the pole moved it the fraction required to ensure that it span into the calm water inside the elbow. The other barge, with two men poling on the side facing the lake, was likewise forced into the sheltered water.

As his vessel touched the shore, Quintus was powerless to stop first the dog, which, at the smell of earth, splashed into the water and swam ashore, then the horses, which were equally keen to find dry land. 'Follow, men,' he ordered, as they looked to him.

Crassus was first to disembark, not wanting to lose the horses. The other men followed. Felix also ordered his men ashore. He sought Quintus. 'Do we rest? Do we camp? It is still early in the day.'

'We rest and eat, men and animals — we need to unload whatever fodder is left. No fortifications, not yet anyway, but we post guards around our fires.' He called beyond Felix, 'Maxim, Jovan, fires and hot food. Is there meat?'

'Some, dominus,' Jovan said. 'We brought meat from their camp. We have meal still.'

'Then we need breakfast — get to it.' Quintus addressed Felix again. 'Set pickets around the perimeter in pairs. We do not need to watch the water; anyone following will be visible for a long time.' He looked out over the expanse of the lake, seeing the tips of the mountains that bordered its far northern reaches, and the detritus of the forest being drawn past by the river currents. 'We were fortunate, my friend.' He put his hand on Felix's shoulder. 'We could easily have ended up like that branch, heading who-knows-where in the river. I will set the seer to work.'

Felix grunted his agreement. 'I will leave you him — and the scout and the blacksmith.' He saluted and went to set pickets.

Quintus called Sextus to him first. 'Have the archers bring down something we can sacrifice, and thank the gods for our good fortune. If they cannot do it, it will have to be a libation, but it must be done.' Sextus nodded. Next Quintus called Crassus. 'Check the horses out; make sure they are fed and watered. We are likely to be riding them before the end of the day. Use the Cantabrians to help, they know horseflesh.' Finally, he called Agnus across. 'Find out what you can. Are we in enemy country? Are we threatened at all? Are we anywhere nearer our goal?' He turned to look at the river being borne behind him. 'Would that this were the Rhenus, but I do not feel it is.' He raised a hand to stifle the scout's objections. 'I do not know why, Agnus. It is just a feeling. Take someone with you.' He dismissed the scout with a wave of his hand.

Agnus fetched his black colt from Crassus' care and shouted to Rufus to accompany him, who, in turn, whistled Salix. The dog bounded after them, excited and desperate to run. They rode off as the slaves coaxed flame from kindling and Felix, with a series of commands backed up by Marcus, brought order to the camp. They were all glad to be off the water.

Maxim approached with a question. 'The barges, dominus. The timbers above the water will burn. The poles will burn. Should we?'

'Not until the scout returns,' Quintus said after a moment's thought. 'Though they are hard to manoeuvre, we may yet need them.'

He hoped not.

XXXV: PAVIMENTUM

It took less than an hour for the spot on the riverbank to look familiar and ordered. The Macedonians lit two fires and were each cooking, one boiling a shallow iron pot of meal and water, the other rotating the meat found in the enemy camp. There was a perimeter of logs and felled trees — small ones, but big enough to provide a platform if necessary. The horses were tied, and the guards were posted.

Salix announced the return of the scouts, the hound bouncing into the camp, seeking a friend who had meat to spare. Agnus and Rufus followed and reported. 'We have found something, sir. Something you need to see.'

'Good or bad?'

'Good, we think,' said Rufus. 'But you will have to judge.'

Quintus mounted up and signalled Felix to join him. 'Is it far?'

'Half an hour's ride should bring us close enough,' said Agnus.

They rode and Salix ran, the centurions intrigued, until suddenly they emerged into a treeless plain, a long gentle slope falling to the south. They halted and looked on the landscape with wonder. This was not a natural break, but a manmade one, trees felled along a straight line that vanished into the distance. They proceeded on foot into the cleared area cautiously. Agnus and Rufus had ridden a little way ahead; their shadowy outlines could now be seen pulling up and dismounting, waiting for the others.

'Take care,' Quintus said to Felix and both drew their swords. 'This looks open and dangerous.'

'I do not think that we have anything to fear, sir,' Felix said. 'Look.'

Where he pointed, Quintus could see that they were on the edge of a deep ditch that ran across their path. The ditch sloped upwards to a surface, tamped down by many feet, curved to allow water to drain.

'It is without doubt a road, Quintus. A Roman road. Not yet paved, I grant you, but a Roman *pavimentum* nevertheless. It must lead to the legions.'

The road ran down the valley in which they now marched, between the two tall hills.

'We crossed it, sir,' Agnus said. 'We have peered further down the valley. There is a camp.'

'We thought that it must be General Tiberius,' Rufus added. 'But it is in a valley, shrouded in mist, so it is hard to be sure. We could see no standards, no eagles. We could hear no trumpet calls, and we were stopped by no patrols. It is an army, and I can confirm a Roman army, but how many legions strong it is impossible to say.' He shook his head. 'In the mist we could not even see fortifications. We could not see for the fog. Sir, it might not be the general; we just could not tell for certain.'

'But it is someone, and someone Roman. Who else could it be?' Quintus asked. In the failing light, he cursed that they had not thought to bring torches. Then he made a decision. 'Mount up. Let's go and look.'

The four of them trotted across the road, following Agnus to where he and Rufus had viewed the camp. As the sun travelled towards the horizon, it dipped under a bank of low cloud. Beneath it was suddenly bright, and Quintus could see to the plain below. At the foot of the valley, two rivers merged, glowing silver in the sun. One flowed from the south, the other from the east. To the north, a steep mountain, shaped like a spear point, struck up through the clouds. To the west, a solid massif cast a broad shadow. The western-flowing river was sluggish and wide, great curves and meanders showing the flatness of the plain. The other tumbled quick and merry down the mountain through rocks and narrow ravines.

The reflection from the point where the waterways met was dazzling, enough to make Quintus need to shade his eyes. But as his eyes adjusted, he was amazed by what they saw. In the triangle of land between the two silver trails was a castra — a Roman camp of at least two legions, perhaps more. He shook his head with relief and turned to Felix.

'Look at it, friend. At last. One of those must be the Rhenus, and this must be Tiberius.'

Felix peered across the valley. 'It could be. But it looks more like a colonia than a castra to me.' He shook his head. 'I don't know what in the blessed name of great Jupiter it means.' He was mounted, knee to knee with Quintus, the dog sitting patiently at the feet of the horse.

'It means that the scouts were right,' said Quintus. 'It is a legionary camp without a doubt, and a big one. It means that we have found the general. Soon we will be eating proper hot food and perhaps even drinking wine. Our long, damp days of posing as the enemy may finally be at an end. Can we make it tonight, Felix? What do you think?'

'Why camp in the open when we could be under a roof — or at least decent canvas?'

'I agree. Agnus, fetch the troop, by my order. Tell them we have found Rome and that, if they hurry, tonight we could sleep indoors. Bring torches — we will need them.'

Within an hour, the two centurions could see a line of lights approaching. As they came nearer, they saw that Marcus and

Crassus rode at the head of the troop, with the men in a column of two behind them. They soon joined Quintus and Felix on the road.

The men stopped and stared at what lay below. The road ran in a straight line until it was lost in the dusky red haze of the west. It ran from the mountains that loomed on the horizon to the main gates of the huge, populated square that lay far beneath them. It drew their eyes to the camp. Pinpricks of light were beginning to appear in the valley as torches were lit on the perimeter of the castra. As the gathering gloom deepened, myriad fires within could also be seen.

The fortification was marked out in traditional fashion. It had two main streets running at right angles to each other, but then other streets criss-crossing these, dividing the area within into ever decreasing squares. Yet none of these squares were small; most would have swallowed the oppidum in which they had spent the winter.

'Do you see any buildings, anything solid?' Quintus asked Felix.

'No,' Felix replied. 'Although it is hard to make out from here.' He shaded his eyes. 'I think the porta decumana appears to be closed with a tree trunk, rather than a gate.'

As fires were lit another camp, much less well organised, could be seen spreading to either side of the western gate.

'Look down there,' Quintus said, indicating the unofficial camp. 'There are followers, natives. It will not be long before all of us will be able to drink and gamble to our hearts' content.'

'There are women there,' Sextus said with a grin. 'There are bound to be women. The "wife" that Rufus left behind in Lucus Augustus will by now have declared him dead and separated herself from him. But here he might find another. So might I.'

Rufus allowed himself a smile. He remembered his wife with affection, even though his 'marriage' was forbidden and had led to him being demoted as punishment.

'Perhaps I will take a mistress, Sextus, rather than a wife.'

Marcus rode forward for a better view. 'Look, a patrol is leaving by the south gate of the via principalis. There are more men in it than our company. There are standards at the head of it, but I cannot see how many. Nor can I see if any is an eagle, although there must be at least one in the castra.'

The patrol that Marcus saw was kicking up dust, with many standards and vexilla flying above the horses' heads. He was right; it was probably fifty men.

'We will be stark against the sky,' Crassus said. 'If they see us, we will look like Germani and that patrol could well turn on us. We should drop beneath the skyline.'

'Agreed,' said Quintus, turning the head of his horse and crossing the ditch that marked the edge of the road. The others followed and, dismounting, made their way in a low crouch back onto the crest.

The darkness of night meant that they could clearly see all that was lit, but little else. But they could hear. The breeze had turned and now carried sounds from below, floating up in ghostly snatches. There were animal sounds: horses and cattle. There were the sounds of fowl: geese, chicken and ducks. Suddenly, with great clarity, there was the clang of metal on metal from a forge. A dull background hum of voices was punctuated by the shouts of officers and the clear notes of cornua. It was evening; the gates were being closed and an assembly being called. It felt like a homecoming.

The men returned, still low to the ground, to where their horses were being held by the Macedonians.

Marcus urged a swift return to the legions. 'We should go down there tonight,' he said. 'It cannot be too long a ride. We would be welcomed.'

Crassus did not share his optimism. 'Maybe we would, but maybe not. We do not look like anything that might be greeted with open arms.'

'Perhaps we would be recognised and honoured as an irregular troop of heroic legionaries marching from a great victory over the Germani,' Sextus said sarcastically.

'Felix, what do you think?' Quintus asked.

'Tomorrow, in daylight, I think that we would have a better chance of not being seen as a threat.'

'What if they are striking camp in the morning?' Marcus asked.

'Then we follow,' said Quintus, simply. 'Felix is right. We wait to present ourselves at an appropriate time. Sadly, we need to camp here, in the open, at least for one more night. The men will be disappointed, but we could go back to the water's edge.'

'We left that camp,' Marcus argued. 'The men will not wish to go backwards. At least from here we can see Tiberius' camp and know that we will be in it tomorrow.'

'Very well, but make sure we are well away from the road. There should be engineers here...' Quintus left the thought hanging.

Marcus shrugged and reluctantly gave the command. 'Make camp, men, away from the road. We will visit the castra tomorrow.'

Felix added to the instruction. 'No half measures, men. We are still in enemy country, however close the legions might be.

We still need a ditch and other protection. We still need guards, and we remain in twos.'

The night was short and the men slept little, full of excitement at what they saw as a homecoming. Despite their losses in the forest, they were still a company of almost thirty in total, enough to put up a fight.

At daybreak, Quintus called an informal assembly with those legionaries not on guard or picket duty. The dismantling of the temporary camp was put on hold.

'Take a look at us,' Quintus said, waving an arm to encompass all those there. 'We must be wary of how we approach this castra, or we will be dead as soon as we are within range.' The men looked at themselves and realised that Quintus was right. The furs had kept them warm throughout the winter, but they were ragged now. The rest of the native gear was also of dubious quality and, despite the efforts of Jovan and Maxim, in poor repair.

Marcus had a suggestion. 'The Cantabrians are in their own clothes and recognised as auxiliaries, as are the Anatolians. Perhaps we should send them down first?'

'If anyone other than you made that suggestion, I would have said they were using them as bait, to see if they survive,' Quintus said, with just the hint of a smile. 'But as it is you, I am sure that is not what is in your heart.'

Marcus began to speak, then thought better of it, setting his mouth in a grim line. He would not give Quintus the satisfaction of either confirming or denying his intentions.

'We have to convince them that we are Romans, citizens,' said Felix. 'It will not be easy, dressed like this.'

'Sir, sir!' The meeting was abruptly interrupted by Maxim, shouting and waving his arms. 'They have taken them captive. They will surely kill them.'

XXXVI: LUPERCALIA

'Who?' Quintus demanded. 'Who has taken who captive?'

Maxim was breathless. 'Soldiers, sir. Legionaries. They have taken Rufus and Agnus and my cousin. They trapped them by taking the dog. Our men were on patrol with Salix. These men held her prisoner, used her as bait to lure them in. They came from nowhere.'

'Not from nowhere, Maxim, but from the castra below.' Quintus shook his head, annoyed with himself. 'I should have expected it.' He raised his voice. 'Crassus, take men and confirm his story. See if they are still there. If they are, free them if you can. If not, come back quickly.'

Crassus wasted no time. 'Marcus, with me. You, you and you.' He tallied off three of the men. 'Show us,' he ordered Maxim.

The Macedonian led them out of the clearing and down towards the sound of water. They could hear the fast-flowing stream from their camp. It would be one of many that fed the great river that dawdled beneath them. The group followed his lead, crashing into the bushes. Crassus called the dog's name as they fought their way through thorny thicket, which closed behind them as they made their way downhill.

'They were by the water,' panted Maxim. 'It is down here somewhere.'

They burst out onto the sandy bank of the stream, still calling the dog. But it was not there; neither were the legionaries or their own comrades. They did find some signs — footprints, broken branches, disturbed ground — but that was it. There was nothing for them to do but report back to

Quintus. They found him in front of a fully armed party of men, ready to fight.

'There is no one there,' said Marcus. 'No one to fight. They have gone — and taken Rufus, Agnus, the Macedonian and the dog with them.' He did not need to add, '*this is your fault Quintus*', it was in his narrowed eyes and clenched jaw.

'They must be taking them to the castra,' said Felix.

'They thought they were capturing Germani,' said Maxim. 'That is what I heard them say. They thought they were capturing enemy tribesmen and escaped slaves.'

'Tell me what happened,' commanded Quintus, signalling to the men at the same time. 'Stand down for now. Finish striking the camp. We must go down to the castra today. Now we have no choice.'

Maxim was shaking with anger. 'It was unfair, sir. It was shameful. Our men only sought the dog. She had gone ahead, "chasing her dinner" according to Rufus. She was running after a squirrel or rabbit and vanished into the dense undergrowth. Her master called her, tried to tempt her back with bits of meat.'

'What of it?' Quintus snapped. This seemed irrelevant. The men were more important than the hound.

'It was the dog that trapped them, sir,' Maxim said very quietly.

'Go on,' ordered Quintus brusquely.

Maxim continued nervously. 'Sir, I joined in with the hunt, as did my cousin. It was light-hearted, as if we were celebrating a festival in the morning air. Today we would sleep once more under Roman skies, Master Rufus had said. We were confident we could find Salix.' He hung his head. 'We had no thought for our safety. I was caught on a thorny vine a few paces behind them when they reached the river, but I could see, sir. They burst out onto the bank and pulled up sharply — and then I saw why they stopped so suddenly.'

He paused for breath. 'There were two legionaries on the far side of the stream, fully equipped, swords drawn. Between them a third held Salix by her neck, as she wriggled and whimpered. The sight of her master was enough for her to squirm with greater energy, and for the man handling her to loosen his grip in shock. The result was that Salix freed herself and ran to Rufus, splashing through the shallow water with her tail wagging. As Rufus was distracted by the dog, two more legionaries appeared to either side of the three of them.' He lowered his voice. 'I drew back, sir. I hid to escape capture.'

'Maybe not a noble action, but the right one,' said Quintus. 'Carry on.'

'I heard them, sir. "This one is an escaped slave," one said. "He carries a blade. Look, he has a slave mark; RRE is inked." And another said, "These two are Germani spies, wearing stolen Roman gear."'

By now a small crowd had gathered, listening to the Macedonian's story. They all knew that RRE stood for *Res Romani Exercitus*, 'Property of the Roman Army', a standard slave marking.

'The new men who arrived were fully armed, their swords drawn. Rufus, Agnus and Jovan had almost no Roman equipment between them. The signifer even wears Gaulish moustaches.' He held his hands up, offering an apology as if it was his fault. 'I am sorry, sir. Two of the legionaries reached across and disarmed them. Jovan first, roughly.'

'Not your fault,' muttered Quintus as he gestured for the man to continue.

'The middle soldier on the far bank asked, "Who or what are you?" Agnus replied, "We are Roman. We are of Legio Nine

Hispania, on a special mission for General Tiberius." But they did not believe him, sir. They mocked him. They mocked his northern accent, saying he was no Roman but a tribesman masquerading as one. Then the biggest of the men reached for his helmet. He was a centurion, sir. An officer. I thought he would see sense. But he did not. Instead he laughed and said, "This is no camp of Tiberius. General Tiberius is not here. But we do have an escaped slave and two renegade tribesmen with a dog. This will be a story worth telling." Then he ordered his men to take them.'

There was an audible intake of breath in the clearing.

'This could mean nothing but death,' Crassus said. 'They mean to make an example of them, a spectacle.'

'Perhaps they have built an arena,' said Marcus bitterly. 'Perhaps they intend to make them fight for entertainment.'

'They are no gladiators,' fumed Quintus, desperately hoping that he would not have to defend his leadership again. 'And I doubt that a marching camp is staging funeral games. Repeat what you said about Tiberius,' he ordered the Macedonian.

'He said "This is no camp of Tiberius. General Tiberius is not here," sir.'

'You are certain?'

'Yes, sir. "Tiberius is not here."'

'Then who commands? Who has Fortuna sent to stand in our way?'

'It may be *bon Fortuna*, Quintus,' Sextus offered gently. 'It may be that a different commander treats us better.'

Quintus sighed at his own decision to spend another night as irregulars. 'You are right. It could be a turn for the better. Perhaps I should not always assume the worst of the gods?' He looked upwards quizzically, then back at the men. 'But I have seen the castra. It is large enough for at least two legions and auxiliaries, maybe more. There is no way we could mount a rescue. Whoever commands, we must go down to them openly and declare who we are. General Tiberius sent us on a mission. We have accomplished it and now we return. Their commander must recognise us.'

'Like this?' Marcus asked, spinning round to better show off his tattered furs and patched trews. Despite the seriousness of the situation, there was a ripple of laughter that he did not expect. He glowered.

'More like this,' offered Crassus as he removed his furs. He pulled the Germani shirt over his head as he explained. 'At the moment we are Germani tribesmen speaking Latin. Jovan and Maxim are not even that; they are Macedonians marked as slaves.' He tugged at the leather cross ties on his legs as he spoke. 'I do not think the legionaries were acting out of spite. I think I would have made the same assumptions.' With difficulty, he pulled off the brightly coloured trews and adjusted his baltea and cingulum over his undershorts. His baldric crossed his bare chest, carrying his gladius. Already he looked more Roman. 'We need to look more like this,' he said, presenting himself to Quintus.

'Crassus is right. Look at him. He is no native.' Quintus shook his head. 'I do not blame them. They did what they thought was right. They captured spies. But let us not fall into the same trap. Let us not be taken as enemies.' He raised his voice, demanding the attention of all the company. 'Men, our journey as Germani tribesmen is over. Today we go down to the castra. We will time our arrival for their evening assembly, when most of them are lined up before the praesidium and discipline prevails.'

He pointed to his amicus and optio. 'Do as Crassus does. Strip down to all that is Roman and no more. Discard the furs and leathers. Remove the trews. Even the short tunics and shirts must go. We have time to cut the worst of each other's hair, to wash, to shave. Leave the round shields and short spears that mark us as native behind. Make sure your gladius is worn properly, as if on parade. Polish and clean your baltea and cingulum. The auxiliaries will march and ride behind us, as they should.'

He addressed Maxim directly. 'The slave we have left will also walk behind us, clothed in the cleanest of the tunics remaining, but not trews. He will be unarmed. His head will be bowed.'

Maxim nodded in understanding.

There were few murmurings amongst the men and no questions. They could see what needed to be done.

Quintus turned to Felix. 'If you had been that centurion, Felix, what would you have done?'

'Sought a reward,' Felix replied, cynically. 'For that I would need to deliver the captives to my commander.' He pursed his lips. 'That is easier to do if they are alive. I think that they live but are being held prisoner. A centurion seeking a reward or commendation would not ask any but the commander to judge. A junior officer would not dare to pass sentence in case he was wrong, so we must pray that the commander is absent, or too busy to deal with such a thing at once.'

'I agree. There is little we can do but approach the fortress as I have said, and hope our comrades have been kept alive.' He turned to the men. 'Go, make yourselves Roman again. Hurry.'

The men dispersed, some already calling to Maxim to make them more presentable. He wished he had his cousin for company. Whilst hair was cut and beards trimmed or chins shaved, the men revelled in throwing off the trews and furs of the enemy and discarding the round shields and short spears.

'I am a little reluctant to discard the trews,' Alba said to Crassus. 'They have proved remarkably warm throughout the winter and are very good at keeping away the malign intentions of brambles and thorns. I have had little in the way of stings and scratches to deal with.'

'Yet they must go,' said Crassus solemnly, half drawing his pugio. 'I can cut them away if you wish…'

'That will not be necessary,' laughed Alba. Like the rest of the men, he was now in high spirits. By tonight they would once more be part of the Roman army. They would be fed, housed, warm and safe. There might even be wine — there would certainly be posca. Alba undid the leather ties and pulled off the trews, tearing them to force them past his caligae.

'It is like Lupercalia,' laughed Sextus as he pulled off his roughly mended shirt. 'But at least my undershorts appear intact.' This was not true of all the men. Some found themselves more naked than they would have wished once the trews had gone. Like schoolboys let out early, the men began to chase and tease each other, laughing.

The Anatolians just shook their heads. 'Sir? What is happening?' they asked Quintus plaintively, the three of them crowding close.

'These fools are just enjoying the moment, pretending it is Lupercalia, the spring festival of fertility. String your bows. Make yourselves look as much like auxiliaries as you can.'

'We are as we are,' said their spokesman. They wore dyed belted tunics of dark red or forest green over loose trews. A long blade, more knife than sword, was thrust unsheathed into each of their belts. Their great bows were over their shoulders, unstrung for now. Their full quivers were on their backs. In battle they wore a round helmet but were now bareheaded.

Quintus smiled, understanding what they meant. 'You could not be mistaken for any other,' he said kindly. 'Nor could the Cantabrians.'

The horses, too, had any extra accoutrements removed, though none — not even the Cantabrians — had emulated the Germani by taking heads and hanging them from the horses' necks.

The activity and jollity kept them warm, but as the afternoon waned and the westering sun threw ever longer shadows, they realised that they had little to keep them from the cool of night. They needed to move soon.

XXXVII: ROMANI SUMUS

The legionaries were bare of chest and head, each wearing baltea and cingulum over either what was left of their undershorts, or loincloths fashioned from Germani shirts. Each had a baldric with its gladius and a pugio in a sheath at their belt. Their cloaks were long gone. Their bare legs ended in military caligae. This, above all, should convince the legionaries that they were Roman.

The officers had no insignia, no plumed helmets, vine staffs or hastilia to proclaim their station. There were no standards or vexilla, and certainly no eagle.

'I miss the Eagle of the Fifth, Sextus,' said Quintus, as he pulled himself aboard his horse. 'With it I felt we were if not blessed, at least protected.'

'We were both,' agreed Sextus, as he also mounted. Behind the horses the men fell into a column of two.

'Quick march,' Quintus ordered as he led them towards the castra. 'And sing — as filthy and loud as you like.'

Crassus led the verse and the men were soon singing the chorus. Only Marcus marched along in morose silence. The rest sang the raucous tale of how a great general of legend had mounted every animal on Jove's earth, one after the other, from the mouse to the elephant. The veterans knew that this was a song of General Caesar's men, before he became divine. It would not do now to mention him by name, so another general, a work of fiction, was substituted.

They looked, marched and sang like legionaries as they came out of the forest and began to cross the ground.

Quintus and Felix rode side by side, eight more men mounted behind them, this being all the horses they had. A column of two on foot followed, each man singing loudly. Behind came the Anatolians with their great bows and the remaining Cantabrians, mounted on their rugged ponies. Finally there was Maxim, in a simple grey tunic.

Patrols of men were busy digging ditches, fetching timber and foraging for food. They did not see this parade as a threat; they merely goggled at the strange sight. The legionaries stopped their work and gaped at the spectacle, then raised a ragged cheer for the song.

When the troop had descended sufficiently, they could see that some groups were working with boats and cargoes on the river. These, too, stared in amazement. Another group — engineers, by the look of them — stood measuring and recording distances for a project to one side. Whilst they also stared open-mouthed, they made no move to intercept Quintus and his men. There were no challenges. The column was at the gate before guards halted it. Seemingly they were so fascinated by the sight and sound that they temporarily forgot their duty.

'Hold,' ordered one, by rank a tesserarius. At a signal from Quintus the men halted; another signal made them stop singing. The guard spoke officiously. 'The river flows ever to the sea.'

Quintus happened to know this one — he had heard it before — and was tempted to provide the correct answer. Felix, who also recognised it, said firmly, 'No. We do not know it, Quintus. We are not of this camp. We need to be met, not admitted.' He addressed the guard. 'We do not have the password.'

'Then declare yourselves,' said the guard. 'Are you friend or foe?'

'*Romani sumus*,' said Quintus proudly. 'We are Roman. We were once a cohort of Legio Nine Hispania but were transformed by General Tiberius into a special group. We were sent disguised as tribesmen to punish those who dared oppose him on the waters at the head of the Rhenus. He called us his scutarius, his shield-bearer.' He added, 'I am First Spear Centurion Julius Quintus Quirinius, cohort commander in the absence of our noble officers, fallen in battle. This is Centurion Marcus Caelius Felix, commander of Century Four.'

Felix dipped his head in acknowledgement. Quintus continued in plain tones, trying not to sound boastful. 'We have completed our mission, taken the oppidum of the enemy, and driven them into the snow. Now we are back at the Rhenus and General Tiberius will vouch for us.'

'General Tiberius is not here,' said the first guard, a crooked smile on his face. He seemed pleased to give them this information. 'And neither of these rivers is named Rhenus.'

His companion was equally amused. 'These are the legions of General Drusus and he, too, is not here. But I like your story. Look behind you, friend; this is no cohort. Look at yourself and your companion. You are not centurions. Where are your crests? Where are your vine staffs?'

The first picked up the refrain. 'Which enemy oppidum? Cherusci? Chatti? Suebi? What are you really? Deserters? Tribesmen? Spies of the enemy?'

'We are as I said we are,' Quintus insisted. 'We even have our own auxiliaries.' He pointed behind.

The legionary laughed. He was dismissive. 'You cannot just dress up as people and claim to be them. These men on horses are masquerading as … what? They look like tribesmen of

Germania to me.' He called out a command. 'Dismount. All of you.'

'Do as he says,' ordered Quintus, when none moved. With a clatter, the men dismounted and stood by their horses. A legionary, beckoned by the guard, pulled them to one side. The unit looked even smaller without its cavalry.

The movement seemed to reveal something to the tesserarius. He peered theatrically, his hand shading his eyes. 'You seem to have a single slave to your name.'

His comrade sniggered. 'I think we may already have the rest.'

Quintus was about to reply when a languid voice came down from one of the raised platforms that framed the gate. 'Disarm them; they should not be carrying Roman weapons until we determine who they are.'

Quintus heard. Immediately he ordered, 'Form square, defend.' At once and with a smoothness borne of familiarity with the manoeuvre, the men fell into a rough diamond shape, the two centurions at its apex, Cantabrians to the rear, Anatolians in the centre, arrows nocked.

'We will die first!' Quintus shouted up to the hidden officer. 'You will have to wipe us out!'

'We could,' came the same voice, dripping confidence. 'As you well know.' But the tone changed and an instruction was given to the guards. 'Bring them in; confine them but leave them their blades. They will not use them.' Quintus caught a glimpse of a crested helmet. 'You will swear an oath, centurion. By Jupiter, Mars and Caesar Augustus. Your blades will stay sheathed in this place. Do you so swear to keep the peace?'

'I do.' Quintus' fist went to his chest. 'And for these men also. By Jupiter Optimus Maximus, by Mars, by great Caesar Augustus, *divi filius* and by Ceres, protector of my household.

By my household manés and larés and the spirits that the Cantabrians and Anatolians revere, by…'

'That is enough,' said the voice sharply. 'Do not descend into mockery, centurion. The auxiliaries and horses I will accept back into our ranks. You must wait to be judged.'

The crested helmet turned away, but not before Quintus caught a fleeting view of its owner's face in profile. 'That nose,' he blurted out. 'That voice. That is Centurion Atticus, without a doubt.'

'It is,' said the tesserarius, amazed. 'How could you know that?'

'I have dealt with him before. But he does not belong here. If these are the legions of General Drusus, Atticus cannot be here. He is one of Tiberius' men.' Quintus was jubilant. Clearly they had been lying to him. This was Tiberius' army after all.

'He is of both,' said the guard dourly, puncturing Quintus' sudden euphoria. 'He will be of Tiberius' army once more when General Drusus sends him back with messages. He is an envoy that travels between the brothers, even sometimes to the father, to Caesar himself. Enter, centurion.'

A single gate swung open and, on Quintus' command, the sorry remnant of the once proud cohort formed a column of two and marched smartly into what Quintus could only think of as a city. The auxiliaries were led off elsewhere, the Cantabrians without their ponies. The Anatolians, looking wistfully at their colleagues, were ordered to sheathe their arrows, unstring their bows, and follow behind. It was an orderly, efficient, emotionless dismantling of Quintus' company.

Two more legionaries met them inside and bade them follow along the via principalis, turning off it onto one of its narrower offshoots. In this area there were simple buildings made of wood, rather than canvas, and the ground underfoot was beaten hard. They stopped when they reached an open area in front of a door, barred on the outside.

At the direction of one of the legionaries, the column marched into the wooden building, a barn or stable. The Roman state, including its army, had no need of prisons. Few were held incarcerated for any length of time. Captives were sold to slavers, high-status hostages entertained by noble families. Even those awaiting their time to die in a Triumph were kept comfortable until the day came for them to be dragged to the Carcer. This was a temporary prison, built for other uses, so barely secure.

As the door was stopped from the outside, the bar being placed across it, Quintus could hear the imperious notes of the cornua calling the evening assembly as the sun set. He felt a warm touch of pride as he realised that he had to order the column to fall out.

Inside it was dark and smelled of animal dung, the only light coming from narrow openings between slats high above the door. This place had apparently been used as a stable only recently. A movement in the corner alerted them to danger and, despite the oath, they were ready to draw swords. A nest of rats was not covered by the promise to keep the peace.

But it was no rat that spoke. Instead a deflated and miserable Rufus appeared out of the gloom.

'Put up your swords,' he said, his voice strangely muffled. He stepped into the red light of the setting sun that crept through the gaps in the walls. He was naked but for a loincloth, and dirty. The angry bruise on his face accounted for the curious tone of his voice.

'What have they done?' Sextus demanded.

'I spoke too much,' said Rufus. 'I tried to convince them I was a citizen. *Civis Romanus sum*, I said, time and again. I also told them to leave the hound alone. I do not know where she is, or what they have done to her. I think they were bored of listening to my complaints. This was the blunt end of an optio's hastile.' He touched his face. 'They took everything about me that was Roman — my baltea and cingulum, my gladius and pugio, even my caligae. I am barefoot in here.'

Quintus grunted an acknowledgement of the injury to his face and the other indignities visited on him. The bruise looked more serious than it was — and he sounded worse due to the effect on his speech.

'What happened?'

'We were seeking the dog. She had gone missing. We stumbled across legionary soldiers drinking from the stream, perhaps foraging. One was a centurion. He it was who had captured the dog and held her to make her whine.' He shook his head. 'We were not careful enough, Quintus. We were thinking too much of the benefits of the camp we had seen. We were stupid — blinded by the hound and our own anticipation of a return to Rome.'

'I understand,' Quintus said. 'I, too, dreamed of a homecoming — and I have been in thrall to animals all my life. What about the others?' He looked beyond Rufus to see if the other men were there.

'Not here,' said Rufus. 'They decided Agnus was a slave. He has a mark on his back, between his shoulder blades — did you know?'

'I knew,' said Quintus. 'He shared the story with me once when we were bathing and I could not avoid seeing it. His family were taken by pirates when he was a boy, and he was marked for slavery. But he escaped. He was never a slave. He is a Roman citizen as much as you or I. Romani, not *quirites*, as Divus Julius would say.'

'They stripped us both, baring his back in the process. They were triumphant, claiming another escaped slave had been found. They took him and Jovan elsewhere,' said Rufus. 'However rough they were with me, they were more thorough with them. I think Jovan was knocked senseless — he had to be carried.'

'Quintus,' Sextus said from the shadows, the light having all but vanished with the setting of the sun, 'Maxim is not here. He, too, has been taken.'

Maxim had been following the party, the last of them. But he was clearly no legionary and had not been included in the same place as the others. Sextus had only just noticed.

'Is everyone else here?' Quintus asked, concern in his voice. There was no roll call, but none were reported as missing.

The company, or at least what was left of it, was intact. It was not the homecoming they had hoped for.

XXXVIII: IMPERIUM

A rattle at the door as the bar was removed lifted the men's spirits, as they thought their case was to be dealt with at once. But it was only an optio, escorting a pair of slaves — not Jovan and Maxim — who brought hunks of two-day-old bread, two large bowls of cold beans and, to the delight of the men, two skins of posca.

The bar was secured with not a word passing between the optio and his prisoners. Quintus knew that there was no point in talking to the man. He merely did the job he had been ordered to do and left. The men shared the resources as best they could, making sure that everyone ate and drank.

'I would rather have had water,' said Marcus. 'This stuff does nothing for thirst.'

'And this,' said Felix, indicating the cold beans, 'does nothing for warmth. We should at least have a fire.'

'We could burn this place,' suggested Marcus, kicking at the structure. 'It would do better as firewood than a prison.'

'I have given my oath for all of us,' said Quintus sternly. 'They could leave the door open if they wished. We are sworn.'

'I did not give you leave to make promises on my behalf,' Marcus muttered, as he made his way to the back of the building.

Quintus decided, with a sigh, not to hear him. 'There is nothing we can do until someone decides to deal with us,' he said. 'This must be the camp of General Drusus if they say it is. Tiberius is his brother. We are endorsed by the second so must be accepted by the first. We are told he is not here. We just need to speak to whoever is the officer in charge in his absence.'

This did not cheer the men. 'We all know how difficult that is,' said Crassus. 'First you have to speak to the man who thinks he is in charge, and then to the servants of the man who protects the man who is actually in charge.'

'I spoke with General Tiberius straight away,' said Quintus. 'He saw me and shared wine with me and Aquila. It could happen again.'

There was no reply from the men, who merely shuffled themselves around the stable, trying to find a place neither too damp nor too foul-smelling to spend the night. Quintus took a breath to explain further, then decided against it. It was pointless. Crassus, of course, was right. They were unlikely to be able to speak directly to the officer in charge.

Morning came and the cornua sounded the reveille, followed by the sounds of marching feet. There were shouted orders and other raised voices. A set of cracking sounds followed by groans indicated a flogging taking place. And again. There was more than one punishment. The cornicen blew once more and, to further shouts, the tramping feet approached and receded. Then all was quiet.

The morning was old before they heard the bar once more being lifted — but it was only for food and water to arrive — poor food and brackish water. No-one was interested in answering Quintus' enquiries. The men muttered amongst themselves. If there was a way out of this, they could not see it, though some suggested options.

'We could throw ourselves on their mercy,' suggested Alba, hopefully.

'When has that ever done anyone any good?' spat Crassus in response.

'We are not their prisoners for them to grant mercy,' Marcus exclaimed. If he thought that they were captives, he would have fallen on his sword. 'We have been left armed, bound by an oath given by our commander,' he added with a sneer. 'They will recognise us.'

In the late afternoon the men heard the bar lift and the door once more creaked open. But it was not, as they expected, food. Instead it was a centurion, almost as tall as Quintus, helmet tucked beneath his arm.

'Atticus,' said Quintus, recognising the wide-shouldered man with the imperious nose. 'You at least know who we are.'

'I do,' said Centurion Atticus. 'That does not mean that I can convince those who hold power here. Come, Centurion Julius Quintus Quirinius, walk with me. It is a warm afternoon.' He held the door open for Quintus to follow.

The two men walked side by side around the inside of the walls, attracting sideways looks from the legionaries working, exercising and patrolling within. Although Atticus had said it was warm enough, for Quintus it was chilly. At this time of year, although the sun shone brightly, the wind carried a bite of the north and he had no furs, no cloak, not even a tunic. He tried to at least walk in the scattered rays of the weak sunlight.

'What is this place?' Quintus asked. 'And who is stationed here?'

'It is not my place to tell you,' said Atticus. 'Although you can see it is a marching camp.'

Atticus looked splendid in his polished armour and red cloak. Quintus looked like a vagrant at his side, wearing baltea, cingulum and arms, but little else, his chest bare but for the lanyard of his baldric. Quintus held his peace for now, waiting for his fellow centurion to speak, hoping that he might elicit more information this way.

'I have spoken to the praefectus castrorum,' Atticus said at last. 'He is currently the most senior officer here. He is one of us, not a senator or well-born boy from the Palatine, but one brought up in the Suburra who attained rank through bravery and battle.' He looked sideways at Quintus, whose expression was doubtful. 'Yes, I was born down by the docks and brought up within sight — and smell — of the Tiber. I work for the brothers and their father on merit, not family connections.'

Quintus was both impressed and taken aback by the casual way in which Atticus referred to great Caesar. He glanced briefly at the centurion, half expecting to see some sign of Augustus' favour. Quickly he pulled himself together. 'What did you ask him? What did he say?'

'I told him that you were a unit of irregulars, sent on a mission by the noble Tiberius. That yes, you were Roman — or at least mostly so — and could be absorbed back into the army at any time. I did not tell him of the success or otherwise of your mission, as I cannot confirm it.'

'When you say "mostly so", you mean the auxiliaries?'

Atticus was clear. 'They belong to the army. They have already been allocated to units here. They should not have been with you and should count themselves lucky that they have not received a flogging, or worse. Technically, they are deserters.' He waved a hand in dismissal. 'The three slaves are also technically escapees. They are army property. They could have been executed and might yet be crucified. They are lodged in the slave quarters until we determine what skills they have.'

'There are only two slaves, Atticus,' Quintus pointed out quickly. 'Both precious to us. The third so-called slave is a Roman citizen, taken and branded by pirates as a boy. He was never a slave. Did your men not notice that he wore caligae?

No slave would ever be issued Roman footwear. Yet they took the footwear from a fellow legionary, an officer. How can you explain this?'

Atticus was noncommittal. 'No slave would ever be issued weapons, yet one of these wore a knife. The other bore Roman arms.' He waved a hand to end the discussion. 'Anyway, I doubt the men had time to notice, especially with a vicious dog attacking — or so they told me.'

Quintus raised his eyebrows. 'Salix is anything but vicious. She is soft — and missing,' he said. After a pause, he went on, 'The man your men stripped and clubbed is a signifer. Your third slave is legionary Agnus. He is a trusted comrade. He is my scout.'

'Interesting,' said Atticus, indifferently.

'Interesting?' Quintus flared, his voice rising. 'Rufus should have his clothes and arms back. Agnus should be freed at once.'

'That may not be as easy as it seems. Your fault, I am afraid.' The centurion spoke condescendingly.

'How is it my fault?' Quintus demanded.

'When you named an authority as high as Caesar's son as your protector, you immediately made everybody below that rank nervous. The prefect is not about to make a decision when there are two commanders above him — both equités at least — and various members of the general's staff, some of senatorial rank, before anything reaches the general himself. A general that holds powers as Caesar's legate, I remind you. The prefect will claim — not without justification — that he does not have *imperium* in this matter.'

They stopped. Atticus turned to Quintus and shook his head slowly. 'It is obvious, my friend. That you cite such a personage as Tiberius as your mentor makes those in authority reluctant to make decisions of any sort, let alone major ones like recognising a citizen, freeing a captive or crucifying escaped slaves-who-may-not-be-slaves. If they make a decision and it is wrong, it could be the end of their career.'

Quintus was deflated. 'Sadly, your logic is impeccable.'

Atticus set off again and Quintus fell into step beside him. 'I suppose if we are, as we claim, the personal project of General Tiberius, then no other would dare to harm us. On the other hand, it does not mean that we have to be treated any better, just in case we are telling lies.' He shrugged. 'I suppose that we remain as we are, alive and unpunished, even bearing arms still, yet not quite free. Yet one of my men is all but naked — and injured.'

Atticus raised his palms in a gesture of futility. 'He looks like a tribesman,' he said drily, then interrupted Quintus before he could speak. 'Yet I will see what I can do to alleviate your position.'

'Of course,' said Quintus cautiously. 'Of course you will.'

He tried hard to keep the sarcasm from his voice, but it crept in anyway. Atticus noticed and fell silent as he turned and started to retrace their steps. Quintus kept up with him. Apparently the walk was at an end. He did not know how much he had offended Atticus by showing doubt in him, but he had to ask the question anyway, whatever it cost.

'It is no decision, really, to recognise my man Rufus. He is an officer, a signifer. He was beaten and stripped by your men when they were all taken. He told them who and what he was, but they denied him. He needs his clothes, his weapons. My oath covers him. Nor is it much of a decision to return our scout to us. I have told you who he is and vouch for him also. He is a citizen, thrice sworn to Rome, the army and his comrades. It would not be just of me to abandon him. It would be unworthy of me not to try and have him released from the slave quarters. If either of them is not restored, it would dishonour me.'

The appeal to the honour of his fellow officer was deliberate. He hoped that it might soften the attitude of the centurion.

'I will, as I said, do what I can,' said Atticus, noncommittal as ever.

Quintus tried another tack. 'The signifer,' he said. 'An optio silenced him with his hastile. We have a capsarius amongst us, but he needs clean water and herbs — charlock, perhaps, or verbena for the bruises. This at least.'

'Only bruises? Nothing broken?' Atticus asked. 'Will he survive the beating?'

'He will survive and should at least be able to wash.'

Atticus nodded but still made no commitment. Quintus did not dare make representations on behalf of Maxim and Jovan, not yet anyway. Certainly he did not dare to mention Salix again. The priority was to have Rufus restored and Agnus returned.

Their stroll had brought them back to where they had started. The gate of the rickety barn in which his men still festered was now once again blood-red in the setting sun. Two legionaries stood ready to lift the bar.

'I have an assembly to attend. The praefectus castrorum is keen on discipline, and on seeing those who flout his wishes punished.' Atticus lowered his voice. 'Between you and me, I can tell you that the men long for the return of the senior officers. They believe in discipline also, we all do, but they are not quite so unforgiving as the old man. Of course, he was in the ranks himself; he served under Marcus Agrippa and Marcus Antonius. Antonius was a notorious flogger of soldiers.'

'Will he make a decision without the tribunes or legate here?' Quintus dared to ask, as Atticus began to turn away.

'I will make sure that a decision is made, whether the tribunes and legate are back or not,' said Atticus as the bar was lifted. 'The men know you are Roman, and it does not do to have you idle here whilst they have duties. I will bring you news after the morning assembly tomorrow.'

Quintus had no choice but to re-enter the barn, his questions mostly unanswered.

XXXIX: SICUT IUPITER VOLUNT

It took Quintus a moment for his eyes to adjust to the darkness, even though it was the dull red of sunset outside. He blinked and several faces came into view, accompanied by several voices, all asking for information on when they were to be released and re-clothed. It was Marcus who managed to quiet the voices, insisting that he be the spokesman. His first question concerned Agnus and the slaves.

'Never mind us,' he said, hushing the men behind him. 'We are safe for the moment at least. What about Agnus? Does the scout still live? What about our slaves? They have been with us for a long time.'

'They all still live,' said Quintus. 'Though they are threatened with floggings and crucifixion. The Cantabrians and Anatolians have been returned to the auxiliary units, and may yet be flogged for their insolence. The slaves — and Agnus — are in the slave quarters, awaiting a decision.' He raised a hand as the tide of questions again began to rise. He turned to the signifer. 'I have demanded, Rufus, that your gear is returned.' Then he addressed the rest. 'I have told the centurion that Agnus is our scout, that he is a Roman legionary, and that he is sworn to his comrades and Rome.'

'And he will be returned?' Felix asked.

'I do not know,' replied Quintus. 'We are to find out in the morning. The camp is currently under the command of an old soldier, so he dares not make decisions lest he be overruled. For now, we wait. We may have to wait for the return of one of the tribunes, or the legate himself.'

Felix nodded. 'As he says, we wait, men. It is all that we can do.'

Quintus was glad of the intervention. The men, grumbling, split up into small groups and made their way back to the corners they had decided to occupy. They were not happy.

Food and drink was delivered as it had been the night before, although this time it was water in the skins, rather than posca. A pile of linen, a mixture of cloaks and blankets, was deposited inside the door. Apparently their captors did not wish them to reman half-naked. When slaves entered to remove the empty skins and bowls, an optio arrived with further supplies wrapped in sacking. Wordlessly, he dumped the package on the floor. A bowl of heated water, smelling of mint, was also brought.

'The water must be to bathe Rufus' wounds,' said Alba. 'Although it is too late for that to do any good.' He sighed. 'The healing is already taking its own path, slow or fast, as it wishes. I will bathe the bruises anyway. What of the package?'

Quintus tipped out the contents. 'It is Rufus' gear,' he announced.

Inside were Rufus' weapons along with his belt and apron, even his caligae. Marcus came across and took charge, helping Rufus on with the kit and sandals, even as Alba cleaned the wounds. Finally Quintus dipped into the pile and presented the signifer with a makeshift cloak, a horse blanket, draping it across his shoulders.

'At least I have been partially heard,' Quintus said quietly to Crassus. 'There may be more concessions to come.'

Sextus was downcast, even though he had been able to secure a blanket in reasonable condition for his own shoulders. 'So your information may well have been met with indifference,' he said. 'Or at least procrastination.'

'Not with indifference,' replied Quintus, himself wrapped in a thin blanket and missing his centurion's *sagum*. He was forced to accept this rag until a proper cloak was made available. 'At least when I asked for Rufus' gear, and for something to soothe his hurts, they listened.'

'A bowl of heated water will not restore us to the colours,' complained Crassus.

Marcus grunted agreement, and Quintus nodded sadly.

They endured another chilly night, still with not enough sacking or blankets. On Alba's advice, they relied on the heat of each other to keep warm, all huddled in one corner to sleep. The sounds of the camp once again woke them, the cornua calling an assembly at first light. There were floggings followed by the tramp of caligae and the clatter of horse's hooves. Then there were voices shouting orders, and finally there was quiet as the camp settled into its routine.

'Perhaps one of the senior officers will return today,' Felix said hopefully, as they breakfasted on the gruel brought to them after the assembly. He, too, had opted for a tattered substitute around his shoulders whilst he waited for a real cloak.

'I am not sure I want them to,' said Quintus. 'I think we might have better luck with an old soldier.'

'Will the general return, do you think?' Crassus asked as he mopped up the last of his pottage with a heel of stale bread.

'Not our general, no,' said Felix. 'But the one who commands here is his brother, so he may have a better opinion of us…'

'…or he may not,' interrupted Quintus, who knew what it was like to have a brother who warred with you rather than providing fraternal support. 'They may hate each other for all we know. Look at these two.' He indicated the friends who had been forced to fight each other.

'We share a horse blanket; we are friends now.' One of the men gave him a gap-toothed smile. 'We just needed someone to remind us of it.'

'My own brother was no friend to me,' said Quintus.

'Nor mine,' Crassus added. There were several murmurs of agreement.

The sound of the bar being lifted again made them alert. Food and drink had already been brought, so Quintus expected another talk with Atticus. But the centurion was not there. Instead, as soon as the doors opened, they could see Agnus, being held firmly between two legionaries. Apparently, these men still did not believe that the slave-marked, bare-chested, caligae-wearing individual was not a spy of some sort.

'He speaks our language well,' one of the men said to Quintus, keeping a firm grip on the scout's arm. 'Although it is a strange accent.'

'I am from Asculum, in the northeast,' Agnus spat angrily, as he struggled to free himself. 'Famous for its two rivers and its victory over Pyrrhus. My accent is well enough known to not be unintelligible.'

'I am from the city,' said one of the men gruffly. 'I find you hard to understand.'

'Let him go,' ordered Quintus. 'He is to be returned to us.' As the men hesitated, Quintus raised his voice. 'I outrank you,' he said. 'Whatever I may look like, I am a First Spear Centurion, sworn to Legio Nine Hispania. Release him at once or I will have you flogged.'

The men looked at one another doubtfully, and the surlier one muttered, 'The Ninth Hispania is not here, centurion. We are of Fourteen Gemina.'

'But,' interrupted the other, unwilling to take the risk of being wrong, 'we have been ordered to deliver this man to his commander, and apparently you are him.'

He released Agnus' arm and stood back. As he let go, the other man managed to spin the legionary around.

'And this? This slave mark?' he barked. 'Also from Asculum?'

Agnus was slim and narrow-shouldered, not as bulky as many legionaries, a scout and a runner rather than a wrestler. The mark was clear in the middle of his shoulder blades.

'It is a pirate mark, but I was never a slave. I escaped,' growled Agnus, twisting out of the man's grip. He faced the two of them defiantly, fists clenched in rage. 'I am a Roman citizen, a sworn legionary.'

The men began to back off, their duty done, their package delivered.

'Hold,' commanded Quintus. 'His weapons. This man is no captive to be disarmed. Where is his gladius? Where is his pugio? You have even taken his baldric and sheath.' He let his anger show. 'Return them or I will have yours.'

The men backed away a little more and began to turn. They froze when they heard the whisper of a sword leaving its sheath. Quintus stood with a naked blade next to Agnus.

'You.' He pointed the tip of the sword at the nearest man. 'Fetch his gear. Be quick.' He moved to the other. 'You stay. Surety.'

The first looked to the second for guidance. Anticipating the question, he hissed, 'In the tent. Be quick, you fool. These men are legionaries.'

The man ran, returning a few minutes later with Agnus' arms. He handed them over gruffly, with no apology.

'Go,' Quintus said, narrowing his eyes at the men, sword still raised. 'Go, quickly, before I report you to your commander.'

The two legionaries tasked with lifting and lowering the bar looked nervous. They were not certain they would be able to force this centurion and his man back inside. But Quintus knew they had nowhere else to go, so he sheathed his sword, put an arm around Agnus' shoulder, and escorted him in. 'Come,' he said. 'This is home for now.'

The doors closed and they heard the clatter of the bar being hurriedly dropped.

Inside, the men greeted Agnus as if he was returning from a victorious battlefield, their welcomes quickly turning into jests at the scout's expense. There were jokes that Jupiter was angry with him for always praying to Juno, and the Reds were jealous of him for always betting on the Greens. There were jokes about the sparse grey interlopers amongst his otherwise dark hair and about the unaccustomed stubble on his chin.

There were no jokes about the weapons taken from him that Quintus had recovered or about the slave mark on his back. Instead, his comrades helped him to put the former back on and found a rough blanket for his shoulders which covered the latter.

'No tunics yet,' Alba jested. 'We have put the order in, but the seamstresses are slow.'

Agnus smiled, pulled the blanket tighter around his shoulders, and joined Quintus and Rufus in the corner that they currently occupied. He squatted down beside them.

'How was it in the slave quarters?' Rufus asked softly, when the scout was settled. 'Were you badly treated?'

'Not as badly as you, by the looks of it,' Agnus replied, looking at the bruises, now turning deep blue and purple. 'None of us were beaten — not like this — although neither were we handled gently.' He shook his head with a mixture of sadness and bewilderment. 'It was just — different. They fed us and watered us, and spoke to us as if we were children or soft in the head. It was more like being a well-kept dog than being a person. The dog...' he added, remembering Salix. 'Does she live? Is she not here with you?'

'We do not know what happened to the hound,' Rufus said sadly. 'She was not brought in with me. I hope that she had enough sense to hide in the forest until her master returned, but I am not sure. She is young. They have not mentioned her, so she was not taken.' He lowered his voice. 'I know you are no slave, my friend, but is it true how you came by the mark?'

Agnus lowered his voice also. 'I boarded a ship with my mother and father as a ten-year-old, sailing from Surrentum to Ostia to join in with the celebrations for the opening of the great theatre of Pompeius Magnus. I never made it, and nor did my family. Pirates boarded the ship not long after it left port and took everyone captive. The slave mark is a code. To those that know such things, it says I am already sold.'

'You escaped?'

'With the help of others, yes — although I have still never seen the theatre.' He sighed and shook his head sorrowfully. 'What it is, what it says, I do not like to share, though not many know what it means. It shows a moment when I was weak and helpless, so I try to keep it covered. I was going to have it burned off, but the scar would still remain, as would the questions.' He finished in a whisper. 'My family were not so lucky. That was the last day I saw most of them.'

Rufus nodded gently and said no more.

Quintus returned to the question of their own slaves. 'Did you see Maxim and Jovan? Our Macedonians?'

'No, we were not together. I'm not even sure I received the full treatment. Quintus, I think they knew I was no slave. They just wanted to play games.'

'As I think we are no prisoners, Agnus,' Quintus responded with a bewildered shake of his head. 'We are here all together, and armed. We could break out of here at any time. That door could not withstand a concerted attempt on it by the likes of Felix and Crassus.'

'Yet we know that the other side of it is at least one legion, if not more.' Agnus snorted. 'Men that we would have no chance against. These are not natives. We could not fight a legion.'

'So why are we confined?' Rufus asked.

'Because they do not yet know what to do with us,' said Quintus. 'Because maybe we are special to Tiberius. Because they may yet have a mission for us. I thought Atticus — the centurion I spoke with — was on the staff of General Tiberius, but it appears he serves both brothers, and Caesar Augustus directly.'

Rufus whistled softly, impressed. 'Really…?'

'So,' said Sextus, coming across to join the conversation. 'They know that there is no point treating us as prisoners. We are fed. We are armed. We are even clothed after a fashion.' With a nod in the direction of Marcus — who had sworn after his experience in Britannia never to be a prisoner again — he added, 'We should consider ourselves confined rather than captive. I think perhaps you are right, Quintus, and we are still useful to the honourable General Tiberius, so we should not be too much offended.'

'I am sure of it,' said Quintus. 'We are being held ready for use whenever they — or he — wishes.'

'So, you think they will return us to service?' Agnus was eager, Rufus no less so, and other ears in the barn pricked up.

Marcus and Felix both voiced the same thought, almost at the same time. 'Will we be re-sworn?'

Quintus stood up to make sure everyone could hear. 'I think we will be re-sworn to the legions, yes. We have been away too long for them to trust us without the ceremony. But I also think that when such a thing happens, we will be split up. They will not want us to stay together. We know that our own legion, the Ninth Hispania, is not here, so we would likely be scattered...'

There was a general murmur of agreement with his assessment of their situation, and disagreement with its possible outcome.

'It cannot be helped,' Quintus said, palms held up in resignation. 'We are in the hands of the gods. *Sicut Iupiter volunt.*'

XXXX: CIVIS ROMANI

The men knew it to be the truth and went back to talking softly in their friendship groups, keeping their spirits up by devising ways in which they could stay together. Many fantasised about escape and made plans, but cooler heads prevailed.

'Although we could walk out, we will not,' said Marcus firmly. 'It may well be that they want us to try. We could force the door, of course, but we would be cut down outside. That would solve their problem.'

'If we are indeed a problem,' said Crassus.

'Anyway, the honour of our beloved commander — his sacred oath — demands that we stay put,' Marcus added sarcastically. The others wisely chose to ignore the mockery, to take what the optio said at face value. It was enough to end the debate.

So they endured the barn, without even the respite of exercise, until Atticus again appeared and took Quintus for a stroll.

'They need movement, physical activity,' was the first thing Quintus said. 'Otherwise they may break out of there just for the fun of it. You know the door could not hold them.'

Atticus raised his eyebrows. 'Of course I know. I was relying on your discipline.' His smile did not reach his eyes. 'And of course I was relying on your oath, your honour.'

Quintus sighed and dipped his head. 'Of course. But that does not make it any less true. I thought we would be moving by now. The tribunes, the legate…?'

'Have not yet returned. Though they are expected.' Atticus paused. '*I* have made a decision, though,' he said, clapping Quintus on the shoulder with sudden bonhomie. He seemed unaware of Quintus' discomfort at the gesture, continuing as if he was the centurion's best friend. 'You will be moved outside today. And I do not just mean outside the building, but outside the fortress.'

He came to a halt, so that he could face Quintus and make his orders clear. He had resumed his serious face, although Quintus thought it was not an honest one.

'You will no longer be within the castra's walls and you are not to mix with any of its men. You will not go near the native camp, on pain of death. You will have three tents. Organise them as you wish, centurion.' Quintus made to speak, but Atticus raised a hand to stop him. 'No questions, now. Your orders are not yet complete.' He continued, as if reciting. 'You will be fully equipped — helmets, cloaks, shields, spears, even horses. When you leave, it will be on horseback, so I would suggest round cavalry shields to help you move with better speed.' He lowered his voice and cocked his head. 'But I will give you the choice of either — I know how the infantry feels about its scuta. I was an infantryman myself.' He narrowed his eyes. 'And you claim to be designated scutarius by Tiberius himself.'

Quickly he returned his head to a military bearing. 'You will not take any of the army's auxiliaries with you, so you have seen the last of your archers and Cantabrians.' He smiled a mirthless smile, almost reptilian. 'I say "yours" but they were never yours anyway.'

Quintus frowned but held his tongue. After all, these auxiliaries had come to him; he had hardly kidnapped them. But they had been good allies and, with their arrows and horsemanship, a useful addition to his troop. He would miss them.

'The men who bring the equipment will show you where to camp. There you will await further orders. You must be patient. If General Drusus arrives, he will determine your fate. If he does not, then you must wait.'

'So, no senior officer has yet returned,' said Quintus. 'It is by your command, Centurion Atticus, that we are set free?'

'You are *civis Romani*. You were never imprisoned,' Atticus said sharply, stopping abruptly and turning his gaze on Quintus. 'Remember that.' He turned on his heel and began walking again, expecting Quintus to follow. 'It is I who have decided to carry out the command. I did not say the command itself was mine. You may not know who commands you, Julius Quintus Quirinius. Not yet anyway. Although clearly you know it was not the tribune or the legate. Nor I.' Again he turned to Quintus. 'Remember that I do not report to anyone here, but that I am acting on behalf of another, more senior, much more senior.' Once more, he lowered his voice. 'Know also that I do not always agree with what they decide. It is not always … honourable. My principal knew all along who you were, including your slave-marked man. I think he just wanted to see how you would prove your identity — out of amusement.' He smiled again, this time with a semblance of warmth. 'Discarding the Germani clothes and arriving half naked — but wholly Roman — was inspired.'

They completed the rest of the circuit and stopped by the barred door. 'I wish you *bon Fortuna*,' said Atticus, amicably enough. 'You may not see me again, but know that, when your orders finally come, they must be obeyed.'

Not long after he had left, an escort arrived — eight legionaries, fully armed, plus a centurion and an optio.

'Ten men,' Quintus laughed with genuine amusement. 'Do they fear us so much?'

'The army is preparing for war,' the centurion explained. 'Any work on this castra will cease for the time being. We will be on the march soon enough. I think perhaps my superiors fear disruption to their plans.' He arched his eyebrows. 'Or your malign influence.'

He was an affable man of indeterminate age, with a craggy face. When he took off his helmet, it revealed a head so bald that it must be shaven. He was confident, whereas the men who had fetched Agnus were shifty and nervous. 'Bring your gear — what there is of it,' he added, peering into the gloom of the barn.

'Up,' Felix ordered. 'Look smart, men. We are moving.'

The men, armed, hardly armoured and in a motley collection of cloaks and blankets, fell in behind the smart troop of regulars. They were glad to be outside and ready to make fun of these soldiers. Felix heard the first line of a jest and scotched it at once. 'No mockery,' he ordered sharply, sensing the atmosphere. 'These are comrades.'

The march was short, but enough to take them outside the gates of the castra to a peninsular that jutted out into the wide, still waters of the slow-moving river. It was almost an island, formed by one of the great twists to which these waterways were prone. The nature of the ground meant that there was a narrow entrance of sorts, one that could easily be guarded, and a screen of trees hiding them.

'Your tents and military gear — and your orders — will arrive before nightfall,' the centurion told them. 'I am leaving men posted at the entrance, but I am told you have sworn an oath, so I doubt they will be needed.'

'They will not,' said Quintus.

Three tents was barely enough, but the men would have to make do. Quintus ordered the ground marked out. Their further orders were subject to much speculation. Sextus took the opportunity to take bets on the various options suggested. No-one had any coin, so each guess had a fixed price of an hour's duty; the one closest to their actual orders would win the 'pot' and could take his ease — at least for a little while.

A noise at the entrance alerted them to the arrival of whatever gear had been allocated to them. A covered cart was being pushed by two figures, immediately familiar to the men.

'Maxim, Jovan,' several voices called at once as the Macedonians manoeuvred the cart inside. 'How do you fare? What are you doing here? Will you stay? Must you go back?' Questions bombarded the pair as they let the shafts drop.

Jovan smiled broadly as he spoke, at the same time tugging away the cart's covering. 'We were tasked with bringing this cart to this place, but they did not tell us who it was for. Our guards left us at the entrance — a senior officer dismissed them. He told us we could make our own way back once our task was complete, or we could choose to stay. If we stayed, we were at risk of being reported as escaped — but the choice was there.'

'You will stay,' said Crassus.

'A man in centurion's garb with a long nose?' Quintus asked.

'That is him,' they chorused.

'Atticus,' Quintus said. 'I think you will be safe, but you should keep a low profile. I do not trust him.'

Maxim agreed. 'I do not think that we will be missed.'

'But stay well out of sight,' said Crassus.

'Do you carry our orders, too?' Quintus asked, as the men fell upon the contents of the cart.

'We were told that your orders would arrive with the horses,' said Maxim, helping to unload.

There were three tents, pupillae as the men called them, due to the way they unrolled like an emerging butterfly. There were tunics and cloaks, shields both tall and round and to their delight, helmets and armour. There were even new undershorts. Felix and Marcus ordered men to erect the tents whilst Crassus took over the distribution of the armour with the aid of his blacksmith's eye.

'They did not say when the horses would arrive,' Jovan added with a shake of his head. 'The whole camp is in a state of disturbance. I think it will be on the move within a few days. I do not think we will be left behind, so we must move with them.'

'More likely ahead of them,' said Quintus, whose own guess in the draw was for them to be a forward scout group, vulnerable to attack. 'They will send us out soon.'

To the increasing consternation of both officers and men they were still camped on the almost-island six days later. Worry about their putative role increased with every day's delay as the imaginations of the men conjured up ever more bizarre tasks for them to do.

'We are for forest-clearing…'

'Or river-draining…'

'Or frog-catching for the general's supper…'

The bald centurion brought messages on a daily basis. They were always the same. 'Wait. I do not have your orders yet.'

He was generally accompanied by slaves with provisions. Jovan and Maxim hid themselves, but they were not mentioned. It seemed like, as they had supposed, they were not missed. The centurion also brought, for the ears of Quintus and Felix, rumour and supposition.

'The senior officers are not yet returned,' he told them. 'Though they took a cohort with them as escort, some are beginning to fear them lost. They fear that this campaign — barely started — will finish before it has begun.'

'What is the campaign?' Quintus wanted to know. 'Is it a single tribe, or a whole region? We have experience; we could help.'

'I could not tell you,' said the centurion. 'All I know is that we began a long march and have paused here. We wait. Perhaps the war is lost.' He laughed. 'Who would ever think that we would need to know?'

One thing that was not lost, however, was the dog. On the sixth morning, Salix appeared on the far bank of the river, barking furiously, lifting the spirits of the men.

'Rufus,' Crassus called. 'Your dog is here.'

Rufus, along with a number of the men, rushed down to the water to see the dog running backwards and forwards along the waterline. He called after her, as did many of his comrades.

'Here,' said Sextus, who had thought faster than the others and now arrived with an animal bone.

'Come,' coaxed Rufus, waving the bone, but the dog would not venture into the water, instead feeling at it with a paw and then withdrawing as though stung.

'She can swim, can she not?' Quintus had joined them out of curiosity and a wish to see the dog returned to her master.

'Of course she can,' said Rufus. 'I have seen her swim. She enjoys it.'

'Then it is not the water she is afraid of,' concluded Quintus. 'It can only be us.'

'Or the uniform,' said Sextus.

'Stand back a little,' Quintus said to the men. 'Let her see it is safe.'

'What if those men harmed her in some way?' Sextus said. 'That might account for her fear. I will go and fetch her, Rufus.' He began to strip off.

He swam across to where the hound barked and ran along the shore and stood waist-deep in the river, trying to coax her into the water. Eventually, he decided to pick her up and bring her back, so he waded out and hauled himself up onto the bank. What followed caused great mirth amongst the men who watched. As Sextus gained solid ground and stood up, Salix took one look at him and launched herself into the water, swimming strongly past the point he had just vacated. Within a few minutes, she made landfall at Rufus' feet, soaking everyone by shaking the water off her fur. Whilst the men cheered and laughed, Sextus could do no more than shake his own head and re-enter the water. Back next to both Rufus and the dog, he pulled on his clothes whilst remonstrating with the hound for her mischievousness.

'At least she is back with us,' he laughed.

XXXXI: PRINCEPS LEGATUS AUGUSTI PRO PRAETORE

A couple of days later, still with no orders, the bald centurion returned with news.

'The general is in the camp, Quintus. Of course he was actually visiting his semi-divine father and fragrant mother, not fighting Germani. He also wished to spend time with his noble newborn son.' Quintus could not tell if the man, who remained straight-faced, was being sarcastic. There was more. 'General Drusus is made Augustus Caesar's man in charge of the whole of Gallia and Germania. He is *princeps legatus Augusti pro praetore* of Tres Galliae, legate and Governor of the province and this region.'

'A great honour,' said Quintus, guardedly. He did not quite know what to say, or in what tone — other than that of utter respect for the nobility. The title made Drusus the senior representative of Caesar in the region — senior even to Tiberius. He wondered how this might affect their own standing.

'It means we can have as many legions as we want.' The centurion was jubilant.

'What legions are here already?' Quintus asked, hoping to at least get a number.

But the centurion wagged a finger. 'You know that is information that only the army should know,' he said in remonstration. 'I do not think I can share it until you are re-sworn.'

'So we are to be re-sworn?'

'Too many questions.' The centurion placed his plumed helmet on his head. 'Although I think you will get some of your answers sooner rather than later,' he said as he retreated from the camp.

'No orders, again?' Felix arrived at Quintus' side as the centurion departed. He looked at his retreating back. 'This is getting tedious.'

'General Drusus is back,' Quintus told him, as they turned back into the camp. 'Caesar has made him governor of the whole province.'

It did not take Felix long to see the implications. Enough for him to come to a halt and face Quintus. 'So Tiberius is no longer master in Germania?'

Quintus shook his head. 'I am not sure that Tiberius is even still present in Germania. He could be in Rome for all we know.'

Unfortunately for him, it was Marcus who overheard the conversation. 'So now we have lost our protector, our patron,' he said bitterly. 'Never mind, at least we have the dog.' He turned on his heel and walked off before Quintus could say anything.

'This rift will have to be healed once we are on active duty again,' Felix said plainly. 'Otherwise it will lead to indiscipline, factions forming.'

'I would not be surprised if such factions already exist,' Quintus told him. 'Marcus first began undermining my authority years ago. I don't think he has ever forgiven me for his loss of rank — or for being his superior.'

Felix laughed. 'Yet I have seen you march together, fight together, smile together.'

'Of necessity. And that was then,' Quintus muttered, parting from Felix. 'This is now.'

Quintus expected that they would receive orders on the following day and was already preparing the men to strike camp when the bald centurion instead brought news of his own mobilisation.

'I am sorry,' he said. 'I still bear no news for you. Still, the slaves have brought you wine instead of posca. We broke some out to celebrate the general's return.' He waved two slaves forward, each carrying three skins.

'This is indeed generous,' Felix said, showing the slaves where to go. 'Sextus, stay away,' he called. 'This is for everybody and to be shared equally.'

Sextus had already appeared as if by witchcraft, and was making his way to where the wine was being delivered. He smiled at Felix and shrugged, veering off in another direction — although Felix noted that his eyes never left the skins.

The centurion was continuing. 'The legate finds that the mountains in the west are not all yet conquered. He tells us that his brother has left a little piece for us to earn some glory. There is a tribe below a small range of mountains that runs to the south. They occupy a land called Liguria, a land that stretches down towards the warmth of the sea. They are called the Comati, relatives to the other Comati, the long-haired Gauls. These we will go and —' he paused, choosing his words carefully — 'chastise. Apparently their chieftain swore allegiance in the past but has now decided otherwise.'

'And us?' Quintus said bitterly. 'What do we do?'

'Wait,' said Felix.

'Tell the men to stand down,' Quintus said with obvious disappointment. 'It seems we will not be leaving today.' He kicked at the ground in frustration.

Felix passed on the news, to more mutterings of discontent. In the afternoon, the men occupied themselves by swimming, exercising, wrestling and practising weapons drills. Mostly, these activities were desultory and soon finished. The waiting had become tiresome, the drills monotonous. They were looking forward to the wine. They built fires and heated water for shaving. They washed, and a few still swam. Rufus and Sextus were both in the water with Salix.

Then, to their surprise, the centurion came again.

'Quintus, sir,' a voice called across to where he and Crassus were one of the few pairs still engaged in combat practice with gladius and pugio. 'The messenger, sir. The centurion.'

Quintus halted the exercise to see that the bald man was once more at the gate, waving with urgency.

'I have your orders!' he shouted. 'You move today.'

The men all stopped what they were doing and listened, hushing those who were not immediately silent. It was late in the day, well past noon, and by the time they had struck camp it would be dusk, if not full dark.

'Why today?' Marcus called. He was stripped to the waist, washing himself. It was not his place to ask, but Quintus said nothing — the men would all have posed the same question.

'Because that is what your orders say, soldier,' the messenger replied gruffly.

'Let me see.' Quintus held out his hand for the orders, but the man passed him nothing.

'Your orders are by word-of-mouth only, centurion. Nothing written down,' he said with a knowing smile.

'Of course.' He was resigned to this. It did not surprise him that there should be no record of the orders, nor did it particularly concern him. He recognised that they were still to be an irregular unit. The positive side of this was that they would therefore most likely be kept together.

'You may speak,' he said, nodding to Felix and Marcus, who now stood on either side of him. 'I keep no details from my men.'

Marcus bridled, muttering, '*Your* men,' beneath his breath. Felix shot a warning glance at him. Both turned to face the messenger. The centurion was at least a little apologetic.

'Suddenly, it seems, there is need for haste. You leave tonight, centurion. But not before it is dark. Horses are being brought. In fact, they are already here.' He stood aside to let legionaries through the entrance, four men, each with a string of seven or eight horses. 'The general is generous. There are enough for all of you to ride and a couple spare to carry some of the gear.'

'My black colt?' Agnus asked, looking at the string of horses.

'Stays here, legionary. He was never yours.'

'Crassus,' Quintus called, but the blacksmith had already come forward and was busy telling the legionaries where to tie the beasts.

Felix also gave orders. 'Marcus, have the men strike camp. We leave tonight.'

Quintus saw the reluctance to obey flash briefly across the optio's features. But he turned quickly and began shouting the orders to strike camp and pack gear.

Whilst Quintus took further details from the messenger, Felix looked at the dripping figures that stood by the river with the dog. 'Sextus, Rufus, get dressed, you fools.' Sextus bridled and began to object, but Felix imperiously called him across. 'To me, to attention, soldier.' Sextus arrived quickly, carrying half of his clothes and looking foolish. Felix spoke in low tones. 'Never mind your pride, Sextus. Make sure the Macedonians are well hidden. Do not let them be taken from us by men who know no better.'

Sextus understood at once. 'Of course, sir.' The salute he attempted was thwarted by the clothes he carried, but at least he tried. 'Rufus!' he called. 'We have a job.'

The camp had become well established; paths between tents and down to the latrines were obvious. The riverbank had become muddy, a place of many footprints. Still, there were but three tents to strike, and not a lot of gear to pack. The men who had brought the mounts were curious about the strange company they knew had been camped outside their own castra. They lingered, trying to find out who or what these men were. Felix made a point of shooing them away.

'You have no business here,' he told them sternly. 'You have delivered the horses. That is enough. Now go.'

Quintus backed him up with barked commands of his own, as did the bald centurion, although it seemed he had no intention of leaving.

'You can go, too,' Quintus told him,

'I may not,' the man replied. 'Orders. I must see you leave.'

Sextus and Rufus had found the Macedonians quickly and told them to stay out of sight, at least until the visitors had gone. The bald man gave a wry smile and nodded towards where the horses were being loaded. 'I know about them,' he said. 'It is not a problem.'

'I don't know what you mean,' Quintus replied.

'As you wish.' The centurion continued the details. 'You ride when I deem it is dark. You travel through the night. The general wants you at least six hours ahead of the legions, who will depart after the morning assembly, so it will be a while before you can rest. Your orders give directions and timings.' He pointed away from the river. 'Go southeast, where there are mountains to cross, but not tall ones, and good passes between the peaks. Use the valleys but keep watch over the slopes. This enemy is a wily one. In three days, you will see a high mountain, distinctive. It is twin-peaked and looks like a child's drawing of a mountain, like a pyramid. Turn south beneath it and you will be in Liguria. It will be easier going.'

'And then?'

'General Drusus wants to know where they are, in what numbers. These natives have a history of not fighting, of striking at weak points and running away. They like stealing food, equipment and horses. Your primary role is prevention of ambush. Know where they are, their strengths, their dispositions. Warn the general. The legions will be following you. We will bring them to battle on our terms, when victory is assured.'

The troop was ready to go at dusk, but their minder had orders not to let them leave until dark. He waited until the cornua rang out for the evening assembly, and for what seemed an age after that. Only when he was satisfied that it was full dark, did he wave the company on its way. When they went to light torches, he forbade it.

'Not until you are well away from the camp,' he said.

Crassus and Marcus had dropped smoothly into their roles as optiones, organising horses, men and materials. Felix, as camp prefect, supervised returning the site to nature — which involved such things as ensuring fires were extinguished and latrines filled in. Rufus, though still signifer by rank, had no standard. When Quintus had requested one from the bald centurion, the man had shaken his head sadly — none of the legionary standards could be spared. Rufus, undeterred, had made a long streamer out of an old cloak and fixed it to a pilum.

They rode carrying the heavy rectangular shields of the infantry rather than the lighter round cavalry ones. There were fewer of them than the last time they had departed on duty and sadly no Cantabrians or Anatolian archers. There were twenty-two riders in total, plus the two Macedonians. Quintus waved an arm at the troop, asking Sextus, 'Is this some sort of lucky number?'

'Not one that I can put a finger on,' the seer replied with a sad smile. 'We will have to make our own luck. I have, of course, made an offering on our behalf to Janus. After all, this is, after our confinement and inactivity, a beginning.'

Quintus nodded his thanks as they left the river camp and the castra behind. The men would be happier knowing it had been done.

XXXXII: INLECTAMENTUM

The bald centurion was right. The going was rough and rocky, but the valleys led in the general direction that they wished to go. The horses were fresh, the men eager and, at this time of year, the nights short.

They had to ride slowly while picking their way through the darkness, so the men were relieved when the bulk of a hill hid them from their starting point and Quintus could allow the lighting of torches. Once it came, the risen moon, three quarters full in a clear summer sky, helped mark the way.

Though often they were forced into single file, there were also tracts where they could ride three and four abreast. At first they followed the winding course of a river, sometimes confined within steep valley walls, sometimes sluggishly making its way through wide lands of bog and reed. In places it broadened sufficiently to be called a lake; in others it flowed swiftly through narrow passes. All the time the mountains loomed up to the west, ranks of cloud-scraping peaks with caps of white snow glistening in the moonlight.

Quintus took the lead, with Marcus deciding that he would take charge of the rearguard. A pair of horsemen rode a little way ahead, and a pair a little way behind, both pairs within striking distance of the main body of men. These observers would give at least some warning of danger.

Quintus rode now with Felix on one side and Crassus on the other, discussing the mission they had been given. Felix was blunt. 'We are bait, of course,' he said. 'A small troop, clearly Roman, unable to defend itself. We are meant to draw these tribesmen out so that the legions can destroy them. We are temptation, *inlectamentum*.'

'And yet it may be that our very weakness has them being cautious,' said Crassus thoughtfully. 'Our existence has all the telltale signs of a trap.'

'So they will shadow us first,' Quintus said, a smile on his face. 'They will watch from high points. If they wait long enough, they will see the legions. They will certainly hear them. If they are cautious, they will recognise us as bait, and we will survive. If the legions are not spotted, then they are likely to swallow us whole. It is in the hands of the gods.'

The morning rose red and golden on the shining peaks of the high mountains first. The men caught glimpses of it as the valleys twisted and turned in light and shadow. There was evidence of movement high on the slopes, dust being kicked up and hanging in the still air.

'Enemy?' Crassus asked.

'Goats,' Felix declared. 'An enemy would not be so careless.'

Once one of the animals, long-horned and long-haired, leapt across the path in front of them.

'I hope that the tribesmen are not crafty enough to pretend to be a goat by deliberately kicking up dust,' Quintus said speculatively as the beast vanished round the shoulder of the hill.

'That way lies madness,' Crassus laughed. 'An enemy pretending to be a goat in order to disguise its movements would be so full of guile that it would be impossible to defend ourselves.'

Sextus and Agnus were charged with keeping them on course throughout these meandering valleys, which entailed choosing the most likely option at the many junctions. Sextus used his knowledge of stars and sun, Agnus his experience as a scout.

Usually they agreed. They were standing shading their eyes from the risen sun when Quintus called a halt by a small stream.

'Water the horses and stretch your legs. No tents, no fires, no sleep. Not yet.'

They took short rests only during the day, more for the sake of the horses than themselves, but they risked a camp for around four hours in the deepest part of the night. When they rounded a sharp elbow in the valley, two nights and two days since leaving the river behind, ahead of them they saw what could only be the mountain their orders had mentioned.

'That must be it,' said Quintus. 'It is definitely taller than all of its companions, with a secondary peak alongside it.'

'And very much the shape of an Egyptian pyramid,' said Felix.

Quintus called over Sextus and Agnus. 'The next time we can do so, we swing due south. Tell the outriders. Tell them to come in closer, too.'

Rufus and Alba were the two that currently rode ahead. They were probably around a quarter of an hour in front, too far now they were in enemy territory, or nearly so. Quintus would rather have them in sight. 'Tell the rearguard to close up, too,' he ordered.

The ground, although it was still rocky, was much easier going than it had been. The steep-sided valleys were replaced with shallower, gentler, slopes. The bite that was in the air in the high passes had gone and it was no longer cool. The wind changed direction and was warm enough for them to stow cloaks in packs. It spoke of Mare Nostrum, whispered Italia. Buzzards circled high above their heads, turning and floating on the wind, their plaintive calls echoing down the valley.

'If only we could see what they see,' Quintus said, staring at the wheeling shapes.

Crassus nodded. The men were wary. Outcrops, boulders, bushes and stunted trees were scattered on the hillsides, enough to hide enemy scouts at least, if not whole armies. Two riders had already been sent back to tell the general of their position, and that no enemy was sighted. These pairs of mounted messengers met with the forward scouts of the legions and exchanged orders and information. They returned now and reported to Quintus.

'No change to our orders, sir, except some advice that we search as widely as possible.'

'Advice!' Quintus spat in frustration. 'We do not have the men to risk by spreading them thinly.'

Yet he did what he could. They continued to head south, but now they were spread out to explore as far as they dared east and west across the landscape, following the command to cover more territory.

'So we are made even more vulnerable than we were,' Felix commented bitterly.

'I have no illusions about how disposable we are,' Quintus replied. 'We are *inlectamentum*, and the wider such bait is spread, the more likely we are to catch something.'

'The legions themselves are still a good three hours behind,' the riders reported.

They at least had learned a little more information. The first couple of times, the legionary scouts had been taciturn, accepting the information and offering none of their own. When the pair of riders had been Agnus and Alba, both previously of Legio Five Alaudae, they were both curious as to whether the Larks marched with Drusus. They could have comrades there, friends, even.

By chance, one of the scouts knew that Legio Five did not march with them but was still in Germania. It had been left behind in one of the many coloniae that Rome was establishing across the lands of conquered tribes. These were camps marked out as cities-to-be, with walls, gates and wooden buildings. Gradually the wood would be replaced with stone. Some even had city delights, like temples and racetracks. Each was the base of at least one legion, but time-served soldiers, other citizens and natives were all encouraged to come and take up residence, to build businesses and trade.

'It is in Germania still, that much they knew,' Agnus told Quintus. 'They also revealed that General Drusus leads two full legions behind us. The messengers carried the standard of one, Capricorn or the goat. This he said was Legio Fourteen Gemina, of which I know little, except that it must be an amalgamation of two or more legions.'

'And the other?'

'Legio Twenty-one Rapax, which —' and here he paused for emphasis — 'we last saw under the command of Varus, part of the army of Tiberius.'

'So our patron is truly no longer here,' Quintus said. 'I had hoped that he might still at least be close — but if he has given command to his brother…' He trailed off. Now it was certain that their very existence was down to a man that none of them had ever met and were never likely to meet.

'Our only link to him is Centurion Atticus — if he even marched with them,' added Felix.

'I would not trust that man this far,' Quintus said darkly, holding up a pinched thumb and forefinger with barely any daylight between them.

In the evening they all came back together to camp, apart from pickets that guarded their flanks.

Agnus shared the information about the legions.

'Fourteen Gemina is unlucky,' grumbled Marcus. 'It was defeated by the Gauls at Atuatuca, then joined with one of Antonius' defeated legions.'

'And Rapax?' Agnus asked.

'Also Capricorn,' said Sextus. 'Caesar's own. Perhaps a lucky legion if he favours it. What do you think, Marcus?'

Marcus grunted, but otherwise did not reply. Since his friend Tullius had fallen, he had become taciturn.

Deep into their fifth night Agnus came and shook Quintus awake. The centurion was not sleeping in the tent; he claimed it was too warm, but his comrades knew that it was because Felix had allocated him to the same tent as Marcus. Somehow, along with other complaints, Marcus had come to blame Quintus for the loss of his friend, and now the very air between them crackled when they were close.

Quintus was sitting with his back to a rock and his feet near the embers of the fire, dozing with a cloak across his shoulders.

'Look, sir,' Agnus said, pointing east to where the tall mountains still grew. On a nearer peak, there was a flicker of light. 'It can only be a fire. It can only be the enemy.'

Quintus followed his gaze and agreed. 'So, we make contact at last,' he said.

'Our messengers should tell the general at once. I could go — and take Alba with me.'

'Not so fast, Agnus. We could do with finding out more information about them. This could be a single family; it could be a hunting or foraging party — it is only a single fire by the look of it. We would look stupid if the general brought the legions to bear on a handful of bowmen or, worse, a set of parents and children. We need to be closer, to gain some details. Then we will send the messengers.'

In the morning Quintus refused leave for fires, and Marcus made no pretence of hiding his annoyance. With difficulty, he ignored him, instead turning to order Maxim and Jovan to break out the twice-baked hardened biscuit that was the staple in such times. He then called an informal assembly so that they could take stock.

'Men. Sit, squat, be comfortable,' he began. He narrowed his eyes at Marcus and Caius. 'All of you.' Reluctantly, they complied. 'In the night we caught our first glimpse of the enemy, high on the hill to the east.' He pointed to where the flickering had been in the dark. 'We can only assume that if we can see them, they can see us — hence no fires this morning.' He smiled. 'You should realise by now that we are not only bait, but we are wriggling on the hook.' Some of the men laughed nervously. 'We do not know their numbers or dispositions — whether this is the main body of their people or a sliver, an outlier. Three things we must do.' He ticked them off on his fingers. 'One, we need to know their numbers — whether they pose a threat to us or not. Two, we need to let the general know. The legions should pause in their march until we have more information. Three, we need to conceal and protect ourselves.' He turned to his fellow centurion. 'Felix.'

Felix took over. 'The last first. We move west until we find a valley where we are hidden — in particular from that ridge.' He nodded in the direction Quintus had pointed. 'There are tall hills there, so there will be deep valleys. We have less chance of being taken from the hook if we hide. A valley also gives us a chance to defend ourselves. Secondly, as soon as we are established, we send a warning to the legions.' He turned to his optio. 'Marcus, choose two fast riders.'

'I will go myself,' Marcus said. 'Myself and Caius.' He stood. 'We could go now, Felix. If we know you are going west, we will find you.'

Felix looked at Quintus, who hesitated, then nodded assent.

'Go now,' Felix said. 'We do not want them crashing into us.'

XXXXIII: MERCATUS EQUUS

Marcus signalled to Caius, who also stood. Caius had kept himself quietly away from any attention since his flogging. Gradually, he had been accepted back into the company. The men acknowledged that he was not really at fault, that Vetruvius had been the true culprit. The loss of their hostage did not sting as much as it had. She had been destined for Tiberius, who was not even in the country anymore. They grew to doubt that the woman would ever have brought them glory.

Whilst Quintus continued, the pair of riders took extra biscuit and waterskins from the Macedonians, mounted and set off.

'Agnus, as soon as it is dark I want you up on that ridge, soft and secret,' Quintus ordered. 'Take another with keen eyes with you. See what you can discover.'

Agnus saluted and turned to the man who sat next to him. This was one of the few whose name Quintus did not recall, but Agnus certainly knew him. They were already speaking animatedly.

'It's lucky that Marcus has gone,' Sextus muttered to Rufus, stroking the head of the dog that sat quietly between them. 'Or he would have had something more to say, I am sure.'

Rufus shook his head. 'Until it affects me, it is none of my business,' he told his friend. 'Come,' he said to Salix. 'Let's find you something for breakfast.'

The troop now swung west. It was harder going as the valleys did not run in this direction, but they needed to find a hiding place. By noon they were in a steep-sided valley, one of the lesser valleys that ran off the main ones, with a stream bubbling through it and high sides hiding them from the ridgeline and the mountains. Each end could be defended and, although they could not light fires during the day since the smoke would betray their position, they could do so at night, so at least they could cook.

Before dark, Marcus and Caius returned. They had met with the legionary scouts, who promised to advise the army to pause its advance. But they warned that the general might not listen to their advice, and that the current commander of Twenty-one Rapax, Varus, was known to be hot-headed. The legions might decide that their strength was sufficient whatever the numbers of the enemy, and that they would engage anyway.

'Though they were but messengers, they were both centurions and advised that we stay in the open,' Marcus added. 'They say that our usefulness as bait to draw the enemy's forces out would be diminished if we concealed ourselves.' He stared hard at Quintus. 'We cannot be bait if we cannot be seen,' he added pointedly. Caius just stood and listened, his head bowed.

Quintus sighed. He had not expected his message to Drusus to generate controversy. 'They must understand, optio —' he spoke carefully and slowly — 'we cannot find out their numbers and arms or the threat that they pose without guile. This is my decision. I stand or fall by it.'

Marcus shrugged, turned his back and slouched off, clearly disgruntled. Quintus could have called him out for insubordination, but he did not. He needed harmony, not discord in his ranks.

As soon as the sun had set, Agnus and his companion set off on their mission. Quintus had learned the comrade was named Cato, as his own dead comrade Nox had been called. This

322

made him shiver at the memory of his loss, even though this man looked nothing like the other.

'Ursus,' he said to himself softly as he gripped his talisman, the armlet that he kept hidden. 'Let me not lose any others.'

The spies intended to work their way up onto the ridge from north of where the fire had been spotted. There was little cover, but at least they would be above the place that they had seen. None of them, Quintus included, expected the enemy to still be there, but there would be signs of the camp, and hopefully indications of where its occupants had gone. It would also give them an idea of numbers.

As they rode off, Quintus once more took up station by the glowing remains of a fire. Sextus joined him, with words of advice that he did not wish to hear. He put a friendly hand on Quintus' shoulder.

'You will have to settle it, Quintus. There are definitely factions forming. Before you know it, we will be like Rome in the time of Cicero. We do not want civil war.'

'Nor do I. But there is not enough insubordination for me to chastise him, and if I did it would only make things worse. What should I do? Demote him? Flog him?' He spread his hands in frustration. 'I do not wish to fight him.'

'You will have to find a way,' Sextus insisted, rising and leaving his friend to dwell on it.

Agnus and Cato returned at a gallop just as the first red line of dawn split the land from the sky. They were challenged by the pickets, a shout that tugged Quintus from his reverie. He rose and urgently beckoned them across.

'Come, come, quickly. What did you find?'

The two legionaries dismounted and walked swiftly towards him.

'It is a meeting or market of some sort,' said Agnus. 'There are many tribesmen, and many more arrived as we watched. Long lines of torches on hillsides showed many parties heading for the place.'

'Jovan, the horses.' Quintus spotted the slave and set him to work, then demanded, 'How many is many?'

'The fire we saw — the single fire — they are stupid to have it there.' Agnus shook his head as Jovan took the halter of his horse and led both animals away. 'It is a lookout. Any decent commander would flog them for lighting a fire where they did, for it can be seen, of course, across the entire valley.'

'So it is not just a single campfire?'

'No,' Cato continued, his words sliding into each other in his eagerness. 'That fire is in a space between two tall, jagged rocks. There are other lookouts that we could see but which are hidden from the plain. This one, thanks to the fire, we could see through the gap, from our position in the valley. Beyond that gap — the lookout — the land opens into a plateau, flat and wide. The area is as big as a legionary castra; there is tent after tent and fire after fire vanishing into the distance. And everywhere there are horses, many horses, including foals.'

'Slow down, friend,' said Agnus, putting a hand up to halt Cato mid-flow. More slowly he confirmed what his comrade had said. 'There are many people there, Quintus, perhaps as many as two hundred. It is recently established; although there are some tents pitched they are still erecting more. There are warriors, but there are also women and children, babes in arms, boys and girls. It is a veritable township of Germani and horseflesh.'

'There are some cattle also, in pens,' said Cato, then his excitement returned. 'But many more horses. The horses are not in pens. They are not even tied; they each have someone at their head, a man in most cases, although even the foals have boys and sometimes girls leading them around.'

The light had strengthened and other legionaries, hearing the reports, arrived to listen. They had thoughts of their own.

'It is a fair,' Crassus said, with confidence. '*Mercatus equus*. A horse fair. It helps them to breed better horses. I have heard of such things amongst the Cantabrians. It is a pity they are no longer with us.'

'It is likely to be a religious thing, as well,' said Sextus. 'There will be a festival of some sort attached to it.'

'Are they warriors? Are they armed?' Rufus asked.

'There are pennants and trophies —' Cato began.

'They are men of the Germani, so of course they are fighters,' said Marcus, interrupting the scout. 'Whether armed or not at the moment, I am sure that they soon could be.' He rubbed his hands together. 'If they are off guard, we can attack them.' This suggestion elicited a chorus of approval from the group of comrades, as if they were ready, at that moment, to arm themselves and go after this camp.

'There are not enough of us.' The men turned to see Felix, hands on hips, looking sternly at them. Quintus was immediately grateful that it was his fellow centurion who had decided to douse the idea of an attack. Stupid as the idea was, he knew that had it been he who had burst the bubble, it would have come down to a stand-off between himself and Marcus.

'How many are there, Agnus?' Marcus began indignantly, as if the scout would alter his numbers to make an attack feasible. The answer was drowned in a hubbub of voices raised to question Agnus and Cato about numbers, dispositions and finally, in the case of Rufus, the quality of the womenfolk.

It was this last that broke the spell as men laughed and indulged in ribaldry, then split up to wash and eat and tend to their own horses and fires. The thought of an immediate attack was well quenched. Quintus was left with the two observers, along with Felix and a glowering Marcus.

'We must let the general know,' said Felix. 'We should send riders now.' He looked at Marcus, hoping that he would volunteer.

Marcus did not put himself forward. Instead he said, 'I would like to see for myself.' Before anyone could interrupt, he gave his reasons. 'I am a veteran of long experience. No disrespect to these two, but I would like to see for myself and estimate numbers and weapons and threat.'

'I am in command,' said Quintus quickly. He tugged his tunic straight, a tic that revealed a decision made. 'I must also see for myself. I must have first-hand knowledge to send back to the general. I will go tonight and you, Marcus, will come with me.'

Marcus visibly bridled at the command but said nothing.

'Do I send any riders to the general?' Felix asked.

'Not yet. Tonight we will confirm what Agnus has said. If they are truly here in such numbers, the general may want to attack.' He looked sideways at Marcus. 'He has the numbers.'

Marcus snorted and walked away. 'As soon as it is dark,' he threw over his shoulder.

After this, the day proceeded slowly. Agnus and Cato were interrogated by the men, but they could not reveal more than they had already said.

Felix ordered morning exercises: swordplay, wrestling and throwing the pilum, and the men dropped into their normal routine. They rested in the heat of the day, seeking shadows and water as the sun rode high.

Crassus and Quintus built up a sweat with sword practice and now sought out shade together. Unprompted, Crassus shared an opinion. 'Of course you should go, but it should be me with you, to cast an eye over the horses.'

Quintus nodded noncommittally. His *amicus* was fishing.

'You know that Marcus has it in his head that this was his idea, and that he is leading you on this mission. He has said as much to the men.'

'I tried not to think so, Crassus, but yes, I am sure you are right.' Quintus shook his head. 'Does it matter?'

'It matters to him,' Crassus replied. 'It makes him centurion and you optio. In his eyes, that is how it should be. You have to show him that you are in charge.'

Quintus could only shake his head once more. 'He is a professional. He will be a professional. I am confident of it. Let it lie.'

XXXXIV: CAPSARIUS MARCUS

The sky was still light, the sun barely below the horizon, when Marcus arrived, leading two horses. Quintus was still sitting and eating with Crassus.

'Too early,' he said. 'We will be spotted as we cross the valley. Sit. Eat.'

Marcus did not speak; he merely wheeled around and walked away. Crassus put a heavy hand on Quintus' shoulder to stop him rising and going after him.

'Wait here, Quintus. He'll be back.'

The same horses led by the same hand returned within the hour. Now it was fully dark.

'We should go. The moon has not yet risen,' Marcus said, adding, as if as an afterthought, 'sir.'

This time Quintus rose, and Crassus watched the pair of them mount and leave the camp. His apprehension showed in the set of his shoulders.

Agnus had ridden the path the night before so had told them which way to go to avoid detection. As long as they could not see the single fire flickering in the lookout, they knew that they could not themselves be seen. At the foot of the climb, the horses were tied; the rest would be achieved on foot. The indistinct track ended near the top of a large, jagged rock, splintered and irregular, one of several planted on this side of the gathering place. The last part of the climb was a steep scramble, the men needing to use their hands. Near the top, with the angles of the rock sheltering them from view, they could look out on the camp from above. They had arrived at this point in near silence, partly due to the need for secrecy, and partly due to the obvious tension between them, but now they both let out gasps of surprise at the scene beneath them.

The moon had risen ahead of them and now shone on a huge camp of the Germani. Agnus had not exaggerated. This was no tribe; this was a nation. The tribesmen had seemingly been gathering for some time, and the site was dotted with tall fires and many tokens of their numbers. As the scouts had observed, there were many men, many horses, almost all with a man or boy at their head. The numbers were already twice what Agnus had estimated.

There were also signs of the camp becoming more established. Tents had long pennants and streamers, and were flanked by carved beast's heads on poles. Areas to the front of the bigger tents had been flattened and swept. There were even several much-prized human heads decorated and mounted at some entrances. The head of a Roman legionary was both precious and magical. Every warrior aspired to own at least one.

Some of the horses were separate, still not tied, but held in paddocks next to the bigger tents and the central pavilion. Quintus whispered, 'Crassus tells me that the chieftains of a clan each have pride in a special mount, a stallion or warhorse.'

'Caius tells me the same.' Marcus was dismissive, not about to give ground. 'He also tells me that the larger pavilions and the best horses belong to tribal chieftains. What does your blacksmith say to that?'

That it is obvious, Quintus thought, but bit his tongue. 'This is much more than a family gathering,' he said instead. 'This is a gathering of the clans — there are many chieftain's tents and many fine horses. Look at that stallion…'

Without thinking, he let go of the rock he gripped to point at the beast. As he did, he slipped — just enough to dislodge a flurry of small stones that scurried down the steep side of the rock face towards the camp. Then, his studded caligae failing to find purchase, he fell awkwardly, landing with a jarring thud on one of the outcrops up which they had climbed. He let out a stifled cry. Immediately, ten faces were turned up towards the sounds, voices were raised and a number of torches converged on a spot below them.

Marcus reacted instinctively to suppress the noise. He dropped on top of Quintus and clamped a rough hand over his mouth. Quintus grunted again in pain, but the weight of the legionary immobilised him. Marcus had always been the stronger and heavier of the two, and he now kept Quintus silent and flat whilst curious voices drifted up to them both. After a moment, it sounded like someone was starting to climb. Marcus did not dare look; instead he found himself half leading, half dragging Quintus down the slope and back towards the horses, his hand still firmly fixed over his mouth, keeping him silent.

It was a short but rough scramble. They slithered down the jagged rock face, landing with a crunch on the grass below. Marcus could feel Quintus wanting to cry out. He turned his face so that they were eye to eye, nose to nose. He narrowed his eyes and Quintus nodded, understanding. Marcus lifted his hand gingerly, relieved that Quintus remained silent. He let go and wiped his wet hand on Quintus' tunic.

'Come,' he hissed. 'Stay quiet.'

He half-carried the centurion to where their horses were tied. Quintus kept groaning involuntarily, whilst Marcus kept exhorting him to stay silent. Reaching the horses, Marcus let him go and untied them. He turned and mounted his own horse with ease, grateful that this had been a core part of his training. As he pulled its head round, he realised that Quintus was still standing next to his horse, trying to pull himself on board.

'Get a move on, you idiot,' Marcus hissed. 'That rock did not look difficult to climb. If we are discovered, we are dead.'

'It's my arm, Marcus. It's useless.' Quintus' left arm hung limply by his side, whilst he clutched at the horse's mane with his right.

Marcus cursed in the dark. 'Is it broken?'

'Not broken. Out of joint, I think.'

Marcus let out a frustrated breath. 'I can get you on the horse. Can you ride?'

'I think so.'

Marcus reached across the back of Quintus' horse. 'Give me your good arm.' They clasped arms, hand to wrist, and Quintus was unceremoniously hauled aboard. Again, he involuntarily cried out in pain.

'Shut up and ride,' Marcus ordered, grabbing the halter and pulling the horse along with his own.

Together they cantered back. Quintus held on tight with his good hand but relied more on the grip of his knees. He needed Marcus to pull him along, as he could not steer — trying to work the reins made the pain in his shoulder even more excruciating.

Soon the twists of the land meant that they could no longer be seen from the rock, should someone manage to climb it. Instinctively feeling they were safe from pursuit, Marcus slowed them to a trot.

'By all the gods, you clumsy oaf,' he spat. 'What were you doing? You could have killed us both.'

He half-turned to see the effect of his words, only to find that there was no-one to hear them. Quintus' horse was empty.

'By Mars Invictus and Father Dis!' Marcus cursed angrily. 'Where is the cursed blockhead now?'

He turned around, looked in the direction they had come to make sure there was no pursuit, and sought his companion. The moonlight revealed Quintus lying on his back a short distance away, trying to lift himself up on his good elbow. Marcus dismounted and strode back to him. 'By all the gods, can you not even stay on a horse?'

'My shoulder,' was all Quintus could say, reaching across with his good arm to support the other.

Marcus looked sideways at the misshapen shoulder with a semi-professional eye. He had seen such things before. He squared his own shoulders, hands on hips. 'Shall I put it back, or do you want to wait for the capsarius?'

'The capsarius,' Quintus said without hesitation, fearing what Marcus — if he still held enmity towards him — might do.

'Too late.' Marcus placed his foot against his comrade's armpit and, with a swift move, grabbed Quintus' wrist and pulled the arm. The patient yelled in pain.

'Hush, boy,' Marcus ordered, looking round nervously. He held up the flat of his hand, threatening to clamp his comrade's mouth shut again.

'No need,' said Quintus hoarsely, although there was pain in his voice still.

'Is it back in?' Marcus asked.

'It is back in, capsarius. Thank you.'

'Then ride, centurion.'

Quintus needed help to mount, and could still only use one arm, but they no longer needed speed, so he could cope. The sharp pain in his dislocated shoulder had become dull and more widely spread, but it was manageable. Marcus rode a little way ahead. Only when they were within sight of their own camp did he rein in, and the two men spoke at last.

'Twice, you know,' he said, mysteriously.

'Twice?'

'Twice I was tempted to leave you.'

There was a long silence. Eventually Quintus spoke.

'But you didn't, Marcus, and I am grateful.'

'We go back too far, Quintus. And you are my officer, I own that. I realised at once that I could no more leave you than I could leave a piece of meat on the end of my knife.' He laughed briefly and humourlessly. 'I think I will never like you, Macilentus — but I would not leave you. I know this now. Although I still do not know what stupid thing you were doing.'

'I slipped,' said Quintus quietly. 'That is all. An accident. I should have been more careful.' Then he brightened. 'The stallion has given me an idea. We can bring them to battle, Marcus. We can fight.'

XXXXV: STRATAGEM

The information — the position, size and composition of the camp — was couriered to General Drusus on the morning that Quintus and Marcus returned. Felix insisted on it, although Quintus wanted to gather more detail. They had neither Celt nor Gaul nor Germani in their number, not even amongst the slaves, so none could confirm the nature of the festival. Sextus could see nothing in the sun or the stars.

'You don't see everything, augur,' Rufus ribbed him. 'The last time you failed to see something, we were buried under eight feet of snow.'

'I could not know of the significance of the fire festival,' Sextus argued indignantly. 'None but the Germani could.' Had they understood the fire festival, they might not have had to spend the winter trapped. He tapped his temple. 'It is in here now. I would not be ignorant a second time.'

Quintus worried about sending the information. 'If the legions arrive in force, that camp will disperse. The enemy will vanish in every direction. We will be no further on than we were. While they are all together, I think we must make them attack — on our terms.'

'You can only send advice,' Felix said, with a shrug. 'We are not senior enough for anything else.'

So the message went as plain fact, unencumbered with guidance on strategy or tactics, and the centurions prayed quietly to their patron gods that cool heads would make the decisions.

They were therefore gratified when, instead of the ranks of Rapax and Gemina appearing on the horizon to the sound of buccinae and cornicenes, it was a party of three red cloaks that rode into view. Atticus, his paludamentum immaculate, was flanked by two senior centurions, the bald one recognisable as their previous liaison officer.

The party did not want to go and see the camp for themselves; instead they closely interrogated the four legionaries who had observed the enemy. They were equally sharp in their questioning, having no regard for rank or station, closely cross-checking numbers and estimates. The younger centurion — this one with plentiful black hair and a black beard — took notes on a tablet. The three then spent an hour apart, discussing tactics and possibilities, before Atticus invited Quintus to join them.

'This is the place I spoke of, Atticus,' said Quintus, pointing towards the mountains. 'This is where we can break the enemy's resistance for good. They are established behind the line of jagged rocks that marks the top of the valley.'

Centurion Atticus looked at the ground with a critical eye. Two rugged hills rose to the north, joined together by a rocky ridge. Between them was the cleft of a wide valley, running towards them, opening out into a plain. On one side was thin forest and scrub, on the other a bubbling stream, its bank sloping away to more trees. At the foot of the slope it turned and ran broad and shallow across the land.

'They are taking part in some sort of meeting, or market?' Atticus asked.

'It is more than that, sir,' Quintus replied. 'It is a horse fair, and my man thinks it has religious significance. It is some sort of annual festival. If we can lure them here, down that valley, we can engage them on our terms. Even the flanks are protected.'

'What is your stratagem? How will you do it?' Atticus asked.

'We will act as bait,' said Quintus. He smiled lightly. 'Worms on a hook. After all, that's what we are.'

Atticus raised an eyebrow. 'Yes, that's what you are. I know it, and you know it. Although you have proved to be better as scouts than bait.'

The bald centurion shared his knowledge whilst the black-bearded one added salient points when the discussion required them, often referring to the notes he had taken. The bald man's deep knowledge showed that he had served in Germania for long enough to have a good idea of what was happening.

'I have seen similar gatherings before. It is a sort of festival of faith. They are renewing their oaths to their chiefs, who renew their oaths to high-chiefs and ultimately, to their king, who dedicates himself to their gods.'

'They have a king?' Quintus asked curiously.

'I know it would be anathema to a Roman, of course, but they have a sort of king, an extra-high chief above them all, like Vercingetorix was to the Celts. He will be king of this small country. This tribe that has resisted Roman rule for so long is called the Ligures, and thus he is high chieftain of Liguria. To him they will have presented the best two horses, a stallion and a mare, as a token of their continuing loyalty. Then they make sacrifices, sometimes human ones.'

'I saw the stallion,' Quintus said. 'It was he who caused this.' He tapped his left shoulder with his right hand. On the advice of the capsarius, his left thumb was firmly stuck in the top of his baldric to rest the arm, which still carried a dull ache. 'A fall put the shoulder out of joint. Felix's optio mended it. It was the stallion that gave me the idea.'

Atticus temporarily dismissed the two centurions of his escort, and he and Quintus walked side by side to a point where they could better view the land. Atticus was interested in the detail.

'They are up there, and we are down here. There is no way on Jove's good earth that we are going to attack them. So how do we make them attack us? How do you propose to make this happen? I know you have done it before. In the northern forests you used effigies and symbols of their gods — Týr and Wotan — to enrage them. Would that work again?'

'How do you know...?' Quintus began, but he was stopped dead by the look on Atticus' face. Of course he knew. 'Then presumably you know that it barely worked last time — and there were losses.'

'So how will you do it?'

'The horses are precious to them,' said Quintus. 'The horses are the key.'

'And if your tactic does not work?'

Quintus matched the centurion's smile with a lopsided one of his own. 'We are still irregulars, are we not? Still deniable? Still disposable? If it does not work, then you — and the general — will have to think again. We will not be around to help.'

Atticus nodded sagely, lips pursed, eyes narrowed. 'You are right, of course.' He looked once more at the ground, the hills, the valley, the way the slope of the plain dipped sharply towards the river behind them. 'The river ensures there will be no escape for them.'

'Do you mean to annihilate them, sir?' Quintus asked matter-of-factly.

'No. I would, but the general does not wish it. Some will be crucified, as an example to the others, but he wants to save the rest. These Ligurians are good fighters, particularly in close combat when we have caught them in their raids. The general says that we could use them in our auxiliary forces, so we are to take alive as many boys and men as possible.' He swept an arm across the terrain. 'This will help.'

The two men turned and set off back to the camp, a picture of contrast. Quintus, a head taller than Atticus, had his helmet tucked under his arm in an unconscious effort to equalise their heights. His face was tanned, his hair lightened by the sun, contrasting with his skin. His cloak was a mixture of different shades of red, patched and worn; his armour was dented and scarred. Atticus wore a bright scarlet paludamentum of tightly woven wool — one which looked newly issued and to which one of his rank was not entitled. His own armour was not lorica laminata but an anatomically sculpted torso piece, the chest shining, the straight lines of hard stomach muscles outlined. Though putatively the same rank as Quintus, Atticus was on the staff of the general, the rank a courtesy rather than a reality. He was a prize stallion to Quintus' workhorse.

As they walked, Quintus explained the plan. Both men were pleased. Atticus because victory here would bring an end to the interminable raids and hit-and-run chases that had so dogged the campaign. One action, one considered and calculated gamble, could end the Ligurian resistance. There would be minimal losses and little risk, most of it falling on the exploratores — this irregular group of scouts that had so far served him so well. Whatever happened, they would fulfil their role as scutarius, if not to Tiberius, then to Drusus. Quintus was pleased because he could present his men with a chance of battle, perhaps a path to being reinstated as regulars.

'I will put your plan to General Drusus. I do not think he will take much persuading. When can you be ready?'

'It should be daybreak,' said Quintus. 'That will give us time to mop up the survivors. It will take us a day or so to prepare.'

Atticus was impressed by his confidence. 'Tell me what you need,' he said.

XXXXVI: VISPILIO

Two days later, the rising sun chased away the shadows of the mountains from the dew-speckled grass, revealing a line of legionary fires across the base of the valley. The river flowed sluggishly at their backs, the land empty behind them apart from the low bushes and tall grasses that thrived in the wetness of the floodplain. Between the fires moved the grey ghosts of men — few in number and appearing to sport no standards or vexilla.

There were perhaps ten fires in total, burning at regular intervals across the valley floor, a string of horses, and a solitary hound. There were no more than thirty men altogether. The legionaries were a foraging party, perhaps, caught for a night away from their base and forced to rough camp.

Suddenly one of the men, squinting into the distance, raised a shout. Seeing where he pointed, the rest of the men leapt up and broke into a loud cheer. They waved arms and weapons and flung shouts of encouragement as two figures came into focus — a pair of riders, galloping furiously down the slope. A black horse and a grey, a stallion and a mare, kept pace with each other, their hooves throwing up chunks of grass and dirt, their riders flat against their backs. The riders rode bareback, precariously clinging to halter and mane, yet still daring to lift an arm in acknowledgement of their comrades, whose cheers were redoubled at this audacity.

It was Quintus who had conceived the idea of using the prized animals as a lure. With a crooked grin, Crassus had pointed out that Sextus was *vispilio* by experience and inclination, a thief-by-night. Sextus had raised his eyebrows at the slight, but agreed, with a nod to Crassus and a prayer to Mercury, that theft could play a role. Agnus had offered to be the other thief. Quintus accepted Agnus for his pioneer abilities and Sextus for his cunning and, though he did not like to admit it, his luck. Both were experienced and expert riders.

Marcus offered to go, but Quintus would not let him.

'These are my decisions still, whether or not you agree with them. I think these two, for craftiness and guile, are our best chance of success.'

At night the thieves rode with two others to the place where Quintus and Marcus had tied their horses on their previous visit. Their comrades took their mounts back, and they climbed the rocks, then crept into the enemy camp. They found the horses soon enough, then remained quiet and concealed for hours, in order to ride into their own camp in daylight. This was important. The theft had to be seen.

The riders now slowed to a trot, waved a further salute and parted, parading to either side of the row of fires. They rounded the ends of the encampment and dismounted. They were almost overwhelmed by pats on the back and cries of praise, the men parting to let Quintus through.

'No pursuit,' he observed. 'Just as we planned.'

'We stole them away silently,' said Sextus. 'They will only now be discovering their loss, perhaps even blaming each other.'

'They should have seen you ride in,' said Atticus. He was, without his escort, still amongst them. 'If they put the fault on their own people, they will never attack. We have to goad them further. You, and you.' He pointed to Marcus and Felix, both big men, even for legionaries. 'Wear full kit — armour, helmets, spears — and ride them up and down.' As the two ran off to fetch the rest of their gear, Atticus turned to Quintus. 'They can ride without saddles?'

'Of course they can.'

'You two.' Atticus turned his attention to a sweating Agnus and a grinning Sextus, both dressed only in belted tunics. 'Well done.' His praise, to the surprise of everyone who heard, was genuine. 'Now get yourselves armed and armoured. I hope we will have a fight soon.' He beckoned over his shoulder to Rufus, who once more was signifer, holding a long-tailed vexillum, the dog Salix sitting dutifully by his side. 'Bring them here,' he commanded.

Rufus lifted and dipped the flag. The signal was echoed in acknowledgement from behind him, the *signum* appearing above the waving reeds, then vanishing again.

Shortly a group of twenty men appeared from their hiding place in the reeds of the wetland. To the legionaries they were strangely attired, clearly auxiliaries. They each had a version of baltea and cingulum over a longer and baggier tunic than the Romans wore, one that reached their shins. They wore light armour, conical helmets with cheekpieces and deep collars of linked mail that protected their upper chests and shoulders. Instead of caligae, they wore tall leather boots; instead of a gladius, they each carried a blade that was short and thin, more dagger than sword, with a round pommel. They were Syrians, cousins to the Anatolians lost to Quintus, but archers just as effective as them.

Each of them carried on his back a quiver of arrows and in his hand a sturdy bow. The bows were not as long as Anatolian ones and had a curved horn at either end, but Quintus had no doubt that they would be just as deadly.

His strategy relied on them.

The archers carried no shields of their own, so took up position behind the tall, curved, rectangular shields of Quintus' men. Each protected by a sturdy scutum, they could concentrate on their aim without the worry of being hit.

Quintus' plan, at least at this stage, did not involve close combat.

'Do it now,' Atticus ordered, and Marcus and Felix each climbed aboard. Marcus took the black stallion and Felix the grey mare. They were now fully kitted out, their tall, crested helms marking their rank.

Once mounted, they paraded the horses in front of the men, walking them slowly and waving their arms in greeting. The men cheered and shouted in return, beating spears and sword hilts on shields.

Quintus and Atticus waited, hoping that their plan would work. The Syrians crouched behind the shields, arrows nocked. At the top of the slope, movement could be seen in the growing light. At first what was happening was unclear, then men and horses began to emerge, their number uncertain but rapidly increasing. The group that milled about carried banners amongst them, and long spears. Mostly, sounds could not be heard below, but some shouts, and the clang of iron on iron carried down the valley. More shouts, orders perhaps, came to the legionaries on the wind.

'If they all come, we are dead,' Quintus said to the Syrian archer who shared his shield. He spoke matter-of-factly, although his heart was thumping. The Syrian responded with a grunt. He understood that he had been spoken to, but that was all.

From the top of the hill, a rising dust cloud signalled that the riders were underway. The two legionaries brought the horses back and dismounted. Their job was done.

The day was fine still, the ground dry. The weather would not play a part this day. Quintus could not hope for a storm or a bolt of lightning to bring deliverance, but he prayed to Jupiter anyway, and to his own patron, Ceres. Of course the men had sacrificed to Janus, Juno, Jupiter, Mars and Father Dis. Of course Sextus had sought a sign in the skies to demonstrate that this enterprise had the approval of the gods. Of course he had found one: three Roman eagles circling lazily, the gods themselves having come to bear witness. Quintus squinted at the birds cynically. 'Do not the spreading feathers at the ends of their wings probably make them Germani buzzards?'

Sextus tilted his head skywards with a smile. 'Eagles, my friend. Roman eagles. My eyes are better than yours.'

Jovan and Maxim added entreaties to Father Zeus and Hades.

'Why not Ares, your god of war?' Quintus asked.

'He is here,' said Jovan darkly. 'You will see him soon enough.'

'Ares is not the same as Mars,' Maxim explained. 'He will smell blood and be here anyway, turning men's hearts to evil.'

XXXXVII: AUT VINCERI AUT MORI

The men stood in a line across the valley. They had marched forward, away from the fires and stolen horses, so that their meagre numbers could spread from forest to stream, so they could not be outflanked. They stood shoulder to shoulder, shield to shield. Quintus was in the centre, Felix now marking one flank, the bald centurion the other. Quintus — and others — were amazed that the officer had chosen to join them. They had expected him to be at the back of them somewhere.

'It is as much my plan as yours,' the man told Quintus. 'If it fails, my worth to the general, and to Atticus, will be at an end. I helped to persuade them both. If it succeeds, I can reap the rewards of taking part. You know what General Scipio said, Quintus, *aut vinceri aut mori*, death or victory. It is no different for me than it is for you.'

Atticus was not amongst the company. Somehow they had not expected him to be.

None had yet drawn a blade, but each soldier grasped a pilum, a javelin capable of puncturing armour and certainly able to bring down a horse. This was a weapon designed to bend on impact, whether it hit flesh or shield or the ground, causing havoc. It would resist removal and, even if it missed its target, it would trip and interfere. More of the spears were stacked in tripod shapes behind them. Atticus had delivered a cart full of them at the same time as he had brought the Syrian archers. The first part of the plan was the theft of the horses, the second to stop this attack. Both archers and spears would be crucial to the success of the stratagem.

Atticus had also provided a cornicen, a trumpeter to relay the signals essential to co-ordination. He sounded a note now, and the Syrian to whom Quintus had spoken drew his arm back and nodded to the centurion, a sign for him to make room. The tall centurion understood and turned his shield, the ensuing gap filled by the straight arm and taut bow of the auxiliary. He had an arrow nocked already. He pulled back his arm and let fly, the arrow soaring high before landing, quivering in the ground. Two further arrows followed in quick succession from either side. These, Quintus understood, were rangefinders. The shields turned again, protecting the archers. They would waste no ammunition in trying to bring down the enemy until he passed the markers.

At the top of the slope, the group of horsemen began to pick up their pace. They spread across the hillside, weapons drawn, kicking their mounts to gain greater speed.

To his relief, Quintus now saw that not only were the enemy thinly spread, but a gap had opened up behind them and the ridge. 'Thank Jupiter Optimus Maximus it is not all of the Ligurians,' he told his Syrian. 'They have sent just enough to smash this thin line and retrieve the stolen horses. We must make sure that they fail.' Suddenly Quintus actually believed that their plan might work.

The shouts of the attackers — insults, challenges and roars — reached the ears of the waiting line, along with the thunder of the horses' hooves, soon close enough that the men could feel the trembling of the ground.

The sight of the enemy was shocking. They screamed from full-bearded faces framed by flowing streams of hair. Few wore helms, but the morning light glinted off their chests and shoulders, showing that most wore at least some armour. Many of the horses had human heads tied in front of the riders. The

Romans knew these to be battle trophies that the Germani believed would bring them good fortune and protection. Some could even have belonged to their comrades, men of Alaudae and Rapax and Gemina, victims denied the crossing of the Styx and forced to wander as headless ghosts.

'Stand!' Quintus shouted, knowing that the sight of these gruesome trophies would enrage the men and was intended to make them reckless. 'Stand! Hold!'

Spears were grasped more tightly as the charge neared the line of markers. Jaws were set, eyes narrowed, deep breaths taken, final prayers muttered through dry lips. The archers would be the first to fire, their range greater than the spears.

'Not yet. Not yet.' Quintus spoke now to himself as much as to the borrowed signaller as he watched the enemy approach the three arrows. 'Now!' He yelled the order as the first hooves churned the markers into the earth.

The cornicen blew the call: a pair of contrasting notes, one low, one high, the high note long and falling. This signalled Zama, the open formation invented by General Scipio to counter the elephant cavalry of the Carthaginian Hannibal Barca. Each legionary stepped back and sideways. It was enough to create a gap for the bowmen, who immediately let fly. Arrows arced skywards, dropping in a shower of death that whistled into the Germani.

Some of the enemy took arrows in their shields; some were unlucky enough for a barb to find exposed flesh. Many of the arrows thudded into horseflesh. It was enough to pause the charge, but not enough to stop it before it renewed its momentum. Immediately the Syrians let fly a second volley, and confusion again took hold. Fallen horses and riders hindered other horses and men, with cries of pain and shouted commands coming from all sides. The tribesmen's speed was slowed and gaps had appeared in their ranks, but the charge once more continued.

'Signal to close the ranks, then *iacite pila*,' Quintus commanded, and the cornicen blew again.

On this note the legionaries stepped forward and to the side so that once again the shield wall was complete. On the second note they hoisted the spears and flung them as one at the enemy. Even before they had hit, the men turned and grabbed another spear from behind, sending it to follow the first. If these hit a man, they unhorsed him and sometimes killed him outright. If they hit a horse, it was at least slowed or turned if not stopped dead. Those that found the ground obstructed the riders and tripped horses.

After the second of these volleys, the charge was no longer worthy of the name. Many men were unhorsed, and many horses were injured beyond continuing. The bellows of challenge had gone, replaced with shouts of anger and pain. There were frantic but failed attempts to regroup the remaining riders.

Spears in such numbers were not expected, arrows not at all. And yet into the mêlée more spears were thrown, more arrows flew. The names of Týr and Wotan and everlasting curses on the Roman demons punctured the air before fading away in defeat.

Rather than shooting volleys, the Syrians were now picking off individuals, stepping into gaps created for them between shields, aiming and withdrawing. The shield wall was still untouched, easily re-formed after each shot, but would not remain that way. There were enough of the enemy to make sure that at least some of them reached the line of legionaries, and now they were angry and desperate. None could with honour return to their camp, so now it was *aut vinceri aut mori* for them too, death or glory. They did not mind death as long as they went down fighting. Many were now on foot, but a few were still mounted — these were the most dangerous.

'Bring them down!' Felix shouted at the Syrians. 'Aim for the horses if you must, if you want to live.'

'Do it,' Quintus echoed. 'We will not survive against cavalry. Let them shoot.' The shields parted again, and the Syrians fired.

'Now it is our turn. Close ranks, legionaries. Draw. *Gladium stringe.*'

With a sound like wind through rushes, the swords were drawn. They were pointed at the Germani like a line of sharp teeth, ready to feast on the enemy.

'Stand! Hold!' Quintus ordered again. The plan depended on them holding this line, not stepping back, not creating room on their flanks. 'We can take these.'

Attackers reached the legionary line only to be cut down, stabbed with the short Spanish sword that had brought Rome its empire. The blades shot out from between the shields, tasted blood and withdrew, the shield wall never wavering. Germani warriors were despatched as they tried to clamber over it, or to hammer on it with sword or axe.

The greatest danger came from horses, with riders able to strike from above, but the Roman shields could take such blows whilst Roman blades found a way under Germani defences. The attackers shouted in anger and frustration, the riders turning their horses to better get at the legionaries — but the line held. The horses were not armoured and the warriors only lightly. They had thought they would be attacking a patrol caught unawares, a few men who had decided to steal their prize horses. They had not expected such fierce resistance.

A blade cut through the air next to Quintus' head, bouncing off the side of his helmet harmlessly. Crassus, standing next to him, stabbed the attacker's thigh, a wound that would bring death soon enough. The man turned to face his new opponent, only to feel the deadly thud of an arrow in his side. He could no longer stay mounted and fell forward, still stabbing with his short spear. Another arrow felled him.

The horse, relieved of its rider, bolted back up the slope, joining several other horses fleeing the noise and smell of battle. Through the gap created Quintus could see to the top of the hill. The enemy had broken, although he could only see horses making their way back up the slope. The warriors were not retreating. They would die, taking as many Romans with them as they could.

Individual fights were taking place along the length of the line, and Quintus could see that the action could be finished quickly if they broke ranks. But he wanted minimal casualties, minimal injuries. Holding the line would assure that. As he watched, Germani continued to fall, pierced by Syrian arrows. Without the auxiliaries, they would not have stood a chance. But his own men also fell, and gaps had appeared that could not be closed by their fellows.

Finally he made a decision. '*Contendite vestra sponte,*' he ordered the cornicen and the man blew the call — the signal for 'every man for himself'. They were to break ranks, choose an opponent, and take him down. 'Work with your *primus amicus*; work as a unit. Do not bother about killing the enemy; just make sure that he cannot fight.'

They knew what to do and, although there were casualties, the enemy was soon overwhelmed. Legionaries now stood back-to-back with their fellows, seeking opponents. The Germani still fighting came to them, lifting spears and axes against the nearest Romans, willing to die in battle rather than taste the shame of defeat. They skewered themselves on Roman blades, attempting to take a Roman head with them into the afterlife. None were still mounted.

On the order the legionaries moved left and right to return down the hill to their fires, Felix leading one half, the bald centurion the other. Marcus led the stolen mounts. The plan required the forces to look casual — insultingly so.

'Take the injured and bring the dead,' ordered Quintus. 'The archers will do the rest.'

Looking at the twisted bodies, many of them young, Quintus understood the nature of Ares, and why the Macedonians had been so certain he would be here to represent the horrors of war, rather than its glory.

On the field wounded men were attempting to rise, only to be pinned by Syrian arrows until there was no further movement. Some of the fallen horses managed to scramble to their feet, while others succumbed to their wounds. Syrian blades put an end to the agony of beasts injured beyond recovery and men still breathing. The injured warriors were finished off without emotion. There could be no prisoners.

As the last two of the enemy were despatched, an eerie silence fell over the field of battle. It had not been a long engagement; it was not yet noon.

XXXXVIII: QUEM DEUS VULT PERDERE, DEMENTAT PRIUS

Back at the fires, Quintus and Alba tallied their losses. Two men were dead; it would be up to their comrades to provide them with coin and a funeral, but not at once — there would be no time yet. One of them, to the sorrow of Quintus, and especially Sextus and Marcus, was Caius the veteran.

'Caius Sergio Nerva, late of Legio Five Alaudae, the Larks,' Sextus announced sadly as he turned over the body. The man had been pinioned with one of the Germani short spears, the blade puncturing his neck through his focale — a lucky but deadly blow. The blade was long gone, pulled out, but the focale and his beard were both dark with blood. His eyes were closed, his face for once pale rather than ruddy.

'He looks to be at peace,' Quintus said.

'I hope so. He had become my friend,' said Marcus.

'Will you take care of his body?' Quintus asked the two of them.

'Vetruvius cannot, can he?' Sextus replied. 'He was his primus amicus.'

'He cannot,' said Quintus gently, putting a hand on Sextus' shoulder. '*Sic vita*, my friend. Life is short.'

'I will see to it.' He and Marcus lifted the body between them and withdrew.

The other man, a comrade of Felix, bled out from a leg wound. He was known to Quintus but only as a loyal member of his unconventional unit. His own friends claimed the body.

The capsarius began dealing with the injured. Most cases were relatively minor, although at least two deep wounds he dressed might later prove fatal. Only two of the wounded were unable to stand, so unable to fight. They were sent to the back, passing Atticus on the way. The staff officer sought Quintus.

'We need them angry, centurion. *Quem deus vult perdere, dementat prius,*' Atticus said, quoting the Greeks. '"Whom the gods would destroy, they first make mad." We need them to attack today, in rage and revenge.' He indicated the corpse-strewn field. 'Don't be squeamish. I want their heads on spikes; we need to show them the sort of disrespect they would not hesitate to show us.'

Quintus understood why; he owned his own mistake in not taking the head of the renegade Dagaz. Nevertheless, he hesitated at the barbarity of the order.

'I know that Divus Julius made a rampart of enemy heads at Munda, but this level of savagery tarnished both the victory and the reputation of the Tenth Equestris,' he said.

'A head is a head. The men are dead. Have you never seen heads on the Rostra?'

Quintus had seen a few, when he had been in Rome at times of unrest. 'Yes. Enemies of the state, quickly unrecognisable.'

Atticus was dismissive. 'Don't worry. The Syrians will do it. They have no qualms about such things.' He called out an order and at once the archers moved onto the field with their long knives. 'We must have them incensed, my friend, if we are to have total victory.'

The Syrians looked across and smiled at the crows and magpies that were already descending onto the field. They waved their arms to send them flapping away. Then they worked quickly and as efficiently as butchers, moving from body to body, carrying their gruesome booty by the hair, not bothering about the blood that smeared their long tunics. They chattered merrily in their own tongue as they brought their haul of enemy heads to the line of fires and made a pile of them, joking as they made sure the faces were all turned outwards.

'Show them dishonour, men,' Atticus commanded. 'Mount them on spears. Throw them around. The Parthians used the head of General Crassus as a football after Carrhae. Follow their lead.'

The Romans were not averse to dishonouring enemy dead, although it was usually done in the white-hot forge of battle, or in the passion of that strange fire that burned in men's hearts after victory. But this engagement was over; the fire burned low and their eagerness for such antics was diminished. But they knew why it had to be done. The Syrians did not know the reasons, but they were cousins to the Parthians and made up for the lack of enthusiasm of the legionaries.

Felix and, this time, Quintus, mounted the stolen horses, each with a head on a spear that they waved from side to side as they rode insultingly where the enemy could see them.

'Extinguish the fires,' Atticus ordered. 'Make a lot of smoke; it must look like we are celebrating, then leaving.'

Rather than dishonouring the enemy dead, Sextus and Marcus had been honouring their own, although they could do little but place a coin under Caius' tongue and sprinkle a few handfuls of earth on him. They covered their heads and added the prayer *sit tibi terra levis* — may the earth sit lightly on you. It was brief, but it was done, and poor unlucky Caius, betrayed by his friend over a woman, stepped into Charon's boat at last.

Rufus also avoided the task of dishonouring the dead — something which he felt brought ill fortune — and instead took Cato with him to cut reeds. 'These are wet,' he said. 'Not only will they put out the fires, they will also create a lot of smoke.' They distributed bundles of reeds and soon every fire was pouring clouds of smoke into the air.

Crassus went to where the horses were tied and began to make a great play of loading them. A careful eye would have seen that it was all a mime, and the repeated movements did not result in any change; a less than careful eye would assume that the animals were being made ready for departure. Agnus was sent forward by Atticus to keep a watch on the movements of the Ligurians. He returned with the news that the men were desperate to hear.

'There is movement, sir, and lots of it,' he grinned. 'I think they may be coming.'

'You are sure? You must be certain,' said Atticus.

'I am certain, sir. They are gathering. There are already many more assembled than came down the hill this morning.'

'Then ride, scout. Go quickly.'

Quintus dismounted and handed the mare to Crassus. Agnus saluted and mounted the horse held for him. '*Bon Fortuna*,' said the blacksmith, slapping the rump of the animal to send it on its way.

'Now we are committed, Quintus,' said Atticus. 'Deploy your men. The Syrians and your two riders will keep up the insults for as long as they can. Stand firm, centurion.' He patted Quintus on the shoulder, then walked away from the line. Mounting his own horse, he rode south, splashing through the shallow waters and vanishing into the reeds.

'Now, Crassus.' Quintus called his amicus over. The blacksmith carried two leather bags full of something small and heavy, which he began distributing amongst the men.

'Caltrops,' he said as he passed them round. 'Throw them as far as you can when I tell you.'

He had spent the past two days in his makeshift forge fabricating a crude version of the wicked spikes meant to halt cavalry. Atticus had provided the metal and the charcoal for the forge, Jovan and Maxim the muscle, and Crassus had done the rest.

'Sound the command,' Quintus ordered the cornicen. 'Form a defensive line.'

The men, though weary from the morning battle, obeyed the sound of the cornu, relieved to leave off their abuse of the enemies' remains. Felix continued to wave the head that he carried as he rode the stolen stallion whilst the Syrians were playing some sort of throwing game behind him.

The troop formed a shorter shield wall than they had done earlier. There were fewer of them, and they were further down the slope, nearer to their fires. Quintus took up position in the centre, with Crassus and Rufus now marking either end. The bald centurion had fought well and been treated by Alba for injuries to his face and arms. He had just now fallen into step behind Atticus, before mounting and riding away from the fight.

Being further from the top of the hill, the men could hear and see even less than they had during the previous attack. They could hear some voices, and the clang of metal. They could see the dust swirling, spreading all the way from forest to stream, covering the breadth of the hillside. They could feel the same sense of comradeship as they locked shields. Quintus called the Syrians to order and with gestures deployed them to either side of his shield wall. They had the benefit of clear lines of sight to the enemy, the disadvantage of being exposed. They did not seem to mind.

Rolling thunder reached the men from the enemy horses' hooves, the ground shaking as if an earth tremor was in progress, as if great Jupiter had stamped his foot. The noise of men merged with it; they called on Týr and Wotan and other gods that Quintus did not recognise. The undoubted insults and challenges were hurled in a language he did not understand. Angry spears were thrown, even though the range was still too great, the leading riders wanting to be the first to strike.

It was a wall of rage, frenzied and disorganised — exactly what Quintus and Atticus had planned.

The line of horses barrelling down the slope was wider and deeper than that of the morning attack. The horses of the Ligurians were not big, not like the cavalry mounts of the Romans, and the feet of their riders seemed to almost brush the ground. The men, hair flying, screamed and challenged. Their faces betrayed their utter fury. They were being forced to guide their mounts round fallen horses and to ride over their headless comrades. In rage they cut down the heads mounted on spears. There were ten times the number of those that had already been annihilated. This time the Germani were taking no chances. The Roman line looked small in comparison, easy to overwhelm.

'Hold!' Quintus shouted, a command which Crassus and Marcus at either end as optiones and Rufus as signifer in the centre echoed. 'Stand firm. Wait. Hold.'

The Syrians had the range from the morning action and shot as soon as they knew their arrows would reach their targets. But this time, even after several volleys had been fired, the charge barely paused. The legionaries braced themselves.

Quintus knew what to expect. They all did.

XXXXIX: RAPAX

With a sound like a great tree falling in a forest, taking smaller trees with it, the first rank of the line of enemy stumbled and fell. The front legs of horses gave way and riders were pitched forward. The entire line tumbled like water over a precipice as if the ground had opened up beneath it. It rolled and crashed and churned, the air filled with cries of anguish and surprise.

Those immediately behind the leaders collided with their stalled comrades, horses and men crying to the heavens. Behind them, riders had time to pull on reins and horses were halted abruptly, rising up on their hind legs. They turned, impeding those behind who crashed into them. Weapons and round shields were dropped as both hands were needed for halters, and knees gripped flanks in desperation.

The charge was at once broken, its momentum stopped, but the press of numbers from behind was inexorable. It kept pushing men and horses forward, kept tipping them into the deadly maw.

More and more of the enemy were forced into the ditch that had opened up in front of them. The fascines that had hidden it, made from the marsh reeds, were broken and churned; the sharpened ends of the spikes buried in the ditch could now be seen, bodies impaled on them, their deadly intent obvious.

This was the weapon that Quintus and the troop had protected from the first charge. This was why they could not step back. Now it swallowed the enemy. Impaled on stakes, pierced with arrows, and pinioned with spears, the Ligurians screamed their rage and frustration.

The Syrians continued to shoot, both into the ditch and beyond it. The legionaries continued to fling spears, but still some of the Germani, maddened to the point of recklessness, came forward to engage in close combat. Though punctured many times with arrow and spear, some crossed the ditch using the bridge of dead riders and injured horses, or managed to leap their mounts across it.

'Now,' Quintus ordered. 'Throw them now.' The order was repeated down the line in both directions and, as it reached the men with the caltrops, they threw them high. They pitched them towards the ground in front of the ditch, a rain of sharp metal, their points finding their way into the hooves of horses and the feet of men, making both scream and stumble.

Even then, a few warriors reached the line, ready to avenge their fallen comrades with the slaughter of this arrogant little troop of Romans.

But they found that they had gone.

When the ditch opened up and the charge broke, Quintus ordered his men to fall back, their job as bait done. The borrowed cornicen sounded the withdrawal and the line of men parted and ran to either side.

In their place, led by Atticus and the two senior centurions on horseback, marched two cohorts of Legio Twenty-one Rapax, fresh, fully armed and armoured. There were a thousand men, plus more auxiliaries, and a wing of cavalry, divided to guard the flanks. The cavalry had been hidden in the forest, the infantry in the reeds. Now, standards, banners and symbols were carried aloft. Cornua and buccinae glinted in the sunlight, sounding the advance. Shields were held firm, and caligae tramped forward in double time.

Three centuries, each twenty men wide and four men deep, formed the front line, three more centuries behind them completing the cohort. Then there was a space in which centurions and signallers marched, before the second cohort followed in the same formation. A centre and two wings, deep and wide, traditional but effective.

There was a gap between each of the three centuries in which optiones marched along with signiferi, who each carried the *signum* of their century. At the very front and centre were more signiferi, these carrying the cohort standard. There was even an aquilifer, carrying the eagle of Legio Twenty-one Rapax, riding between the two leading centurions. Rather than staying behind with the remainder of the legion, it had come to battle, to bring fortune to these men.

The Germani saw their deaths approaching and vowed to their ancestors, their dead comrades and to Wotan and Týr that they would take as many of the enemy with them as possible. But the orders that Atticus was following would not allow this. General Drusus wanted prisoners, not deaths. The legionaries marched forward, swords drawn but used sparingly, slowing or disarming those who were too enraged to stop. By sheer weight of numbers and discipline, they pushed the enemy back towards the ditch in which their comrades had perished.

As they trapped the Ligurians between their own ranks and the enemy dead, a new noise reached the ears of the legionaries, the sound of crying and wailing.

Coming down the hill were hundreds of Ligurian women, old and young, some holding onto each other, some carrying suckling infants. At their feet were children, some supporting old men. They were being driven by two more cohorts; these had been fetched by Agnus to invade the camp when the warriors left, to drive the two halves of the nation together.

Seeing this, and that Rome was not interested in killing them, many of the men still armed fell to their knees and thrust their own blades deep into their bodies, or stabbed each other in pacts of mutual death. The legionaries rushed to disarm as many as possible, knocking swords and spears away. Without their blades, the Germani warriors sank to their knees, denied their places in the hall of heroes. Once disarmed, they did not want to die.

Quintus and his irregulars watched from in front of the wetland as the cohorts formed a ring around the Ligurians, the fighting men separated from their families by the deep ditch, filled with their own dead and dying.

'Tell our men to stand down, to rest, Crassus,' he told his optio. 'Tell them that they have done all that Rome asked them to do. Perhaps now we will be returned to the colours.'

From the west a line of carts appeared, pulled by mules and guarded by legionaries. A slave held the head of each animal.

'What do they bring?' Marcus asked.

'Manacles,' said Crassus. 'Manacles and chains. The blacksmiths have been making them for days. The general means to have his prisoners.'

L: EXPLORATORES ET SCUTARII

On the following morning, the rest of the legions arrived in full pomp. The heavy tread of marching feet was accompanied by banners and standards and vexilla, the jingling of cavalry harness, raucous singing and, at its head, the polished eagle of Fourteen Gemina. Quintus assumed that one of the shining officers that rode ahead in a haze of red and gold and silver was Caesar's noble legate and son Drusus, and another was legionary commander Publius Quinctilius Varus.

For once in this damp and dreary land the bright sun bounced off arms and armour, and the advance looked more like a parade than an invading army.

Quintus and the rest of the men watched as the camp sprang out of the ground. A compound for the captives was first — a ditch, a rampart and guards. There would be nothing else — this was meant to be temporary, and was designed to keep the captives in, rather than an enemy out. They were manacled together in groups of twenty to make it easier to count them and impossible for them to escape. Not that they looked like they would try.

The legate's pavilion followed, a huge tent, many-roomed and well guarded. Meanwhile the surveyors and their teams marked the boundaries of the castra.

One legion made camp at the side of the marshland and reed bed; the other would occupy the land where the horse fair had been. The battlefield itself lay between them. Troops swarmed across it and a great pile of arms was made on the field, whilst the bodies of the enemy were dragged to the ditch. They would occupy it, then it would be filled in.

Ten crosses were erected in the centre of the field, above the ditch, and ten men nailed to them. Some of these had been found hiding in the huts, so the Romans deemed them cowards. Some were chieftains; others were chosen by nothing more than ill luck. Their cries were terrible to hear as they bemoaned their lack of weapons. Without a blade, they would wander as dishonoured ghosts forever.

'The crucifixions send a message. The rest are no longer defiant.' Crassus stated the obvious as he and Quintus viewed the captives. 'They are no longer men.'

'I think you do them an injustice, Crassus. They are men, still. They are defeated men, that is all. They will make fierce fighters.'

'Or die in the arena. *Sic vita.*' Crassus shrugged.

The captives were all sitting or squatting. They stared at the ground disconsolately. Some of them rocked gently backwards and forwards, moaning or singing softly.

'If they could reach a blade, they would use it on themselves,' he finished. 'I think they still have honour.'

'Do we?' Marcus joined them. 'Are we to be re-sworn at last?'

'I think even better than that, Marcus. We are to be part of the escort of these captives.'

'To where?' Crassus demanded.

'Rome,' Quintus answered simply. 'Atticus spoke with me as soon as the legions arrived. He had already spoken with the commanders, already given his report on the action. He told me that General Drusus was pleased with the way the stratagem worked.'

'Does he even know our part in it? Or is the credit all for others?'

'He knows, Marcus. It was a success, so he knows.'

'So are we to be re-sworn to the colours?'

'Atticus says it is not his decision. For now, our orders are to join the escort of the prisoners to the ships; apparently our knowledge of the Germani will be valuable.' He raised a hand to stop the questions. 'We will still be irregulars. Our orders are to help to board them, and to make sure that they arrive safely in Ostia. There we will be met by the representative of Caesar Augustus. Then perhaps we will be re-sworn.'

'We are to sail for Rome?' Crassus was incredulous. 'When?'

'Tomorrow, our troop marches to the harbour that is currently under construction. The captives will follow. We must be ready to receive them. They are building boats, military craft, not slaver scows. These prisoners are going to be soldiers or, if they do not submit to discipline, gladiators.'

'As soon as they are armed, they will kill themselves,' said Crassus.

'So they will start with wooden swords and the discipline of the lash,' said Marcus. 'They will learn.'

'Atticus tells me their high chieftain — the king — is dead and half of his client chiefs were crucified. The other chiefs have been taken to Drusus' pavilion as "guests". If they value their lives, they will join the praetorian guard. They will get plenty of opportunities for a more noble death than a self-inflicted one.'

They watched as the women, children and old men were separated out. Legionaries made decisions as to whether a boy was old enough to be trained as a warrior, leaving behind only the very youngest and smallest. There were tears from both those taken and those that remained. The boys chosen joined the menfolk in manacles.

The women and old men were to be allowed to stay. Time-served legionaries would join the women as husbands, become sons to the old men. In this way the tribe would become civilised, become part of a Roman province.

The three companions took the news back to their own camp. Once more, it was not within the legionary camp, but set apart, provisioned with its own tents and supplies. They would tend their own fires, guard their own gates. Drusus had ordered wine to be issued to celebrate the victory.

'The general will sacrifice at sunset,' said Quintus. He smiled at the men as the wine was distributed. 'We are not invited.' He raised his wineskin. 'Tomorrow we march for the coast, where boats await us. Boats that will take us to Ostia. Jupiter be praised.'

There were loud cheers from the men, many of whom had served their time. Pay, land and retirement beckoned them. Sextus offered to sacrifice to Janus at the same time as Drusus made his offering.

'It is a new beginning. We should at least pour a libation.'

But by the time the sun sank below the horizon, the men were already drinking and carousing, the thought of religion far from their minds. Sextus would have asked Quintus, but his friend was happy for once, so he let it drop. That night, he and all the men drank their fill and slept heavily.

In the morning the usual weather returned, damp, dull and cloudy, a soft drizzle blurring the edges of the landscape. Once more a malign influence was wielded and an unpleasant fate awaited the troop. A group of gnarled legionaries, some carrying injuries, arrived at the gate of their camp. The bald centurion led them.

'I am the bearer of good news, Quintus,' he said, though he did not look happy. 'You are to be relieved of your onerous and less than honourable duty as slavers. These men are time-served veterans, many of them injured in the line of duty. General Varus has commanded that it is they who should escort the captives; there are farms waiting for them in Italia, and they cannot wait. They will take your place.'

'We are not to sail?' Quintus asked, his heart sinking.

'Centurion Atticus says that his principal is happy with your status as irregulars. He is impressed by your work. So impressed that you will remain as you are — *exploratores et scutarii* — scouts and shield-bearers to the noble sons of Caesar Augustus. Tomorrow you travel west, not south. Your orders will be with you by daybreak; that is when you will move.'

'West,' said Quintus, crestfallen. 'How will I tell the men?'

'You will find a way,' replied the bald centurion. 'Caesar Augustus has great faith in you.'

Quintus kicked the earth disconsolately. 'Caesar Augustus does not know we exist.'

'That may be true. It won't change your orders, centurion. West, it is.'

The word travelled quickly to the men, their replacements carrying it. There was a mixture of disappointment and anger.

'I knew that I should never have trusted you,' Marcus shouted, striding towards Quintus, his gladius half drawn, his eyes blazing.

'It is not his fault.' Crassus rushed across and grabbed the sword arm before his friend wrote his own death warrant. Sextus had also seen what was happening, and grabbed the other arm. They struggled to hold him back.

'Then whose is it? Yours?' Marcus turned his fury on Sextus. 'You have hardly brought us luck, how ever many sacrifices and ceremonies you have held.' He half-turned. 'Or yours, Crassus? You are his friend after all.'

Quintus stepped close, putting up a restraining hand. 'Stop. Our fate is no more than what a general wants, or a Caesar. We are just caught up in their wishes, like eddies in a stream. If you want to blame me, I will carry it, but I can no more prevent the will of the gods than stop rivers flowing to the sea. You oppose them if you want, Marcus. I have a vow to Ursus to fulfil. I *will* do it, though the gods rain fire down on me.'

His *auctoritas* was severely undermined. His faith in the gods equally so. He turned his back on Marcus' fury, the better to hide his own.

'*Deorum voluntatem*,' he muttered angrily to himself, as he walked away. 'Let the gods have their way.'

HISTORICAL NOTE

The battle on the water that opens the action is mentioned by a number of ancient sources, although on which lake it took place is not clear — both Lake Constance and Lake Garda have been put forward as candidates.

Augustus Caesar's two stepsons, Tiberius and Drusus, both still young men, had been tasked with subduing the Alps, the intention being to create a safe overland passage from Rome to the new province of Gaul (divided into three as Tres Galliae). Drusus traversed the high passes from Italia and founded Augusta Vindelicorum (the present-day city of Augsburg) whilst Tiberius came north from Lugdunum (Lyon). The geographer Strabo implies Lake Constance as the venue, and a naval engagement involving the Vindelici. Cassius Dio mentions the construction of transports and the crossing, but neither confirms the sequence of events. The battle could easily have unfolded as described.

Augustus had, by this time, defeated all opposition and become sole ruler of Rome. Tiberius did indeed (at the age of just twelve) ride the trace horse in the triple Triumph to which he refers, which was designed to underline Augustus' prestige. A traditional Triumph started on the Campus Martius and wound its way to the Capitol, where the laurel wreath was dedicated to Jupiter Optimus Maximus and any captives (sometimes kept for years for the occasion) were executed. The triumphing general rode in a chariot, his face painted red to make him 'Jupiter' for the day. He was led into the city by the consuls, then followed by his legions. Augustus turned this on its head, riding rather than being carried, and with the consuls behind him. It may not sound like much of a change but was a huge statement of his power.

The action at the end of the book takes place in modern-day Liguria. Drusus was made *legatus augusti pro praetore* — the personal representative of Augustus in the region — sometime in late 15 BCE, taking over from Tiberius. He is known to have visited Augustus and Livia at Lyon, to perform the ceremony accepting his new son into the family. On his return to Germania no record of his first few months in office exists (an open goal for a writer of historical fiction). What is known is that he was keen to complete the subjugation of the Alps.

Liguria, which stretches from below the Cottian Alps to the Mediterranean, still resisted and had to be conquered (the twin-peaked mountain mentioned is the Punta Marguareis, marking the edge of Ligurian territory). By the winter of 14 BCE, according to Cassius Dio's *Roman Histories* the native Comati tribe had been not just defeated, but the surviving men made to serve as auxiliary units.

GLOSSARY

Agmen formate — the order to form square. This would be a hollow square, with shields facing outwards.

Aquilifer — the standard bearer who carried the legionary eagle (aquila). He was also often entrusted by men as a banker, and with their wills.

Auctoritas — having the authority to issue commands and be obeyed, acquired rather than bestowed. Augustus accrued more *auctoritas* than any contemporary. Quintus has gained *auctoritas* with his men.

Aut vinceri aut mori — 'Either conquer or die', attributed to Scipio Africanus before the battle of Zama against Carthage in 202 BCE.

Buccina (pl. buccinae) — a curved brass instrument used to sound watches in camp and convey orders in battle.

Campus Martius — Mars' field, the sacred civic space outside Rome where voting took place, temples and monuments were raised and soldiers were recruited, billeted and trained.

Capsarius (pl. *capsarii*) — a field medic, essentially a first aider. In a full legion he would be under the command of a specialist centurion, the *medicus ordinarius*. A *capsarius* can be found bandaging wounds on Trajan's column.

Castra — a camp, *castra hiberna* is a winter camp; *castra incognita*, a hidden camp, *castra inimica*, an enemy camp.

Collegium Augurium — the College of Augurs in Rome: Marcus Antonius was a famous member.

Congrega — the order to assemble or muster in a particular place.

Cornicen (pl. *cornicenes*) — a trumpeter. In a full legion there would be a number of brass players of different instruments. This one played the *cornu* (q.v.).

Cornu (pl. *cornua*) — a brass instrument roughly in the shape of a capital G, with a vertical brace to take the weight on the player's shoulder. It had no holes or stops, so produced notes through the action of the player's lips. *Cornua* is also used to mean the warding sign of the horns made with the little and index fingers pointed downwards.

Cursus honorum — the 'greasy pole' of Roman politics, a set of steps from the lowliest magistrate to the Senate and ultimately the Consulship.

Cursus publicus — the road used by imperial couriers. It relied on citizens providing horses and post stations.

Deorum voluntatem — the will of the gods. In the Christian era it became '*Deus vult*' or 'as God wills it'.

Dies Februatus — the annual festival held to purify Rome, the *februa* were originally strips of skin from a sacrificed goat, used to strike people to 'purify' them. It was later called Lupercalia and became an excuse for salacity.

Dignitas — there is no direct translation. It does not mean 'dignity' but social standing, influence and reputation. It would be built up throughout a citizen's life.

Divi filius — 'son of a god', apparently Augustus' favourite title. His adopted father Julius Caesar was deified.

Equités — members of the equestrian order of Roman 'knights', holding lesser offices and responsibilities than the senator class.

Evocatus (pl. *evocati*) — a legionary who has served his time and been honourably discharged, then voluntarily rejoined the army.

Exploratores — scouts.

Fides — acting in good faith in all dealings of business or state.

Flamen — a type of priest.

Focale — legionaries wore this scarf at their necks; it caught sweat and prevented armour from chafing.

Gladium stringe — the order to draw swords. One of the most effective tactics of the legions was for a rank to draw swords (*gladii*) simultaneously and strike in concert.

Gravitas — being serious or earnest when required, a sense of the importance of acting appropriately in a situation.

Hastile — see *optio*.

Honestas — not honesty but respectability, the action of projecting an honest image of oneself.

Iacite pila — the order to cast javelins; the pilum (pl. pila) was a heavy spear around two metres long with a metal tip designed to pierce armour.

Imaginifer — see *signifer*.

Imperium — having the authority to act in a certain sphere, granted by the state or (later) the emperor.

Inlectamentum — temptation, to tempt someone into doing something.

Ius iurandum — see *sacramentum*.

Janus primus Vesta extremisque — Janus first, Vesta last. Many rites invoked Janus, god of doors, first and Vesta, patron of endings, last.

Lemurés — the malign spirits of the unquiet dead, i.e. those who have not crossed over.

Lex exercitus — military law, literally 'the law of the army'. Commanders held absolute power, including the death penalty, over all their subordinates.

Lugubri sono — the mournful note, a call for the absolute destruction of an enemy fortress or position. It is the equivalent of 'give no quarter'.

Lupercalia — see *dies Februatus*.

Lustratio — a ceremony of purification, specifically to bring good fortune to an army before a campaign. The *suovetaurilia* (q.v.) was a specific version of this.

Mákhaira (pl. mákhairai) — a sword with a single cutting edge specific to Hellenistic warriors.

Mare nostrum — 'our sea'. The Mediterranean Sea, considered by Rome to belong to them.

Navis actuaria — literally 'ship that moves'.

Noli dare misericordiam — the spoken order for *'lugubri sono'* i.e. 'give no quarter'.

Optio (pl. optiones) — the second in command or 'chosen man' of the centurion. His helm was crested and he carried a *hastile* (pl. *hastilia*) a long staff whose original purpose was to push men who might be wavering in battle back into line.

Paludamentum — the thick hooded cloak, usually red, worn by a commander or senior officer.

Pietas — although often translated as piety, this has a wider meaning of respect for state and family and an acceptance of the way it is ordered.

Praeceptum — an order or command, verbal or written. If passed in written form, the writing itself becomes the *praeceptum.*

Praefectus castrorum — an officer responsible for military logistics who commanded a legion if the senior commanders were absent. He was usually a seasoned soldier, promoted from centurion.

Princeps legatus augusti pro praetore — literally 'the legate of Augustus, the First One, acting as praetor'. In effect, governor of a province, with *imperium* (q.v.).

Quadratum defende — the order to defend a square formation.

Quem deus vult perdere, dementat prius — whom the gods would destroy, they first make mad — an idea first mooted by the Greek tragedian Sophocles in his play *Ajax.*

Quirites — Roman citizens in peacetime. Julius Caesar famously quelled a mutiny (47 BCE) by referring to the mutineers as '*quirites*' implying that they had left military service.

Sacramentum — and *ius iurandum* are both cited as military oaths, the first made the soldier sacred to the gods (and bound to the state), the second was an oath to his comrades.

Scutarius (pl. *scutarii*) — shield bearer. The role harks back to the Greek hypaspist, originally a sort of squire, later a heavily armed soldier. In the Late Roman Empire, they were a type of gladiator.

Scutum (pl. *scuta*) — the legionary's shield. It took various shapes through the ages but at this time was rectangular and tall, with a curve that helped protect the soldier's flanks.

Sicut iupiter volunt — the will of Jupiter; as Jupiter wishes.

Signifer (pl. *signiferi*) — a standard bearer. There were specialist bearers such as the *imaginifer*, who carried the image of Augustus.

Sol Invictus — the sun unconquered, a pagan rite or festival later folded into Rome. On the shortest day of the year, the sun completes its journey across the sky and begins to rise again.

Suovetaurilia — a ceremony of purification involving the sacrifice to Mars of a pig (sus), a ram (ovis) and a bull (taurus).

Tesserarius (pl. *tesserarii*) — a junior officer whose key task was to set watchwords. These were usually not words as such but questions that required a specific answer. He derives his name from the early republic when watchwords were written on tesserae or tiles.

Testudo — a formation made by interlocking shields to imitate the shell of the tortoise, thus providing legionaries with protection from missiles.

Virtus — excellence of character and courageous leadership.

Vispilio — anyone who carries on a disreputable trade, originally an undertaker of

A NOTE TO THE READER

Dear Reader,

I cannot thank you enough for taking the time to read this, the fifth Quintus novel. I hope you enjoyed it.

While I try my best to be accurate, if you find any errors I shall be delighted to hear from you and, if you're right, correct future editions. I can be found on **Twitter at @NeilDenbyAuthor** and **Facebook at NeilDenby-Writer**.

Reviews by knowledgeable readers are an essential part of a modern author's success, so if you enjoyed the novel I would be grateful if you could spare the short time required to post a review on **Amazon** and **Goodreads**.

Neil Denby

Sapere Books is an exciting new publisher of brilliant fiction and popular history.

To find out more about our latest releases and our monthly bargain books visit our website:
saperebooks.com